Reply All

CAROLINE FRANK

To Tracey.
Thank you for your friendship. There are no words to describe how thankful I am for it.

CONTENT WARNINGS

- Sexual Content
- Loss of Parents (off-page)
- Parent in a wheelchair
- Complex family relationships

1

EMAIL ETIQUETTE IS A REAL THING

It takes about half a second for me to realize that I've messed up. Big time.

And isn't it always the case when you accidentally "reply all?" Practically as soon as you hit that send button, you know—you just *know*—that you've broken the first rule of email etiquette: *never* reply all in a professional email, unless expressly told to do so, unless the email chain demands every member of the trail to be a participant in the conversation. And certainly, absolutely, and resolutely, you should never reply all to an email as a new junior hire with the sentence "OMG GIIIRLLLL! How cool!!!" and nothing else.

"Shit shit shit fuck fuck fuck," I mutter under my breath, searching frantically for the fateful "recall email" option in Outlook, the one that could potentially save me from ending my career before it even begins.

Getting fired now certainly isn't an option for me—especially not after the years it took to find some stability. It's been three months since I started this job as an associate production manager, and I can now say it's the longest I've had a job without having something or someone in my life make it go wrong. Not just that, but it's also that this role I somehow managed to get by the grace of god or some higher power (probably karma—it was high time the universe threw me a bone) is *actually* the dream job I never even dared hope for. For the first time in my life, I'm doing something I want to do. For the first time in my life, I'm not living for anyone but myself.

Which is why, with shaking hands, I quickly find the recall option and double-click it with the speed of light, praying to the fashion gods that the silly response didn't get sent out to the twenty-something people on the email trail—the clients, my company's VP, our design team, and, more importantly, Lena Bouras, my boss.

I look over my shoulder into Lena's office, watching as she reads something on her computer screen while talking on the phone, furiously waving her hands in the air. Knowing my luck, she's already discussing my mishap with HR, telling them what I did, and asking them to prepare my paperwork to fire me.

Lena lives by a rule of perfection. The entire company ethos does, in fact. Which is why I'm certain I'm a goner if anyone finds out what I did.

Email etiquette is a real thing in corporate America. Perfect perfection, even more so in the fashion industry.

But when 10 minutes pass and no one's stopped by to pull me away into an office to have a "special talk," I call my friend Molly in design, my old friend from high school and the person who helped me get this job. The person I *actually* meant to email.

"Molly Chan, ready-to-wear junior designer," my friend answers with utmost confidence.

I would never be able to answer the phone as easily. I probably would've stuttered through hello. Mumbled my name. Maybe even forgotten it altogether. Sure, Bridgett Quinn is an easy name to remember, but with me, anything is possible.

"Hey," I squeak, my voice smaller than a mouse's.

"Bee? Why are you calling me? I'm only on the other end of the floor."

"I'm trying to keep a low profile," I whisper into my headset, looking over my shoulder to make sure no one is listening.

Molly takes a beat before asking "What's wrong?"

"Um. So. I made a mistake," I tell her, twirling my long red hair around my finger.

A heavy silence comes from the other end of the line because Molly is well aware of Lena's reputation. And my history with job retention, for that matter.

"Jesus, Bee, already?" she whispers. "I thought you said you weren't going to mess this one up. That you loved this job."

"I do. So much." And it's true. More than I ever expected to. Finding out how the production process in fashion works might not seem fascinating to most, but it's become everything to me. Learning the tricks of the literal trade; understanding how things are made; how materials are chosen and why. There is so much that goes into it, so many people involved from beginning to end, and it's my department's job to make sure it flows. It also helps that the company I work for, Sartoria & Co., is a strong believer in sustainable fashion, which, as a big thrifter myself, makes me feel better about working at a company that responsibly produces and sells new clothing. They aren't exploiting factory workers; they hold themselves accountable and regularly make sure all their manufacturers are complying under their own stringent set of ethical norms—or at least that's what their website and employee introductory packet said.

It's a dream company, which is precisely why I groan, running my fingers through my now-messy hair—because I don't want to mess this up.

"What did you do?"

"I didn't mean to. I was just so excited that..." I sigh deeply.

"Lena added me to the email trail you're also on—the one with the Stevenson project?—which, *finally*, because she hasn't let me in on any external comms since I started working here three month ago—and when I saw the details and sketches of the designs you sent over, the ones we're proposing for them... I thought I was replying just to *you*, but—"

"Oh my god, please tell me you didn't 'reply all' on that email trail."

My silence is confirmation enough for Molly.

"Bridget. *Dude*."

"I know. And to add insult to injury, I may have used exclamation marks. Four of them. And definitely threw an OMG in there, I'm sure."

I can practically hear Molly facepalm from the other side of the phone. "Lena has fired people for less."

I try to swallow the knot in my throat, to clear it, but nothing seems to help.

"I tried to recall the email. Can you see if luck was on my side today? If I was able to get it just in time before it went out to everyone?"

Molly exhales over the phone. I can hear her clicking viciously on her computer, then typing away. After a few eternal seconds of silence, Molly exhales again—this time, it's a clear sign of relief. "I don't have anything from you from today. I think you got it just in time."

"Oh, thank god." I sag in my chair, closing my eyes. "I can't believe I did that."

"Don't worry. You're safe."

For now.

Something about this job makes me feel like it's constantly on the line. Maybe because, even though I'm twenty-nine and have been working since I was fifteen, it's the first job I actually enjoy? It's either that or the life-or-death attitude people in this office seem to live by when it comes to this job. It's so bad, I've sometimes heard people remind each other that "we're not saving lives—it's just clothes" when things go south and the higher ups come down hard on them.

"You told me you'd try this time, Bee," Molly tells me. Her voice is soft, but laced with concern all the same—concern for herself. She's the one who put herself on the line to get me the job, after all.

"And I promise I meant it. *Mean* it. Present tense," I say, doing my best to reassure her. Though, if I'm being honest, I resent her comment. It's not like I mean for these things to go wrong in my life; they just happen. Life just seems to always have other plans for me and things end up imploding in the most vicious of ways. "I was just so genuinely excited. The design you sent the team was wild, and I wanted to show my support. Plus, like, you never told me how cool this job would be. I guess I was really pumped."

She laughs softly. "You literally have probably the most boring job in the world of fashion. Maybe the second most boring after pricing."

I gasp, bringing a hand to my chest. "Are you serious? I work in production for the private label side of our company. That means that I get to have a hand in every step of the garment making process. My team talks to the customer about what they're looking for, then we talk to you guys in design, then coordinate with the factories and pricing, and it's aaaall like a dance. An intricate, beautiful dance," I say, my voice taking on a dreamy tone. "And because it's private label, no one knows we did it—they just think the client did. It's like being in on a dirty little secret. So when you walk into a random store and see the product there, you know you had a hand in its creation, but no one else does. What's not to love?"

"You're insane and delusional," she says, but I can hear the smile in her voice.

I grin and nod, even if she can't see me. "Oh, I am fully aware of my delusion. I am aware that I have truly zero say or influence in anything at this point in time and that I am a twenty-nine-year-old woman doing the job of a recent college grad. But I mean that by working as Lena's assistant, I have exposure to all of this and... it's been nothing short of amazing. So, I know I've already thanked you for helping me get this job. But I feel the need to thank you again for helping me find something I *love*."

"Wow, Bee. That's... That's amazing. I'm so proud of you."

I bite my lower lip to keep from smiling, admiring the to-do list in front of me full of important tasks (at least they seem that way to me), a computer screen filled with boring-looking spreadsheets that are actually full of fascinating information once you understand what they mean, and an inbox full of emails regarding collections people don't know about that won't hit the stores for at least another year. But *I* know. I know what these brands are planning. And it's like I told Molly: it feels like being in on a dirty, delicious secret.

"I'm sorry there weren't any roles I could recommend you for earlier. But I'm so glad it worked out in the end because you sound so happy. I know it's been tough with everything that's happened—especially in the last couple of years—but—"

"Oh my god," I cut her off, my stomach dropping when, in the middle of my screen, at the top of my inbox, there's a reply to my original, mortifying email—from someone on the *client's* team.

Shit.

"What? What happened now?" Molly asks, but her voice is distant, as if trying to break through a layer of thick fog.

Not wanting to stir the pot again after listening to my best friend wax poetic on how much I've changed for the better, I tell her, "Nothing, nothing. I... I had a burrito for lunch and it's hitting me now. I have to use the restroom."

"Oh, no. Remember to use the bathroom on the fifth floor. It's cleaner and no one ever uses it."

I nod, wanting to get her off the phone as fast as possible. "Yes, yes. I have to go."

"Good luck! And next time, just message me through Teams."

I slam the phone down hard, making several of my coworkers turn to look at me.

"Sorry," I mouth.

A cold sweat breaks over my back as my mouse hovers over the message, hesitating to open it. Right now, it's Schrödinger's email. So long as I don't check what's inside, I am both fired and *not* fired at the same time. So maybe, I decide, it's best to just leave it at that. Leave it alone until I get called by Lena to have my ass—and pink slip—handed to me.

I walk away from my desk, do a lap around the office—partly as a last goodbye, partly to be reminded of what I'd lose if I truly messed this up. After raiding the free snack area in the office kitchen (I would lose all access to free chips and granola bars—unlimited Diet Cokes, too!), I realize that if I'm not getting let go for a dumb email, then I certainly will for shirking my responsibilities. Reluctantly, I stomp back to my desk to face the inevitable.

With a deep breath, I bring my screen back to life and immediately click the email reply open.

From: <w.jacobs@stevensonclothing.com>
To: <b.Quinn@sartoriaco.com>
Subject: Your Reply All

. . .

FOR THE SECOND TIME THAT DAY, I SLUMP IN MY OFFICE CHAIR from relief. The sender, unlike me, did not click "reply all."

Wincing, I brace myself for its contents, not sure what to expect. Maybe a curt "Please refrain from emailing stupid things to the entirety of the twenty people on this list." Or even maybe a "I have contacted your superior for this extreme lack of professionalism." Honestly, I wouldn't even be surprised to read something like "Consider yourself fired." The world of fashion is much more ruthless than you'd expect. Though I will say that, though it is occasionally toxic, most of the time I've found the hard work and competitiveness motivating—exhilarating, even. It's simultaneously been grossly misrepresented and accurately depicted in the world of entertainment.

In the time it takes me to eat three small bags of salt and vinegar kettle chips and down two Diet Cokes, I imagine a whole slew of possible replies. I do not, however, imagine the words in front of my screen.

In simple Times New Roman (and who the hell uses Times New Roman in their emails anymore, anyway? Calibri—sure. It's the default. But TNR? How old *is* this person?) are the words:


```
From: <w.jacobs@stevensonclothing.com>
To: <b.Quinn@sartoriaco.com>
Subject: Your Reply All

It really is cool.
But please be mindful of your email etiquette.
Wouldn't want you getting in trouble over it.
;)
```

```
Best,
- W
```

IRRITATION FLARES ALL OVER MY SUDDENLY HEATED SKIN. HOW dare they—But really, how *dare* they email me that? How dare this person stick their (presumably) big nose in *my* business? Sure, I made a mistake. But it's not the end of the goddamn world. And yes, I love my new job. And yes, it's given me a new sense of purpose that I've never felt before in my entire life. But I've also never felt more stressed. Never felt more anxious. Truthfully, it's the first time I've felt like I *really* have something to lose. There's no way I'm going to let some loser from the other company—who can't even sign with their company signature, by the way (another big corporate email etiquette no-no)—tell me how to do my job.

Rage coursing through my veins, fear driving my actions, I click on the *reply* button—with a bit too much force.

```
From: <b.Quinn@sartoriaco.com>
To: <w.jacobs@stevensonclothing.com>
Subject: Re: Your Reply All


W (or whoever you are, because you neglected
to add your company signature) -


FYI, it wasn't my intention to reply to every-
one. OBVIOUSLY. That email was intended solely
for my friend's eyes. She was the one who sent
the updated designs, and my intention was to
reply only to her. I tried to recall the email
```

and was mostly successful, but I guess you slipped through the cracks. Apologies for the inconvenience.

Bridget Quinn
Assistant to Lena Bouros
Sartoria & Co.
(212) 555-1234 ext 321

THERE.

Thinking that's the end of it, I *humph* once and nod, satisfied.

From: <w.jacobs@stevensonclothing.com>
To: <b.Quinn@sartoriaco.com>
Subject: Re: Re: Your Reply All

Dear Ms. Quinn,

I'm sorry to have offended you. It wasn't my intention. I simply wanted to point out that perhaps your "reply all" might not have been a good idea—especially given you work for one of the most demanding women in the industry. It's the first time I've seen your name on these emails, so I thought you might be new. I wouldn't have wanted for you to get in trouble just as you're starting out.
PS. The name's Will. Please don't call me W. It makes me cringe.

. . .

OF COURSE W IS A DUDE. TYPICAL.

I resent the fact that he just assumed I'm new. Correctly, but still.

From: <b.Quinn@sartoriaco.com>
To: <w.jacobs@stevensonclothing.com>
Subject: Re: Re: Re: Your Reply All

Dear *Will*, Thanks for looking out for me, but I don't need it.

(Also, if you didn't want me calling you W then why did you sign your initial email with it?)

Sincerely,

Bridget Quinn
Assistant to Lena Bouros
Sartoria Co.
(212) 555-1234 ext 321

IN SECONDS, I RECEIVE ANOTHER REPLY:

From: <w.jacobs@stevensonclothing.com>
To: <b.Quinn@sartoriaco.com>
Subject: Re: Re: Re: Re: Your Reply All

Are you, though?

No salutation. Not even a signature. And he didn't even answer my question. He thinks he can lecture me on email etiquette and professionalism, but not follow the same rules?

From: <b.Quinn@sartoriaco.com>
To: <w.jacobs@stevensonclothing.com>
Subject: Re: Re: Re: Re: Re: Your Reply All

Will -

Am I what?

Best,

Bridget Quinn
Assistant to Lena Bouros
Sartoria Co.
(212) 555-1234 ext 321

From: <w.jacobs@stevensonclothing.com>
To: <b.Quinn@sartoriaco.com>
Subject: Re: Re: Re: Re: Re: Re: Your
Reply All

New.

. . .

I CONSIDER MY REPLY. I COULD JUST LIE. SAY I HAVE OVER FIVE years of experience under my belt. That this isn't my first rodeo —I'm a new VP of something. Anything. I could do all of that, and mislead him to save face. But then I realize my title is in my signature and groan.

From: <b.Quinn@sartoriaco.com>
To: <w.jacobs@stevensonclothing.com>
Subject: Re: Re: Re: Re: Re: Re: Re: Your
Reply All

Obviously.

Best,

Bridget Quinn
Assistant to Lena Bouros
Sartoria Co.
(212) 555-1234 ext 321

From: <w.jacobs@stevensonclothing.com>
To: <b.Quinn@sartoriaco.com>
Subject: Re: Re: Re: Re: Re: Re: Re: Re: Your
Reply All

Thank god.

I frown, sitting back in my chair. Before I can stop myself, I type back an email, forgetting all formalities.

From: <b.Quinn@sartoriaco.com>
To: <w.jacobs@stevensonclothing.com>
Subject: Re: Re: Re: Re: Re: Re: Re: Re: Re: Your Reply All

What is *that* supposed to mean?

Best,

Bridget Quinn
Assistant to Lena Bouros
Sartoria Co.
(212) 555-1234 ext 321

From: <w.jacobs@stevensonclothing.com>
To: <b.Quinn@sartoriaco.com>
Subject: Re: Re: Re: Re: Re: Re: Re: Re: Re: Re: Re: Your Reply All

It means I've been suffocating and in dire need of a breath of fresh air. And I get the feeling that's what you are.

WILL

He has no idea why he chose to reply to her email. Maybe a part of him was caught off guard by the enthusiasm in her message, the almost-naiveté of her words and tone. Maybe he was pulled in like a moth to a flame wanting so very much to feel the same passion she exhibited— the one he had lost long ago, or more accurately never even felt.

Or maybe the darkness inside him craves to tell her the truth: that this entire industry is a nightmare and she should get out while she still can. That the enthusiasm that so clearly bounced off his computer screen is too precious for it to wane as quickly as it will.

Either way, he's at a loss. One thing is for sure, there is no way he can deny that, even based on their very limited email exchange, the entire interaction made his day a little more tolerable.

2

—————

SOMETIMES WE JUST NEED A FRIEND

t means I've been suffocating and in dire need of a breath of fresh air. And I get the feeling that's what you are.

"And what was *that* supposed to mean, anyway?" I mutter to myself as I pick up a couple of oranges from the produce section. I sniff them while my mind wanders back to the odd email exchange between *Will*, whoever he was, and myself. When I tried stalking him through LinkedIn like any rational, normal person would, I didn't find anyone by that name and definitely not one working for Stevenson.

It's honestly surprising. Stevenson is one of the oldest and most luxurious department stores in the US—so much so that Sartoria almost lost their minds when *they* approached *us* wanting to be our client a few months ago. They wanted us to help them develop their own in-house clothing brand to sit next to other designer, high-end brands and the opportunity had the company in a tizzy—we all wanted to scream it from the rooftops. Any person in fashion, at least. If I hadn't signed an NDA regarding our company making their branded clothes, I'd certainly be doing the same thing by adding it to my LinkedIn page (especially since this is my first "*serious*" job, as Molly would say).

"Excuse me, miss?" A pimply teenager with dark, curly hair interrupts my musings. "You—You can't just *sniff* the produce like that."

I gawk at him and then back to the orange in my hand. "I'm testing the quality of the produce, my man. To see how fresh it is."

"Right, but your nose is almost making physical contact with the fruit, and we really can't allow you to—"

I sigh deeply and lift a hand to stop him, not wanting to argue. "'Nough said. It's going in my basket. See?" And really, can I blame him? I wouldn't like eating an orange that someone else had sniffed, either.

He exhales, his entire body relaxing. "I'm sorry," he whispers, looking nervously over his shoulder. "My boss was the one who made me come over here and practice my... assertiveness." He winces like our conversation caused him physical pain.

I laugh once. "I understand." Slapping him once on the shoulder, I smile at him. "I've been in the same boat, but I promise you it will get better." *Or so they tell me.*

It's not like working with Lena has been a *total* nightmare—it's not like my job has taken over my life, and I've been working crazy hours. Surprisingly, she's been very respectful about keeping work outside office hours to a minimum—something I pray never changes. But she certainly isn't someone easy to work for.

This morning, for example, was no walk in the park. I made the colossal mistake of handing her some documents in a branded black folder instead of a normal manila one. This ultimately led to a ten minute lecture on attention to detail, the importance of continuity and consistency, and good taste.

Sigh.

Walking away from the fruit stand, I hope both me and the supermarket kid will soon be able to find some kind of balance or happiness with our bosses. Me in particular because I really do love what I do.

It isn't long before I reach my place—a sixth floor walk-up studio apartment in Chinatown whose lease I took over from Molly's college roommate's uncle's friend. A sub, sub, sublet. It came with peeling paint, water damage, and a colony of ants, but at least it's rent-controlled, right next to the subway station (a luxury in New York City), and pet friendly.

The latter is the most important part, of course, seeing as there's no way I would ever abandon Ginger, my twenty-five pound Maine Coon love of my life. Named after her orange coat and Ginger Rogers, she's the best present I've ever received from the person I've loved the most—my grandmother.

Ginger was one of the last things my grandmother gave me before she was diagnosed. When things were *really* bad, the moody little rascal never left my side—especially on nights I would cry myself to sleep. Ginger would curl herself in my arms and let me hold her until I calmed down.

I hear my favorite girl meow as I attempt to unlock the two locks and deadbolt before kicking the door open. The layers upon layers of old paint cause the decrepit piece of wood to stick, but beating it down usually works. A regular person would complain about having to put in so much effort, especially after hiking six flights of stairs every day, but it truly is the cheapest workout around. There's no denying my ass has tightened, my calves look great, and I'm in the best shape of my life—all because I'm broke AF and New York City is basically unlivable. I guess you could say it's the bright side to the housing crisis?

I try as often as I can to do so. See the bright side in everything, I mean. Which, living in New York City, makes me not so likable all of the time. Not to perpetuate the stereotype of a "true

New Yorker," but most people I meet around here are jaded and angry. So when I smile and attempt to reframe certain circumstances to make them more tolerable, it's not always so well-received. Some people just want to sit in misery, whereas I've had so much of it, I would probably not be able to handle any more of it. My body just *needs* to repel it in order to survive. In any other story, this is where you'd start the slide show of my sad background and cue the tears. But that's not who I am.

My point is: I try my best not to sweat the small stuff. Which is why I don't mind kicking my door and jiggling the keys a million times to get it open, because as soon as I do, I dump my stuff on the ground and Ginger jumps in my arms, rubbing her face against mine.

"And who could ever be depressed or angry when they've got you to come home to, huh?" I ask her, baby talk in full force. She purrs in my arms as I rock her like a baby. "I *loooove* you."

Yes, I am your regular crazy cat lady. And proud of it.

I set her down carefully and triple lock the door, making sure the chain is locked regardless of how flimsy it looks. Would it be able to stop an intruder from busting into my house? Probably not! But you never know.

Ginger follows me into the kitchen with a happy trot, tail in the air. It's as I'm pouring her wet food into her pink bowl that I hear the familiar sound of the email notification on my phone. I tense, back ramrod straight. Part of me wants to ignore the email, not wanting to risk the aforementioned work/life balance I was just internally marveling at no less than half an hour ago. I know I won't be able to help myself. Sure, Lena is terrifying, but she's still super smart and a badass, and I want her to like me. Plus, the other part of me wants to know what it can be, because in the short time I've been working at Sartoria, I've become a bit obsessed with what I do.

Heaving a sigh, I lose the battle with myself and reach for my phone, expecting a demanding email from the woman who makes my blood run cold from nerves but also swell with pride when I see her command a room and kick ass. (Note to self: research Stockholm syndrome—there's a chance I might be suffering from a mild case)

To my surprise, it isn't a message from Lena but one from Will. The mystery man from Stevenson Clothing.

From: <w.jacobs@stevensonclothing.com>
To: <b.Quinn@sartoriaco.com>
Subject: hi

Hey Bridget Quinn from Sartoria.

- Will

I drop the phone on the counter. It clatters loudly but Ginger remains unbothered, too focused on her dinner to care. I, however, stand shellshocked, confusion flooding my system. What is he doing?

Brows raised, I pick up my phone and decide to reply.

From: <b.Quinn@sartoriaco.com>
To: <w.jacobs@stevensonclothing.com>
Subject: Re: hi

Um, hi?

- Bridget

. . .

I CHEW ON MY FINGERNAIL, EYES FIXED ON MY PHONE SCREEN. Every couple of seconds I swipe down, refreshing the app, until a new email from him comes through.

From: <w.jacobs@stevensonclothing.com>
To: <b.Quinn@sartoriaco.com>
Subject: Re: Re: hi

What, no company signature this time?

- Will

Is he for real?

From: <b.Quinn@sartoriaco.com>
To: <w.jacobs@stevensonclothing.com>
Subject: Re: Re: Re: hi

Why are you emailing me?

- B

I worry it comes off as abrasive, but I'm genuinely curious. And while I believe he's probably an entry-level person like me, given that I've never seen him come to the showroom whenever the client comes in for a meeting, he's still a member of their team. I need to proceed with caution.

His answer doesn't come as quickly as the first, so I find myself pacing my small apartment like a lion in a cage, my mind running through every possible scenario—each one more unlikely than the next.

From: <w.jacobs@stevensonclothing.com>
To: <b.Quinn@sartoriaco.com>
Subject: Re: Re: hi

The truth?

- Will

I reply back in seconds.

From: <b.Quinn@sartoriaco.com>
To: <w.jacobs@stevensonclothing.com>
Subject: Re: Re: Re: hi

Always. The truth is *always* better.

- B

Can my life take another person lying to me? Who knows. But also, what does it matter when this is a random person I don't even know?

My stomach turns as I wait. This is our *customer* emailing me, though. If Lena found out we were emailing on the side she'd… What, exactly? I mean, it's not like there's explicit rules about this, right? But… still, it doesn't feel right.

```
From: <w.jacobs@stevensonclothing.com>
To: <b.Quinn@sartoriaco.com>
Subject: Re: Re: hi

I'm not sure.
I guess I needed a friend.

- Will
```

My fingers hover over the screen as I think of what I could possibly reply to that. He needed a friend? I know what that's like, but what can I possibly say that would help?

In the end, I decide not to reply, but I toss and turn all night in my Murphy bed, going over his words in my head a hundred times over.

He needed a friend. And I guess I've been in more situations than I can count where I've needed support and been lucky enough to get it. But I've also been in situations where I've lost friendships due to things that have happened to me because of my bad luck that were out of my control. Like, right after Roger left, a few of my friends ghosted me after he swindled them out of some cash. They blamed me for bringing him into their lives and cut me out of it for good despite not having anything to do with his grifting. Which is why, despite not owing this stranger anything, the following morning the people pleaser in me can't help but reach out to check in on him because I've been through some very lonely lows myself.

```
From: <b.Quinn@sartoriaco.com>
To: <w.jacobs@stevensonclothing.com>
Subject: Re: Re: Re: Re: hi


Do you want to talk about it? I'm a good
listener (or reader, I guess).


- Bridget
```

I feed Ginger her breakfast and get dressed. Once she's done, she jumps with grace on the teal tufted reading chair I inherited from my grandmother. I, on the other hand, keep refreshing my app, waiting for his reply to come through—but nothing ever does. It isn't until I'm back in the office, several hours later, that I hear from him again.

```
From: <w.jacobs@stevensonclothing.com>
To: <b.Quinn@sartoriaco.com>
Subject: Re: Re: Re: Re: hi


Haha you're sweet. But I'm good. Work is just
a lot. This industry can sometimes be… well.
You know.
You excited about the new collection? Haven't
received any emails today from you expressing
how cool you think things are going lately.


- Will
```

I blush a deep crimson, grimacing at my computer screen as I sink deeper into my office chair. So this is gonna be a thing between us now? Him teasing me about my mistake? I sigh. Still, though, I won't let him distract me from what's going on. Because if it's work related, I absolutely understand. Plus, his comment and the way he phrased what's frustrating him is confirmation enough that he must be a little minion just like me, puttering about, trying to survive every day. So there's no way I'm letting him off the hook that easy.

```
From: <b.Quinn@sartoriaco.com>
To: <w.jacobs@stevensonclothing.com>
Subject: Re: Re: Re: Re: Re: Re: hi


Nice deflection.

And yes. I am excited.

What's going on over there?

- Bridget
```

```
From: <w.jacobs@stevensonclothing.com>
To: <b.Quinn@sartoriaco.com>
Subject: Re: Re: Re: Re: Re: Re: hi


I'm not deflecting. But these are corporate
email accounts. And I don't want either of us
to get in trouble for talking.
```

I'm sorry I said those things and made you
worry. But I'm totally fine I promise. Maybe
it's best if we go back to our regularly
scheduled professional relationship.

- Will

God.

I squeeze my eyes shut and bite my lip, feeling bad. He isn't
wrong about getting in trouble for using the company emails for
this, but for some reason it feels wrong to just let this go. Like I'd
be breaking some unspoken junior employee/minion support
group code. I mean, what kind of person would I be if I just left
things like that, knowing that this guy is having a hard time?
What if his boss is just as ogre-like as mine?

I take a deep breath and murmur "Don't make me regret
this" before replying with my personal email.

In just under a minute, I refresh my personal email and find
a new message:

From: <will.jacobs0516@xmail.com>
To: <bees_knees_0214@xmail.com>
Subject: (blank)

Hey.

- Will

WILL

It was just a one word email, but something about it felt monumental.
Hey.
A simple hello, three letters, one syllable.
It feels like the beginning of something big.
And honestly, thank god for that.

3

WHO'S THE REAL G.O.A.T.?

```
From: <will.jacobs0516@xmail.com>
To: <bees_knees_0214@xmail.com>
Subject: Re: Goats are the G.O.A.T.


You can't be serious. There's no way that's a
real thing. This video is definitely doctored
or something. It's got to be AI.


- Will
```

I giggle on my bed as Ginger sleeps peacefully beside me, twisted on her back with her paws in the air. Though I shake the mattress with my laughter, she barely acknowledges my existence.

```
From: <bees_knees_0214@xmail.com>
To: <will.jacobs0516@xmail.com>
Subject: Re: Re: Goats are the G.O.A.T.
```

I am telling you, goat yoga is a real thing. Baby goat yoga is even better. I've done it before.

- Bridget

From: <will.jacobs0516@xmail.com>
To: <bees_knees_0214@xmail.com>
Subject: Re: Re: Re: Goats are the G.O.A.T.

I'm sorry, but I'm gonna have to call bull-shit, here. Where would you even do it in NYC? Where do people keep livestock here? I work out often and I have never heard of "goat yoga." Hot yoga, yes. Never any type of farm animal yoga.

- Will

I snort as I re-read his words, focusing on the part where he admits to working out often. Immediately, my mind drifts to wondering what Will, this man I've been speaking to only via email, looks like. I've tried not to. Tried to not think about his build or hair color, stopped myself several times from looking up his socials (besides that one time I tried searching for his LinkedIn) or asking Lena if she's met him by chance at client meetings. And I've been surprisingly successful at keeping myself in check. I know it sounds crazy, but I feel like finding out what he looks like would shatter part of whatever spell exists between us in this odd friendship. Like I'd be losing an anonymous confidant and ruining it with a real life person.

But then I wonder whether he's secretly an evil demon on the other end of my emails, like that one episode of Buffy the Vampire Slayer in season one when that green guy tries to get out of the computer in order to take over the world. Part of me wants to make sure I'm not responsible for bringing about the end of civilization as we know it. (Hey, it can happen. You never know.)

So yeah, my mind has gotten away from me sometimes in an uncharacteristically negative way, but it isn't often. For the most part, talking to Will has mostly been so much *fun*. So I get ahead of myself and start imagining *other* things. *Good* things. This usually happens when I learn something brand new about him. Like just now: he says he goes to the gym and does it often. Does that mean that he's a The Rock type of gym-goer, built large and hard? Or is he just in shape? And that's even *if* he's being honest about the frequency with which he attends, because I'm always conscious of the fact that this man could be the world's biggest liar. He could be telling me exactly what I want to hear. He could be a serial killer or something.

And yet... I still can't kick the habit of speaking to him. I wouldn't care what he looks like. Not if he's still the guy he is in our interactions.

From: <bees_knees_0214@xmail.com>
To: <will.jacobs0516@xmail.com>
Subject: Re: Re: Re: Re: Goats are the
G.O.A.T.

One thing you should know about me is that I
never tell a lie.

- Bridget

From: <will.jacobs0516@xmail.com>
To: <bees_knees_0214@xmail.com>
Subject: Re: Re: Re: Re: Re: Goats are the
G.O.A.T.

Fine. I'm sure it would probably smell the
entire time, but I guess you're gonna have to
take me there yourself, then. I gotta see it
to believe it.

- Will

My whole body tenses as I read and reread the words in his
email. He wants to meet? Like... in person? Like... face-to-face?
Or was that just an expression?

I can't be too surprised, though, right? I mean, we were probably going to meet anyways. Our paths are bound to cross any
day now, given our work. It's just a matter of time until Lena
decides I'm ready to go to an in-person client meeting or the
same happens for Will. From what he tells me, we both work for
difficult bosses (although I'm not quite sure yet who his exact
supervisor is). Neither one of them are the easiest people to get
along with. Still, it won't be long until we're in the same room at
the same time, and after weeks of talking, it might be weird if

our first interaction is in front of other people. Especially since things have turned a little flirty.

Or maybe it's just my imagination. Even a bit of wishful thinking, if I'm being honest with myself.

I chew on my bottom lip, fingers hovering over my phone screen, searching not only for the right words, but for what I truly want from this friendship. Should I *carpe* the hell out of this *diem* or keep this distance and let our relationship progress professionally? Or is *this* the natural progression of it all?

Just as I click into the message box to reply, however, my phone buzzes again. This time with a text from Lena.

LENA

Need you in the office ASAP. And get me two extra hot flat whites and a warmed coffee cake.

Phew. Saved by Crazy Pants.

"I can't have you lose focus on the Stevenson account, Bridget. I know you're just an associate, but you *do* perform vital tasks to this project." Lena sits behind her desk, arms folded in front of her, her eyes pinning me to my seat. "I know we started off slow, working what some would call *reasonable* hours. But things are getting choppy with the client. This is our first season ever with them, and if things don't go to plan, we might lose them altogether."

I suppress a sigh because I know what she's telling me: no more of that same work/life balance I was just thanking my lucky stars for. And while that may suck, in its own way, it's actually amazing. It means Lena needs me. It means that she's going to be giving me more responsibility. I shouldn't be surprised, to be honest. After all, she did start including me in the emails. Like she said, I perform vital tasks. I am an *essential* member of the team. I need to be on call to bring her food when she needs it.

Sigh.

"I'm going to need you to be flexible about hours; I'll need you to get my coffee and lunches most days since I'll be stuck to my chair, working. Of course, you'll have to continue handling my calendar and scheduling."

"Oh," I say, deflating a bit. I already perform those duties as an assistant sometimes, but is she referring to doing them *all* the time? "I thought..." But I trail off, not knowing how to proceed.

She raises a brow. "You thought what, exactly?"

I shake my head. "Nothing. I just... I thought you needed me to be more involved in a direct way."

Lena purses her lips and sits back in her chair. "And what exactly do you think you'd be able to bring to the table, Bridget? Besides the past three months of work you've done here, you have no experience whatsoever doing this kind of work. Frankly, we hired you in a moment of desperation because I needed an assistant quickly as the Stevenson account was fast-approaching and your friend Molly gave you a personal referral. Right now, you're nothing more than a blank slate. You will have zero input on anything. Your job is to keep me informed and the other teams in line."

I try to control the stinging behind my eyes, tears threatening to make a very unwelcome appearance. Something about Lena tells me that she wouldn't take too well to someone crying in her office (though the same instinct tells me she's no stranger to it, either).

In a surprising turn of events, however, Lena's eyes soften—infinitesimally, but still. "You're not *young* young, but you *are* green. New to this industry. I can't trust you yet. You haven't done anything to prove that I can. And this project is too risky for me to let you take on any big responsibilities on a leap of faith. Can you understand that?"

I press my lips together and nod, too scared to open my mouth and say something for fear of letting her hear my voice break. With a nod toward her office door, she dismisses me.

I dash through the office floor, looking for somewhere to hide so I can break down where no one can see me. The bathrooms would be a logical choice, but the risk of someone finding me mid-breakdown is too high.

On a whim, I decide to spend the next few minutes of my work day crying in the sample closet—a nice, dark place filled with awesome clothes, each one so beautiful it helps to settle my nerves.

I sit in the corner of the walk-in, hidden behind a rack of ballgowns, and put my face in my hands as I cry. I consider texting Molly to ask her to meet me back here so I can vent, but she's made it clear that she doesn't trust my ability to keep this job—at least not 100%. *Just like Lena.*

For a moment, I allow myself to be sad, to absorb the situation. I'm gutted I got my hopes up thinking Lena was opening the door for me to receive more responsibilities, to give me more autonomy over certain duties that fall under my role, but at least I still have a job. I've never held one down this long, and for that, I need to be thankful. And she just told me what I needed in order to get to where I want: earn her trust; prove my worth. So I'm sure I can get there.

When my phone vibrates in my pocket, I pull it out immediately praying for a positive distraction.


```
From: <will.jacobs0516@xmail.com>
To: <bees_knees_0214@xmail.com>
Subject: A case of the Tuesdays
```


A HINT OF A SMILE PLAYS AT MY LIPS AS I SNIFFLE, HIS NAME ON MY screen instantly making me feel better. Without giving it another thought, I open Will's email as I sit in the corner of the sample closet, in the dark, hidden behind pounds of luxurious, responsibly manufactured, materials.


```
From: <will.jacobs0516@xmail.com>
To: <bees_knees_0214@xmail.com>
Subject: A case of the Tuesdays
```


```
Dear Bridge,

I'm currently writing this email while in a
"very important" meeting. I'm supposed to be
taking notes, but I swear to god I cannot
stand another minute of having the same
conversations over and over again. My brain is
fried and my soul close to being wiped out so
I figured I'd do something I enjoy and email
you, my friend (pen pal? Vendor? Who knows),
and tell you all about my day instead.
I can vent to you, can't I, Bridge?
```

Anyway. Here goes:

I hate Tuesdays. I hate Tuesdays with a passion. And I know what you're going to say: "Don't you mean Mondays?" And I will whole-heartedly reply with a "hell no."

Mondays are glorious days that offer us a fresh start. The opportunity to start the week off better than we did the one before—an unlikely POV that someone as negative as myself would have. But it's true, nonetheless. I love Mondays because they're all about starting off strong.

Tuesdays, however… Tuesdays have a nasty habit of knocking all the optimism you gathered on Monday right out of you if you're not careful. You started the week off the day before by making a plan, organizing yourself, only to have Tuesday meetings pop up to fuck up your life. Why are Tuesday meetings almost always filled with bad news? Granted, it's not every time, but when they are, it's disheartening. Like today's most recent meeting—the one I'm currently in—where our finance department is making what I believe are really dumb fucking decisions, but I can't say anything about it because I answer to some all powerful force here that will not take my disagreeing with him too kindly. Retaliation tends to be the name of the game around these parts of town, and I don't consider myself to be a masochist— or a sadist for that matter.

(Not that I kink shame. We all have our *thing.* I'd ask you what yours is, but not sure if

we're at that point in our friendship yet. Do
let me know when we are, though.)
So, here I am. About to lose my mind as I see
a group of people make decisions that are best
for themselves and not our consumer or shareholders, and I can't do anything about it. All
I can do is channel my new friend Bridget and
try to find the good—that silver lining—which
is that today is one less day I have to work
at this damn company. And hopefully next
Monday will set the tone for a better week.
Tell me about your day. It's bound to be
better than mine.
- Will
PS. Will accept any other cute goat or animal
videos you have that may cheer me up. :)

A WET LAUGH BURSTS THROUGH ME AS I SCROLL THROUGH HIS
message once again. Maybe a cute animal video will cheer the
both of us up.

From: <bees_knees_0214@xmail.com>
To: <will.jacobs0516@xmail.com>
Subject: Re: A case of the Tuesdays

Will,

How irresponsible of you to fake work! I'm
appalled (LOL). If only I could do the same.
I'm honored, however, that you've been

thinking of channeling me today—I keep
telling you that focusing on the bright side
will make you a happier person. Manifest the
life you want! It hasn't fully worked for me
yet, but I'm hopeful. Plus, life could be way
worse! Focusing on the silver lining sometimes is the best way to keep going when
things are hard.
In the spirit of remaining positive, today has
been *interesting*. There's a growth opportunity
at work, so that's good! Also, I wore my new
(old) vintage dress that I found on eBay to
work today and felt like a million bucks! If a
million bucks were a cashmere dress from the
seventies with a high, yet still professional,
slit and a flared collar that cost me $25. It
had a few snags, but I managed to sew them up
and revamped it with some delicate beading and
it looks great.
So you can see, all good things.
And as requested, here's a link to another
video—this one's about a German shepherd and a
black cat and how they travel all over the
world camping in these amazing places with
their human parents and are best friends who
cuddle in the woods and stuff.

- Bridget

ONCE I HIT SEND, I STAND, RUN MY FINGERS THROUGH MY HAIR,
and wipe the tears from my cheeks. Time to head out to the

bathroom and get myself cleaned up before going back to work. But as I reach for the door, my phone vibrates once more.

```
From: <will.jacobs0516@xmail.com>
To: <bees_knees_0214@xmail.com>
Subject: Re: Re: A case of the Tuesdays
```

What's wrong? Are you okay? What does *'interesting'* mean, exactly?

```
From: <bees_knees_0214@xmail.com>
To: <will.jacobs0516@xmail.com>
Subject: Re: Re: Re: A case of the Tuesdays
```

Everything's fine, I swear! Just tired. Your team is apparently turning up the heat, so my boss is stressing a bit. She's so scared of losing this contract. Not sure why, since she won't tell me much, and I'm sure you don't know either, being part of the finance team. But it looks like there's some tension between our two companies.

Anyway, Lena's getting a lot of pushback from you guys, apparently. She made the sourcing team work until late last night so that they could have a call with our overseas suppliers and negotiate a lower cost of materials. No one thought she'd be able to, and everyone was hating on her behind her back for making them stay late, but she got it done.

Anyway, she's been extra stressed and I guess
taking it out on me.
Not gonna lie, Will. Your bosses are proving
to be impossible to please. We're getting you
everything you ask for, but pricing never
seems to be good enough.
(And this is the last I'll go into semi-
detail, btw. I would never want us to cross
that line. I like this friendship we've got
going for us.)

- Bridget

From: <will.jacobs0516@xmail.com>
To: <bees_knees_0214@xmail.com>
Subject: Re: Re: Re: Re: A case of the
Tuesdays

Yeah, I heard something along those lines with
regards to pricing… But I promise I won't say
anything more. I agree—let's be careful about
what we share regarding work. This odd thing
we have going for us? There's not a thing I
would do to ruin it. I enjoy talking to you
too much.

- Will

My heart flutters in my throat as I read and reread the last two sentences of his email. As soon as it does, I push it back down because *what am I thinking?* A pen pal relationship with someone I have a cool connection with is fine. But having a crush on a literal stranger who could be anyone? Nope, that definitely isn't cool.

Still, I can't help my reply:

```
From: <bees_knees_0214@xmail.com>
To: <will.jacobs0516@xmail.com>
Subject: Re: Re: Re: Re: Re: A case of the
Tuesdays

I enjoy talking to you, too. A lot.
```

We don't talk again until the following day, the longest we've gone without speaking.

WILL

If you'd have asked him just a few weeks ago to describe what the best part of his day is, he'd have told you it's the scalding hot forty-five minute shower he takes after his hour-long workout session. It's the only time Will allows himself to decompress properly and soak in any type of true feeling of accomplishment he may have earned throughout the day or even week.

Lately, however, the best part of his day has been whenever Will receives any message from her. From the assistant that works for Stevenson's vendor who he has yet to meet in person. The notification of an email on his phone or computer no longer fills him with dread and disappointment. Now, all he feels is a rush of adrenaline—the kind he gets during one of his workouts, but better—just from the thought that it might be a message from Bridget Quinn.

4
———

MURPHY BEDS ARE SEVERELY
UNDERRATED

Whe my phone goes off during lunch, a thrill courses through my entire body. I don't even have to check my phone to know it's *him*. My face breaks into a giant grin.

Will.

Instinctively, I reach out to read his text—probably his response to the link for goat yoga classes in Brooklyn I went to yesterday just to prove to him they existed. I did not invite him to come with me.

> **WILL**
>
> That's insane. Those poor goats! You've goat-a
> be kid-ing me.

I snort at his excessive use of goat puns, my heart doing more somersaults than an olympian—something that's been happening way too often when we talk.

He's so adorable with his stupid dad jokes.

"Um, ma'am?" Molly eyes me suspiciously over our salads on our lunch break. "What's going on here? Who has you smiling like that?"

My entire face falls, whatever flip was happening in my chest moved down to my stomach at the possibility of getting caught, of having to reveal this secret friendship. Because even though Molly and I have been close for several years, I'm sure she wouldn't approve of whatever Will and I have. Not when it can affect my job and, in turn, hers for having been the one who helped get me hired. "Um. No one?"

"No one? Your face was about to split in two from how big you were smiling, and you literally just giggled. *Giggled.* Who even does that anymore?"

Admittedly, it shouldn't be that difficult to hide this secret pen pal relationship I've been carrying on with a member of our client team. I mean, among the million things I could've done, I could've also just *not* checked my messages while in close proximity to anyone else. But my guard was down in front of Molly since she's also a real life friend, and it was just too tempting to ignore the obnoxious personalized ringtone I set for Will—the chorus from *Get Knocked Down* by Chumbawamba (it's a long story that revolves around him telling me about the time he performed a dance in a talent show to this very song in parachute pants and me promising to never let it down. He refuses to send a picture of said performance, but I've vowed to obtain it one day).

Recently, we've evolved from email buddies to texting buddies, which has somehow opened up our relationship even more. Besides the fact that communicating has become faster and easier, having each other's numbers has given way to the possibility of actually *calling*, of hearing each other's voices. For some odd reason, though, I don't feel ready enough for that yet. It's like the stakes have been raised, but I'm not ready to push the limits. Still, knowing that it's a possibility, that the opportunity to take this to verbal communication is there, is thrilling. It could be that it all feels like a secret neither of us can tell. It could also be that there's an obvious attraction via text.

I sigh. "Just someone I met through Tinder." *As if I'd ever be caught dead on that app again. Vom.* "We've only been chatting, though. No IRL communication, yet."

I know I told Will I never lie, but this is different. I'm just trying to protect my job—and, honestly, probably my relationship with Molly. What would she say to finding out I have a flirty virtual friendship with someone from one of our clients? Would she tell me I was doing something wrong and chastise me? Tell me I'm going to get fired and ruin her reputation?

Still the guilt of the lie begins to eat at me, because it's not in my nature. My throat tightens as if I'm having an allergic reaction to it or something. I swallow hard a couple of times and force a smile that I hope says *I am not hiding anything—I promise!*

Molly eyes me suspiciously because she knows I'd die before joining another dating app. My only experience with them was short-lived and with good reason. I mean, what about meet cutes? Whatever happened to those? I understand that over fifty percent of relationships start like that now—possibly even more —but I want my movie moment.

"Tinder?" She asks, definitely not buying it.

"Yup."

"Let me see that." She reaches over the table to grab my phone, but I pull it away just in time.

"That's *private*. Just focus on… on finishing your sixteen dollar salad!"

Molly frowns, looks down at her overpriced, yet delicious-looking chopped salad, and back at me. "Seventeen-fifty. They increased the price of avocados again."

I gasp, bringing a hand to my chest. "I didn't know you came from old money," I tease. But also, who in their right mind would pay that much for a salad?

She pokes at her lettuce with a sigh. "No more good fats for me. I'm gonna have to start bringing lunch from home like a normal person."

I think for a moment I've saved myself, distracted her enough by changing the topic to the same thing she eats every single day, until her eyes flash back at me.

"You're deflecting," she accuses, through narrowed eyes. "What's going on? I thought you were holding out on dating again after the whole Roger thing."

Ah, well. There's that, too. Because "the whole Roger thing" is a euphemism for how the guy I was dating eight months ago kinda, almost destroyed my life. Three months into our relationship, he had already lied, cheated, scammed people around me into giving him money for a fake business, and somehow managed to get me kicked out of my previous apartment, leaving me homeless, before disappearing into the night with all my money and whatever material valuables I had (which admittedly weren't many).

Thankfully, he didn't take the only thing that truly matters to me: Ginger. That, and Grandma's old teal chair.

"Oh. That. I forgot about that." I sink in my seat.

"You *forgot* about that? How could you just forget about something like that?" she asks, a brow raised so high it almost gets lost beneath her bangs.

I shrug once and spear a piece of lettuce with my fork. "You know me. Always trying to focus on the positive."

"The positive? The guy took off in the middle of the night with your grandmother's necklace and pearl earrings which she gave you the night before she died. Wasn't she the only family member you liked?"

"Dating Roger at least taught me what I *don't* want in a relationship: a liar and a criminal—"

"Way to set the bar super high," Molly deadpans.

"And I've never *disliked* people in my family, necessarily. They've just historically... not been good to me. Except for Gran, of course." I close my eyes and shake my head, not wanting to let thoughts of Mom ruin what started off as a great day. The hurt is inevitably followed by guilt, because I know Mom had her own demons to fight since her mental health problems were left untreated. She couldn't help who she was or how she acted, and I was too young to find access to the right care. But even Gran couldn't do anything, she'd told me. For years, she'd tried to get Mom to go to doctors, put her in a hospital. Nothing stuck, though.

When Mom died, I went to live at Gran's which left me feeling both depressed and relieved at the same time. My mother was gone, but I was finally in a living situation where I didn't have to be scared 24/7.

"I only met my mom's brother a couple of times and he was whatever. And I don't know who my father is," I go on. "So there's hope that, if I ever meet him, he could be a nice guy."

Molly scoffs. "Doesn't the fact that he also disappeared into the night negate the possibility of that?"

"We don't know that. My mom was the one who said he ran away when he found out she was pregnant, but who's to say with her? She was unstable and unreliable. Maybe he doesn't even know I exist, you know? What if she never even told him? Or what if she never even knew who he was?" Molly looks at me with a sympathetic expression, like she wants to reach over the table and hug me. "Oh, stop it," I tell her.

"Stop what?"

"Stop looking at me like I'm some sad three-legged puppy in a shelter that you want to adopt. I'm totally fine."

"But you *are* a three-legged puppy in a shelter—or at least the human equivalent."

"I highly resent that. Roger leaving turned out to be a good thing. Especially for Ginger, who hated him and resented having to share a bed with him. I lead a fantastic life now." I say it with my whole chest because I believe it to be true. I've never been more mentally exhausted, but it's a good thing. Every day I'm being challenged, working in a difficult environment—absolutely—but one that will take me places so long as I keep going.

"You live in a pest-infested shoe box where you sleep on a shitty Murphy bed, work at a demanding, low-paying job, and have been fucked over by too many people close to you."

I mean, she's not wrong. *But...*

"First of all, you were the one who found me this place—"

"Because you had no other choice."

"—and Murphy beds are *fun*. They're basically magic: they come out of a closet, so I don't have to make my bed every day because I can just put it away. Outta sight, outta mind. And my apartment is no longer pest-infested thanks to some basic insect repellant and Ginger's hunting abilities—seriously, you should see that cat kill a water bug. She's a pro. And as for the job? Sure, it doesn't pay much. But I'm positive once they see how hard I'm working and how well I'm doing, they'll reward me for it."

Molly bursts out laughing and pats my hand. "Oh, sweet, innocent, sunshine child of mine. You think the world of fashion is that simple? Nuh-uh. But I envy your positive energy. I just don't want you to get hung up on this false sense of hope or toxic positivity. Yes, I love that you love your job and you're doing your best to, quote, *look at the bright side of things*. But don't let that deter you from taking chances or asking for more. Don't let yourself just accept how things are with a smile and a good attitude—you deserve better."

I look down at my salad and spear some more of it before stuffing my face. "Thanks," I say, mouth full. "But I got this."

I understand where Molly is coming from—I do. But after the life I've had, I can't let myself sit in stress for too long without doing my best to get something good out of it. Which is why I want to be careful with the whole Will situation. What we have is an odd friendship or dynamic. Something delicate that I'm not sure I'm ready for Molly to know about just yet. I'm not *scared*; I'm just trying to protect this *one* thing.

When I get back to my desk, I see I have another message from Will:

WILL

Did you stop replying because you thought my brilliant goat puns were baaaaad?

"OH MY GOD."

I giggle and I hit reply.

WILL

She's brought him back to life.

5

———

DID WE TAKE IT TOO FAR?

Balancing my bags, I manage to open my apartment door after an interminable day at work. Ginger greets me at the door, but with a glare this time.

Meowww.

"I know, I know. I'm late. But to be fair, you only had to wait an extra—" I check the time on my phone. "—forty-five minutes for dinner. Your water bowl is half-full and, even for a Maine Coone, you're a few pounds overweight. So, no offense, but you can handle a little delay in your dinner."

I swear she shoots me a look before walking ahead of me into the kitchen.

"I'm not trying to fat shame you. You know I'm all about body positivity here. I just mean to say that—"

She turns back to hiss softly at me, her tail swooshing in the air as if to say *No more excuses, human. Just feed me.*

Heaving a sigh, I dump my things on the floor beside the door after locking it behind me and proceed to feed Ginger before even heading to the bathroom. It doesn't matter that I've been dying to pee for the past three subway stops—I'd rather avoid death by cat at this point.

Once I'm settled, I dig into tonight's dinner: a bag full of Valentine's Day candy (it was a long day at work and the pink and red wall of two-for-one candy and chocolate at Walgreen's seemed way too good to pass up).

It's not like things have been *bad* at work, but it's been a lot, that's for sure. Lena wasn't joking around when she warned me the stakes had been raised with the Stevenson deal. Our client's team had liked the preliminary designs so much that they'd increased their orders from five articles of clothing to nine, with a total of twenty SKUs. This meant we had to develop a full high-end and environmentally friendly collection, rather than the experimental pieces we had agreed to start with. This *also* means that the client has gained a bit more negotiating power, which they used to press us for deeper discounts and shorter turn-around times. We want to impress them, to keep them as clients for next season, so everything has to go just right.

And while more products and a bigger line might seem like a completely wonderful development, our team wasn't prepared to take on so much work. Each product requires development, tech pack creations which need to be sent to the factories, sample productions, and quality controls—all things that take time, energy, and money. On top of that, they require us to reserve more factory space than expected, which means having to move around lead times for other clients who don't have as pressing delivery times as Stevenson. And this is all based only on projections. We haven't even solidified a collection yet! Again, it's a beautiful dance, but it takes a lot of coordination, and I just need a shot of dopamine in the form of sugar—and the cheap bottle of wine I splurged on when I stopped by a liquor store on my way home.

The entire thing has been an incredible learning experience, where I've been absorbing every possible thing I can from working with Lena. It's taught me that, despite her abrasive personality, she's incredible. There's not a single person who doesn't listen to her in meetings, who doesn't follow her every word and expression. Lena is a wealth of knowledge and a true force to be reckoned with. It leaves me wondering why the hell she's stuck in this upper management role and isn't killing it at the top. Could it be her less-than-sparkling personality? Or has she been passed up for someone better (which seems highly unlikely)? Either way, I took her words to heart and am now trying to absorb any and every single little thing around me.

I'm on my third Reese's cup and second glass of wine, when *he* texts.

WILL

Hey, you.

BRIDGET

Hey back! Haven't spoken to you in a while.

I CHECK THE TIMESTAMP FROM OUR LAST TEXT EXCHANGE, WHERE we challenged ourselves to say how our last meetings went with just a meme (Michael Scott screaming *No. No, no no. No* a thousand times for him; Meryl Streep playing Miranda Priestly in *Devil Wears Prada* giving someone a judgmental once-over for me, because not everyone appreciates a good vintage piece in my office).

BRIDGET

Well, two and a half hours

WILL

Two hours is a lot for us tho, isn't it? At least
lately

BRIDGET

Yeah. Unless we're sleeping

WILL

Nah, I'm convinced I talk to you in my
dreams too

A FEELING OF WARMTH THAT'S GROWN ALL TOO FAMILIAR LATELY
spreads through me as I reread his words, teeth biting into my
lower lip.

I want to run my fingers over his words, feel them sink deep
in my skin.

BRIDGET

Do you think we're overdoing it?

WILL

What do you mean?

BRIDGET

I mean, we're like always talking.

WILL

Does it bother you? Bc we can stop if you want.

Though I gotta admit I really don't want to stop.

BRIDGET

No! I enjoy talking to you. But maybe it's too
much?

WILL

Why would we stop doing something we enjoy
doing?

I SIGH. GINGER OPENS ONE EYE TO CHECK THAT I'M FINE, BUT
immediately falls back asleep with an even more dramatic,
dragon-worthy heave.

BRIDGET

What are you up to? How was your day?

WILL

Well, I'm currently on my third beer and second
bowl of Cocoa Puffs. So.

BRIDGET

Oh man. That bad, huh?

WILL

Whatever. Could've been better; could've been
worse.

BRIDGET

That's the spirit

WILL

I just need to stick it out for a few more months
and I'm done.

BRIDGET

What do you mean?

WILL

What about you? You out at a fancy happy hour
with a bunch of fashionistas? Are you friends
with your entire office already?

. . .

I SNORT, THE SIMPLE IMAGE OF ME OUT TO DRINKS WITH LENA almost leading me into hysterical laughter. I don't miss how he avoids my question, but I answer his instead of pressing him again. Our friendship is relatively new and I don't want to mess it up by being too pushy.

BRIDGET

I'm currently in bed drinking wine and eating an industrial amount of Valentine's Day candy. Definitely not in the partying mood.

WILL

So we're basically in the same boat then.

BRIDGET

LOL

WILL

If you're eating all the candy tonight, what are your plans for day of, then?

For Valentine's, I mean.

BRIDGET

Is this your not-so-subtle way of asking whether I'm seeing someone?

WILL

Haha I guess it is

I GIGGLE ALONE INTO MY WINE GLASS, A THRILL COURSING through me. It's honestly so odd we haven't even touched upon the subject of significant others. I guess, if I'm being honest with myself, I've been too scared to ask.

.   .   .

BRIDGET

Wouldn't it be kind of inappropriate for us to talk this much if I was in a relationship?

WILL

What do you mean?

BRIDGET

Well, you're a dude. And we text each other all day. I wouldn't be happy if my partner were texting someone from the opposite sex all the time. It just isn't appropriate.

Unless they were gay. Are you gay?

OMG I'm so sorry that's not appropriate to ask.

WILL

Jfc you need to calm down. LOL

I'm not offended at all by your question.

And I think you know I'm not gay, Bridget

BRIDGET

What is that supposed to mean?

WILL

I am very much straight and single.

BRIDGET

And ready to mingle? Haha

WILL

Maybe.

BRIDGET

Um, ok.

WILL

Do you date much?

. . .

I take a beat because this feels like we're entering dangerous territory. I may have been lying to myself before, but I'm not anymore. I absolutely do have a crush on this man, so this topic of discussion? Probably not something I want to get into. Still, I reply:

BRIDGET

Not really. Tbh, my dating life has been a notorious nightmare. Despite all the disastrous men I've dated, though, I'm still looking for the right guy. But I'll admit I'm still too much of a romantic for the current dating scene. I blame it on all bad experiences and the old movies and romcoms I grew up watching. That's kinda the love I'm looking for.

Watching those movies were my favorite hobby to keep myself busy during the long periods of time my Mom was MIA on one of her downward spirals. This was all before Gran knew exactly how bad things were, before Mom died, and before I moved in with the woman who changed my life. I still watch romcoms and old romantic movies, but now it's because I want to and not because I need someone to keep me company while I'm all alone at home. And that feels better than anyone will ever know.

WILL

Oh, yeah? Which movies?

BRIDGET

IDK. Anything Audrey Hepburn or Nora Ephron.

WILL

So movies that are anywhere between 70 to 20
years old?

BRIDGET

God, SEVENTY???

WILL

Yeah, I think. Definitely not about modern love.

BRIDGET

Yeah, I guess I'm not a fan of modern love. The
eighties song, yes. The current state of our
dating world, no.

WILL

Preach. It's a nightmare. Nowadays, it's all
about apps.

BRIDGET

OMG. I can't deal with apps.

WILL

I feel like there's a fun story there.

BRIDGET

Doesn't everyone have one with dating apps?

WILL

Yeah, but I only wanna hear yours.

BRIDGET

sigh fine.

WILL

Wow. You caved easily haha

BRIDGET

I mean, it is pretty bananas. So buckle up
buttercup.

WILL

clicks seatbelt

I SNORT AS I FLUFF MY PILLOWS, GETTING COZIER BEFORE I HIT HIM with my first and last app dating story:

BRIDGET

I swiped right on this one guy my very first time using the app. Seemed innocent enough—very guy next door, nothing threatening about the way he looked in his pictures. Five seconds into our conversation, he asked to see a picture of my pussy.

WILL

Jesus. I'm opening my fourth bottle of beer after that. I'm sorry on behalf of all men.

What did you do?

BRIDGET

I sent him a picture of Ginger, just like he asked. LOL. He called me a bitch and a tease even though it was literally our first time talking and I never hinted at anything sexual. Then he blocked me. Needless to say I haven't been on another dating app since.

WILL

Jesus. I don't blame you.

BRIDGET

Tho I feel like dating apps have nothing to do with my luck with guys, honestly. I met my most recent ex organically through friends we had in common and he turned out to be a grifter who ruined my life

So

WILL

Fantastic. We're gonna have to circle back to that whole "grifter who ruined my life thing," tho

BRIDGET

Wow, ok. I can't believe you used "circle back" in one of our conversations. You really did have a long day at the office, didn't you? Too much corporate lingo for one day?

Next thing you know you're going to tell me we should "sidebar" this conversation before "double-clicking into it" further.

WILL

Fuck, I can't even control myself anymore. I need to get out of this hellhole.

If I ever use the word "synergy" in a sentence, please shoot me. That would be the last straw. It would make things official: I'd be a corporate robot.

THE LOGICAL PART OF ME KNOWS THIS WOULD BE A GREAT opportunity to ask why he hates work so much. Or why he keeps dodging the question of how he needs to stick it out a little longer and can't leave now. But there's a louder part of my brain (or maybe it's my heart?) that needs to have this conversation:

BRIDGET

What about you?

WILL

What about me?

BRIDGET

Come on. You know what I mean. Your dating life.

WILL

Sigh

I'd need to have time for a life at all in order to have the sub-genre of dating.

BRIDGET

Hahaha good one.

WILL

Glad I made you laugh. Tbh, it feels like I fill half my day wondering what it sounds like when you do.

I suck in a breath, my phone shaking in my hands. Did he really just—?

WILL

Most of the time, I'm at work. When I'm not, I'm at the gym. Which means I don't have the time to take anyone out.

I swallow the lump in my throat, convinced he only meant the thing about my laughter as a passing comment. It had to have been, right?

. . .

BRIDGET

You can multitask. Find someone at work or the gym. You can take her on lunch dates in the office or take a work out class as a date.

WILL

Nah. Not interested.

BRIDGET

So what, you're just celibate?

WILL

I didn't say that

BRIDGET

Oh wow. Forget I asked. I thought we were in the same boat.

WILL

You're celibate?

BRIDGET

I mean, not by choice??

A WILDFIRE SPREADS ACROSS MY CHEEKS. MORTIFIED, I SLIP beneath my comforter, covering myself as if it could protect me from the embarrassment of admitting that I clearly have not had sex in ages.

BRIDGET

God why are we even talking about this? I'm mortified. Byeeee.

WILL

Stop, don't be ridiculous. We can talk about
anything. You know that.

This is a safe space.

LOL

I SNORT, FEELING A BIT MORE RELAXED. AND THAT'S THE THING
about Will: no matter what, he manages to appease me, keep me
calm. It's not the words he uses but something about how well
we understand each other.

But I won't deny the wine is playing a part in this whole
thing, though.

BRIDGET

Nope. We're not talking about this.

WILL

Fine.

BRIDGET

Fine.

WILL

Fine.

...

But don't you miss it, though?

BRIDGET

Miss what?

WILL

Sex.

.   .   .

SOMETHING ABOUT SEEING THE WORD ON THE SCREEN, IT FINALLY popping up in our conversations, sends a current of electricity up and down my spine.

My breathing quickens, pulse races. I feel the blush creeping up my neck once again as I consider what to reply. Normal Bridget would play it cool, but two-and-a-half-glasses-of-cheap-wine Bridget just... doesn't. She's over this unspoken tension between us.

BRIDGET
Yes. I do.

More so lately.

ESPECIALLY SINCE YOU CAME BLAZING INTO MY LIFE OUT OF NOWHERE.

WILL
I could help with that.

SCORCHING HEAT SEARS MY SKIN, AN ACHE SO DEEP AND LOW IN MY stomach I can barely breathe. Is he...? Am I...? Are *we* about to...?

"Fuck it," I whisper, telling myself I'll blame it on the alcohol in the morning. I knock back the rest of my wine and place the glass on my nightstand.

Oh, yeah? How would you help when we're in completely different places?

BUT I'M OBVIOUSLY NOT AN IDIOT AND JUST PLAYING COY.

WILL

I'd can start by telling you I've been thinking about you all fucking day.

That I haven't stopped imagining what you look like naked. How you'd taste on my tongue.

Would that help?

I STRUGGLE TO PULL OXYGEN IN MY LUNGS, HALF-GASPING WITH each breath. Unable to take the heat, I throw the covers off onto the floor and scoot farther down the bed. I let the fingers of my left hand travel with a delicate touch up and down my chest while I hold my phone and type with the right.

WILL

Would it help to say that I've come to the thought of your pretty lips around my cock every morning this week? It's the first thing I think about when I wake up.

BRIDGET

You've never even seen me in real life. How do you know what my lips look like?

WILL

Because I just do. And it's all I fucking want. To feel the inside of your mouth with my cock.

Now

BRIDGET

How is you admitting all this supposed to help ME?

OF COURSE I KNOW WHAT HE'S DOING, BUT I WANT HIM TO KNOW that I need the direction, that I want him to tell me what to do.

WILL

Take two fingers and put them in your mouth. I want you to pretend they're my cock.

"OH MY GOD."

But still, I moan, bringing my fingers to my mouth as I wait for his next message to arrive. Something in the back of my mind screams, warns me I'm being crazy, but my brain is covered in a fog of lust and want and need and can't listen to reason. I need release.

WILL

You there?

BRIDGET

Yes. Fingers. Mouth.

WILL

Good. I just pulled out my cock and am
imagining my hand is your mouth as I fuck my
fist.

I DO AS HE ASKS, BUT I TAKE IT ONE STEP FURTHER: I IMAGINE
being in front of him on my knees, taking him as he guides his
cock into my mouth. My hands are on his hips, his fingers
tangled in my hair as he sets the rhythm, his taste on my tongue.
The need to bring my fingers to where I'm pulsating between my
legs is nearly painful, but I hold back, waiting for his instructions. Thankfully, he doesn't make me wait much longer.

WILL

Now I want you to be a good girl, take those
two fingers, and drag them over your body all
the way down to that pretty little clit. I want you
to start rubbing circles outside of it. You're not
going to do anything more than that now, are
you? You're gonna be a good girl and listen to
me. I don't want you to come yet.

BRIDGET

Yes. I promise.

FOLLOWING HIS ORDERS, I SLOWLY DRAG MY WET FINGERS DOWN
my body, down my neck, over my seventies silk blouse in
between my breasts, and over my stomach. When I reach my
hips, I unbutton my high-waisted jeans and slip a hand beneath
my underwear, doing exactly as he says. Wetness has pooled
between my thighs and, for a moment, I almost panic. I'm

sexting with a man I've never met before and escalated so quickly, and *am I fucking insane*, and what if—

WILL

You have my permission to touch it now, Bridge.
But don't come yet. You understand?

THE RELIEF IS ALMOST IMMEDIATE, BUT ALL TOO SOON I'M ON THE verge of coming, so I pull away. Even though I know he would never know whether I came or not, I do as he says. Panting, I pull my hand away while I settle down before letting myself play again, feeling the wetness on my lips, my underwear completely soaked.

WILL

In my head, I have you on all fours, face down, Bridge. I'm eating you from behind and you taste so fucking sweet.

I lose my mind thinking about it every day

Space out in meetings thinking about this and you and doing it in real life.

I ARCH OFF THE MATTRESS ON A MOAN, EYES ROLLING TO THE BACK of my head as I try to keep myself together or risk exploding into a million pieces. He hasn't given me permission to come yet and I'm way too close. When I open my eyes, I see my freckled chest is flushed red and covered in a sheen of sweat, glittering beneath the overhead lighting of the apartment. I imagine feeling him moving on top of me, running my hands up and down his back, feeling his skin beneath my finger tips.

WILL

What's wrong? Can't type back? Too busy?

Come on. Tell me what you're doing. How you feel.

BRIDGET

Wet

WILL

Yeah you fucking are

BRIDGET

I'm frustrated

WILL

Why

BRIDGET

Because I want that. I want your cock and your mouth and your hands and you aren't the only one who thinks about it.

And I want to come to your voice and feel you above me. I want you to surround me. I want you to pin me down.

I want you to do whatever you want with me

WILL

Oh, I will, Bridget. One of these days I fucking will. You can count on that.

ANOTHER SWIPE OF MY FINGERS OVER MY CLIT AND I NEARLY explode, having to squeeze my eyes shut to keep my release. I grit my teeth, every muscle in my body as tense as a bowstring.

BRIDGET

I need to come.

Please let me come

WILL

Normally I'd make you wait, but I'm so fucking hard, so close to coming just thinking about you like this, alone in bed, getting off to thoughts of me

Fuck, baby. Come. Come all over your hand but pretend it's my face.

"OH MY GOD! WILL!" I CRY OUT INTO MY APARTMENT, BREAKING into a million little pieces and being put back together in the same second. I come harder than I've ever come by myself, writhing alone on my mattress as thoughts of Will—this faceless, incredible man—fill every corner and crevice of my mind. An electric current travels through my body, every nerve on my skin a live wire aching to be touched. I'm sticky with sweat and come, and gasping for breath as I try to recover.

WILL

I need you to fucking tell me what you taste like

I'm gonna dream about this for months, Bridget. For fucking months.

. . .

AND SUDDENLY IT'S LIKE A BUCKET OF COLD WATER IS THROWN over my overheated, sweaty body.

What the hell did I just *do*?

The fall from the high comes just as quickly as it arrived, crashing me into reality as I become aware of the magnitude of what just happened: I just sexted the person I've grown closest to, and potentially ruined what's felt like the most honest and dependable friendship I've ever had. Except he's also a complete stranger.

I am a fucking idiot.

With a groan, I roll over onto my side, my jeans open and just below my hips, and cry quiet tears into my pillow. I throw my phone onto the floor, ignoring it as a symphony of incessant vibrations coming from my phone fills the room.

Gripping my pillow with both hands, I whisper four words I never thought I'd ever say in relation to Will: "Please, stop texting me."

WILL

He's never felt more alone; never felt less lonely.

6

―――

IT'S ABOUT TIME

Last night plays over and over in my head on a loop, going over every moment, every single interaction I've had throughout the day, making it nearly impossible to exist.

What happened between us was a mistake—how could it not have been? Two complete strangers who've never seen each other in real life should never have done anything like that. That and the fact that Will was my confidant, my virtual bestie, made it so incredibly wrong. But it happened so quickly, I couldn't have stopped myself even if I wanted to. And if I'm being honest with myself, I didn't *want* to stop myself.

After I finally pulled myself together by taking a shower and consuming about twenty pounds more of Valentine's Day candy, I managed to fall asleep. It was a restless night, filled with nebulous dreams of me and different versions of Will sitting outside a café somewhere, laughing over coffee and dessert during springtime as cherry blossoms blow around us in the chilly air under a warming sun. Me and Will rolling around in my bed as he and the morning sun kiss every inch of my skin at the same time. His lips soft as they explore, strong when he's in between my legs, shoulders pushing them open as he makes me come harder than he did last night with just a few words.

Sometimes he's a pale, short king with bright blue eyes, or a beefy gym rat. Other times, he's the perfect guy you'd find if you googled "tall, dark, and handsome" or the adorable boy next door type. Regardless of what he looks like, however, he's always *amazing*, every version of him absolutely perfect and sweet and kind. I know that I'll like him, no matter what he looks like. And I ache for that moment; ache for that place where I can see and touch him, where I don't have to keep playing the imagination game, and we can just hang like two old friends.

I want that. I want that more than anything these days. Despite having a few friends here, New York City can get lonely, and I'm hungry to have the easy relationship Will and I have virtually, but in person. And I know it's as simple as asking him to meet up somewhere, but maybe it's for that reason alone that I *shouldn't*. Risking this odd companionship and relationship over just wanting to touch him—or fuck, at least just see his face for once—seems a bit foolhardy—especially after what we did last night. We still haven't talked today—something completely out of the norm for us—leaving me terrified that I've already ruined things. And maybe I'm being stupid; maybe it wasn't that big of a deal to him and I should trust our friendship more and—

The slap of a manila folder on my desk brings my recurring daydream and concerns to a violent halt. I jump about a foot in my chair, almost knocking my Diet Coke over my entire office set-up.

"This folder is missing the pricing sheet." Lena looms over me, her dark brown eyes fierce as she crosses her arms in front of her chest.

With a slicked back ponytail and expertly tailored skirt and silk blouse, Lena doesn't just look like my boss—she looks like *a*

Boss. Capital B. Her commanding presence demands respect, which causes those with smaller egos to misinterpret her as a different type of b-word (didn't I once refer to her as an ogre, too?). But I'm convinced she's just misunderstood. She has to be.

"I need to hand this to the higher-ups in forty-five minutes, and I cannot have one of the most important pieces of information missing from the packet."

"Yes, Lena." With shaking fingers, I pick the folder from the desk and rifle through the papers. "But, are you sure? I thought I printed them out and—"

"Bridget." Her voice is all business. I swallow and look up at her. "Yes, I'm sure."

"Right. Okay. I'm so sorry. I'm not sure what happened, but I'll go ahead and print one out super quick and bring it back to your office as soon as possible."

I turn from her and quickly click through my documents, searching for our most updated pricing sheet on our company shared drive. I expect Lena to walk back to her office and continue with her day, but she chooses instead to prop herself up against my desk. With hesitation, I look up at her to meet her gaze—brows furrowed, eyes narrowed.

"Are you scared of me, Bridget?"

I laugh once involuntarily because, well, *duh.* She can't be that oblivious, can she? She's way too smart to be.

"I—" I hesitate, wondering what it is she *wants* me to feel.

"It's not a trick question," she says, as if reading my mind. Folder in hand, she says, "Come on. Let's step into my office."

Out of habit, I take my notebook and pen with me, ready to take any necessary notes—whether it be instructions on how to brew evil potions or what paperwork I need to file after she fires me (though that last one might just be something to ask HR).

"I'm not trying to terrorize you," she tells me once she's

seated behind her desk and the door to the office is closed tightly behind us. "I'm just trying to train you to be the best at your job, however trite that may sound. Because this industry... This space isn't for everyone. For too long it's been controlled by abusive people, and you need to be tough in order to survive it."

I gawk at her, wanting to ask her whether she realizes the irony in her statement. But there's no need, since it's visible on her face that realization has already dawned on her.

"And I fear I've already become part of the problem," she whispers, wincing.

"No!" I say a little too loudly. "Well. Um, *maybe*. It's just... You can be a bit intimidating sometimes. A lot of the time. Okay, fine, all of the time. And that can make it difficult for people to approach you when they have questions or need help. And maybe... Maybe if they felt like they could talk to you and stuff, fewer things could go wrong? Because, you know, you'd be able to assist them instead of instilling fear and making everyone avoid you as much as possible?"

Wow. How diplomatic of you, Bridget. I hope you liked the free food in the kitchen, because that's the last time you'll be seeing such a fantastic smorgasbord of flavored sparkling water, soda, and snacks.

Lena raises a brow at me, her eyes roaming all over my face as if studying every inch of my expression, soaking up my words.

"Am I fired now? Please don't fire me. I know I might not be great yet, but I can get there because I *really* love this job and I feel like I could really learn a lot from you and I've been making a lot of progress and I promise I will—"

She raises a hand. "Stop." Lena heaves a huge sigh, pinches the bridge of her nose between her fingers. "I'm sorry."

My jaw drops, and I look around, searching for someone else who might be in the room. Because she can't have apologized to me. There's no way. "Did you... Did you just apologize to... *me*?"

She clears her throat and fiddles with a pen. "It has come to my attention that I may not be the nicest boss to work under sometimes. It's not like I don't know that I'm not an *easy* person to work with, but I didn't expect for people to find me so horrible." She groans. "You see, I had an abusive boss when I first started. This person... They took credit for my ideas, yelled at me, and made me do unnecessary work just to humiliate me. Screamed when things didn't go their way, whether it was my fault or not."

I gasp, finding it impossible to believe that *anyone* could take on the legendary Lena Bouros. Was it someone from this company or somewhere else? It was my understanding that she started working at Sartoria straight out of college and all throughout her grad school, so this had to have happened at this company. Did the person still work here? Was it someone I saw every day?

"When I began to grow within the ranks," she continues, "I vowed to myself I wouldn't be the same way, but I guess I didn't even realize it happened to me, too. The thing is, sometimes in this industry, it feels like if you're not the one being feared, you're the one who's going to lose. And I suppose I've gone a little too far over the years."

I stare at her, wide-eyed, unsure of what to say.

"So, if I've... *terrorized* you," she says with a wince. "I... I apologize. I didn't even notice I was doing the same things that were being done to me."

"Um." I hesitate. "Not to ruin this beautiful after school special moment—and I mean that in the best way possible, because I honestly find this pretty healing—but what brought about this self-awareness and need to repent?"

She purses her lips. "I'm not proud to admit this—to be honest, I'd love to say it was all me, and I had an epiphany—but, no. There was an HR complaint. Several, actually. At first, I thought they were insane, but I started thinking and—" She shakes her head and looks off into space. "I don't even want to tell you what it was—I actually am not allowed to—but it rocked me. What I said was very similar to something my old boss said to me once. It wasn't a great feeling when I realized I was doing *exactly* what I swore never to do. In fact, I believe I even used the same words my old boss did and everything, made someone feel small just because they weren't well-versed in something instead of using it as a teachable moment. But at least I'm not taking credit for anyone's work like they used to do with me," she says with disgust.

"Anyway, HR suggested I speak to everyone who reports to me and, well, that includes you. I'd like to know how I can uplift you—not put you down."

I smile widely. "Lena, you have no idea how happy this makes me. This job means everything to me. It's the first time I've ever felt passionate about getting up in the morning and *doing* something that isn't related to my hobbies or my cat."

She shoots me an uncertain look while I think back to all the other jobs I'd had in the past, from admin roles to retail; dog walking to appointment scheduler at a hospital. The only thing that's come even the tiniest bit close to making me this excited is that one time I took a job as a cook for that retired Goldman Sachs banker who had a breakdown and decided to open his own very successful burger food truck. And that was only because I got unlimited fries and was allowed to take any left-over food back home with me at the end of the day.

But anyway, even getting free fries on the regular does not compare to feeling like you're a part of something big. And it *is* big, even if it is "just" clothes. It's something people wear *every* day, it becomes part of their life, it's how they express and present themselves to the world. And to be able to do it in a responsible, sustainable way is the cherry on top of it all.

"Good," Lena tells me. "I'm happy to hear that because I think it's time I start involving you more in projects. So let's talk."

WILL

It's been a while since he's had such a bad fucking day. Not even an extra half hour at the gym at lunchtime can cheer him up; there aren't enough endorphins to help his mood or enough energy burnt to get past his current frustrations.

For the first time, it wasn't work that was causing him grief. No, it's Bridget, his usual daily ray of sunshine, that's ripping him to shreds from the inside out.

Last night had been a fantasy come to life, a dream come true that quickly turned into a nightmare. He admits he lost control, that the alcohol led him down a fast path to something he only dreamed of, but he never expected this result. She seemed to like it at first, but then...

She's gone.

He squeezes his eyes shut and tries to force the thought from his head, but ultimately fails miserably. He never thought he'd lose her over this.

And that's exactly what it feels like. Because even though by a normal person's standards not receiving a text for 24 hours isn't the end of the world (there's still the chance her phone died or something—you never know!), since first meeting each other, they'd always found a way to stay in touch. If something were wrong with her phone, he believes she would've found a way to contact him by now. Sent smoke signals. Something.

He's crawling out of his goddamn skin, stomach in fucking knots, not really knowing how he's going to survive this. He'd never forgive himself if he hurt her, if what they did last night was too much— which it clearly had been. Enough, at least, to have her disappear on him.

And that's the worst part, not knowing whether he's caused her any pain, any harm. Hurting her is the last thing he wants to do.

She is the one good thing he has going on in his life and he's gone and fucked it up just because he was horny and frustrated and aching to touch her, this woman he's never even seen. Now he just wishes he could take it all back. As he looks out his apartment window at the stormy night sky, Will swears to the universe he'll never so much as flirt with her again if it means he getting her back. And just as he makes that vow and sends it into the universe, his phone pings with a message from the only person he's wanted to hear from all day.

BRIDGET

I know last night was weird, and we should probably talk about it. But... Today was the best day EVER at work!!! Can I tell you about it?

With a massive sigh of relief and a loosening in his stomach, Will reaches for his phone and replies back.

WILL

Always

7

FACETIME ETIQUETTE IS ALSO A REAL THING

I practically bounce around the apartment, waiting for Will's reply. Ginger lifts her head with bleary eyes to shoot me an annoyed look from where she lies on the reading chair. After terrifying me with her deathly stare, she covers her face with her large paws and goes back to ignoring me during her post-dinner food coma.

But even Ginger's quiet threats can't lessen the excitement within me, because I *finally* earned Lena's trust, and with it comes even more responsibility—something I've been chomping at the bit for. And now that we've mapped out my career path a bit, spoken about what's next, and clarified how much more involved in the process I'll be, I can't wait to get started.

Lena giving me a shot? Letting me have more of a say and giving me *some* discretion when it comes to our projects? Unimaginable, but there it is. Sure, I won't be running my own accounts any time soon, but this is still a big step—and one in the right direction.

Today was epic.

As soon as Lena gave me the news and I left her office, my

hands reached for my phone, itching to text Will. Even though things have been weird between us, going to Molly with this before him felt weird for some reason. Like despite it all, despite how out of hand things got last night, he was still the one person I wanted to tell as soon as it happened.

WILL

Did you find a new vintage store in your neighborhood that's full of seventies jumpsuits and wrap dresses or something?

I SNORT AND BITE MY LIP, TRYING TO SUPPRESS A SMILE BECAUSE HE remembers my obsession with vintage clothing, teases me about it (but in a nice way), and sends me recommendations for the best shops all over the North East (which I've already earmarked for future shopping sprees the second I have some expendable income). Thanks to him, I've already purchased and revamped three incredible pieces from the seventies to add to my collection.

BRIDGET

No, unfortunately, I have not seen any new seventies Diane Von Furstenberg wrap dresses down at my favorite thrift store.

But it's big. Can I call you?

WITHIN SECONDS, I RECEIVE A REQUEST FOR A FACETIME CALL.

"*FACETIME?!* Ginger, is this guy insane?" I look desperately at my cat, who continues ignoring me.

While the phone continues to ring, I run to the bathroom to check myself in the mirror and squeak in horror. There is *no* way I'm going to let him—or anyone else, for that matter—see me like this. Rumpled red hair in a high bun, no makeup, straight from the shower, and a (albeit cute) baby blue sweat set is not an acceptable look when letting your texting crush see you for the first time ever—*especially* not after what we did last night. So I reject the call because *what the hell is he thinking*, really.

WILL

Um. Why'd you hang up?

BRIDGET

You can't just spring a FaceTime on someone without warning! It's bad communication etiquette!

WILL

I don't think you're exactly in a position to lecture me on communication etiquette. Should I remind you how we met?

BRIDGET

Ha. You're hilarious.

Seriously, Will. I just got home from work and am not exactly in a presentable state.

WILL

Lol I'm sure you look amazing and have nothing to worry about.

BRIDGET

How would you know? You've never seen me!

WILL

Exactly. So what would I compare it to? Come on. We've texted long enough. Do you not feel comfortable with me or something? I just really want to see you.

AN ACHE BUILDS BENEATH MY RIBS AS I REREAD HIS WORDS, processing them.

BRIDGET

You do?

WILL

Of course I do. Don't you want to see me?

HE REALLY WANTS TO SEE ME?
I really want to see him, too. So much it hurts.

BRIDGET

What about yesterday?

THREE DOTS POP ON MY PHONE SCREEN AND PROMPTLY DISAPPEAR. A few seconds later, they're back before disappearing once more. It takes a couple of minutes, but he finally replies:

WILL

Why don't we put a pin in what happened last
night so we can talk about your good news.

That's more important.

A SLOW SMILE SPREADS ACROSS MY FACE AFTER A QUIET SIGH.
Safe. I feel safe.

BRIDGET

Will you at least give me five minutes to brush
my hair and make myself look presentable?

WILL

Two minutes, though I'm sure you don't need it,
and I certainly don't care what you look like. ;)

I RUN OVER TO MY BATHROOM AND SPLASH COLD WATER ON MY
face, gently patting it dry. With no makeup, my freckles stand
out—but I don't mind. Growing up, I used to hate them. As an
adult, I've grown to love them and see them as something that
sets me apart, that makes me unique.

With impressive speed, I pull my hair out of the satin
scrunchie it was in and brush it until it looks perfectly detangled
and soft down to my waist. Exhaling once, I look at myself in the
mirror with a determined expression, and whisper, "You've got
this. It's just a phone call. Just a video call with a man you've
never seen though you've been crushing on him for weeks."

I settle into the center of my bed under my favorite teal, cozy blanket, fluff my pillows behind me, and, with a deep breath, click the FaceTime video call button on his contact profile.

It barely rings before the call is accepted, and I'm rendered speechless by the most handsome, sexy man in the world when he pops on screen. For a second, I swear I'm hallucinating because there is *no way* that the man I've been texting for weeks, the man I haven't been able to stop thinking about, looks like a hotter version of Theo James. I'm not that lucky. And who even thought that could be possible? With high cheekbones and a perfect bone structure that rivals Ancient Greek sculptures, lips that look soft and demanding at the same time, dark, curly hair begging to have my fingers tangled in them, and brown, smoldering eyes that feel like they can read my soul in a split second, Will knocks the wind out of me.

Holy shit.

Suddenly, I want to curse myself out for not listening to my gut instincts, for not putting on normal clothes and at least adding a bit of foundation to cover up the insane blush creeping up my neck and face. The side effect of being a redhead, no emotion goes hidden—and I think the extreme blush I feel heating every inch of my skin is very clearly revealing my thoughts: *Damn, he's hot.* More than I can handle, I think. So much so that it takes me a minute to process his shocked face before it morphs into the most heartbreaking, face-splitting smile.

"Hey, Bridge," he breathes.

His voice...

And I am officially a goner.

"You're..." Will swallows once on the other end of the line. "You don't look the way I imagined."

His voice. God, his voice.

I bite back a moan because something about it, something about its depth and tone, has me suspecting *things* about how he is in bed. I hate that it's the first thing I think about, but I can't help the immediate attraction.

"You imagined what I looked like?" I ask in a small voice, which is, admittedly, dumber than any question anyone has ever asked ever. It would be odd to be talking to someone for just over a month without imagining at least *once* what they looked like. It would be especially odd to sext with someone, say you imagined eating them out on all fours, without having once thought about it. Even if Will had thought about me only a fraction of the times I've thought about him, he must've wondered about my physical appearance.

"I..." Will hesitates. "Kind of? I don't..." He bites the inside of his mouth and runs a hand through his hair, unable to meet my eye.

"Are you... *nervous*?" I try not to tease him. To be honest, though, there's no denying I'm genuinely shocked a man who looks like *that* would ever—

"*Oh*. Now I get it." I nod, somber. I've never been too concerned by what my body looks like. No, I've been much too focused on fashion and clothes my entire life for that. Pulling an entire outfit together that was able to express how I feel or who I am in that moment is what I think of when getting ready in the morning. Besides my initial aversion to my freckles when I was younger, I didn't concern myself with what my body looked like (I had much bigger problems to contend with for that). Tonight, though, for the first time ever, I feel the most self-conscious I ever have in my life. It's odd, this feeling, going from extremely comfortable with who I am with Will to almost afraid to show myself on camera. And I know why.

"You're... You're disappointed." I wince as the other shoe drops, as I realize I actually said that out loud. I mean, it's evident that he is, but I shouldn't have put him on the spot like that.

Horrified, Will brings his phone closer to his face. "What? No. *No.* That's not what I meant. How can you even say that? I just... I don't know what I imagined when I thought of you, but you were never..." The way he sputters his words, the anxiety clear on his face, is what causes me to take pity on him.

So he doesn't find me attractive. So what? That's not what this was, anyway. Right? Not necessarily. At least I made a friend. At least now I know that this weird relationship I'd been in with my work pen pal can progress through the friendship route. And I wouldn't mind having another friend, I guess. It's not like I have many these days.

"A redhead. You never imagined me as a redhead," I say, cutting him off while trying to hide my disappointment.

Relieved I gave him an out, Will nods. "Right. That's what I meant. I never imagined you as a redhead."

And maybe there's some truth to that, too. A lot of guys aren't into redheads.

An awkward silence falls between us when I can't bear to look at the screen. I can feel his eyes on me, though, traveling over my face as he examines every inch.

This is dumb, I think, regretting ever wanting to make this call. I was happy to have a confidant, someone who understood me. And now I've gone and ruined it all by making it awkward and agreeing to something as trivial, yet gargantuan, as seeing each other—even if it's just over a video call.

It's not like Will won't talk to me again after this. No, I know him well enough (even if we've only been talking for just over a month) to be certain he would never do something like that. But it's the disappointment that I find him devastatingly attractive, and he so clearly doesn't like me back—the letdown that I *cared* so much in the first place—and the fear that the relationship we developed might change after Will and I have become so close that gets to me.

But he knows me. He knows me, and I know him. And right now, we're putting a pin on what happened last night, not letting it ruin what was a great day at work for me.

At least we got it out of the way, I think. *At least this way it's done and I don't need to wonder anymore.*

"So," he starts, his grin making me melt deep into my sheets, every joint in my body coming loose. "Tell me about this great day that you had."

WILL

He's never seen anything so beautiful in his entire life.
There's no denying he's even more in trouble than he thought he was.

8

———

AI FRIENDS ARE NOT PREFERABLE

"That's incredible!" Will beams from the other side of the call, his eyes bright despite their milk chocolate hue.

It's the first time in a long time I've felt like I have a genuine cheerleader on my side, not just a fair-weather friend hoping I get my shit together long enough so we can have six months of uninterrupted good times. I haven't felt this supported since my grandmother.

"So what are your plans to impress her? You've got something in mind, don't you?"

I grin. "Yeah, I think so. The more I learn about the manufacturing process, the more fascinated I am by it. And I think I have an easy solution to a problem."

His thick brows pull together, but not in doubt or apprehension. "Please don't take offense to this, because it's an honest question, but... If it's a simple solution to a problem why do you think no one's thought of it before?"

I smile even wider. "Because it's not *really* a problem they think is worth solving. Because it's an absorbable cost. But I have a feeling that if this thing works, it could end up saving us a ton of money while keeping up the quality of our products now that we've scaled quite a bit since the company started using our current method of production. Plus, while it sounds like a factory's responsibility to be more efficient, sometimes they don't care so long as they're getting paid and the client keeps coming back."

"Really?" His brows shift, one raised, the other straight and stern and I wonder how wildly insane it is that I find eyebrows attractive now. Just *his*, actually. Everything about him, if I'm being honest. His deep voice, smooth and commanding, yet soothing. The broad shoulders I can tell lie beneath his button down shirt, opened at the collar after a long day of work. His short, brown, lightly curled hair that's got my fingers wishing they could reach out through my phone screen just to run through it. Lips that make me want to sigh whenever I look at them, slightly larger than I imagined, but still masculine, utterly kissable, deliciously biteable. And that smile... A smile that made me thank my lucky stars I was seated because it made me immediately lose all feeling in my legs—while gaining a pulsating one in between them. It's safe to say that the first time I laid eyes on Will my brain short-circuited because I have never been more attracted to a man before in my life.

And I fucking showed up on camera in a sweat suit, no makeup, and messy hair.

God, I'm such a loser.

"Bridge, that's amazing! If you're able to solve a problem no one knew they had and can save the company more money, you'll be worshiped. I bet it's the perfect thing to make you stand out from the rest of the new hires."

"I know! And I really wanna impress my boss. She's this fire-breathing dragon of a goddess and I know I can learn so much from her."

He shakes his head in amazement. "I'm in awe of you, Bridget Quinn."

I blush once again, something that's become normal since speaking to him. "Why do you say that?"

"Because. You're so passionate about this whole thing. And it's easy to see you've hit the ground running. You're incredible." His smile is heartbreaking because I want it to be mine. I want *him* to be mine. And that is psychotic because, for the millionth time I have to remind myself *Will and I have never met.*

"Hey. How do I know you're not some AI bot that's gone rogue?" I ask, 99.99% serious.

Will huffs out a laugh, his eyes widening. "What the hell are you talking about?"

"I mean..." I sigh. "How do I know you're real? What if you're like this super duper advanced AI bot who was on the email trails to record and write briefs on company correspondence or something? And you replied to my email because I broke an email etiquette rule your programmer told you about so you felt the need to tell me about it? And what if we just kept talking because?"

He presses his lips together, trying hard not to laugh. "What about this call? How do you explain the video chat?"

I shrug, looking away, not wanting to tell him that the video chat is what added to my "he can't be real" theory. A man that gorgeous being that kind to me? History has taught me not to trust this.

"Stevenson is a very big company with deep pockets. You could be one of those video AI people. I don't know!" A product of generative AI having pulled every single handsome man in the world and made this one, specific, perfect specimen just for me.

He's quiet for a moment, processing. Maybe the chip where his mainframe is located is shorting because someone's finally found him out. Or maybe he doesn't even know he's an AI bot.

Maybe we're in the middle of a Cylon type of situation. He can't be real.

"Bridge." His voice is soft, imploring. "Look at me, please."

It takes me a couple of seconds, but I manage to turn my face back to the screen, tears stinging behind my eyes.

"What part of this doesn't feel real?" he asks. Sad, wary eyes stare back, and it kills me.

The simple fact that, so far, this relationship has been a texting one, for one.

"Last night could've ruined everything," I whisper. One of us had to bring it up, rip off the Band-Aid. "What we did..." I shake my head. "It's dumb, but since meeting you I've realized that the people in my life I thought were my ride or dies... aren't. My life has never been without drama, and though they understand it's never been as a consequence of my own actions, I can see the way people pull away, not wanting to be dragged into my problems. And I guess it's my fault for picking the wrong type of people as friends—I see that now—but somehow the universe led me to you and... You have made me feel so safe, so heard and seen even when we didn't even know what we looked or sounded like... And just..." A tear runs down my cheek, making me hate myself a little. "I don't want to lose whatever weird thing this is." I finish my rant with a sniff and another damn tear, waiting anxiously for his response.

It doesn't come for a few minutes. In fact, I wait so long I begin to wonder whether he is an AI bot after all and he's having connectivity issues—or maybe his creators never thought to program him to deal with a psychotic woman like myself. Until...

"It's definitely unconventional, this thing we have. We've talked about it at length. And last night..." He blows out a breath. "I'm not gonna deny I didn't enjoy it, Bridge. Because I fucking did. I don't want to make you feel more uncomfortable than you already do, but in the spirit of honesty, I got off to the memory of it this morning, too. It was *hot*."

Not as hot as my cheeks are now, I think.

"But I'm not gonna lie, the longer you went without texting back, the more and more I thought about how what we did might've made you run away from me, the less I thought it was worth it. This might sound super fucking weird—believe me, I know—but I... care about you. And like you said, we're friends. *Human* friends, by the way—I'm definitely not an AI robot. So how about we agree to never do what we did again? And just... continue to be there for each other? Because, Bridge, having you pop in my life the way you did... It's what I needed. You're who I needed. I was... not well. And now I am. Because of you."

I nod, sniffling. If I'm honest, I'm a little upset he didn't fight me on it a bit more. Clearly, he isn't as into me romantically as I am him. Getting off to the memory of sexting someone is not the same. From what I gather, he probably did share my crush, but one look at me was enough to kick him of the habit.

"I needed you, too, Will. More than you know."

WILL

At least he knows what she looks like now.
Unfortunately, it also means he knows what she looks like.

9

LEARNING HOW TO #GIRLBOSS IS HARD

"This proposal looks really good," Lena says, a small smile on her lips as she reviews the contents of the folder (manilla) in her hands. "Not sure how you did this research, but if all the facts are right, it could save us a lot of money. I wonder why the factories hadn't considered this yet?" she muses.

"My guess is that they're not getting paid to do that small extra leg work, so they wouldn't, even though they were my first source when doing this research. Also, they don't really care about increasing the efficiency of an arguably already efficient process just so we can sell back usable scraps of material to other companies."

She looks up suddenly, a frown on her face. "You emailed the factory reps?"

My stomach drops. "Was I not allowed to? I'm so sorry—" I rush to apologize. "I just didn't want to waste your time by going to you first in order to get an intro if this wasn't a doable thing and—"

Lena waves a hand in the air, dismissing my concerns. "Stop, it's fine. I told you I was giving you more freedom and you've clearly used it well, taking some serious initiative." She looks back down at the folder and nods once. "I'm going to double-check these numbers and then hand it over to Jenna if they're good. Next week is our in-person follow up meeting with Stevenson—they're coming in to discuss business and look at the updated Fall line. Jenna and Sascha, our CEO, will also be in attendance. I want you to present this to them before the meeting."

I inhale sharply, eyes wide. Jenna is the VP everyone is terrified of, the one who seems to float around the office, dressed exclusively in black, like a sort of grim reaper looking for her next victim. Scary Lena is a bunny rabbit next to Jenna. Thankfully, she works on a different floor.

Reading my expression, Lena smiles and cuts through my doom spiral. "Relax. I'll be there with you and you'll do great."

But when a week goes by, and I never get called into anyone's office, I begin to worry maybe my research didn't make the cut. A crisis comes up for another client, so I'm left wondering whether Lena's even had the time to double-check my work before the meeting, leaving me tied up in knots.

Please don't let this opportunity slip through my fingers.

"I'm telling you, she's not going to cave on that pricing. Lena is ruthless—she's not even going to take it to upper management for consideration," I tell Will over FaceTime as I get ready for work.

"It doesn't make any sense, though. Our team is increasing the order by 10%. That's enough to amortize the cost—or it should be. And that's on top of the original increase of SKUs. You guys *should* be able to give us a bit of a deeper discount," he argues.

His phone leans against his bathroom mirror as he does up his tie, eyes focused on his reflection. I wonder briefly why his office is more business and less fashion casual like ours is, but he mentioned working in their finance department as middle-management. Maybe the less creatives live by a more formal dress code at Stevenson? Either way, the fact that his eyes aren't on me means that I can take the time to appreciate Will without him noticing. It means I can drink up how sexy he looks in his suit—equally as sexy as he looked late last night on our call while dressed in a black t-shirt and wet hair straight from the shower right before he went to bed.

Will is all tan skin, perfectly chiseled angles, and dark hair that's begging to be mussed by strenuous activities I find myself more and more willing to participate in every day—I get to ogle him now without him noticing him. It's a true blessing.

Over the past week, I've grown both devastated and ecstatic because our relationship has moved to the next level of communication. In all honesty, it feels like I'm never *not* in contact with Will—unless either one of us is in a meeting or something, that is. The growing closeness has turned me inside out, making it consistently more and more difficult to maintain a positive outlook on everything. Because where can this relationship go? My crush has evolved into severe *like*—especially after our sexting session—but I don't think I'm strong enough right now to let him go in order for me to move on. Which I *have* to do, right? He so obviously isn't into me. I mean, he used to mention meeting me in person before, but that's stopped seeing each other over FaceTime.

He's lost interest. Or doesn't find me attractive.

With this thought in my head, I sigh in frustration. Luckily, he takes it as a consequence of the conversation at hand.

"I'm sorry, but I just think this whole thing is crazy," he tells me, eyes kind.

"You're telling me this as if I have any say in the decision-making process, Will. I'm barely even allowed to look at the first cost pricing sheets." *They probably would be able to get a discount if my plan were approved,* I think. But I can't cross the line and reveal too much about work. Even if it is Will.

"That's weird. Isn't that kind of part of your job?"

I shrug, copying his getting ready routine by leaning my phone against my bathroom mirror on the small counter. Pulling a brush through my hair, I explain, "Not really. I'm more like an assistant, still learning. Pricing is out of my scope for now, though I'd really love to learn more about it eventually." Is that why I haven't heard back from Lena? Because my research didn't pan out? "But it's fine—they're teaching me a lot. Also, I looked up some courses at Parsons and found some really cool ones that would help. When I spoke to HR about it, they offered to pay for the summer semester since it covered retail math and other valuable skills that will be helpful for this job. It's on the weekends so I could—"

I look down at my phone and catch him smiling fondly at me, the way he does every time I get excited about work. The look in his eyes does something to my heart and suddenly I can't speak.

After a pause and intense glare, I break the silence. "Stop smiling like that," I grumble.

"What?" he asks innocently with a shrug. "You're cute when you're all excited."

"That is extremely patronizing of you. I know I'm younger than you, but only by five years or something, and I got a late start here, remember? I'm just starting out, so yeah, I get excited." I hate the bitterness and bite to my voice, but I can't help it. The ache in my chest makes it harder to stay positive these days, not to mention the fact that I've been professionally ghosted by my boss.

Will's smile slips a bit, eyes meeting mine with sadness. "I didn't mean to make it sound like I was making fun of you or patronizing you or something. I'm sorry. I wouldn't do that knowingly. I hope you know I deeply respect you." His brow furrows and he swallows, his Adam's apple bobbing visibly.

I sigh, frustrated with myself. "I know."

And I do, because no one has ever spoken to me like Will has. No one has ever listened to me or taken me seriously or even cared about what I have to say. But Will? Will's always cared, since that first email where he cautioned me on my email etiquette.

"No, I'm sorry if I made you feel... any sort of way. You had to rebuild yourself, and that isn't easy to do later on in life. Not like you're ancient or something—you're not even in your thirties yet —but I mean, because it doesn't come easy. And you're doing such a great job. I had to... readjust my course at your age, too. And it was really difficult. More than I ever expected it to be."

This is the thing about my relationship with Will: though it's been amazing to get to know someone on a deeper level, it's also been hell. I wouldn't categorize myself as a shut book with anyone, but with Will? I'm a leaked ultra-classified document. I don't think there's anything I've ever hidden from him, and as far as I know, there's nothing he's hidden from me. We *know* each other.

For example, I know that he loves to eat a bowl of Cocoa Puffs as a midnight snack when his job really gets to him and does so often while on calls with me. I know he also serves it like a serial killer, pouring the milk into the bowl first and the Cocoa Puffs second instead of the *right* way like a normal person would. I know he works out often and the name of his child-hood dog (Neo, because *The Matrix* was his favorite movie back then). On nights when it's raining, I can sense his restlessness when we speak. And I know I can count on him no matter what based on how supportive he's been during my very rare rants about work. He knows I feel guilty when I do, because I truly am blessed to even have a job—especially in this economy. *Especially* in this industry.

Will is sweet and understanding, really listens when I talk about being at Sartoria (stressful, but exciting), my relationship with my parents (mother, ostracized; father, unknown; siblings, none that I know of; grandmother who practically raised me, dead) and the event that happened a while back, which led to my current financial instability (an ex with an addiction problem who took my Social Security Number on a wild ride without my permission).

Meanwhile, Will seems to have grown up in a normal household—or at least, I assume so. He doesn't talk about his family much, which makes me think they're unexciting—and I mean that in a privileged way. When he does share any tidbits, they're always with a small fond smile on his face. Nothing I've heard about his family life suggests him going days on end without adult supervision or a parent with mental health concerns. Other than the brief mentions of his mother's fantastic cooking and how he tries to go up to Connecticut to visit her as often as possible, he doesn't say much. Honestly, though, I understand his reticence. Despite having shared deep things about ourselves and speaking nearly twenty-four hours a day, I'm still a stranger from the internet, and stranger danger is a real thing.

"Anyway, today should be interesting," I say, changing the topic back to work. "Your team is coming in for a meeting and after that email your Chief Merchandising Officer sent last night, I'm sure it's going to be a blast," I say, my voice dripping with sarcasm. "I'm bummed you're not coming in, though."

"Is Lena still giving you a hard time?" His concern is adorable, forcing me to bite down on my lip to keep from grinning like an idiot. But I also don't miss how he ignores my disappointment with his absence from today's meeting.

"No," I continue, as if unbothered. "Not since our talk. She's been great. And I've realized that though her delivery sucks, she really *does* want me to succeed."

But then I remember my research and frown, remember how all my hard work has been largely ignored this week and today is the day we should be presenting it to our client.

"Well, if she does anything... You'll tell me, right?"

I snort. "And what, pray tell, would you be able to do? Ask your boss to talk with her? Or tell Lena to meet you in the parking lot after work? Challenge her to a duel?"

Will's face falls. "Well, I suppose the higher ups in our company could say something to her about not liking how she treats her employees and, as consequence, not wanting to associate with them. But I... Yeah, I guess you're right. I don't see how I could make that happen, and there's not much I can do in my position."

I snort and put the cap back on my lipstick. Phone in hand, I walk into my bedroom, searching my closet for the perfect outfit.

"Stop moving around so much. You're making me nauseous," he groans.

This makes me laugh as I look over my shoulder to check the clock on the oven, subtracting thirty-seven minutes from the display (I still haven't figured out how to change the settings). "It's fine. I need to hang up anyway and finish getting ready or I'm going to be late for work."

"Oh. Okay. Yeah, I guess it's about that time." He laughs awkwardly, scratching the back of his head. Will's mouth opens as if readying himself to say something important. But what comes out instead is a rushed, "Have a great day at work and good luck in the meeting," before hanging up without another word.

As I zip into a floral dress that might be too light for February, I think glumly of ways to bring up meeting in person again. Unfortunately, I find that I've taken way too many hits in life lately to bring the subject up again.

WILL

This morning, he almost asked her to meet in person. If he's being honest with himself, the virtual part of his friendship with Bridget is getting tiresome. He craves her the same way he craves that first cup of coffee of the day to give him a morning jolt.

More accurately, if he's being honest with himself, he craves her the way he craves air to breathe.

And yet...

The smallest chance that he'd be a disappointment to her, that he wouldn't live up to her expectations, is enough to stifle the need whenever it reaches its boiling point. Will has already disappointed so many people in his life; he doesn't want to add this perfect woman to the list of humans who regret ever meeting him.

He wonders how much longer he'll be able to take without knowing her in person. Wonders how much longer he'll be able to keep the truth hidden. Most of all, he wonders whether she wonders as much about him as he does about her.

Bridget.

10

CAN SOMEONE GET THIS KNIFE OUT OF MY BACK? IT'S REALLY UNCOMFORTABLE

Most of the work day has gone by the same way it had every other day: running early morning sales and shipping reports, checking in with production statuses and asking design for updates. Not to mention *carefully* crafting and replying to emails to the correct people (I doubt every accidental unprofessional email etiquette interaction will end as happily as establishing a pen pal friendship as it did with Will, so I've been really careful with that lately).

Thankfully, after almost four months at Sartoria, I seem to have finally slipped into an easy routine. Of course, it's not without its ups and downs; there's always some issue with a factory or material vendor, or a human error when inputting numbers into our system that needs mending. But it isn't boring work—more of a DIY project on a macro level (i.e. trust the process, as they say). It's fun and requires major problem-solving at times, requires a certain ability to properly pivot when things go wrong—but that's what makes it great; it's like a game.

I'm in love with my job. Though I think I might be more in love with what it could become.

When the meeting with Stevenson is fast approaching, I'm

disappointed Lena never brings up my proposal. I handed it over to her two weeks ago and have heard nothing, meaning we're going into this meeting with our original plan—which, in my opinion, is the wrong thing to do. Worst of all, now that we're being joined by the CEO *and* the VP, everything has to be perfect. Going into the meeting, it was already clear to me, though, that there would be issues. After all, Will had told me this morning that their team still had concerns with the pricing we'd quoted.

As a Hail Mary, I decide to address Lena's lack of response to my proposal minutes before the meeting, just as we're finishing setting up the showroom.

"Lena, were you able to double-check the numbers and research on my proposal?" I ask her, my voice barely a squeak. *I should probably work on that whole confidence thing.*

"I'm so sorry I haven't gotten back to you," she says with a sigh. "I presented the proposal to Jenna—I thought it was that good—but she said she wasn't interested in changing our strategy. I pushed her, and she promised she'd think about it, but that's just her way of saying no." Lena pats me on the shoulder. "It was a good idea, though. A *very* good idea, actually. Kinda jealous that after twelve years of me working here I didn't even see it."

"Right," I say with a sad nod.

"This is good, though. It shows you've got good instincts and you showed amazing initiative. You've also shown me I can trust you with more." Lena gives me a rare smile and my chest fills with pride.

But you can't live off of just pride in a job well done in life, can you?

"FANTASTIC. TRULY FANTASTIC," IRIS, THE CHIEF MERCHANDISING Officer of Stevenson, says. "I love the updates to the collection. Looks even better in person."

Our head of design sits in the meeting, smiling proudly at the compliments.

"This is exactly why I wanted to come to look at them in person. Because unfortunately," Iris continues, "we still have several concerns surrounding pricing. Maybe we should pick another material, one that costs less, if we're going to keep our planned MSRP?"

Our CEO, Sascha, gets to her feet and pulls down a suede leather jacket from one of the racks in the showroom. "Iris, feel this leather. *Feel* it. In fact, slip the sample on. This isn't some second-rate brand where we skimp on materials just to increase our margin. That's not what we want to be known for as a private label company, and it's not what you should be known for, either. You should not be charging this high an MSRP for a jacket with lower material because you want a higher margin and think you can justify it because it has the company name on it. On the contrary, you should be living up to said name, making people happy they spent this money on a *great* quality jacket from a well-known brand. You and I both know what brand loyalty is, and this is how you both build *and* keep it. Don't be like so many other fashion houses who have begun to inflate their prices and drop their quality just to make more money. Yes, this is business, but let's maintain some sort of integrity, yes?"

Whoa.

Iris slips on the item of clothing and runs her fingers over the soft, chocolate material—a moto jacket perfect for fall. A deep sigh bursts through her lips. "You know I still have young Liam to deal with. Ever since he joined the company a few years ago, we've been fighting with vendors left and right, Iris. We can't budge in this regard."

Our CEO nods thoughtfully. "I understand it's *his* family's company he's trying to protect, but that's my whole point. You should tell him that, unless he becomes more flexible, it will be his fault he ruins his family company's reputation. Does he want to be another joke of a nepobaby? One who runs the company into the ground? Or does he want to show the world he's capable of running a multimillion dollar company despite just having it handed to him?"

Iris shoots her a look, and for a second I almost gasp. Sascha and Iris *must* have a close relationship if our CEO feels comfortable enough to insult their company's leadership.

"Well, he's not all bad—he's actually quite smart. But I agree with you. The boy needs to learn. I'll have to bring this up to him for the third time—you know that, don't you?" Iris shoots Sascha a look.

"I don't mean to pressure you, but we have until tonight before we need to submit the orders to our factories. To secure the materials and the space for production," Lena breaks into the conversation. "Unfortunately, we don't have much time to go back and forth on final numbers."

This I know for a fact, is not necessarily true. Because of situations just like this one, we often pad our due dates by a week or two, meaning Stevenson actually has until next Wednesday to give us final numbers. We make the client feel good by telling them we're making "an exception," but the truth is we always schedule them farther out than projected. It's a white lie I'm not fully comfortable with.

"You know what? I think I have an idea for how to reduce

production costs," Jenna finally speaks up, taking a matching suede skirt from the rack, inspecting it closely. "It's a bit out there because it will require a lot of coordination with our vendors and such, but I think if we work with our factories, we can figure out how to make our die cutting process more efficient so as to use every available bit of material possible, as well as buy up the same material other customers use at a discounted price for our own use. It would also help us in our mission of keeping our production as sustainable as possible." Jenna pulls a folder that looks suspiciously like the one I gave to Lena last week and hands it over to Sascha.

My stomach drops, blood runs cold.

There is no way. No fucking *way.*

"That sounds interesting, Jenna." Sascha smiles, pleasantly surprised. "And you've spoken to the factories about this? They're willing to facilitate these sales and adjust their processes?"

Jenna's smile is the picture of innocence. *What? Me? Steal a junior employee's idea? That's crazy talk!* "Yes, of course. In fact, I was hoping to present it to you after this meeting. I have a folder with the actual proposal in my suitcase, but I wanted to make sure we could work things out before. Would you like to quickly review it before we continue the meeting? See whether we can proceed and perhaps reduce the wholesale for Stevenson so we can all win? It will take some coordination with the factories, but I've estimated the new costs if we're able to pull this new strategy off."

I feel my jaw drop, rage-induced adrenaline coursing through my body, hands shaking so much I need to fist them at my sides for fear of losing control. I turn to look at Lena, begging her with my eyes for an explanation for her betrayal, but I find some relief in seeing she's clearly just as horrified and surprised as I am.

Jenna Morris just fucking used my idea and took credit for it in front of our client and CEO.

"Well, that's an *amazing* idea, Jenna. Lena," Sascha addresses my boss now, "why didn't you think of this sooner? You're head of production, are you not? I mean, this proposal has amazing value."

Lena presses her lips together, fire in her eyes as mine sting, tears threatening to run down my cheeks. "I suppose Jenna and I are sometimes misaligned on what *values* are," Lena bites back, too low for our CEO to hear.

"Well, I'm so glad to hear we have Jenna on our team," the client says.

Jenna smirks at Lena and then at me, daring us to challenge her in front of the client, to make a scene in front of the leader of our company. Helpless, I stand there, in the corner of the show-room, fighting back tears. Following Lena's lead, I attempt to control my emotions—which, given her frequent outbursts, I would've never found her possible of doing.

This growing love for what I do has broken my heart.

WILL

The call comes in around five pm.
Will is neck deep in paperwork, fighting back the urge to pull his hair
out of his scalp and curse himself for ending up in this position to
begin with. He wants to curse the obligations tied to this job. He wants
to yell at the universe for everything that led to this moment in time.
But most of all, he wants to say no. He wants to go against his
grandfather and do the right thing rather than be the scapegoat. He
wants to figure out what it is he loves and pursue that rather than be
strong-armed into doing things he feels aren't right.
So when her name flashes on his phone screen, he more than welcomes
it, her ever-positive outlook on life a gift she doesn't even know is more
valuable than anything he could ever buy.
"Bridget," he breathes, hearing her name spoken aloud alone is a
healing balm for the burns accrued throughout the day.
"Will?" She sobs. His stomach plummets, her cry a starting gun to his
heart. "Will, I need you."
And with just those four words, he's up, all the work he needed to
complete by the end of the day forgotten.
"Tell me where to meet you; I'm on my way."

11

IF THIS WAS A LESSON I HAD TO LEARN, I THINK I'D LIKE TO TRANSFER TO ANOTHER SCHOOL, PLEASE

"I'm really sorry this happened to you," Lena says. "Truly, I am speechless."

I lift my head from where it rests on my crossed arms on the sticky pub's tabletop to shoot her a desperate look.

"Is this real life?" I ask her. "Did the vice president of Sartoria seriously just steal my idea? What kind of people work at this company? Is there no one I can trust? Am I the idiot here?"

Lena shakes her head, taking another sip of her martini. "It's not you, and it isn't the company. Sure, you're still green AF and the fashion industry is far from easy, but it isn't any of that. You did beautifully. This is all her. It's who she is. Jenna is probably the most insecure person in all of fashion. She did the same thing to me five years ago when she was my direct supervisor, and it's why she's where she is today. And also where *I* am today, for that matter."

"What?" I gasp.

"Yeah." Lena nods. "She was the one I told you about. One day after work, we were at happy hour. I told her about this idea I had on how to maximize profits while keeping costs low for our clients—just like you did—and before I could tell anyone, while I was out on PTO, she took my idea and walked it over to our bosses." She pauses and looks at something over my shoulder, a shadow of betrayal in her eyes. "While I was in Palm Beach enjoying my much-deserved time off after she had been running me ragged for an entire year, my supposed mentor was double-crossing me and getting promoted for it. She felt threatened, so she took the opportunity to shoot me down before I had a chance to rise."

"Sure, okay," I say, still in disbelief. "I get why she did it when she was younger. She was a devil person looking to get ahead—nothing new there. There's always a couple in every company. But what I'm more confused about is why do this now? Why to me? I'm a nobody. I'm barely one step above an intern. I've been here for less than half a year. I am in no way a threat to her or her career."

"It isn't about you threatening her career. It's about what *she's* done to it all on her own." Lena sighs, looking down at her martini glass as she uses the cocktail stick to stir its contents. "I shouldn't be saying this, but I am angry and disappointed enough to break the rules on this. From what I hear—and please don't judge me because this sounds like water cooler gossip, even though I know for a fact it isn't—Jenna has been struggling to bring innovative ideas in a time where retail isn't doing great and bonuses haven't been paid in years. Also, I wouldn't be surprised if management has started to catch on to how much 'research shopping' she does with the company card."

My jaw drops, shocked by her words. "She's been using the company credit card to buy stuff for herself?"

Lena looks nervously at me and shakes her head. "We use the card sometimes to buy items from other brands for research—that's pretty standard of any fashion company—but some of us have noticed she tends to *keep* these 'competitive samples' instead of leaving them with our product development teams for them to study."

"Oh my god."

She shrugs. "My guess is she was desperate to bring something new and innovative to the table, given the trouble she's been in. Trying to save her job by stepping on other people's necks."

I stifle a wail. My first opportunity to prove my worth, and it was stolen by a fucking wolf in Chanel clothing.

"Am I gonna regret telling you these things?" She narrows her eyes at me, the terrifying expression in her eyes that once made me shake back in her eyes.

"God, no. I promise not to say anything." But even as the words leave my lips, I think *Will is never going to believe this when I tell him.*

"Good," she says, "because I felt like we've been having a moment lately." Her smile is soft and barely there.

I do my best to smile back, but it turns out that having someone in upper management take credit for your idea really knocks the enthusiasm out of you.

"Listen, I hate to do this because I know today has been a shitty day—"

"Understatement of the century."

"But I have to go now." She checks the time on her watch and frowns. "I'm actually running super late."

While she slips her leather jacket over her shoulders, I ask, "You got a hot date?" I regret asking her about her personal life immediately after I do. This whole experience might have caused some brain damage somehow, because even though Lena and I have been cool lately, we haven't been *girl talk* cool.

Her smile is small, her cheeks tinged with a light blush.

"Maybe," she says coyly before winking at me once. "What about you? You going home or staying?"

I shake my head and sigh. "Nah, I'm staying here. I'm waiting for a friend."

Lena nods in understanding. "That's a great idea. I think a girls night is exactly what you need right now. Plus, the fact that it's Friday night means you can get drunk and not worry about being hungover at work." She laughs softly at her own joke, and I force a smile.

I don't correct Lena by telling her I'm waiting for a man. Too risky—an opening for more questions I don't think I can answer without getting in trouble. After all, Will is not just any man. He's the one who's consumed every free moment of my time for the last six weeks, yes. The one person I've felt closest to in my entire life despite the fact that we've never met in real life. But he's also part of our most important client's team.

So telling her about him in a small way would invite a round of questions I'm not prepared to answer. It would be moronic, since I'm not prepared to lie about it, either. Today has been shitty enough as it is without having to mention to my boss that I've had a secret pen pal relationship with a member of our client's team.

"Don't let this get you down," Lena tells me. "I mean, I know it sounds impossible and you should give yourself a few days to mourn, but... I think you have a bright future ahead of you—you just need to keep going. Take this as a lesson. I sure as hell will, too. This will be the last time Jenna pulls anything like that on me or anyone on my team again." Her eyes are fierce, and definitely something to fear.

I thank Lena once more before she says goodbye and raise my hand in the air, looking around for the waiter and wordlessly order a second glass of wine. I'm going to need it if I'm going to finally meet Will face-to-face.

WILL

It's pouring outside, just the beginning of the February blues coming down over the city. It's unsettling, the rain—too many bad memories tied to it for Will to be able to take it as a regular meteorological event. As he walks over to the pub, he wonders whether that's the reason this day has been extra hellish for him. The cherry on top of an already miserable position he's in. Perhaps it's why he was so close to throwing it all away in a moment of desperation this morning. Either way, it's added an extra layer of anxiety in an already overwhelming nine layer bean dip of restlessness.

None of that matters now, though, because he has to pull himself together for her. For Bridget.

When he spots the pub from across the street, he stops and stares at it for a moment.

This is it. They're about to meet face-to-face for the first time. There's no going back after this.

12

THE BIG REVEAL

I already knew what he looked like, obviously. We've been FaceTiming nonstop since last week. Every morning, Will and I get ready for work together, talk through what our day looks like, what we're hoping to achieve, and gossip about our companies' collab—without ever crossing any lines, of course. And then, at night, we sometimes have dinner together while on a call and talk right all the way through to bedtime, slipping into our respective beds after changing into our PJs off camera, heads laying on our pillows as we yawn and wish each other a goodnight. He's become the first person I speak to when I wake and the last before I go to bed—excluding Ginger, of course. So after hours of seeing his face every day for the past week or so, I did not expect to be so rattled by his looks.

And yet...

All of the oxygen in the room is sucked out when I see him open the door to the bar, his eyes searching through the crowd until they land on me. I try to control my expression, to not reveal how my skin has turned blazing hot in a split second, but I'm one and a half drinks deep and a bit of a lightweight, so who knows what my face looks like now?

Picking up my jaw from where it fell on the sticky bar floor, I wave him over. With a tentative smile, he walks slowly toward the high top, stopping just a foot away.

He takes a deep breath, eyes wide as he takes me in, before speaking. "Hey." His voice is soft and rich, and I want to dive into it head first. I want to let myself sink in that single word and never come back for air—not if it means never hearing him say it again with that look in his eyes, like he can't believe this is real, either. Like he never wants to look away.

He runs his fingers through his wet hair, waiting for me to reply with something. And I try—I really do—but nothing comes out.

He's here. Will. Is here. In front of me. Right now.

And I'm blowing it.

Finally, I manage to whisper, "Hi."

With the grace of a bull in a china shop, I attempt to slide off my stool to... hug him? Kiss him on both cheeks like a European would? Shake his hand? Anything... But my legs turn to jelly when I catch the deep brown of his eyes, the curve of his lips, and lose my balance. On instinct, Will catches me just in time, right before I fall face first onto the dirty floor.

"You okay?" His brows pull together as he helps me to my feet, his big hands comforting as they wrap around my biceps. How can they be this warm when he's just come in from the cold? How does he look this amazing even after so clearly being rained on outside with no umbrella in sight?

"Yeah," I say with a shaky laugh. "Thank god you caught me before I touched that filthy floor. I would've probably ended up needing a tetanus shot from it."

He snorts and shakes his head, eyes bright even under the dim bar lights. "Too true. Why'd you pick this place, anyway?"

He's so beautiful. Yes, Will is six-foot-a thousand and while I think it's safe to say he isn't Arnold Schwarzenegger, he's definitely a gym rat in the best possible way—lean, strong as a tree, yet still has a welcoming softness to him. He's still beautiful—a word I never would've thought I'd use to describe a guy. A sculpture of a man with angular cheeks, straight nose, smooth tan skin. His thick but tidy brows accentuate every single one of his expressions when he speaks. Will's dark curly hair looks so inviting, I have to fist my hands to keep from reaching out and running my fingers through it.

When I first saw him through my phone screen, I was surprised by how attractive he was. Now that I have him in front of me? I'm speechless. How can a man so kind, so sweet and intelligent, be this good looking? I thought God didn't give with two hands, yet here he stands, Will Jacobs, evidence to the contrary. And he's here for *me*.

As friends, but still.

I try for a settling, deep breath to calm the sudden swell of emotions, but it turns out to be a massive mistake. A wave of orange blossoms and vanilla falls over me, and suddenly I can't produce a rational thought, let alone move.

"Bridget? Are you okay?" he asks, glancing furtively at the half empty glass in front of me. "Uh, are you... are you drunk?"

Mortified, I clear my throat and try to get it together because I sure as hell don't want Will's first IRL impression of me to be of me drunk. Because I'm not, by the way—just a little tipsy.

(Although there's no denying his arrival has made me feel a different kind of intoxicated.)

"No. *No*." I sigh. "Sorry, I'm just taken a little aback. It's been a long, shitty day, and now you're here and..." I trail off, unsure of what else to say.

Hurt, he takes a step back, releasing the grip he still held around my arms. "Do you want me to leave?"

"What? *No*, of course not."

"Then..."

"I'm thrilled you're here. Really. I'm just confused. Because…" I sigh again, even deeper this time, trying to organize my thoughts. "I have other friends—friends I've known for years, even—but my first instinct was to call *you*, to ask for *you*. It's your shoulder I want to cry on. And… it's *weird*."

"Weird?" I hate the way he still looks hurt.

"Not weird," I say, frustrated I can't seem to form a normal sentence. "Just odd. I… I don't know you." I regret the words as soon as they leave my mouth, the hurt on his face even more clear and present than before.

"Don't you?" Will takes a step closer, his scent surrounding me even more.

"I just…" I can't look away, his eyes hypnotic. My brain tries to work through a rational thought, a way to express how confused I feel because I don't *want* anyone else and it scares me. But I don't want to scare him in turn and… "I just think it's a bit odd."

"Maybe it's a good odd? Because I would've hated knowing you were crying on someone else's shoulder. And I'll admit it's a little *odd* for me, too. I don't really… talk to anyone. At the risk of sounding like a fucking loser, I don't have time for friends. Or *other* friends, I guess. You are…" he exhales, his eyes bouncing over my face, as if taking me in.

"Conveniently virtual?" I ask.

He laughs once and shakes his head. "I was gonna say an exception. But the fact that I've had you in my pocket this whole time, that up until now our entire relationship was all through texting and emailing and FaceTiming? It's definitely made things more convenient than a regular friendship, yeah. This thing —this friendship—is also odd for me. So maybe two odds make a right?" He smiles at his own attempt at a joke, and I can't help but smile, too.

"That wasn't even funny." I bite my lower lip to keep from smiling. Will and his dad jokes.

"It kinda was. It rhymed with the original saying." His smile is heartbreaking as he pulls out a stool for himself.

"You know, if you have to explain it, it almost certainly means it's a sign the joke isn't funny."

He rolls his eyes and laughs. "You know you love my dad jokes. Now let me order a beer so I can catch up to you and you can tell me everything about your day and who I need to kill."

WILL

Will has half a mind to flush this whole deal with Sartoria down the drain just to get the VP fired. He wants Jenna to pay for taking credit for Bridget's idea, of course. But more than that, he wants to make her pay for taking away Bridget's light. For breaking her heart, which he so desperately wants to protect at all costs.

Despite all that, despite the hunger for vengeance growing inside, he knows he couldn't do that to Bridget. If he were to help pull the project, she would also end up losing. Her passion project would be cancelled, an investigation would surely happen, and her reputation, unfortunately, could be ruined.

Either way, it's not like his boss would even allow it, anyway, would he? It's not like he can walk over to him and say "This company's manager hurt the woman I care about's feelings so we must cancel our order and find a different vendor."

There isn't much that Will could do for Bridget, realistically. What he can do is be there for her in any other way. And there is nothing in this world that would ever stop him from doing so.

13

PRO TIP: TRY NOT TO DEVELOP A MAJOR CRUSH ON YOUR NEW BEST FRIEND

Once I finish my story, Will gulps down the last of his beer, slamming the glass down with a loud enough bang that our neighboring tables turn to look at us. Eyes on the table, he grits his teeth as if biting back words, bushy brows pulled together as he processes the events that led me to hate my job for the first time since I started. Did I have moments of dislike towards other jobs I had in the past? Yes. But never until today, I'd never felt anything close to hate or heartbreak until Jenna took from me what I'd worked so hard for.

"Will?" My voice is small and careful. Slowly, I reach out to place a hand on his forearm, which breaks him free from whatever path his mind took him down. He turns to look at me and places a hand over mine before taking it between both of his.

"Are you okay?" Just listening to the sound of his deep voice feels like crawling under a cozy blanket on the couch during a rainstorm—comforting, warm, and reassuring. Like I know there's a lot going on outside, but nothing can hurt me while I'm there.

"No," I say, my voice breaking. I dig into the bowl of pretzels in front of us with my free hand and shove a few into my mouth.

I chew viciously, thinking over my answer before correcting it. "But also yes? Like, it's horrible and it kind of feels like my heart is broken. Like I was betrayed, because I suppose I was. But, I mean, I guess I should look on the bright side, right? My idea was so good that an executive from the company felt compelled to steal it and claim it as their own." I shrug and try for a pathetic laugh, trying to make light of it.

"Stop. Don't diminish what happened by trying to spin it." His no nonsense attitude derails me, a bucket of cold water over the fire I feel in my heart for this job that I'm trying to stoke. "Your ability to find good in difficult situations is one of the things I like the most about you, but you can't make light of what happened. None of this is right."

I stop and sit up straight. "I'm not making light of the situation. I'm just... What else am I supposed to do? Looking at the bright side is all I can handle right now."

"You can report her. Say something to HR or something. Talk to the CEO." He raises a hand and signals our waiter for another beer while I scoff in disbelief.

"Are you crazy? You really think it's that simple? You want me to just walk into the CEO's office or HR all willy nilly and tell them that the VP, who has been at the company for over a decade, stole some random associate's idea she developed in a week? Like, who do you think they're going to believe? The inexperienced one who's barely above an intern and has had more jobs in different industries than she can count on two hands, or the woman with years of experience under her belt that are exclusive to not just this world, but the company?"

He sits up, his jaw set in determination. "It's wrong, what she did. And when you show them all of the work and research you put into the project, they'll believe you."

I roll my eyes at him. "You don't get it, do you? That's not how things work, apparently. Otherwise, my boss would've said something, told me to do the same thing you're telling me to do now."

The waiter places a beer in front of Will, and he slumps in his seat. "It's not that I don't get it. I do, believe me. It's that I don't want this for you. When we first met, I loved how excited you were about your job and this industry—which I have grown to seriously resent. So I'm upset it's getting to you. I'm frustrated that you're finally facing some of the negative things that come with this world, and I don't want that for you. I don't want you to get to a point where all this bullshit will eventually dull your shine."

"Dull my shine?" My lips quirk upwards, cheeks blushing once again. He thinks I have a shine to be dulled? Before I can help it, my little quirk turns into a goofy grin, despite the subject matter of our conversation. Even through this stressful conversation, Will can make my body light up like a freaking Christmas tree. My mind drifts back to our dirty and flirty exchanges and I realize I miss them. I want them back.

Will looks down at his glass and clears his throat. "You know what I'm saying. You're almost annoyingly positive," he says, a teasing smile playing at his lips while his eyes remain intense. "But I think having people like you in the world brings a balance to it we are in desperate need of. Like vegetarians."

I sputter a laugh. "Vegetarians? What the hell does that mean?"

"You know," he repeats, as if those two words should explain everything. His cheeks blush as he shoots me an almost rueful smile, and I think I almost die. Because even though it *looks* like I'm cool now, my mind is still reeling from seeing him in person for the first time. From the instant swirl of... *something* that I felt run through every inch of my body.

"I literally have no idea what you're talking about," I tell him, doing my best to hide the storm of confusing feelings brewing inside me. "I frequently enjoy a double Shake Shack burger and cheese fries. *Plus* a vanilla shake. This ass doesn't happen from just eating vegetables, you know. Or going up and down my walk-up at least twice a day." Laughing, I look down at my bottom with meaning. I cut myself off when I see him look away, though, the tension in his body making it seem like the action itself took every ounce of strength he had.

When he turns back to look at me, he reaches for a pretzel from the bowl, chewing before speaking again. "First of all, cheese fries and shakes *are* vegetarian. Second, I used 'vegetarian' as a metaphor for your positive attitude, because it isn't really normal for humans to be the way that you are."

"Flattering, thanks," I say, deadpan.

"We're omnivorous creatures. So if you being this positive person means you're a vegetarian because you're *rare*, then the rest of us realists—some would call us jaded—individuals could be called omnivorous or even carnivores. Depends on the level of bitterness."

"I feel like this metaphor is way too complicated than it needs to be. Might be taking a turn."

"It makes sense, I promise. Stay with me for a moment." I raise a brow, but he keeps going. "So if we live by the theory that vegetarians bring some balance into the ecosystem so we don't deplete the world from animal protein as quickly as we actually could, we can say that you exist to build the rest of us up by having a positive attitude and keeping us from falling into a depressive mental health crisis similar to the food crisis we're in."

"Aren't we in *multiple* food crises?" I ask, trying not to let my mood be dragged further by thinking too much of how fucked the world is and how mankind is responsible for most of it.

He shrugs. "Probably. But, to clarify, when I compare you to a vegetarian, I mean you're one of those bright, shiny people who never lets anything bring them down. And in this bleak, jaded, fucked up world, we need metaphorical vegetarians to keep us going or else we'd all fall into a depression spiral."

I pause and take another sip of my wine as I think his words over. "That was way more convoluted than it needed to be."

He rolls his eyes. "Did you understand what I meant?"

"Yeah, I guess."

"So why does it matter?"

This makes me laugh into my wine, my skin buzzing as his smile grows wide. "Okay, but if you want me to stay bright and shiny, as you say, then why are you giving me shit for looking at the bright side of things?"

Will shakes his head so fast and hard, in my tipsy state I worry whether it could actually come off. "No. It's not the same thing. Looking at the bright side of things is not the same thing as doing nothing when bad things happen to you—which is what you're doing now. You can't just let this Jenna thing slide and go on with life and work and pretend like everything is okay."

I chew on my bottom lip, tasting the salt from the pretzels that would've paired so much better with a beer than the shitty wine I ordered.

"Do you want me to talk to Lena? Or someone?" he asks, his voice serious.

I burst out laughing, waiting for him to break, to laugh with me and tell me he's joking. When I'm met with nothing but stony silence, I stop. "What do you mean '*talk to someone*'? What exactly do you think you can do? First of all, you don't even work at my company. Second, aren't you middle management? Plus, you work in the finance department. What do you expect to be able to do?"

He purses his lips. "There are many options I could go with."

"What? Even though I still don't know exactly what you do

at Stevenson—and I probably wouldn't be able to understand it because finance is *definitely* not one of my strong suits—I'm sure there's nothing *you* could do to... avenge me? Or whatever." We haven't gotten too much into detail about Will's job—he's cagey about it, probably not wanting to cross some corporate espionage line or something, which I totally get. I don't want to cross that line either. Which makes me realize something... "Actually. If we're going to continue to be friends, I think we need to set some ground rules regarding work. Outside of what we *both* see in the email exchanges or very generic venting about our days, I think we should keep it separate from our relationship."

Will perks up a bit at this. "That sounds... like a great idea."

I smile. "I could tell you've been nervous about revealing too much info. And I guess I shouldn't be discussing work stuff to a client, even if it's you. It makes sense."

"Yeah." Will forces a smile, looking visibly uncomfortable. He looks away and runs both his hands through his hair.

He struggles to meet my gaze when I say his name, ask him to look at me. "I know you want to help," I tell him, "but there really is nothing you can do. I'm just going to have to accept that my boss's boss is a dick and will need to learn how to manage that situation going forward. That is, if I stay in fashion."

His eyes swing back to me. "*If* you stay in fashion?" Will's eyes widen. "No—you *have* to stay in fashion. I've known you for less than two months and I already know how much you love your job. Stop. You can't let this affect the rest of your future. You can't let her win."

I heave a sigh, weary. "I'm not going to quit," I admit. "But I'm just... I don't know. Tired. Achy. Betrayed."

He huffs and shakes his head with furrowed brows. "I wish you'd just let me help."

Exhausted, I laugh. "Will." It's all I say before reaching out to take his hands in mine, both of us staring at the way they naturally fit into each other.

"You're always there for me when I'm the one having a bad day. I want to be there for you, too." One of his thumbs strokes the back of my hand, cheeks flushed.

"Really?" My eyes well, the wave of emotion finally reaching its peak.

"Yeah, of course." Will smiles, squeezing my hands. He exhales once before pinning me down with an intense stare in his eyes. "You've turned my days around so many times, Bridge." His voice is full of awe as he shakes his head. "Before you, I was kind of holding on by a thread. But you've shown me a different path, you know? Yes, work sucks, but I've been creating a toxic environment for myself and others by focusing on how much I don't like my job. And maybe if I focus on the good, remind myself why I'm actually there, I can keep going for as long as I have to."

His words make my head swirl, lost in their sweetness. But then the last part of his statement makes me do a mental double-take: "As long as you have to? What does that mean?"

Will's face shifts into one of concern. "Nothing. I just mean that I probably shouldn't be so negative all the time. That maybe, even though I really do hate my job and don't want to be there, I make things worse for myself. And I love that you've taught me that lesson."

"Oh. Okay." I want to push a little more because he didn't really answer my question, but his hands are still holding mine —or I'm still holding his?—and my skin is on fire, I'm sure of it. Even warmer still is the feeling building deep inside my abdomen, low in my tummy, and between my thighs. And even though I've *known* Will is attractive since the second I saw him over FaceTime, it's the first time I'm able to admit to myself something much bigger: I *want* him. I want him *bad*. More than for a silly sexting session.

Stupid Bridget. He's basically turned into your best friend. You cannot ruin what you guys have by being this attracted to him. Plus, he was so clearly not into you when he first saw you on FaceTime, remember? Drop it and move on. What are you even thinking?

I pull my hands away with a heavy sigh and look out the bar window, see that the rain has not stopped pouring since this afternoon. When I first got to the pub, I could've sworn the weather was matching my mood—dark, gloomy, and a bit end-of-the-world-y. But now that I'm feeling a different kind of frustration and despair, I wonder what it will turn into. 'Horny and disheartened' doesn't really have a matching meteorological pattern, doest it? Maybe a heatwave.

Sigh.

Feeling Will's eyes on me, I look around the pub, taking in my surroundings as I contemplate what to do. I watch a group of people move to the beat of the music, louder now that it's later, on the small pub dance floor. Watch the couples with envy as they sway with their arms around each other, smiling as they do. A dark part of myself I rarely let free peeks out from beneath where I keep it hidden, my ability to keep my head above water in difficult situations waning. Squeezing my eyes shut, I visualize the darkness, push it back down where it belongs, locking the door behind me. With a deep breath, I open my eyes and look straight into the chocolate eyes of the man who's taken over every corner of my brain for weeks.

"Thank you," I tell him.

"For what?"

"For meeting me tonight, even though it's raining outside."

His eyes widen, spine straightens as the muscles in his neck visibly tense. "What do you mean?"

"The rain. You don't like it. And still, you came. I know it must've been hard."

He's stunned, his lips agape as he processes my words. "You know?"

I smile at him. "Only that you don't like it."

"It's... a long story." He looks down at his hands, frowning. "But it's not like I'm *scared* of it or anything. Just... bad memories."

He clasps his hands together in his lap, unsettled. We don't speak for some time until the song changes to one of my favorites, slow and sultry. Without thinking twice, I ask, "Will you dance with me and tell me about it?"

Will looks up, a slow smile spreading across his face. "Yeah. Yeah, I'd love to."

I take one of his hands in mine, and lead him to the makeshift dance floor in the small cleared space in the pub where I wrap my arms around his neck as he slips his arms around my waist.

WILL

The ache in his chest grows tenfold in an instant, making it nearly impossible for him to breathe. He'd rather live with it forever, though, because its presence is exclusive to hers. And now that he's seen her, that he's held her in his arms, he never wants to look away, will always want her around.

14

WHO WOULDA KNOWN MY FRONT DOOR WOULD BE SO COMFORTABLE?

Eyes closed, I let myself enjoy this perfect moment: Will's hands around my waist, my head resting on the place between his chest and his shoulder—what feels like a perfect nook made just for me—inhaling his scent like an addict. *This is Will. All of him.*

His breath is warm on my ear when he finally speaks after a full slow dance in silence. "My mom was in a car crash almost five years ago that left her paralyzed from the waist down."

My breath hitches, and I hold him tighter to my body. He responds the same way, gripping me closer to him as if needing to hold me to him in order to get through the rest of the story.

"It was raining—*pouring*, really—and..." Even over the music and the loud crowd, even over the sound of laughter and dishes clattering from where we stand a few feet from the kitchen entrance, I hear him swallow hard. "And I was driving. We hydroplaned, I lost control of the car, and just... fucked up my mom's life." His voice breaks, but he clears his throat immediately after. Even so, there's no way to hide the pain in his voice. The guilt and shame he so clearly feels for what happened to her.

I dig my fingers into him, pulling him closer still. "Will," I whisper, wanting so much to help him.

"I—I wasn't drunk or anything. I just lost control of the car. But..." He shakes his head, then breathes me in when he dips his nose in my hair.

"It wasn't your fault. At all."

"I know that. Still doesn't mean I don't feel like shit over it."

"Is your mom okay now? I mean, you said she's paralyzed from the waist down, so obviously not. But... is she okay?"

He understands what I mean.

"Yeah. It was touch and go for a bit. And things got really dark when the medical bills started piling up. The stress was..." He exhales, squeezing his eyes shut and shaking his head as if wanting to shake off the memory. When he seems to finally collect himself, he continues. "Mom's a retired teacher, so it's not like she had a ton of savings. Whatever she had was quickly depleted. And my dad's been gone for a while—died when I was three—so it was just us dealing with everything and stuff. I had a different job back then and didn't make much..." He frowns, his gaze lost as he stares over my shoulder for a moment before looking back at me. "Anyway. That's why I don't like the rain. Brings back too many bad memories."

"I understand. And I'm so sorry it happened." Some deep instinct wants to reach out and place a kiss on his cheek, wants to run my hands through his hair to make him feel better. But I can't. "And are you guys okay now?" I ask, trying to distract myself.

"Yeah. She's fucking amazing, honestly. She got used to a wheelchair in record time and does her physical therapy every day. Never complains. Bounced back with an amazing positive attitude. Honestly, there's no one like her. She's kinda like you in that way." He smiles. "Scrappy."

"But are *you* okay?" And it's like hitting the nail perfectly on the head.

He almost slumps in my arms, the devastation in his eyes goes so deep I almost wish his guilt were a tangible thing I could physically fight off. It's not like I have a particular talent in hand-to-hand combat, but I'd like to at least *try* and help.

"My mother is paralyzed because I wasn't able to control the car enough to avoid hydroplaning. So, no. I'm not. But that isn't fair of me to say. I'm not the one in a wheelchair," Will says, his voice breaking. "She's way too forgiving. Constantly tells me it's not my fault and that I shouldn't be putting myself through hell for her."

My stomach twists at the pain radiating off his body. Every ounce of me wants to be the balm that heals it. "I agree with your mom. It's not healthy, this guilt. I mean, the look on your face just now..." I shake my head, pulling back so I can press my palm to his cheek, feel the prickle of his five o'clock shadow beneath my fingertips like spikes pressing against my already aching heart.

We're touching a lot. We've *been* touching a lot. Is this something normal friends do? Is it the alcohol that's made us handsy? I know why *I* want to keep touching him—I'm crazy about the guy. But he clearly took one look at me weeks ago and decided he wasn't attracted, so why do I feel him holding on to me like his life depended on it?

"You can't hold onto this guilt."

"I know. But it will never not be my fault."

"Will. Stop. You're not being fair to yourself." I rub my thumb across his cheek, almost on instinct, in an effort to soothe him.

He takes my hand from his cheek and brings it between us as we sway with a soft, sad smile. "It's okay, Bridge. I'm almost done paying for my sins."

"What the hell does that even mean?" I ask, wanting to push, *needing* to push.

"Don't worry about it. Soon enough, it won't even matter."

I huff a sigh, ready to burst in exasperation and demand he stop being so cryptic sometimes, but something takes over me. I don't know if it's the alcohol or the music, if it's the dark lights or the comforting warmth of being in his arms, but I let myself get lost in his furrowed brow, in his dark eyes, and decide not to press him for more answers. Instead, I focus on how Will's lips could be just half an inch away from mine if I just raised up on my tiptoes. If I just stretched up a little and—

But the slow song ends, transitions into something fast-paced and upbeat; the crowd around us begins to move faster, bumping into us, breaking whatever magic or moment had started to build. It's like waking up from a dream you never want to let go of. And I almost wail as I feel his arms slip away from my waist, see the corners of his mouth drop, and hear his voice over the music as he tells me it's late and he better get home, but can he walk me back to my place before?

True to his word, he walks me all the way from the Garment District to the hell that is the Times Square subway station, and even takes the train with me down to Chinatown. I tell him it isn't necessary, that I'm fine, but there's no walking him off the edge of that cliff. And it *is* a damn cliff in the sense that I feel we're in danger.

Our friendship has, once again, evolved—but in a different direction. It's obvious I've been having non-friend friendly feelings for Will for *a while* now. But this is different. We almost *kissed*. And he pulled away.

I want to dig a hole and bury myself there, a thousand feet below ground. I want to never see him or anyone else ever again after how embarrassingly idiotic I acted. He had just told me about his mother's tragic accident, just opened up to me about something huge, and I almost kissed him!

I am, it's clear, beyond a next level idiot.

No wonder he wants nothing to do with me.

A couple of blocks from my apartment building, as thoughts of all the mortifying ways in which I embarrassed myself run through my mind, I exhale loudly.

"Bridge?" He stops in the middle of the sidewalk and gently takes hold of my arm. "You good?"

I force a smile because, on top of not being able to control the urge to kiss my friend, I can't control the urge to sigh—a fully controllable bodily function.

I'm a mess. An absolute nightmare. I'm beat up and tired and heartbroken. Yet still, he stands there in front of me, cold, humid wind pulling at his hair, rain long gone, with a look in his eyes I wish I could properly read. In anyone else, I feel like I could confidently identify it. But after everything that happened tonight and the last two weeks, there's no way he's looking at me with the kind of affection I think I see. *It's just wishful thinking*, I tell myself. *You think he's looking at you that way because you want him to.*

"I'm fine," I tell him, faking my best smile. "You don't need to walk me the rest of the way, though. I promise I'll be okay. I can even text you when I get to my apartment. Even share my location with you, if you want."

He grins, encouraged by my tone, but he doesn't budge. "I wouldn't mind having your exact location in the palm of my hand for whenever I want it. But nice try—I'm still walking you home." To my dismay, he lets go of my arm and continues walking.

When we reach my apartment on the sixth floor, I half expect him to be out of breath, but he doesn't even seem to have broken a sweat. And why would he, considering the amount of time he spends at the gym? And while he doesn't look like he's physically exhausted after going up six flights of stairs, when I slide my keys into the lock, ready to kick open my door, when I look up at him over my shoulder to thank him and wish him a good night, I do notice he's almost panting. His cheeks flush as one of his hands grips the frame of my front door, arm tense as if he were losing his hold on himself and his grip on everything around him.

"Will?" I gasp when his pupils dilate as he leans in closer. He isn't touching me, yet I feel the heat of him all over my body.

"I had a good time tonight," he manages to say after appearing to struggle through his words.

"Me too. Thank you. For coming to see me."

"Anything. Anytime. Whenever you need me, I'll be there."

In all honesty, for a moment I almost forgot why Will and I even met up in the first place. Why we broke our rules and decided to leave our virtual relationship behind in place for an actual, in real life one. He made me forget about anything else that wasn't him.

"Right. Work. Thank you for listening to me."

He reaches out and pushes a strand of hair behind my ear, following his movements with his eyes as he does. "You okay, then? For me to go?"

I catch his hand by the wrist before he can take it away, move it down to the nape of my neck where he digs his fingers into my hair.

"Do you *want* to go?" My eyes widen as I see the shift in his expression from sweet and caring to hungry and animalistic. Is this happening? I mean, he sort of rejected me at the bar, but now...

His eyes study me as he leans forward, almost pressing me against my front door. His hand moves to cup my jaw this time, forehead pressed to mine. I feel the inevitable crimson blush spread up my chest and neck, travel all the way to my cheeks.

He moves his lips to my ear and whispers: "Do you know how many times I've imagined running my tongue over that perfect fucking skin just to taste your blush?"

A breath gets caught in my throat, though no oxygen appears to make it into my lungs. I drop my keys and bag on the floor, freeing my hands to clasp them behind his neck. His hands fly to my hips beneath my open coat and he pushes me against my door with a thud, fingers digging into me. And that's when it feel *it*. Pressed against my stomach, hard and long. And it feels *incredible*. Our lips are less than a centimeter apart now. The heat radiating from them almost burns. I ache, I whine, as he teases me, pressing a small kiss on the corner of my mouth, running his tongue on my bottom lip. I can barely breathe when he presses me harder still. He is predator and I am prey *and I fucking love it*.

"Please," I beg him.

"Please what?" he murmurs, placing a kiss against the side of my neck. I close my eyes and swallow as I feel his teeth graze the delicate skin before following it with a kiss.

"You *know* what," I whine, two seconds away from bursting into tears. I've wanted this man for what feels like a lifetime. And for some unthinkable reason, he's here in my arms, and based on the *very* hard and very, *very* promising erection pressed up against me, he wants me, too.

While he's kissing my neck, gliding his nose up and down, telling me he never would've imagined I smelled this good—*So fucking good, Bridge; better than I ever could've dreamed*—I still haven't been able to do more than hold on to his broad shoulders for fear of passing out. "Will, *please*, god."

"You are..." he huffs, his hands digging into my hair, hips pressing me into the door. "You *are*." He practically growls the word, like my existence alone is enough to drive him wild.

Finally, he takes my face in his hands and presses his lips to mine, parting them with his. I can't help the moan in the back of my throat when he nips at my top lip before soothing it with his tongue, or when I lick the inside of his mouth and he answers with a growl. I can't help the way one of my legs wraps around his hip, the skirt of my dress riding up and exposing my thigh. The way I try to relieve some of the tension with friction. I can't help the heat that builds between my legs and I think *Oh my god, this is going to be the best sex of my life. The best sex ever that anyone has ever had. I just know it.*

But something breaks through the fog of lust, a noise I'm all too familiar with. I hear the scratches and the wailing coming from the other side of my apartment door and some motherly instinct I didn't even know I had manages to pull me away from thoughts of devouring this man. Ginger is howling aggressively, begging for food.

"Shit," I say when I pull away, trying to catch my breath. "I— I have to feed her. It's almost ten o'clock. Way past her dinner time."

Will looks a mess, with his hair mussed, perfect lips red and swollen. His shirt somehow untucked and coat half pushed off his shoulders. When did *that* happen? I watch him try and process my words—it takes him a while to get there. "Ginger?"

"Yeah." I clear my throat, run my fingers through my hair.

"Right. Your cat. Okay. I... Do you want me to go then?"

"No!" I say, a bit too enthusiastic. "I mean... No. Come in. It's not the most luxurious apartment around, but it's home. And I don't want you to go."

He grins and reaches for my hand. "You don't?"

"No. Come inside; let me introduce you to Ginger."

WILL

Yes, he kissed her. Yes, he now gets to live for the rest of his life with the knowledge of how Bridget feels in his arms and the way her lips feel against his (twelve out of ten, by the way). But it doesn't mean anything. Not yet. Especially not after they decided a while back ago to keep things in the friend zone.

Whatever happens in the next twenty-four hours will finally determine who they are to each other. He's sure of it.

15

REVISITING CERTAIN DISCUSSIONS CAN BE A GOOD THING

Ginger, it turns out, barely even notices Will's presence, choosing instead to glare as I come in, silently giving me shit for neglecting her dinner time and leading me into the kitchen.

My place isn't "company ready" by any means. There are clothes strewn about everywhere, my bathroom counter is covered in a layer of cosmetics, skincare, and hair clips, in an uncharacteristic move, my Murphy bed is down and unmade, and the only other piece of furniture I have, Ginger's chair, is covered in orange and white cat hair.

But I don't care. Because I know somehow that Will doesn't care either. By the look on his face—a little less frenzied now, a little more fascinated—he's just happy to be here. From the corner of my eye, I watch him examine my place as I feed my little monster, who finally stops for one second to stare at our guest suspiciously as I pour her food into her bowl.

"Relax," I whisper to her after she jumps up onto my small kitchen counter. "He's not going to kill us and he's not here to take your tuna and whitefish pâté." She practically rolls her eyes before proceeding to attack her food.

"Were you just talking to your cat?" he asks. His smile is fond as he stands by the window. The neon lights from the restaurants outside cast a red glow on his face that remind me of the deep flush he sported just a minute ago. Just when he had me pressed against my apartment door.

"Duh. It's not like that's weird or anything," I say defensively. I prepare myself for the ultimate red flag: he doesn't like cats.

But I should've known better, because Will laughs softly, walking over to me before placing his hands on my hips and says, "Nah. It's cute." He looks over my shoulder at her. "And cats are awesome. Are you gonna introduce me?"

"Mmm, she's pretty busy at the moment."

With a wistful smile, Will shakes his head. "Alright then. I'll try not to take it personal." He brushes a strand of loose hair behind my ear, following its movements as if it were the most fascinating thing he's ever seen. "You're so goddamn beautiful, you know that? I thought so the second my screen filled with your face. Even before then, I think, when I didn't even know what you looked like."

I snort. "You're just saying that."

Looking alarmed, his hand drops to his side. "No, I'm not."

"It's okay if you didn't find me attractive, Will," I say, trying to play it off as if it didn't gut me when he pulled back from his flirty texts. "It was kinda obvious you weren't into me."

"What? Are you insane? What the hell makes you think that?" Genuine shock spreads across his face. And I'm just as baffled by his reaction, honestly.

I lean back to stare him straight in the eye. "Are you kidding? You stopped being all flirty the second we saw each other for the first time on camera."

"Because it was the day after we sexted, and you had ghosted me! I'm not gonna be the dick who pushes themselves on someone after they were asked to back down. You said you wanted to keep things friendly and weren't interested in pursuing anything sexual or beyond."

Fuck.

"I did say that."

And now that he brings it up, it means we obviously need to reevaluate our agreement from a few weeks ago. Or stick to the plan, stick to just being friends, because it feels like Will is the only person I can depend on lately and, based on personal history, my romantic relationships never seem to last. It's too much of a risk. I should nip this thing in the bud right now, before things get too serious. Before we jump into bed and... But I don't want to stop and think about it. I don't want to think of the consequences of my actions. I've been waiting for this moment and now we're finally *here* and *he's* here and—

"I'd like to revisit this discussion, if that's possible," he says, his voice several octaves deeper, eyes dark and hungry. He pulls me closer to him, my breasts pressed up against his chest. I slide my hands up his arms, over his corded biceps, to his shoulders. His coat is long forgotten, hanging on the hook by the front door, mine tossed haphazardly onto the kitchen counter.

"Sure," I murmur against his lips, eyes closed as I dig my fingers into his hair. "Maybe later, though."

With a groan, he presses his lips to mine, his kiss destructive to my soul, because I've never felt anything quite like this. He bends to carry me in his arms, holding on to my ass when I wrap my legs around his waist, thighs exposed as the skirt of my dress rides up to my waist. The slight bounce as I settle in this position ends in a delicious friction where I'm already so wet and ready. I can feel my thin lace and cotton panties soaked through from before, and now I just want them *off*. My whole body cries out for him to do it again, to feel the ridge of his hard cock hit my clit over our clothes so I can feel that release I crave more than oxygen. He tenses, sensing exactly what I need because that's him. That's Will. My confidant, the only person who truly *knows* me. But I want him to know me everywhere and I want to know him too. Bouncing me once more in his arms, he does it again, his hardness hitting me right where I need him most. This time, I don't hold back the way I moan his name into his neck, begging him for more.

"Fuck, Bridget. *Fuck.*" We turn and he walks me over to the bed. Thankfully, my apartment is practically closet-sized, making it a bearably short trip. With gritted teeth, he tosses me onto the mattress where I fall with a bounce. In the back of my mind, I thank my lucky stars I forgot to put the Murphy bed away.

The mattress squeaks below me, but I barely notice, too focused instead on the way Will's dark eyes lock on mine when he removes my high heeled boots, throwing each one over his shoulders. I can't think of anything else as his hands travel up my thighs, parting them and lifting my skirt up once more as he does. When he reaches my underwear, he runs his index and middle finger over the fabric up and down, before moving it to the side. "You're so fucking wet for me, Bridge. And you have such a pretty pussy, don't you?"

I squeeze my eyes shut and nod my head desperately, biting down on my lip for fear of screaming out in desperation. Will sits up and pulls my underwear off, before throwing them over his shoulder as well; then, he settles back between my legs, as comfortable there as if it were his second home. His fingers tease my clit. Circle it in a slow, torturous rhythm. Feeling the wetness there, sending shivers up my spine despite feeling completely engulfed in flames. It doesn't make sense, how I feel. Everything is in disarray yet in perfect order. I can barely understand anything, yet it all makes perfect sense. I feel so alone, yet am surrounded by his arms around my hips, his scent in my apartment, and his growls as he kisses around my pussy before finally putting me out of my misery and running his tongue over me in one, perfect, slow lick.

My back arches off the mattress, and I cry out Will's name, pleading for more than just that one touch, more than just the way he holds me open. *I want you to hold me tighter. To lick me longer. I want your fingers inside as you taste me.*

And I guess I've said it all out loud because his grip tightens like a snake around my thighs and hips, a hand pressing down on my abdomen to keep me still. His mouth comes down on my clit with a moan, where Will makes himself comfortable. Finally, the fingers of his free hand join his tongue in completely overwhelming me, giving me something to tighten around as little bursts of a precursor to an orgasm start coursing through me.

He eats me like a starved man, while savoring me like I'm his last meal.

Way too soon, I find myself barreling toward an orgasm, careening wildly towards a place I'd clearly never been to before in my life. Because sex—at least oral sex—has never been like this for me. At once animalistic and perfectly measured, a series of contradictions that leaves me spent and melted and wet and a sticky mess on my mattress as I watch Will helplessly get to his knees on the bed and wipe his mouth with the back of his hand before licking his fingers clean.

"I used to think you'd taste like strawberries and cream. Maybe cherries." He begins to unbutton his shirt, breathing ragged. Meanwhile, I wonder whether I'm still alive. Wonder how I'm even able to pull in any air. "I should've known someone like you, someone with your passion and brightness, would taste more like cinnamon and something floral. Like magnolia." He peels his shirt off and I lose all sense, sitting up just to run my hands down his perfect, defined, tan chest. I feel the light smattering of hair beneath my fingertips, feel the smoothness of his skin, dewy from exertion.

"I could lick every inch of your chest," I admit in a whisper.

In one wild movement, he manages to pull my dress over my head, leaving me in my bra. His eyes land on my breasts, pupils widening as I fall back onto the bed and they bounce. "Fucking. Ditto."

He leans down to kiss me on the lips, his tongue and mine a tangled mess, before moving down to my neck. "I could kiss every single one of these perfect freckles. Like tiny targets of where I know I'm gonna lick and kiss and bite you." Will moves the cups of my bra over my tits, where he spends a considerable amount of time lavishing them. His tongue plays with my nipples, teeth grazing, giving me just enough pain to make me cry out, but not for it to hurt.

"I used to hate them," I breathe, my hands in his hair, over his back and shoulders.

"What?" His voice is muffled as he speaks against my skin, face between my tits.

"My freckles. I hated them."

He looks up suddenly, anger in his eyes. "You're fucking perfect, Bridget. Every fucking inch of you that I've seen is perfect. And I'd bet everything that I am that what I haven't yet is perfect, too."

"Really?"

Will's eyes soften before he reaches up to kiss me slowly, endlessly—so deep I feel myself sink into another world I never want to come back from. "Really," he whispers when he pulls away. I want to cry because he gets to his feet, and the loss of his body against mine is devastating. But it only takes a second for him to remove his shoes and socks, his pants and underwear, before he's back on me and the relief of it is immediate.

His hands are around my waist when he suddenly flips us, his fingers working the clasp of my bra with ease. It's like it *wanted* to jump off my skin for him. I settle on his thighs, feeling the long hard length of him right beneath my folds. The tip of him touches my clit and if I move *just so*—

I gasp and lean forward, catching myself with my hands on his chest. His hands fly to my hips to keep me stable, to keep my hips from moving. Which is good, because right now, in the fog of pure need, I ache to rock myself on top of him. To feel his cock between my wet folds. To let him make me come just by doing this alone.

"Fuck, you feel incredible. Even just by doing this." He groans and experimentally moves me back and forward. My head snaps back as I call out his name and beg for him to do it

"Again, Will. *Please, please, please*—I need it again."

"Okay, baby. You know I'll always give you what you want, right?"

I melt like sugar in his hands, but he doesn't let me fall. Instead, he digs his fingers into my skin and forces me backwards and forwards on his cock. Will's groans mix with my moans in a beautiful orchestra that bounces off the paper-thin walls of my apartment, my neighbors surely getting a kick out of what's bound to be one of the best nights of my life.

I come for the second time tonight, collapsing and falling forwards on Will's damp chest. I kiss his skin, tasting the salty wetness on my lips as I try to catch my breath. But he doesn't give me time to recover. Before I even know what's happening, Will rolls us so he's on his knees and he's somehow maneuvered me to end up on all fours. Ass up, head down. He slaps my ass once, making me yelp. It's a surprise, that's for sure, but not an unwelcome one.

He kneels behind me and takes a hold of my hips, pressing his cock against my ass cheeks without entering me. Will leans over me, kissing up my spine, licking my neck. "Condom. Need condom..." I thought he was in control, but he's just as lost as I am, struggling to form full sentences, trying to keep his head on his shoulders so we don't make a stupid mistake.

"Nightstand," I do my best to say. After all, my face is pressed down onto my pillow.

He pulls away for no longer than fifteen seconds but the ache of his absence is visceral. I feel empty and wound tight, needing to be filled and used once again. I don't know how I'm still conscious after the two most intense orgasms of my life, but here I am, wanting more. While I wait for him, my brain spirals, despairing because how the hell am I supposed to go on in my life after *this*?

Thankfully, he's back before I've gone too deep down a black hole, the heat of his body behind mine enough to pull me back to the present.

I feel Will line himself up against me, feel the initial push. And though I'm wetter than I think I've ever been before, and even though I've come more than once at the mercy of his mouth and hands, it's still a struggle to fit. It takes a series of false starts, of small and measured thrusts, before he's able to push in to the point where he can move. When he pushes into me to the hilt, my face pressed into the pillow, I grit my teeth as I feel the painful and delicious stretch. His deep, wild groan does something to me I've never felt before; it awakens an instinct to claim Will as mine and let him take me wherever he wants, because I will follow.

It's impossible to keep my eyes open as I breathe through each of his movements once he starts a steady rhythm. It's not long before Will increases his pace, and I don't think it's a conscious decision. Based on the way he holds on to my hips, the way he calls out my name over and over again like a chant that will save his fucking life, Will is on the edge of losing control.

"Can you come again?" he asks, his voice desperate and out

of breath. "I need to feel you come again. I want to feel you around my cock."

I whimper at his words, wanting to give him just that. So I make to slide my hand to my clit, but he stops me, choosing instead to take on that task on his own. "Me. *I* want to be the one making you come."

It's the most difficult thing in the world, talking. He's so deep inside, I feel every inch of him and it *hurts*. It hurts and yet it is so fucking good.

I feel him shake his head when he moves my hand away, leans his sweaty forehead on my shoulder. "I want to be the one making you come," he repeats.

His fingers are steady and the pressure is beautiful and perfect, and pure heaven and hell. It isn't long before I find myself nearing the end of the line, just a moment away from imploding in Will's arms. His punishing rhythm is back, his coordination skills truly award-worthy. He fucks me so intensely while he touches me so delicately, I can hardly make out the words he breathes against my ear.

"Beautiful, Bridge... Waiting forever. *So fucking long...* Coming, coming. I'm fucking *coming*." And when he bares down his teeth on my shoulder, I join him. Together, we fall over as we come, his hips still thrusting, pushing me into the mattress as he empties himself into the condom, in me, as I writhe beneath him.

For a moment, we don't speak or move. Then, I feel Will's large hands travel up and down my arms, skimming me with his fingertips, raising goosebumps on every inch of my body. He moves my hair to one side so he can press soft kisses to my neck and shoulder, and I never want him to stop.

Will anchors the condom and pulls out, making me whimper from the loss of him. With an arm around my waist, he rolls us on our sides and pulls me into him, condom discarded somewhere. On the floor? The table? I don't really care.

When Will's lips move to my ear, he whispers, "What now?"

I shake my head, keeping my eyes on the wall across the room, not wanting to speak—not even knowing if I physically can.

I feel Will nod against me before he presses a kiss to the top of my head. "Okay. Okay. We'll talk about it in the morning." In what turns out to be typical Will fashion, he pulls me even tighter still into his chest, where I happily settle. In the comfort and safety of his arms, I fall asleep after just a few seconds.

WILL

Will can't believe this is his life. He can't believe he's in Bridget's bed, her arms wrapped around his neck, legs hooked over his hips like she needs to hold on to him even in her sleep as she drools all over his bare chest.

Tonight was perfect. Tonight was everything he'd ever hoped for and more.

As he runs his fingers through her soft, flaming red hair, he smiles, thinking over every single event that led to this moment in time. There are many things that Will has done throughout his life that he wishes he could take back. His mother's accident, specifically, which led to a series of unfortunate consequences he will have to live with forever. Since the crash, he's sworn he would give up anything if it meant it would make his mother walk again. And while he still means it, he can't deny that something amazing came from it: he would never have met Bridget if it hadn't been for it. After all, there was no way a sane Will Jacobs would ever have worked for Stevenson—taking on a job at this company was a clear sign of desperation for anyone who knew him—and it doesn't seem like Bridget and Will had any friends in common. So would they have ever met otherwise? Would he have had to go on living his lonely life without her?

The thought is terrorizing and not something he wants to entertain for a second longer. Will just wants to close his eyes and enjoy this moment right here, the intimacy of it all, the pure peace he feels when he's with her.

16

BFFS?

When I wake, it's with great effort. At first, I keep my eyes closed as I try to process why the hell my body feels like I took a two hour intense hot yoga class the day before. I stretch my limbs to measure the full extent of my soreness and almost hiss. But while it hurts and I'd love to pass out again to sleep another hour or ten, it's the kind of satisfying soreness that comes after doing something really, *really* fun. Like sex with an incredible man.

It's delicious.

And it's right then that I remember what happened, and my eyes fly open to double-check whether Will is in bed beside me or whether it was all just a dream. To my surprise, when I turn on my side, I find him asleep and naked, lying on his back, about an inch away from falling off my queen mattress. While the bed is certainly big enough for me, it appears we're *both* the sprawling kind of sleepers, making it nearly impossible to fit in the bed with room to spare. Not that I mind, if I'm being honest. Will smells incredible, his skin is soft yet hard, and his body heat is more than welcome on this cold, February morning. I really don't hate having to share my bed's real estate.

As if wanting to make things more difficult, Ginger hops on the foot of the bed, jostling the mattress. She looks between me and Will, her unwanted guest, with an annoyed look.

He took my spot. Am I supposed to share now? she seems to ask.

"We have a guest. Be nice," I whisper back to her.

It's been so long since a man has been in bed with me, I wouldn't be surprised if she forgot about the existence of other humans. It's not like I bring many friends over here, either. Where would I even put them?

Eventually, Ginger settles at the foot of the bed, curling up into a big, fluffy ball by our feet, accepting that she's been relegated. Meanwhile, I go back to staring at Will's peaceful features as he sleeps. Except—

"Is she mad at me for taking her spot or something?" he asks in a sleepy voice that has me grinning like a goof. Will's eyes are closed, an adorable lazy smile attempting to spread across his face.

There's officially no doubt in my mind that I'm going to want this every day from now on.

"You're awake?"

He yawns and stretches a bit. "Yeah."

"You heard that?"

His laugh is low, groggy. Will's eyes are still closed, but he wraps an arm around my waist to bring me closer. "Yeah. But it's not a surprise that you talk to your cat." He doesn't have any morning breath. How is that even possible?

I place my hand an inch away from my mouth as I speak, just in case I have some sort of fire breathing dragon level gnarly thing going on. "Is that a bad thing?"

He shakes his head in my neck before dipping it in my neck and inhaling deeply, filling his lungs with my scent. "You smell incredible. Like you and sex and me and shampoo." His arms slink around my waist, evolve into two massive snakes I wouldn't mind being constricted by. Once again, Will is predator, and I am hopelessly devoted prey.

Irritated by our bed takeover, Ginger gives up and heads back to her chair for her morning nap (the first of three). Will notices and laughs with me, muttering something about having to win over my jealous roommate.

My grin is wild, the butterflies in my stomach are in a frenzy, and if he pressed his ear to my chest, he'd hear the impossibly loud and fast tempo of my heart while my brain processes his words. Thank god he can't see my face. Would he think I was crazy for the wild blush?

I press my cheek against his soft hair, relish in the feeling of his hard, yet soft arms around me. Close my eyes so I can let the way I feel burn into my brain. Pray I never forget it. Because oh my god, this feels so good.

"How do you feel?" he asks into my neck.

"Fine." *More like joyous. Elated. Safe.* But I don't want to go and wax poetic over how last night was one of the most incredible nights of my life if we're not on the same page. Call me a coward —I'll admit it—but I don't feel strong enough to be able to take the initiative here. Not after what happened at work. Not after having been clobbered in such a way by something I was beginning to care so much about, left feeling betrayed and hurt. If I felt so bad over something that happened at *work*, I don't know whether I'd be able to come back from his rejection. After all, just because we had sex, doesn't mean he has feelings for me. Will said it himself: he hasn't dated in a while, but he isn't celibate. He clearly doesn't believe sex and feelings are mutually exclusive. For him, this could've just been two good friends scratching an itch. A casual hookup. Maybe even a pity fuck after the horrible day I had.

God, my stomach drops at that last one. *Please don't let it have been a pity fuck. Anything else but that.*

Will pulls away, his brow furrowed in disappointment. "Fine? That's it? I thought it was…"

"I didn't mean *fine* as in, like, it didn't mean much or anything or that it was bad," I rush to correct him. Sure, I don't want him to know just how into him I am, but I guess I also don't want Will to feel like it didn't matter. "I feel good. *Great*, even. Just a little tired from the… er, overexertion."

His grin is lopsided and sly. "Yeah, I definitely feel like I did over a hundred sit-ups last night. And I regularly work out."

I snort and cover my face in my hands, trying not to laugh. When I settle, I feel his hands wrap around my wrist, so I let him pull them away gently.

"You're so fucking beautiful. Especially in the morning. Especially after I've fucked you."

The fire is back and it's spread all over my body. From my now-crimson cheeks, to the instant growing ache between my legs, and the way his words make my toes curl.

His thumb grazes my cheeks as he stares at him. "Freckles," he whispers. But he says nothing else. My cheeks heat even more.

With every ounce of strength I have left in my body, I fight the urge to let myself fully go. It's such a good alternative to what needs to be done—talking about last night—that I almost cave. But I know that if we fail to define what's happening here, it could end badly for us both.

"So…"

"So." He grins.

"We had sex last night."

"*Ooh.* That's what that was?"

"Will."

"Bridge."

"C'mon."

He sighs, his smile wistful. "We had sex. And I thought it was amazing. Didn't you?"

I have to bite down on my lip to stop from smiling like a goof. "It was... bananas."

He takes my hands to his lips, kisses them. "I love it when you say that."

This makes me laugh. "You like it when I say that something is bananas?"

"Yeah. It's cute. You're cute."

"And you're cheesin'."

"Only a little." But he kisses my hands again. "So besides it being bananas, as you say. What did you think?"

"Performance wise? You did great. Solid nine out of ten would recommend. Though I gotta say it's not really attractive behavior when someone asks for a review."

"Bridge, you know that's not what I meant. I meant— Wait, *nine* out of ten? Why a *nine*?" He squeezes his eyes shut. "No, you know what? I'm not gonna let you distract me. I know exactly what you're doing."

Shit.

I hate this. I hate that he's putting me in the position to make the call. For the first time since meeting him, I feel vulnerable and exposed with Will in a *bad* way. This is far from the comfortable yet open situations which we put ourselves in when sharing stuff we wouldn't otherwise share with anyone else. "You first," I tell him.

He huffs out a laugh and nods. "Alright. I'll be a gentleman about it and take the first hit." He takes a deep breath and stares deep into my eyes. "I'm not going to deny that I want to do it again. Like I said, I thought it was amazing. And fun."

Fun. But is it just that? I bite back all the questions I want to throw at him, all the things I want to say. If it were any other guy, I wouldn't care. I'd prioritize my mental health and time—I'm not gonna go ahead and waste it on another asshole—and make sure to get all the nonsense out of the way. But I'm on unstable ground, risking losing Will altogether.

"Fun. Totally." Even though I'm putting every ounce of effort I can manage into this, there's no way of hiding the flatness in my voice.

"You didn't think it was fun?" He frowns. "I thought you just said—"

"God. We're going around in circles," I say with a groan. "We both said we were fine and we both agreed it was fun. What we keep avoiding is the question of what now. So... What now?"

He takes a beat to think the question over—finally. When he's done considering it, his answer comes out in a very rational tone. "We've agreed it was fun. And we agreed that we're both okay. And seeing as those two feelings are positive things, I don't see what the problem would be in repeating said activity. Like... would it be so horrible if we did it again?"

My heart plummets. Does he mean do this casually? Like fuck buddies? "Oh."

Now *his* face falls. "Unless you don't want to. Which is also totally okay. I mean, it's fine if you want to just stick to being friends who do not fuck." As opposed to just friends who do, I assume?

A sharp stinging behind my eyes begins to build, my throat constricting itself tighter than the grip he had around my waist just moments before. So this is it for us, then? It's fuck buddies or nothing? Friend zoned all the way?

I want to cry. I want to gently kick him out of my apartment so I can sit in my shower and cry my heart out under steaming hot water. Because I'm an idiot. What did I expect? That he would just fall for me the way I fell for him over a few emails, texts, and video calls? Stupid Bridget. He's a normal person, and you clearly are not. You're delusional and ridiculous and will only ever be his friend. People who fall for strangers they meet on the internet usually end up on a TV show while viewers stare at the screen, begging the person to see the countless red flags.

It's me. I'm that girl. Though, other than the fact that he doesn't want to see me romantically, he *has* no red flags. At least, none that I can see.

I search my brain for a joke, something to relieve the tension. To distract him—and honestly, myself, too—from noticing how much this news affects me to my core. Because I am absolutely devastated. I was just given one of the best nights of my life only to be told I can't have any more of it. Or rather, I can—so long as I skip the emotional component my heart would need in order to enjoy it.

"I mean, yes, last night was great. But I'm concerned about what it would do to our friendship, you know? I guess we've already had this conversation. After the sexting, remember?"

"Bridge, if you think I'm going to cut and run—" He shakes his head, eyes wide with panic. "That's not me. I told you that—"

"That you wouldn't. I know. And I believe that's how you feel —*now*. But we're just getting to know each other. And I think *that's* what we should be prioritizing, right? Making sure we're good, not letting ourselves get caught up in silly things like being fuck buddies. What if we can't survive this if we decide to keep it casual? I don't think it's worth running the risk of it getting messy and losing this." I point back and forth between us. My comforter is pulled up almost to my neck, and I know he can't see an inch of skin, yet I've never felt more exposed.

His expression falls, but I'm not surprised. We had good sex last night. *Amazing* sex. Eleven out of ten, and would not want to recommend because I want to keep him all to myself sex. So I get his disappointment. He's a guy, after all, and he's no stranger to keeping things casual, apparently. But I can't let the people pleaser in me or my feelings for him let me make the stupid mistake of sleeping with him ever again.

"So, what you're saying is…"

"That we should just be friends. Who do not have sex. Ever again."

He blinks once. Twice. Another time. "Okay. Heard, chef. Friends it is." And without another word, he gets out of bed and to his feet, searching for his clothes, buck naked.

"Where are you going?" I can hear the clear panic in my voice, even with the sound of my heart beating a drum in my ears. When he hears my tone and sees the distress in my eyes, Will kneels by my side of the bed. Naked again. And his dick is there and perfect, and his chest is strong and defined, but I said no. And no is no. And I'll never get to see those parts again once he puts his clothes on.

"Hey, don't freak out. Everything's fine." He smiles when he reaches out to hold my hand, but I know better than to believe it's fully genuine. He's disappointed. I want to tell him I am too, but it's for different reasons. Reasons that will probably end with us never speaking again. Reasons better left unsaid.

"I'm just looking for my clothes, okay? Then maybe I thought we could go to breakfast? I can get you a bagel and we can start with you making uncomfortable jokes about what happened and I can pretend like nothing is awkward until we get lost in conversation—because our conversations are even better than that mind-blowing sex we had last night—sorry, that's the last time I'll bring it up—and then everything will be back to normal. Okay?"

Mortified, I realize I'm near tears. "I don't want to lose you," I admit.

"Lose me? Bridge, you're stuck with me for good. No matter

what. If the only way I get to be in your life is by being your friend then consider me your BFF, alright? We can even make friendship bracelets for each other and everything." I snort and wipe my nose with the back of my hand. *So ladylike.* "I'm not going anywhere."

That's what they all say right before they leave.

WILL

He doesn't know whether it's because he went from feeling the happiest he's ever felt in his life to almost the worst, but one thing is for sure: Will has never felt a pain this intense before. This time, he doubts whether he'll be able to survive it.

17

FUN IS JUST A THREE-LETTER WORD

There are many bakeries outside of this city who claim to have NYC-quality bagels. They promise the same consistency and flavor, the perfect toasty, crunchy first bite when you sink into your still-warm bread. They even go so far as to claim that you'll feel like you're right smack in the middle of the City.

They'll say a lot of things—just like people. But let me tell you something right here, right now about these places and brands: they're *lying* to you. Because no bagel will ever taste as good as the one from your local bodega or deli in New York. No bakery outside of the five boroughs will ever be able to deliver quite the same quality or taste. And while there are a million different types of bagel combinations, your order will never fail while you're here. True New Yorkers know it takes one single hot bagel with the perfect filling to make your shitty day turn around. And yet, not even the extra-toasted poppy seed bagel with a thick layer of scallion cream cheese and slices of extra-crispy bacon from my favorite people at the deli can save my mood this gloomy Saturday morning.

I try. Oh, do I try. Because Will's the one who bought me this bagel (and coffee) and suggested we walk around the neighborhood as we talk. Because I don't want him to see how upset I am after the incredible night we shared. Because, even though I'd love for us to be together, I'd rather not risk losing him. I'd rather pine away, so long as we get to share the same orbit. So I endure the pain and nod when he suggests he get me my favorite order "To clear the air and get the awkwardness out of the way," he said.

But as we wander aimlessly around the city, munching away, I begin to doubt his plan. His phone keeps going off, but Will never responds—though he can't seem to ignore it, either. Which obviously makes me obsess over who the hell is texting him so much. Makes me paranoid he'll use it as an excuse to get away. Also, it reminds me of how quick he's been to reply to my messages. A few weeks ago, I started to wonder whether it was because of me. Whether it was because he was as excited to talk to me as I was to him and that's why he always had his phone on hand. Now, I mostly feel like an idiot because it could've just been that he's one of those people addicted to his phone.

This isn't me. I'm not like this. I am not this person at all. I'm not one to sulk and pout and wish things were different. I'm one to accept, find the positive, and move on. And yet, I feel like this one's gonna take more than what it did when I found out everything my ex ever did to me.

"Is the bagel good?" he asks as we take a seat on a bench.

"Sure," I say around a huge bite. I chew quickly and swallow before speaking. "Thanks again. I had, like, no food in my apartment."

Will grins and takes a sip of his coffee. "No problem. I was starving and figured you'd like a good bagel. You mentioned this was your favorite place, right?"

He's so sweet. He's so sweet and—*fuck*—I think I may be mere millimeters away from falling for him—*crashing*, really.

Crashing in love. Definitely a more accurate description of what's going on.

This is such a dangerous game.

"Yeah." I smile and nod, stuffing my face with an even bigger bite of my bagel to stop myself from saying something stupid. From asking the wrong questions. *Why don't you like me? We would be so good together. We would be more than the incredible sex we had last night.*

Will's phone vibrates again, but this time it doesn't stop. He groans when he pulls it out, and looks at the screen.

"Everything okay? You need to get that?" I ask.

He shakes his head. "Nah. Just... I think I have to head back to the office soon."

"Are you serious? It's a Saturday!"

He heaves a heavy sigh. "I know, but I still have a ton of work to do. I left work early yesterday and..."

"Oh, sorry. I didn't mean to pull you away from anything important."

"What? No, don't be sorry. *You're* important. What you were going through was more important. I wanted to be there for you. *Want* to. I knew what I was doing. I just have to pay the consequences for it now." He scratches the back of his head as he reads through his messages. "I'm sorry, it's just if I don't answer now, it will never stop."

"Your boss?" Which seems like an obvious question.

Will looks me straight in the eye and a beat passes before he nods. "Yeah. He's being extra demanding lately."

He proceeds to unlock the phone and type furiously for a couple of minutes. In the meantime, I do my silver lining recalibration. I look around the neighborhood, try to find things to appreciate. And while the sun is out for the first time in a while, the cold seems to bite at my skin even harder than usual. Though I usually love to people-watch and appreciate the melting pot that is this city, I'm suddenly overwhelmed by the crowds. It's like I've lost my positivity superpower, and I'm being sucked in by the harsh realities I possibly refused to accept or acknowledge.

I don't like this.

With a groan, he sits back and looks up at the sky. He pockets his phone and says nothing.

"At the risk of stating the obvious, you seem stressed," I tell him.

This makes him laugh once, a little more light finally coming back into his eyes. "You could say that." He nods. Sighs. "My job…"

I study his expression for a moment, taking in the clear exhaustion in his eyes that goes way deeper than the late night we spent together having sex. It goes beyond a bad week at work —even a bad month. Whenever we talk about work he looks… bone tired. Depleted, almost."Why are you doing this?" I ask.

"Huh? Doing what?"

"This job. You hate it. Why are you still here? You're smart and charismatic. I feel like you could charm the most difficult person in the world to hand you the keys to their entire empire in a heartbeat. You seem like the kind of guy who could do anything he wants. Instead, you're doing something you very clearly hate. Even in this economy, you're a star candidate. Why not find something else in a different industry? Or have you already been looking? This obviously isn't something you want to do forever, is it?"

He presses his lips together and looks away. I feel like a total idiot.

"Sorry. I don't mean to pry or cross any boundaries. Too many personal questions."

"No, it's fine. It's you, Bridget. Anyone else, I wouldn't be down to talk about this."

Something about that—something about the *It's you* of it all really does it for me. So much so, I almost melt—even in the thirty-degree weather.

"I really don't want to be in the fashion industry in any sort of capacity, if I'm being honest. I think that's obvious. This job was born out of pure necessity, though. Or desperation, more like it. And I made a commitment I need to see through, so there's no way I can just..." He sighs. "I have a lot riding on this job right now."

"You hate it."

He stares into my eyes, before whispering. "Yes. Very much so. But not necessarily because of what the job entails. But more what it represents. And more recently, I've grown to resent it for other reasons."

"What exactly does that mean?" Are we speaking in riddles now?

"It just means that... In a nutshell, it's not what I want to be doing, nor is it with people I want to be surrounded by. Not at all. And sure, I'm good at my job, I guess. I mean, I recently got a promotion, right before meeting you. So there's that. But, to be honest, it doesn't mean shit to me. None of it does when it has no meaning."

"So if not this job, then what? I think the whole 'someone handing over the keys to their empire to you' thing is a realistic expectation." I try to cheer him up with a smile, and it almost works. His lips quirk up a bit at my confidence in his abilities. "You're smart and capable enough to find something that will work for you."

Honestly, who wouldn't find this man absolutely charming? Sure, his looks are something out of Hollywood, but his personality is unmatched, his heart is one of a kind, and his mind is a never-ending source of fascination for me.

Will stares quietly at a flock of pigeons fighting over some leftover crumbs a few feet away from us. I don't think I've asked him a particularly difficult question, but it takes him a moment to answer.

When he does, it's after heaving a very big sigh: "I don't think it's that, exactly. I don't think I feel like I've suddenly been put into this box I'll never be able to get out of, if that's what you mean."

"Then what *do* you mean? Why does Will Jacobs feel trapped when it looks like, from the outside, the world is his oyster? Besides this big commitment you said you made, I mean. What did you do before this job?"

He sighs once again and reaches out to grab one of my hands in both of his before meeting my gaze. I feel a warm liquid spread through my veins. Sinking slightly in my seat at his delicious touch, I say a mental prayer to the universe that he never lets go.

"I... I used to be a teacher. Math. High school AP."

I gasp quietly because *what?* Will Jacobs dressed in full teacher mode, shaping the young minds of the world? It might be even hotter than any other version of Will Jacobs I've met or spoken to to date.

Maybe. There's just so much to choose from, really.

With great effort, I hide my sudden and very unexpected need to throw myself at him (even if we are in public) and take a sip of what's left of my hot coffee.

"I... wasn't expecting that."

A corner of his mouth quirks up in a half-smile. "What were you expecting from my past life?"

"I... don't know. Stripper, maybe? You've certainly got the body."

A loud guffaw bursts through him, and you can almost physically *see* the tension leave his body as he laughs. He threads the fingers of his hand through mine and I stop breathing. What the hell is this? Do friends do this? *God*, I should've never slept with him. My mind is a mess.

"A stripper? Nah. Don't have the coordination."

You certainly seemed to have fantastic coordination last night, I almost say.

"Did being a teacher make you happy?" I ask, trying my best to control my breathing before it turns absolutely erratic. My reaction to this innocent touch is almost out of a Victorian era novel, as if it were the most scandalous thing to happen in the ton.

He frowns, completely unaware of the internal battle going on inside me. "Not particularly, no. Is that awful of me to say? That I didn't enjoy it?"

"Why would it be?"

He shrugs. "I don't know. Isn't everyone supposed to find working with kids fulfilling or something? Does it make me a horrible person that I just... fell into it? Like... I like kids in general. Really want to have one with the right woman one day." His eyes flash up to my face, cheeks red. "But teaching high school kids was a nightmare."

I snort because I can imagine. We were all teenagers once.

In an effort to comfort him, I squeeze his hand. "I think it makes you human. And it's okay if you didn't find one of the hardest professions in the world—because teaching is absolutely one of the hardest and most thankless jobs out there—fulfilling."

"Yeah. I don't know. I just have a few things to figure out."

"Don't we all," I say with a laugh.

Will's smile is soft, his words firm. "You're perfect, though. Passionate about work and life and your hobbies and your cat." I grin at his mention of Ginger. "Who is already halfway in love with me, by the way." *Like me. Pretty sure I'm already halfway in love with you.*

I laugh as I hide my pain, basking in his complements.

"How do you do that, Bridge? How do you keep going when things seem impossible?" His expression shifts to something more serious. His tone taking a turn.

I don't like it.

"I told you. Always look on the bright side. The silver lining. Or things can get really dark, really fast."

This makes Will laugh. "Your silver lining."

"Yes, indeed," I say with a grin, taking advantage of this brief, light moment to pull my hand from his. Any longer, and I'd grow even more attached to how comfortable, how natural, it all feels.

Will looks down at his now empty hands, though, and I don't miss the way he fists them a couple of times before slipping them into his coat pocket.

"Anyway, of course there are many silver linings. I know I'm blessed. Just..."

"It's a lot of stress," I say, keeping my voice as soft as possible. Because it's okay for Will to be upset or unhappy even if he has other things going for him.

"Yeah. And it's particularly frustrating because the gym is normally my way of de-stressing, but it just isn't working lately." Will sighs and runs a hand through his fingers.

I wince. "Gross. I don't know how you gym people enjoy the pain of working out."

He laughs again, relaxing even more. "Hey, I need the endorphins. I don't understand why people *don't* like getting a natural high." I give him a look and he smiles. "What do you do to relax then?" He takes a big bite of his bagel, grinning around it.

I snort. "Nah-uh. I'm not telling you. It's embarrassing." My cheeks flush red, the heat of my skin contrasting against the cold gusts of air around us.

"What? How is it embarrassing? Unless it's something super

nerdy like Star Trek model painting or something, I don't see how it can be bad."

"That's not my hobby, but I don't think that one is embarrassing! Trekkies are people, too."

He laughs and shakes his head before taking a final bite of his bagel. Something about my answer pleases him. "You're right. They are. Sorry. But if it's not model painting, what is it?"

I sigh and wrap the remaining half of my bagel in the wax paper it came in, dump it in my purse for later. "It's ridiculous. But... I watch cookie decorating videos." I press my lips together, trying not to laugh. "Hours and hours of cookie decorating videos on socials. *That's* what I do to unwind."

He frowns. "Like... baking and sprinkles and shit?"

"Not *sprinkles*. I mean, yes, sometimes they use sprinkles. But I mean like the super professional ones. With the special icing? Royal icing, it's called. Something about the lines and the flooding make it so satisfying to watch. How they get the most incredible details right. That and cake decorating also helps. The way the bakers will smooth the buttercream over a cake with such ease relaxes me. Also, the insane way they can make ruffles with an icing pipe. I'm really into vintage style cakes lately."

Will sputters a laugh, turning in his seat. He leans an arm on the backrest of the bench to look me square in the eye. "Cookie and cake decorating? That's the best way to get you to relax?" I nod proudly. "You ever thought about doing it yourself instead of watching videos?"

"*God* no. Mastering that looks like it would *add* stress to my life, not relax me. No thanks. I don't want to know how the sausage is made."

His grin is beautiful and sweet, and even though he's laughing I know it's not because he thinks it's dumb.

"You know, it's funny," he says. "Sometimes, I'll think that after speaking to you so often I already know everything about you. Like, even though it's only been just under two months since we've met, it feels like we've known each other forever. But then I'll learn something new about you and just…" He shakes his head, as if in awe of me and my weird obsession. "I like it. I hope this never goes away. I like the familiarity, feeling like I know you and you know me. But I also like learning new things about you."

I smirk at him, but inside, my heart is running wild. Breaking and getting put back together by the same words. How is that even possible?

"I hope it doesn't go away, either. I guess we still have a lot to learn about each other. Even though it feels like we've known each other for a while."

He reaches out and pushes a strand of hair from my face, his smile slipping into a softer one. Eyes shifting, he gives me that same look he did at the pub while we were dancing. The one I so clearly misread.

"I'm glad we finally decided to meet in person, even though the circumstances sucked. It's fucked up because of everything that happened with your work, but I actually had a ton of fun last night. And this morning."

Fun. Fun fun fun fun.

I've never hated a word more.

"I had fun, too."

This is our new normal.

WILL

At least she's still in his life. At least he didn't lose her.
He just needs to learn how to live with the pain of having her while
not having her.

18

OLD FRIENDS DON'T ALWAYS MAKE GOOD FRIENDS

onday morning progress report meetings used to be my favorite part of the week. It's the one time where all teams involved in the development and production process of a collection sit together to talk about where we're at.

Each team presents their updates, challenges, and to-dos, and every time I'm left in awe by everything that goes into making a single article of clothing. Inspiration, sketches, sourcing, packaging design, factory scheduling, pricing, tariffs, shipping, allocation, quality control, distribution, and so much more. After my first meeting, I couldn't go into a store without picking up an item and losing myself in thoughts of all that went into the product, how it got to this exact shelf in this particular store. Why was it placed in this location and who picked the merchandising style.

I loved it. Past tense. At least, I'm not loving it today.

Today, I'm distracted, detached. Bored, even, as I pick at my cuticles. I'm not listening to Molly as she talks about updated sketches based on the client's feedback from last week. I don't care about what Noel, our head of sourcing, says as he talks about ordering extra material. I wince when Lena introduces *my* new idea to the team, ignore the way her voice tightens when she says it was Jenna's.

Today, I don't care. I'm much more interested in my nail polish and how I'm due to give myself a manicure. I mean, Jesus, it's peeled and gross. I can't come into work with these gnarly claws. Picking out a nail polish color in my head right now takes higher priority than taking notes on whatever everyone is saying, in my opinion. I can ask people for updates later on an individual basis.

Not gonna lie, I'm so lost in my thoughts, conflicted over going for a classic neutral like Ballet Slippers (a little boring) or something more daring like Vamp (more appropriate for fall) that I barely notice when people begin to pour out of the conference room. Worst of all, I barely notice Lena looming over me, hands on her hips as she glares down.

"Oh, hey." I get quickly to my feet. "Great meeting." I try for a smile, but the look of thirst for murder in her eyes stops me dead in my tracks.

"Really? And how exactly would you know?"

"I..." I *could* look for an excuse for having checked out. But Lena is so good at reading through someone's bullshit, it would be a joke to even try.

"My office. Now."

I suppress a sigh and follow her out of the conference room and into her office, mentally preparing myself for the worst. *Well,* I think, *this truly would be the cherry on top of it all, wouldn't it? Losing my job after getting my heart broken. Super.*

When she takes a seat behind her desk, she stares at me for a moment, the look in her eyes intense. Instead of anger, though, it's filled with concern. "What's wrong with you? This isn't like you."

I sputter a humorless laugh. "Are you joking? Did you seriously ask me what was wrong with me?" I'm playing with fire, talking to her like this, and I can tell she wants to tell me off by the way she presses her lips together. The way she frowns.

"If this is about what happened Friday with Jenna—"

I cut her off and throw my hands in the air in exasperation. "*Of course* it's about that. What else would it be?" I mean, *I* know that the situation with Will didn't make the work thing easier, but she doesn't know that.

She purses her lips, narrows her eyes at me, and nods. "I'm not usually a touchy-feely boss. I think you already know that though, from experience and probably from what your coworkers have shared. But I just want to make something clear: you're different. I see a lot of potential within you. An internal strength I don't think *you* even realize you have yet. I need you to not let this get to you, Bridget. I need you to keep your head up. Because you've got a natural instinct and passion for this and for doing a job well done. And we both need that."

I look away, tears threatening to make an unwelcome appearance. I've been crying so much lately. More than I ever have. Even more than when Gran passed and I was left all alone in this world. When I feel something warm fall on my hand in my lap, I curse under my breath, hating myself a little for breaking down in front of my boss.

"If you believe so much in me, how can you just stand by and let Jenna take credit for my work? I'm a baby at this company; you're not. You're wildly respected and feared and people trust you and your point of view. And you just... get here on Monday morning with a smile on your face and pretend like everything is super? Like I'm just supposed to move on like nothing happened? I'm *hurt*, okay? By Jenna, this company,"— *by Will*—"but by you, too. How can you just let her do that to me? I thought I could trust you. You're supposed to be my mentor."

Maybe it's because I'm a little bit broken right now, but I'm starting to think Will was right: there is no silver lining to this. I was screwed over by my bosses and that's it.

Her brows rise. "Mentor? You consider me your mentor?"

I roll my eyes and wipe my cheek of the tears streaming down my face. "*That's* what you took from this? I mean, Jesus, we already live in a world where men want to take everything from us. Are we going to let women do it, too? Where's your sense of solidarity? Why are you being so cool about this? I thought she did the same thing to you. You should be outraged."

Lena sighs and nods. "I *am* angry. I *am* outraged. But if you haven't realized that this industry is very much like a game, then you're more naive and green than I thought you were." She gets to her feet and walks around her desk. Sits on the edge and looks down at me, her face somber. "Listen, I need you to believe me that not doing anything *is* in your best interest right now. That pretending like everything is good is the right move. Mostly, I need you to trust me, Bridget. I promise you I will not let this slide. You just need to understand this isn't one of those situations where you can walk in, guns blazing, and demand justice. This is about games and politics and it sucks, but it is what it is. Just... trust me, okay? I'm making some moves. And that's all I can say."

I sniffle and look away, digging my nails into my arms to keep myself from saying anything more.

"My advice? Move on for now. You gave yourself the weekend to mope. Now let's get back to work. Do well. And it will pay off."

She waits for me to say something, but I remain silent, instead. I get to my feet and run to the bathroom, head down, trying not to alert my coworkers to the tears streaming down my face (though I'm sure it wouldn't be the first time they see someone leaving Lena's office crying).

When I open the bathroom door, I crash into Molly, who

takes one look at my face and frowns. "You got fired, didn't you? What did you do this time?"

Not "Are you okay?" or "What happened?" No. An automatic assumption that I lost my job. That I had gotten fired. And that it was my fault. No questions asked.

I take a step back as if someone had pushed me, her words knocking the wind from my lungs. "Fired? Why would you think that?"

She sighs and pulls me into the bathroom. Turns on the sink and wets a hand towel to wipe the tears from my cheeks. "Bridge. C'mon. I helped you get this job, but I knew it would only be a matter of time before you'd lose it."

"Before *I'd* lose it? If you thought that, why even help me at all?"

She shrugs once, pity in her eyes. "Because you were desperate. Because I wanted to be a great friend. Because I thought you could at least make a decent salary and save up before finding a job that's more in line with what you can actually do." She reaches out to dab at my cheeks once more, but I pull back.

"With what I can *actually* do? That's..."

"I know. You're welcome, again."

I was not gonna say thank you, but okay.

"I gotta say, I'm proud of you, though. You lasted longer than I thought you would. I could've sworn you wouldn't make it past the three month mark. It was almost five, right?" She smiles. Molly *smiles*.

What is happening?

"I didn't get fired, Molly."

She frowns, her brows half hidden by her bangs. "What do you mean?"

"I mean, you're wrong." My voice is icy cold because *what the actual fuck?* She was so certain I'd fail?

"Oh my god, I just assumed. You came out of her office

running and crying. If you didn't get fired, then what happened?"

I take the hand towels from her and throw them in the trash, checking my reflection in the mirror. Naturally, my cheeks are flushed crimson. My hair is a mess, so I finger-comb it in an attempt to get it presentable. Meanwhile, Molly just watches me, waiting for me to tell her what went on between me and Lena. But I refuse to go into details. She wouldn't understand. Part of me wonders whether Molly would victim-blame me for the whole thing, and I don't think our friendship would be able to withstand that right now. Not on my end.

"You know what, Molls? I don't think you deserve to know." I slink out of the bathroom and speed walk to my desk, ignoring Molly as she calls out my name. I don't know what the hell that was about, but I don't think it was good friend behavior.

"You know," Will says when he slips into the booth where I'm seated at a wine bar near work, "I'm gonna have to start charging for these emergency therapy sessions."

I groan and let my forehead touch the table as he settles into his seat and peels off his coat. "I'm sorry. I just didn't know what to do."

"Hey, I'm just joking." He laughs softly. "You know you can call me anytime."

I heave a sigh and sit up straight. "I know that, but I also know that my life is a mess sometimes, and if I called you every time something happened you'd hate me and think I'm too much."

"Bridge. Come on. I could never hate you and you could never be too much."

I sigh again.

"Now let me order us both a bottle of wine and you can tell me all about what happened."

After half a bottle and a full charcuterie board, Will and I have decided that a) Molly acted like a terrible friend. And b) we still don't know whether Lena is being genuine or not.

"It's possible she's being truthful," he tells me. "She really may have a plan to stop Jenna."

"I don't know—I'm having trust issues." I take a sip of my wine and follow it with a bite of brie. "I'm suddenly paranoid that everyone around me is lying."

"Including me?"

I narrow my eyes at him comically. "I don't know, are you?"

He laughs once, but doesn't answer the question. "I think you need to give people the benefit of a doubt. Trust that if Lena told you she has a plan, it's because she has a plan. I think sometimes people lie to protect other people. Lies don't always have to be about hurting each other."

I'm taken aback by his point of view. "Are you kidding me right now? Are you saying lying isn't always a bad thing?" Suddenly my cheeks flush, remembering *I'm* lying to him and his company—at least when it comes to when we need orders by.

"Have you never heard of the concept of white lies?" he asks with a smirk so dangerous it could steal my undies in a heartbeat.

I attempt to mentally shake off the image of his body over mine, the memory of the way his eyes squeezed shut as his body turned into a rigid board and he came while holding me tightly to him. I try to push away the memory of the way he repeated my name in my ear, practically chanting it as he fell over. It all turns out to be a little more difficult than expected.

"Yeah, but where do you draw the line? And are we including things like white lies of omission? Because I'm not a fan of either."

"Yes. Sometimes white lies are needed, *especially* ones of omission." Will's expression slightly darkens, but the humor never leaves his eyes completely. "I'm just saying that it's not always important to know every single detail of a person's life. Sometimes keeping things or lying about something is a way of protecting another person."

I'm quiet for a moment as I process the fact that those words left this man's mouth. Because up until this very moment, I thought that Will would never lie to me. But if he's saying that lying isn't always a bad thing, if we're disagreeing on a core value for me, can we even be friends?

"Is this even seriously up for discussion?"

He sighs and takes a sip of his wine. "I'm just saying. It's not always a tragedy if someone lies."

I hate his answer. I hate how dismissive he's being. But most of all, I hate how it's making me doubt everything between us. "I don't know how to respond to what you've just told me. How do I know you haven't been lying to me this entire time?"

He swallows once, regret clear on his face. "That's not what I meant. I don't mean lying is an okay thing to do whenever you please. I just mean... sometimes white lies are *good* things. Like not telling a nine month pregnant woman she looks fat. Or telling your mom the casserole she made is your favorite thing in the world because you feel too guilty after fucking up her life to tell her that it's the grossest shit you've ever tasted. *That's* what I mean."

I chew on my lip, suddenly so close to tears. Stupid wine. "Sorry. You're right."

"Not always," he agrees with a smile.

"Will?"

"Yeah?"

"It would kill me to find out this was all a lie."

"Bridge," he pleads, dark chocolate eyes pulling me in, tempting me to get lost in them and ignore the rest of the world around us. His large hands reach over the table to grab one of mine, warm—a safe haven that wraps around me, grounds me. "You and I could never be a lie. I swear."

A slow smile, wet and sniffly, spreads across my face. "Okay, then."

"Okay." He looks down at my hand, pensively playing with my fingers. "Are we good? Are you feeling better?"

I watch as his index finger trails patterns on my palm now. For a moment there, it feels like he's tracing the same letters into my skin over and over again. I...M...R...Y? But no, I must be imagining it.

We're touching. Always touching. Again.

I want him to keep going. I want him to stop.

"I... I do feel better. Thank you. You always make me feel better."

"That's what I'm here for."

"Thanks," I repeat.

"So, what are you going to do? About this whole work thing?"

I take a deep breath, considering my words. "I think... I think I'm going to pick peace over resentment and this... this toxic anger. I think I'm going to let Lena run with her plan, trust that she's going to do the right thing, and just... not let this experience ruin what's been an otherwise great job. Because it has been so fun, and I've learned so much. About business and project management and just a ridiculous amount of things I never even thought of. So, yeah. I think I'm choosing to let it go. At least for now."

Will nods, lips pressed together as he processes my words. I know what he really wants to tell me. That I deserve better. That I should put up a fight. But I just don't want to stir the pot. Which is why I appreciate it even more when he says, "I understand why you would want to go that route, even though I think you deserve more."

"Thank you," I say with a smile.

"And as for Molly?"

I take a shuddering breath, because my fight with her hurt me in a different, more vicious way. "I think Molly and I need to take a friend break," I whisper, the words killing me. "She just..." I shake my head, keeping my eyes on him.

"She's not a good friend." His voice is deep, with a little anger to it. Protective, and I love him even more for it.

"She's not acting like a good friend *now*. But she is. Usually. Or has been."

"You deserve better, Bridge. You deserve so much more. In every regard."

My stomach swoops and my lungs seize, his words the balm I sometimes don't even know I need.

I love you, I want to tell him. *And I feel like I'm dying from it.*

Will opens his mouth to say something else, but is cut off by a slew of incessant vibrations coming from his pocket. He drops his head between his shoulders and sighs heavily, exasperated.

"Excuse me," he practically grunts, pulling his phone out. "My boss is always riding my ass. Today he—" But he stops short when he checks the name of the person on the screen. Instantly, his face softens. "Shit, it's my mom. I have to answer this, actually."

"Sure, no problem."

With an apologetic smile, he gets to his feet and steps out of the wine bar to take the call, leaving his coat behind. The waitress stops by to ask whether we'd like another bottle, but I pass. It's only a Monday and, while I'm angry at work now, I don't *actually* want to lose my job by showing up hungover. I do love it, after all. We're just going through a rough patch. Building some character.

When Will comes back, his brow is furrowed in concern. "Sorry about that," he says as he retakes his seat. "Just reminding me I have to go up to Connecticut this weekend for my mom's birthday."

"Your mom's birthday is this weekend?" This makes me sit up in my seat, eager. "I *love* birthdays."

He smiles, finally. "Of course you do."

"When is it?"

"This Friday."

I gasp, thrilled. "Valentine's Day!"

He shakes his head with a grin on his face. "Yeah, Valentine's day."

"That's so cool!"

"If you say so."

"Oh my god, does she do a Valentine's Day themed birthday party every year? I know I totally would." My mind races with an explosion of pink and red birthday party decorations, glitter everywhere, hearts on every single flat surface, streamers hanging from any and every corner of the rooms.

Will sputters a laugh. "No, actually. This is the first time she's felt like celebrating in several years. Her friends are throwing her a party on Saturday and she was just making sure I knew when it was."

"Cool!"

"Is it?" He winces. "It's going to be all women—my mom's friends—and their kids, who are all younger than me by at least ten years. I mean, I'm really excited Mom is finally feeling up to it and all, but I'm not looking forward to the girliest birthday party in the world where I'm bound to spend the entire afternoon surrounded by people asking me the same inane questions over and over again. 'Do you have a girlfriend?' 'When are you getting married?' 'How's work?' 'What have you been up to?'" I cackle at the nasally, high pitch he switches his voice to. "Nuh-uh. No, thank you. It's going to be a nightmare," he says, his voice returning to normal.

"But cake!" I yelp, one of the nearby tables turning to shoot me judgmental looks.

"No amount of birthday cake can make up for a night of that kind of harassment," he says, grinning.

"That's not possible. Even bad birthday cake is better than no birthday cake. But if it's such a pain, take a date or something. As a buffer," I say, before I'm able to stop myself.

A date, Bridget? We do not want him going on a date with anyone! Sure, we want him to be happy. But can we at least wait until we're over him?

"You'll go with me?"

I hesitate for a moment. "Me? I—I meant someone you like. Someone you could potentially see as a girlfriend or something."

"I told you—I don't date. And there's no way I'm taking some random dating app girl to a family function. That's just an invitation for drama. I'd rather take you."

"I... Sure. If you want me to go, I mean. I definitely owe you. And I guess I can distract you. Keep you entertained. Field off any unwanted questions about your dating life or work or whatever. It'll be my way of repaying you for coming to my rescue twice this week. Honestly, I don't know how I would've survived."

"Bridge. You don't have to come with me over some sense of obligation. Seriously, I'm here because I want to be."

I smile. "And I know that."

"I'm inviting you because I want you there."

"But also because you need a buffer."

He laughs once. "Sure, Bridge. Whatever you say."

"It's just for the day, right? I don't need to find a cat sitter for Ginger?"

"Just for the day. But... if you're going to come—" he stops himself. Swallows once. Shakes his head.

"What?"

Will takes a deep breath and stares straight in my eyes. "Come because you want to, too. Not just because I asked."

I bite down on my bottom lip to keep from smiling too hard. "I want to."

"Good." He lets go of my hand and orders the check.

WILL

It's exactly the way he imagined taking her home to meet his mother for the first time.

Except that it isn't.

She isn't his, even though he is certainly hers, and he still hasn't told her the truth about it all, even though he traced his apology on her skin with his fingertips.

Will has definitely started to fall for her, and while he isn't able to give her every piece of himself like he wants to, he can give her this. All he has to do is make sure she never finds out the truth. All he has to do is make sure no one blows his cover.

He can't risk losing Bridget over a dumb misunderstanding that has spiraled into something massive. She said it herself: she has a hard time accepting white lies. How is she going to feel when she finds out the truth?

Will shudders at the thought.

19

TRYING TOO HARD, MAYBE?

"I have nothing to wear!" I wail, pulling every single item from my closet one by one, inspecting it, and deeming it not good enough for today. I mean, what *does* one wear to a birthday party of the man you're secretly in love with's mom? A flowy dress? Casual jeans? Heels? Flat boots?

God.

WILL

I'm about 5 minutes away from your place.

BRIDGET

5 MINUTES?!?! You cannot do this to me, Will. I need at least 10 more minutes

WILL

10??? Why??? Did you oversleep or something???

I GROAN AND TYPE FURIOUSLY AWAY, WHILE GINGER HAPPILY kneads (and probably destroys with her sharp nails) my favorite crimson sweater where it lies on the bed. It took me some time to find the right trim to fix the frayed edge of this vintage Helmut Lang sweater, but when I did, it was perfection. And now it was going to be destroyed by the love of my life just because I threw it carelessly on the bed—along with many other articles of clothing—in frustration. I should probably say goodbye to it before I return from the party to find it in pieces. Right now, though, I couldn't care less.

BRIDGET

I still don't know what I'm going to wear. And my hair is a mess. What's the dress code? I asked you like 1093095838 times and you never gave me an answer.

WILL

I would just like to say that I'm using the hands-free function on my car and hearing that number spoken by the rental's robot voice was fully unnecessary.

And I did give you an answer. I told you it was casual.

BRIDGET

That's not an answer! Casual could be anywhere between jeans and a dress.

WILL

Just wear something comfortable.

BRIDGET

Oh sure. I'll go ahead and wear my sweats.

WILL

> Whatever. You look great in anything, anyways.
> No one will notice you're wearing sweatpants.

I FROWN, THE PANG IN MY CHEST KNOCKING ME BREATHLESS.

Why does he keep saying nice things? Why can't he just... I don't know. *Not* be adorable?

BRIDGET

> Fine. I'm wearing a sweater dress. A brown one with a belt and matching boots. Does that sound good?

WILL

> Bridge, please don't take offense to this, but... Who do you think I am? The host of a makeover show or something? I'm not a professional stylist.

BRIDGET

> You should have at least a basic knowledge of clothing and what goes together, William Jacobs. You work in fashion.

WILL

> Not by choice, Bridget Quinn.

BRIDGET

> What's that supposed to mean?

WILL

> It means I wish I didn't know the difference between herringbone and houndstooth. It also means you should stop texting me and finish getting ready because I'm 15 minutes away from your apartment.

BRIDGET

You said 5!!!

WILL

I lied. I knew you'd need longer.

BRIDGET

…

I hate you.

WILL

No you don't. But I just showed you how valuable white lies can be. The pressure of the time crunch made you realize what you wanted to wear.

BRIDGET

No, I definitely hate you

WILL

See you in 14 minutes.

AFTER OVER AN HOUR OF TRAVEL WHERE WILL VERY GRACIOUSLY lets me control the road trip playlist and I agree not to comment on his driving, I half forget where we're going and why. Just being in an enclosed space with him, joking around and talking has already made my day. That and the fact that he looks so handsome I could cry add to my good mood. With just a light blue button down under a cozy-looking navy sweater, Will's broad chest looks like pure heaven—a place I would love to lay my head (again) and rest. I try not to stare at that place in between his shoulders and neck—that little nook that felt like a charging station the night we spent together. My safe space. But I fail miserably, clearly.

"Why do you keep looking at my clothes? Do I have a stain or something?" He glances down at himself before moving his eyes back to the road, swiping at his sweater as if he's trying to brush something off.

Busted.

"No, not a stain. Just staring at your chest, is all," I say casually, without even thinking.

He sputters a laugh. "What?"

I clear my throat once and then follow it with a deep breath. Screw it. I'm not gonna lie. "Your chest. I was staring at it."

He pauses. "Because...?"

"I... don't want to say." I wince.

"Oooh. Now you've *got* to say." He grins that wicked smile of his.

"Nooope."

"Oh, you fucked up because you know I'm never gonna let this go."

"Just kidding. You definitely have a big stain there. Mustard. A big gloopy mess. That's what I was looking at."

"Well, that's fucking weird, since I had an everything bagel with cream cheese and not a fucking hot dog for breakfast. So how about you stop lying?" He asks with a laugh. "Just tell me."

I sigh, putting my face in my hands. "Your chest. Looks comfy."

And while I cannot see him since I'm covering my face, obviously, I just know he's fighting a fit of smug laughter. In fact, it's not long before I sense his body shaking.

"Listen, I had to wake up early this morning and am really tired because I couldn't sleep and was checking you out and remembered how comfortable it was to cuddle together and so yeah... That happened. I'm sorry. I know we agreed to not talk about it again or do it again but that's where my mind went, okay?"

Silence. Painful silence as I look down at my hands.

"I mean, I also look at your chest often. So we're even."

I burst out laughing in surprise and slap him on the arm. "William! What?"

He throws his head back in laughter, struggling to keep his eyes on the road. "What! It's a nice chest." He shrugs casually. "And I thought it would make you feel better to know you're not the only one doing it."

I bite my lip to hide my smile, because I should feel offended, shouldn't I? But I'm not.

Oh god, this is a mess.

"Thank you for the compliment, I think? But also, how about we *not* look at each other's chests anymore?"

"Like, in general or just in front of my mom? Because I don't know if I can promise not looking at it long term. I'll try to be more subtle next time, but..." He laughs when I hit him again. "Okay, okay. I get it. Boobs are off limits. Gotcha."

I shake my head at the ridiculousness of this moment. We are crazy, but I love the way we are—a series of contradictions. Comfortable enough to talk about mutual ogling of chests, yet feeling a tension so tight after doing so that I feel like bursting out of my skin.

"I hope she likes the presents I got her," I murmur, looking over my shoulder at the backseat where I've left them.

"You know, you didn't have to bring her a present —let alone three," Will tells me, eyeing the gifts in the rear view mirror.

"I'm sorry, but in what world is it okay to arrive to a birthday party empty handed? And I'm meeting *your mom*. That's important to me."

He presses his lips together, eyes on the road as he tries not to smile. "Why is that important to you?"

"I want your mom to like me."

"Why?"

"Because."

"Because why?"

"God, why are you being such a toddler this morning? Did you forget your coffee or something? Or have too much of it?" I run my hands down my thighs, smoothing my dress. I don't want to look a mess when I get to his mom's house, which, according to the GPS, is in twenty minutes.

Will laughs at my frustration. "Bridge, I'm just fucking with you. I just think you're cute when you're nervous. But I'm trying to understand why you're even nervous to begin with."

I exhale and look out the window, staring at the bare trees on the side of the highway. It's February, but spring seems so far away.

I don't look at him as I speak. "You're... important to me. And she's important to you. Which means it's important to me that she likes me."

He's quiet for a moment as he processes my words. "Okay, then. I'll stop teasing."

I nod, eyes still firmly looking out my passenger window.

"For the record though, it's also important to me that you guys get along. But it wouldn't change anything between us if you didn't."

Not long after, we arrive to a small, but cozy-looking ranch-style home in a town I've never heard of before. The house is hidden behind a couple of bare, overgrown trees Will frowns at, but the walkway is clear and tidy.

"...told them to prune the branches last month before spring gets here... looks like fucking Tim Burton's Sleepy Hollow..." He sighs and shakes his head, pulling our gifts from the backseat.

"You know," he starts, "at the risk of bringing this up again, you didn't have to get her flowers, a gift, and cookies. I'm sure this bouquet was enough."

"Well," I say, taking the three items from him. "The flowers are like a basic 'Thank you for having me in your home' gift. The birthday present is for her birthday—duh. And the cookies are from that cookie decorator who does all the celebrities' cookies on instagram? Kooky Cookie Queen? You know the one. The famous one. She did a Valentine's collab with that small coffee chain by my house, so I snagged a few before they sold out."

"Famous cookie decorator for *you*, you mean." He smiles, placing a hand on my lower back, using it to guide me up the walkway to his mother's house.

Even through my coat, I feel its warmth. The heat rises up my spine and down between my legs. It causes my upper body to turn into a shade of bright vermillion, I'm sure.

One touch, and suddenly my mind is filled with filthy thoughts of flashbacks and fantasies of him and me together, back in my bed.

Sigh.

I pull myself together and glare at his smirk, but I love our flirting. "Either way, the cookies are gorgeous, and I thought they'd be perfect for today. So hush." I stick out my tongue, and he laughs.

Without taking his eyes off me, his smile full and gorgeous and heart melting, he knocks on the front door.

While we wait, he whispers, "She's going to love you, Bridge. In fact, I can't imagine anyone helping it."

If you believe that to be so true, then why don't you love me, too?

WILL

Will knew that taking Bridget to meet his mother, to his childhood home, was a risk. He was aware that, in doing so, he would be teetering a dangerous line. But letting her get to know this extra piece of him, to show her another part of who he was, was way too tempting.

In preparation for today, when Will had called his mother to let him know he was bringing a guest, he requested the topic of work and careers be taken out of the approved list of conversational topics. In fact, it was his condition for attending the party (not that there was any way he was going to miss it, anyway). He wanted Bridget to know the good parts of him. He wanted her to see that he was not a bad man despite having done many bad things. To her. To his mother. To lots of people.

He wanted her to fall in love with the good sides of him before she realized just how terrible he has been.

20

SOMETHING LIKE IT

Will's mother looks nothing like her son. Or rather, Will looks nothing like his mother.

Sandra Jacobs is platinum blonde and blue-eyed, with pale skin and delicate, soft, round features. And even from her wheelchair, you can tell she has a petite frame. She is shockingly the complete opposite to her son. Will is all angular lines, hard muscle, and Mediterranean skin. His dark eyes are wide, intense, and set below thick brows making it very clear that he takes after his late father. And if that weren't enough, his over six feet two height sure should settle that theory. If it weren't for the same infinitely long and full lashes and the deep laughter that stems from their belly, I would never have assumed they were related—at least by blood. But once Sandra takes one look at her son, it's pure adoration and devotion you can see in her eyes. The kind you only see in mothers' eyes—or so I've been told, since *my* mom was about as maternal as the bow clip currently keeping my hair out of my face.

Due to his height and her wheelchair, Will has to squat to hug his mother hello. She reaches her arms up and wraps them lovingly around her son, closing her eyes like her entire day has been made.

"You're here!" she exclaims, pulling back to look him in the eye.

"Mom. I told you I was coming," he says before kissing her once on the cheek and gently pulling away.

"Yes, but still! I'm excited! My first birthday party in a while and you're here and all my friends are here."

Will smiles down at his mom. "I know, Mom. I'm happy you're finally letting someone celebrate you."

Sandra grins up at her son a final time before her eyes land on mine, bright and mischievous. They say *Aha! Gotcha!*

"And she's here, too." She smiles at me before she glances at Will and back. "You must be Bridget. Will has told me so much about you, I keep asking whether you guys are together or not."

"*Whoa*, Mom! What the actual fuck? We've talked about this. I said no." Will's face flushes almost as red as mine does.

I sputter a laugh, almost gasping for air. Did she seriously just ask that?

"Oh." It's all I can manage at the moment, and honestly, I should receive an award for being able to say as much.

"C'mon, Will. You talk about her all the time. You spend most of your free time with her. And maybe I believed you the eight times you told me she was just a friend. But now that I've seen the way she looks?" Sandra shakes her head, laughing. "No way you guys aren't together."

"Okay, you need to stop this before it even starts or this will be the last birthday party of yours I come to." He's half-joking, half-mortified, and it's so adorable I want to melt. "I do not talk about Bridget all the time." He stops and looks at me. "I do not talk about you all the time."

The only reason I believe him—besides just the idea of having him be as obsessed with me as I am with him is completely ridiculous—is because it feels like we spend any free time we *do* have talking to *each other*. When would he even have the chance to talk to his mother often enough for her to say he talks about me all the time?

Sandra throws her head back in laughter at our expressions and backs into the house, letting us in.

"Are those for me?" She nods towards the gifts in my hand.

"Yes! Sorry, yes. I got distracted from the whole..." I wave my free hand vaguely in the air.

Will sighs and rubs his eyes as he shakes his head in frustration while Sandra looks like she's having the time of her life.

"Thanks so much for letting me crash your birthday." When I hand her the three things, her eyes go wide.

"Honey, you did not need to get me this much stuff. The flowers would've been more than enough."

"She has a whole thing behind each gift, Mom." Will shoots me a smirk, dark eyes shining.

Sandra raises a curious eyebrow at her son, then at me.

"The flowers are a thank you for welcoming me into your home," I begin to explain. "The heart shaped cookies because your birthday is on Valentine's Day. And the other gift is your birthday gift."

"It's too much, is what it is. Thank you, though." She takes my hand and squeezes it, her smile warm and tender. An obtrusive thought instantly pops into my head: *I wish I had had a mother like her growing up.* But the guilt pushes it away as quickly as it came on. My mother couldn't help herself, so it's not fair to feel this way.

"Of course. It's no problem."

She squeezes my hand once more before taking the gifts from me and placing them on her lap. "How about I introduce you to my best friends? They're kind of like Will's aunts and, in addition to myself, will be the ones providing you with a wide array of embarrassing childhood stories for your entertainment."

I snort and follow her into the living room, laughing as Will groans in mortification. "Please don't believe anything they say. And if they bring up the whole bowl of Jolly Ranchers thing, please have mercy on me—it was traumatic, not cute."

THE JOLLY RANCHER STORY TURNS OUT TO BE AN INSTANT CLASSIC —and something I will forever tease Will about. The way he stole and proceeded to eat all of his kindergarten teacher's secret stash of watermelon candy. How she asked everyone to 'fess up, but they all denied it—including Will. The way he tried to hide it but his bright red tongue sold him out. And how the teacher decided to punish him by not letting him participate in the holiday pageant while the rest of his classmates did leaves an image of young, cute Will in my head I never want to forget.

"It was traumatic, Bridge! Imagine standing there, crying, having to watch everyone have fun, but you can't do anything about it."

I smile and laugh, looking down at a picture of five-year-old Will. "I totally get it, Will. It does sound traumatic. But oh my god, look at how adorable you are." I point to the adorable boy with the mop of curly hair, eyes too big to fit his face, and a sweater that screams the nineties so loudly I wonder how I can hear anything in this place. "I can just imagine you being a cute lil' mess in your Rudolph sweater."

He narrows his eyes at me and takes the photo album from my hands. "That's it. No more baby pictures for you."

"Noooo." I reach over him in laughter as he pulls the album

behind his back, losing my balance and falling over his lap, ass up. Realizing the precarious position we find ourselves in, I try to right myself but fail. Instead, I end up slipping off his lap and onto the ground with a loud thud.

"Shit. You okay?" He reaches a hand down to help me to my feet, but I don't take it, choosing instead to right myself. When I sit up, leaning on my hands, I inadvertently push out my chest. Will's gaze instantly drops to it, pupils blown wide. Humor has left the building, replaced by that ever-present sexual tension between us which only ever seems to wax and never wane.

"Will," I hiss in a whisper voice as I readjust my neckline. "I didn't actually think not staring at my tits would be a difficult thing for you to do in front of your mother."

He squeezes his eyes shut and shakes his head, an embarrassed laugh bursting through his lips. "I know, I'm sorry. I didn't mean to—"

"William, we need you in the kitchen!" Alexandria, one of Sandra's oldest friends, calls out.

"One sec," he calls back. He helps me to my feet, hands in his, and smiles down at me. "Thank you for coming, by the way. It's helped in keeping them off my case about a lot of things. Even though I added one by bringing you."

"What do you mean?"

He squeezes my hands once. "Well, now they think we're in love. Or at the very least, something like it."

WILL

Seeing her here, surrounded by everyone he considers family, is unlike anything he could've imagined.
He loves the way this feels. Loves the way she feels and fits in the equation.
And he thinks he might love her.
No.
He knows *he loves her.*

21

SO, THAT'S WHAT YOU MEANT BY BFFS

As I slide another bead onto my elastic, I watch Will from the friendship bracelet making table in the corner of the living room. He's coddled and loved by his mother and her friends through cheek-pinching and teasing. And it's nice, seeing him like this. Most of the time, by the way he talks, I feel like Will doesn't think too highly of himself. Which is ridiculous, since I know bad people, having been surrounded my entire life by them, disappointment, and betrayal. And Will could never.

"Did you use up all the pink beads?" Sandra's best friend's daughter asks with narrowed eyes. "Because I need some to finish mine."

I shake my head and push the container with the different pink beads to her. "Are you kidding? No way." Look at me, playing at the kids table, letting the grown-ups mingle.

Surrounded by pink and red sparkly hearts, confetti, and streamers, I feel like the Valentine birthday decorations reflect the strongest feelings in my heart. As Will stands beneath a strand of cutouts, that all too familiar ache spreads all over my body. I wish they made an NSAID for being lovesick—I'm sure it'd make a killing.

Sigh.

Of course I'm bummed we aren't *together* together. But at least he's still in my life, and that's the silver lining I need to hold onto.

Smiling to myself, I tie off my second bracelet and roll it onto my wrist, this one a little looser than the first. After all, it isn't for me.

When I lift my eyes, Will is looking back at me, a smile on his face. I give him a small little wave, a shy smile, and he takes this as an invitation to leave his group of adoring fans and come over.

"Hey," he says with a grin, staring down at me. "You been hiding or something?"

"Not at all. Just keeping myself busy while I make you one of these." I slip the larger bracelet off my wrist and pass it to him. Will takes it in his hands and holds it almost reverently, fingers running over the three square letter beads with the letters BFF with two heart beads on the side.

"What is this?"

"You told me—BFF's remember? You said we could even get matching friendship bracelets." I lift my hand up to show him, wiggle my wrist in the air. "So I made some. Matching friend-ship bracelets."

Something akin to frustration flashes through his eyes, but it's gone so quickly I begin to wonder whether it was real or I imagined it. After examining the beads a little closer, he slips it on, the light pink and white beads contrasting beautifully against his tan skin.

"You don't have to *actually* wear it." I roll my eyes, but deep down I'm thrilled. "It was meant as a joke."

"Are you wearing yours?"

"I—" I look down at my wrist. "I guess so?"

"Then I'm wearing mine."

My heart does that somersault thing it's been doing way too much of. The Olympic-level kind that leaves me a little dizzy and a lot achy—the one I also feel low in my core.

"You know, I take back what I said before. You actually make a terrible buffer, Bridge."

I grin back. "I know you wanted me to play interference, but c'mon. Look at how cute they are with you! Your mom and your found family aunts adore you."

He laughs softly and shakes his head. "Yeah. But the inquisition has been getting intense. You could've at least stood by my side. Distracted them a bit."

"So they can ask us whether we're hooking up? Wouldn't that have made it worse?" I whisper in the hopes the eleven-year old girl in front of us doesn't hear us. "No, thanks." I mean it as a joke, but he winces.

"Sorry about that."

"Don't be silly. Family members are supposed to embarrass you like this." Or so I've been told.

"Well, I think that—"

"Will." Sandra comes up behind him, her voice filled with humor. She knows what she's doing. Will closes his eyes and takes a deep breath before turning to face his mother.

"Yes, Mom?"

"Lisa and the girls are getting the cake and everything ready to sing happy birthday, but of all the things they got for the party, no one thought to get candles." She laughs softly.

"Do you need me to run out and get some?"

"No, not at all. Alexandria already left a couple of minutes ago. But what I mean is that it'll probably be a while before we sing happy birthday. So why don't you go ahead and show Bridget your room stuff while we wait til everything's ready? On top of that, they keep fighting over how to set up the table for maximum photographic aesthetic appeal, as they claim. I get the feeling it's going to be a while. You'll have a bunch of time to show her all your awards and artistic abilities and stuff."

"Artistic abilities?" I look back and forth between the two Jacobs.

"Will didn't tell you? He's an incredible artist." Sandra's voice is filled with pride.

I look to Will who can barely make eye contact with me. "What? No, he never said anything."

Sandra frowns. "Will?"

"I... It never came up. That's only high school stuff. It's really not that good."

"And college. You did some college stuff," his mom adds.

"But those are in my apartment back home, not in my childhood bedroom." His cheeks are red, his eyes stuck to the floor. "And whatever's here isn't good."

"Okay, you need to stop being so self-effacing," I tell him. "And I can't believe you hid this from me." The hurt in my voice is real. I thought we knew everything about each other? He definitely told me about the nerdy awards when we covered high school, but never about the art.

Sandra *tsks*. "Well, now you *have* to show her. Let her see how incredible your work is."

Will's cheeks redden, eyes panicked. "Whoa. No, Mom. I don't think Bridget would like—"

"Bridget would, actually," I cut him off, a huge smile spreading across my face. "Bridget definitely would love to very much."

He stares down at me, a bit hopeless.

"C'mon," I whisper low enough for his mom not to hear. "I want to know you."

Something about what I say shifts the way he carries himself and the expression on his face—determined, a man on a mission, ready to get things done.

And it's kinda hot.

"Okay," he tells his mom, but his eyes are on me as he pulls me to my feet by the hand and leads me down a hallway without another word to me or anyone else for that matter.

"God, what is up with you?"

We reach a door at the end of the hallway with a hanging Mickey Mouse sign, his name painted on. Clearly, a memento from when he was younger. I reach out and run my fingers over the old sign, its color a little worn and faded, one of Mickey's ears chipped.

When he wraps his large hand around the doorknob, Will pauses for a moment before opening the door. Once he does, though, he lets me inside, a hesitant smile on his face.

"Oh my god, Will." I gasp, bringing my hands to my mouth. "Are these..."

"Trekkie models and figurines?" His smile is radiant as he surveys his collection. Dozens of figurines stand proudly on a shelf above Will's childhood desk, surrounded by medals and what look like academic trophies. "Each of these was hand painted by yours truly."

A laugh bursts through my lips. "Oh my god, this is amazing."

"I thought you said it wasn't an embarrassing hobby." He frowns, shifting uncomfortably on his feet.

"It's not," I say, turning to look at him. "Really. I'm just a little shocked to find out that this was your hobby as a kid after you made fun of it. It's such a wild collection."

"It's kinda dumb, I know."

"No, it's not. It's so cool! Can I touch them?"

He nods once. "Go for it."

With some hesitation, I reach out, taking a model of the Starship Enterprise in my hands to inspect more closely. The crisp lines, the perfectly blended paint, and the neat placement of the lettering leaves me wondering how the hell this was hand painted by a teenager.

"This is incredible. You did such an amazing job." I set it down and pick up more pieces. A Spock figurine first, a Captain Kirk second. "Will," I breathe, setting down the last piece.

He picks up a Sulu figurine, studies it for a moment, and sets it back down on his shelf. "I went through a big Trekkie phase, as you can see."

I laugh as I set down the final piece. "I'll say. Between the Mathlete trophies, the figurines, and the Star Trek prints on the wall, it looks like you were an all-around, cliché nerd—except a hot one, probably." I throw him a smirk and a wink.

This makes him laugh. "I was not hot by any means. Very tall and lanky. Bad cystic acne, too. Not popular with the girls— cheerleaders or nerdy ones—by any means."

I giggle and reach out to touch one of his first place competition diplomas, running my fingers over his name. The thought of Will not being appealing is just absolutely ridiculous.

"Things got better in college, though. I went to a nerdy school so I fit in perfectly. How about you?"

I shrug. "High school was *meh*. I didn't have much of a life, always doing odd jobs here and there while my mom was still alive, you know? In a messed up way, things got better when she passed. My grandmother took over and I had less on my plate. Still, I never went to college. It wasn't an option for me. By senior year of high school, I could tell my grandmother wasn't holding up too well, so I became the main breadwinner. She lost her mind when I told her I wasn't going—the plan was to get a degree from a junior college first and then wrap it up at a four-year—but it got to the point where she needed too much help, and there was no way she could deny it coming from me."

"I'm sorry you didn't get to do the things you wanted to," he whispers.

"Don't be. My grandmother saved my life, basically. Or actually. I wanted to give back to her and if that meant not going to school, then that was fine." It's Will, the person I feel most comfortable with, and still it's hard to talk about my grandmother. "It took me ten years or so, but I finally got to a career that I like and am good at, right? At least I'm here. And that's the bright side."

He heaves a frustrated sigh, running his fingers through his hair. "You and your fucking bright side. I wish just for one fucking day you wouldn't *have* to look on the bright side or the silver lining. I wish that for one goddamn day every single side of your life were bright. That it would be covered wall-to-wall in silver and you wouldn't have to look for any kind of lining." Will's voice is almost a growl, the frustration clear. His hands fist at his side as his jaw ticks. Meanwhile, my heart sprints toward a finish line that doesn't even exist.

And even though my heart rate is also raised, *I* try to calm *him*. "Hey, it's fine." I put a hand on his shoulder and he relaxes his bicep.

A silence passes between us, both revisiting our pasts—and each other's.

"Those aren't prints on the wall, by the way," he murmurs, breaking the silence.

"What?"

"The things on the wall? You said they were prints. And they're not. I sketched them."

I drop my hand—and my jaw—and turn to look at him. "What?" I look between him and the prints, each one more impressive than the next. I stand closer to examine the one closest to me—a satellite—drawn in a fine-tip black marker. I take in the dedication he put in every single one of those lines, in the shading of the curve of the satellite, and the detail of the lights and buttons.

"These are incredible."

"They're okay." He shrugs, biting the inside of his cheek.

"No, no. Seriously. They're amazing. Truly."

Will smiles softly at me and takes a step closer, standing beside me to stare at the same print together. His scent fills my lungs, the notes of it intoxicating. I can feel the air buzzing between us, though maybe that's just me, close to bursting out of my skin for all that I feel for him. In seconds, I'm full of need, aching to wrap my arms around him and beg him to just hug me back.

Instead, I break the moment with a joke.

"So... you can draw? Can you draw me like one of your French girls?" I ask, batting my eyelashes at him in an exaggerated motion.

He laughs and shoves his hands in his pockets, dark eyes warm as he traces my body from top to bottom. "I... don't usually draw people."

"Usually or never?"

"Not never. Just... not usually."

I purse my lips at him, cross my arms in front of my chest. "So, theoretically, you could?"

"I could, yes. To the best of my abilities."

I laugh once at his almost nervous hesitation, the quiet and careful way in which he strings his words together. I decide to run over to his bed and throw myself atop the—yeah, you guessed it—Star Trek sheets. "So. Draw me like one of your French girls, Jack," I repeat.

I get in position, lying on my back, with my hands thrown behind my head à la Rose—a position which inadvertently causes me to push my chest out. Again. Something Will definitely notices. Again.

His eyes darken, they trail up and down over my body slowly. And suddenly, I feel my smile slip because I can feel it like wildfire, scorching my skin.

I clear my throat once. "Or... I mean, you don't have to, if you don't want to."

He shakes his head and takes a seat at his desk, rifling through the top drawer for a pen. When he finds it, he searches in the next one until he pulls out an old sketch pad. Once he reaches a blank sheet, he uncaps the pen and turns back to stare at me once more. Except this time, he holds his gaze with mine.

"You ready?"

No. "Yes." A chill runs up and down my spine, and suddenly this whole thing doesn't seem as funny as I thought it would be.

Will looks up between me and the sketch pad several times, face serious, but tender. Like he's staring at his favorite thing in the whole world. Like I *am* his whole world. With each passing second, I find myself hoping it were true. A stinging grows behind my eyes, and I'm mortified to realize that I just may cry —and I don't even know why.

Each scratch of the pen, each flicker of his eyes as they roam my body, stokes the fire inside. Every single movement of his wrist increases my heart rate and the temperature of my skin. It's so intimate, what we're doing. More than I ever expected it could be. I've given him permission to take me in, to focus on every peak and valley, every flaw I may have. I've given him the green light to look at me and take what he sees and put it on paper.

But what if I don't like what he sees? What he thinks of me? Or worse: what if he sees me exactly for who I am and realizes he doesn't like it?

It isn't long before he sets the pen down on the desk and sits up, holding the sketch close to his chest before dumping it facedown onto his desk. Wordlessly, with eyes so dark and an intense gaze I've never seen before, Will walks over to me, slowly, like a lion about to attack his prey. Lungs frozen, unable to breathe, I watch as he places a knee on the mattress and crawls over me on the bed, covering my entire body with his. Noses touching, I feel something hard press into my thigh. Involuntarily, I arch my hips up to feel it better, to double check that it really is what I think it is.

Yup. That's his cock. Hard. Pressed against me.

"What's happening here?" My voice is barely a whisper, shaky.

Will licks his lips as he looks down at mine before speaking. "Before I even saw you on FaceTime, I used to imagine you in my head often. And I sketched out versions of what I thought you looked like. I have so many versions of you sketched into the pad in my apartment back home, Bridge. You wouldn't believe. But I never would've dreamed you'd be this beautiful. Never."

"I... I thought you didn't sketch people."

"You're not *people*. You're *you*."

My breath hitches, trying hard not to cry. Something about this moment, something about how he grazes one of my arms while he keeps his eyes on me, has me enraptured and overwhelmed.

"Since seeing you for the first time," he goes on, one hand coming up to cup my jaw, thumb tracing my lower lip, "you're all I can draw. All I can sketch. And it's never enough. It never does you justice. You're my biggest frustration, Bridget. For so many reasons, but... You're so fucking beautiful, and I will never be able to draw how absolutely fucking perfect you are. There's just no way."

No oxygen. There's no oxygen left in the room.

I open my mouth to beg for air, for words—for *something*—but nothing comes out or comes in. I need something to bring me back to life because the words I just heard come out of Will's mouth killed me.

As if reading my mind, Will presses his lips to mine, his tongue dipping into my mouth and waking my body from its shocked stupor.

It's me, Will, it seems to say. *I'm here and you're safe and I've come to bring you the happiness you finally deserve.*

With a moan, leaving all rational thought behind, I let myself enjoy the kiss, finally moving my arms from above my head to wrap around his neck. Feeling the way I shift beneath his body, Will's hand travels down my arm, over my ribs, and onto my hip. He pauses there for a moment, gripping me hard, pulling me closer to feel the hard line of his cock. I gasp when I feel it press just shy of my clit, my underwear already soaked after just a few moments of kissing. When he moves his lips to my neck, I hear myself beg for more. And because Will is such a good man, he proceeds to give me exactly what I want.

His hand trails down my thigh and stops at my calf; he hooks it behind my knee and hitches my leg on his hip. I stop breathing for a moment, my dress riding up all the way to my waist. Suddenly, I'm back to that night we shared in my bed which started almost in the same position as this one—except vertically.

He moves his hips in a slow roll against my own, rhythmic and perfect, making me cry out his name once again. One of his hands comes over my mouth as he shushes me, lips pressed to my ears. "You're going to get us caught."

All of a sudden, the awareness that there are people just outside the door washes over me, and while I would've expected myself to let this piece of information put a damper on this moment, all it does is make it all the more appealing. The taboo of it all increasing my need for him, for us.

The hand that was holding my thigh to his hip travels inward, heading straight for where I'm wet and hot and aching for him.

"I don't have time to fuck you like I properly wanna fuck you right now. But there's no way I'm going to let you walk out that door without having come. Hard. I wanna see that special blush on your face. The one that only happens after you have an orgasm. I've only seen it a few times, but it's seared into my fucking brain, Bridget. The most beautiful color red I've ever seen."

I whimper beneath his palm, meeting his fierce dark eyes as his hand moves my underwear to the side.

Will's head dips to my neck with a groan when he feels the wetness between my thighs, growling words that sound like "... can't fucking *believe* you get this wet this fast for me." But I can't be sure, because he says them right as he begins to tease me, run his index and middle finger around my clit, and the only thing I can focus on in that moment is keeping myself from screaming for him to touch it. To rub it. To make me come like he did when we spent the night together in my place.

"You're so fucking perfect."

I wrap both legs around his waist, the stiletto heels of my brown boots accidentally stabbing Will. He doesn't seem to notice, though. Too busy driving me wild with his fingers, teasing at my entrance as he sucks on my neck.

"Hickey," I say in a gasp behind his hand. "No hickeys. Work."

"But I want to mark you," he growls, kissing down my neck. He pulls down the neckline of my dress to expose my tits, cradled in my favorite lace bra. "Can I mark you here?"

A hickey from Will on my tits? *Yes, please!*

I nod enthusiastically, something about the knowledge that I'll get to walk around with his mark on my skin for days after this incredibly hot.

He proceeds to lick at my breasts, biting them as if they were the juiciest fruits, before kissing them and sucking on them.

After doing that in one place, he moves on to another spot a few inches apart. Meanwhile, Will proves his supernatural abilities for multitasking by sliding in two fingers, heel pressed to my clit. Immediately, my back arches off the mattress at the fullness, at the absolute feeling of being surrounded by him and us and everything I still don't understand about our relationship.

This is good. This is so good, and it isn't even really sex. I could do this. I could have Will like this even if I don't have him. And that's okay, right?

My unreasonable reasoning comes to an end, however, when my tolerance for whatever magic he's doing between my legs does, too, playing with my pussy with the same hand that currently wears our friendship bracelet.

BFF might as well stand for Best Finger Fuck instead of Best Friends Forever.

"I want to sketch a full series of you coming," he whispers in my ear after I come the first time. "Of your face when *I* make you come. Sketch after sketch of this gorgeous face and this perfect body and keep it all to myself. Only mine, for no one else to see. And if it's the only part I get to keep of this, of you, of *us*—then fine. I'll take this moment."

I try to tell him he can have it all—he can have me however he wants me—but the words turn to ash in my mouth when a current of electricity runs through my body.

Because I'm close.

So close.

So fucking close I have to bite my lip to keep from moaning, from calling out his name and alerting everyone outside that this incredibly sexy man is about to make me come on his hand.

"Now come for me, baby. Come before you get us caught. And stop moaning so much. *Shh.* That's it. Bite my hand. Bite it and come."

His words, the nickname, the way his fingers scissor inside of me while the heel of his hand adds the right amount of pressure, have me coming like a freight train. I free one of my hands from his hair and hold it over his hand and my mouth in an attempt to stifle a scream. The orgasm comes in waves, in strong pulses that turn me into a melted heap on his childhood bed.

When it's over, when my breathing has deepened and my heart rate has lowered and his head is on my chest listening to it beat, I say "I never expected to have one of the best orgasms of my life on Star Trek sheets."

WILL

She was right, he thinks, any birthday cake is good birthday cake. Especially when you have the wet underwear of the woman you're desperate for in your pants pocket.

22

WE ALL HAVE NEEDS

The rest of the afternoon goes by in a haze. An underwearless, sweaty haze.

No sooner had Will finished getting me off, than his mother called out for us to come sing happy birthday and blow out her candles. I lay there in shock momentarily as Will smugly readjusted himself in his pants, his eyes bright, cheeks flushed, breathing still a little ragged.

I don't remember much of what happened after, but I remember leaning up on my elbows, eyes wide as I asked him, "What about you?" and him replying, "Believe me, that was more than I could have hoped for."

I nodded in a trance-like state until he came back to bed, knelt between my still-spread legs, and kissed my clit over my underwear just once. He pressed his forehead to my hipbone for a few seconds, inhaling my scent deep into his lungs. After, he sat up and gently pulled my underwear down my legs, his fingers simultaneously leaving a hot trail and raising goose-bumps as they caressed my skin.

I watched in awe as Will bunched my underwear in his fist

and shoved them in his pocket. "For safekeeping," he said with a mischievous smile before pulling my dress back down.

From the pad on the desk, he carefully ripped out the sketch he'd drawn and handed it to me. But I couldn't bring myself to look at it. Not yet. That would have to wait until I was alone. So I folded it in four and held it tightly in my grasp. After, he led me out of his bedroom in a lust-drunk and foggy state—mostly shocked.

Now that we're in the car, two blocks away from my apartment after his mother's birthday party, I wonder what the fuck kind of safe keeping he was talking about anyways?

We haven't said much to each other since leaving the party. Only short questions and answers for us. "Want a bite to eat?" "No, thanks." "Air temperature good?" "Yeah." "Stopping for gas if you want to use the bathroom." "I'm okay." All while I've been rocking this road trip commando.

Our fun banter has left the building. In its place, we've got sexual tension by the truck load and the urge to throw a million questions at him at the same time.

What the hell was that?

Did that feel as incredible to you as it did to me?

We should never do that again, but also: when can we do that again?

What does this mean for our friendship?

Instead, I tell him: "You can just drop me off here. No need for the door-to-door service."

"Oh," he says, his face falling. "Yeah, okay."

"Plus, the car rental place is like ten blocks away, right? And don't you need to return the car before end of day?"

He nods, his eyes studying my face.

"So... Thanks for a great afternoon. I had a ton of fun. And your mom is pretty great."

He smiles as he parks the car on the side of the road, angry cab drivers cursing at him. "Yeah, thanks for coming. After having a promising start, you turned out to be a lousy buffer, but good company just the same." He laughs gently, his whole body turned in my direction.

There's a moment of silence that passes between us as we stare at each other. I wonder if I should ask whether he plans on giving me my panties back. Or whether he has plans of us doing this again. I want him to ask whether he can come up because he wants to and not because I ask him to.

But when everything goes unsaid, I open the door and whisper a goodbye. I hear his low, but audible gasp in my ear the second my lips press to his cheek. For a moment there, I think he might reach out and keep me in the car, but nothing happens. So in a state of defeat and confusion, I get out of the car and head back to my apartment.

Ginger happily greets me at the door, jumping on my legs for —you guessed it—food.

"You're not supposed to eat for another half hour," I tell her, checking the time on my phone. "But I'll feed you now since you've been alone all day."

While she purrs on the kitchen counter, chowing down on her dinner, I reorganize the debris of clothing my panic storm left all over the apartment. My morning freakout over what I would wear today seems so long ago, it's surreal. And a bit inconsequential given everything that happened at Will's mom's house, if you ask me.

I focus on folding my sweaters and pants, on hanging my dresses and putting my shoes away, getting lost in a Marie Kondo-level organizational manic episode just to get my mind off of Will and whatever happened. I also focus on *not* opening the sketch he drew of me, choosing to leave it untouched on my kitchen counter. I'll look at it when I'm ready. Someday.

It's when I'm freshly out of the shower and in my bright pink slip that I hear a knock at the door. Not a buzzing in my intercom, but a knock.

Terrified my first floor neighbors have finally been found out by the FBI and need a place to hide, I tiptoe to the peephole only to find a panting Will, both hands on either side of the door frame.

"Will?" I ask, opening the door. "How did you get up here?"

"Came in just as one of your neighbors was leaving."

"Oh. What are you doing here?"

He swallows once, his dark eyes locked on mine with a fire I feel down to my bones. They travel up and down my body, taking in every contour, every exposed freckle—and there's a lot to see, since the slip isn't exactly made for modesty.

"I'm here," he says, voice deep and gravelly, "because of what happened earlier, obviously. I'm here because of these." He takes my underwear from his pocket and holds them between us, dangling them between us with his index finger. The friendship bracelet I made for him is still on his wrist, right where mine is, too. "And I'm here to figure out what happened. Because in the moment, it felt like you enjoyed it." He closes his eyes as if struggling to keep himself in the present, only to open them again with a feral expression. "Really fucking enjoyed it. But then you wouldn't speak to me. Which, I mean, I get. Because previously we had agreed upon never doing anything like that again. But then I don't know how things escalated—it was my fault, obviously—you didn't ask me to crawl on top of you." My cheeks blaze fire engine red at the memory of how he looked prowling toward me, the weight of his body on me. "And then *that* happened. But you didn't stop me. And I didn't even think to stop myself. So now I'm caught between thinking I'm either this fucking asshole who practically attacked you because he can't stop thinking about you or..."

"Or?"

"Or you were into it, too."

I watch him for a moment, measuring what to say. "You can't stop thinking about me?"

Will huffs out a laugh. "Bridget."

And I know we should probably, for the sake of our friendship, discuss what happened and what we would like to happen at length. But I decide to give up on maintaining rational thought or reasoning and simply whisper, "I was *very* into it," before taking him by the hand, pulling him into my apartment, and closing the door behind us.

He places his hands on my hips, fingers digging into my skin through the delicate fabric of my slip. "Good. Because I've been wanting to see you come again since the second you came down from your orgasm that first night. And today was fucking surreal."

I drag my hands up his arms, feeling his muscular biceps as I go, reveling in this moment. "You didn't get to finish today," I say with a pout. "Maybe we can fix that."

He smirks before kissing me intensely, letting me walk him backwards toward my bed. I push him into a sitting position onto the mattress, mentally thanking myself for putting away all my clothes before his arrival. This would be difficult to do on top of a mountain of dresses and skirts.

I stand between his spread legs looking down at him as he grazes his fingers up the backs of my thighs, my core tightening with every millimeter he touches. By the time he reaches my fresh set of underwear, I'm breathing heavily, folding over him as I wrap his head in my arms, my hair falling forward over his back like a crimson curtain.

His fingers move to the front, trailing over my wetness to stop right above my already swollen clit. When he begins circling it over the cotton, I take ahold of his wrist to stop his movements. I bend down and press my lips to his in a gentle kiss. He attempts to deepen it, tongue playing at the seams, but I pull away.

"You were so good to me today, Will. So good. and I want to be so good for you, too. This one's all you," I breathe against his mouth. "Not me."

Without breaking eye contact, I get to my knees in front of him and unzip his pants. Together, we push them down to his ankles, leaving his underwear on. I tilt my head back and stretch to kiss him as one of my hands pulls him from his underwear. When I begin to nip and lick at his lips, my fingers wrap around his hard cock. I balance myself with one hand on his chest, eyes closed, enjoying the feeling of holding him in my hand, the power exchange happening right now. I'm on my knees, but he's at my mercy, and I feel it even more when, on an upstroke, my thumb touches the tip of his cock, and he almost whimpers.

The sound of him starting to lose himself does it for me. In that moment, I know exactly what he's going to ask of me, I know that I want to give it to him, and I know we're both going to enjoy it.

"Be a good girl and suck my cock," he almost growls, knotting the fingers of both his hands in my hair, moving my head down. He doesn't need to push, though—I go enthusiastically.

I moan when my lips wrap around him, when I feel the soft mushroom tip on my tongue. My mouth waters even more when I begin to move, sucking hard, cheeks hollowed, and he groans and cries out my name, telling me I've been so good and now it's his turn to come, and he's going to do it in my mouth.

"I'm going to make a mess out of you. And you're going to fucking like it."

I speed up my movements. His breathing speeds. I tighten my hold on his thighs. He tightens his grip in my hair. I moan around his cock. He groans when I feel him come, filling up my mouth. I try and swallow as fast as I can, eyes squeezed shut as I do.

It's the first time I've ever let a man come in my mouth—I've truthfully never seen the appeal and have always thought it sounded disgusting—but something about it being *Will* makes it different. As I lick my lips while I stare into his low-lidded eyes, I think I've learned something new about myself.

He exhales once, whistles, and shakes his head in disbelief. "That was some high quality head..."

We burst out laughing like two idiots. Heart fluttering in my chest, filled with pride at a job well done and something else, I stretch my neck up to kiss him on the lips. It starts off slow, playful. But I'm still on my knees in front of him, wet and needy, and hearing him lose control has made it even worse.

He knows me, though. So he helps get me to my feet without breaking the kiss. And as he bites my bottom lip and tugs at it, he finishes removing his underwear, kicking them and his pants off without ever letting me go. He pulls away to take off his sweater, and together we unbutton his shirt at the speed of light. Once we're done, Will throws me on my mattress and flips me onto my stomach. Before I even know it, my face is buried on a pillow, my ass in the air, slip all the way up to my waist.

"Will!"

He crawls up over me, kissing up my spine until he reaches my neck where he places a soft bite. "I got you," he whispers against my skin. "You know I fucking do."

He's got me.

He moves away and the loss of his body heat is painful. I need to feel him—his weight, his scent, *everything*—just to breathe. Finally, his hands come over my cheeks and he parts them. But I've never felt more exposed. My legs shake as I wait in anticipation for what he's going to do, for what's waiting for me. I can tell he's on the verge of losing control—and I want that. But I understand his hesitation.

His hands tighten around me and suddenly his tongue is there, running down the length of my pussy to my clit, his entire face buried in me from behind. I scramble to grip my sheets, my pillow—*anything*—searching for some sort of purchase before I melt into a puddle on my bed. He comes at me with more enthusiasm and hunger than I've ever felt from anyone before in my entire life. The way he tightens his grip on my hips, the way he makes himself more comfortable between my legs like he's found his true home, his favorite place in the world, have me crying out his name into my pillow.

Desperate. I'm desperate. Desperate for more. Desperate for him to stop because it feels too good. I'm desperate for him to keep doing this forever for the rest of our lives. It's light and darkness and silence and noise and pain and pleasure all at once. It's everything I've ever wanted and everything I've managed to avoid.

My skin buzzes with the perfection of it all.

I feel my legs begin to slip, and Will notices, grabbing me by my thighs now, pushing my legs a little closer to regain some stability. "Just a little bit longer," he says before groaning into my pussy. "Just a little longer. I need you to come at least a couple of times like this before I fuck you."

I fist my sheets, moaning his name as I lose the ability to say a single word. The noises he makes as his tongue presses against my clit, two fingers deep inside, tapping at that one spot that makes me crazy, has me over the edge after just a minute. When I come, my neck snaps back as best as it can and if it weren't for Will's strong grip, I would've certainly toppled over. But he's relentless, his tongue a champion performer, his grunts and growls the ultimate dirty talkers, and even though his fingers are doing a phenomenal job, they are reminders that when he does get to fuck me, it'll be even better.

"It's all good. It's all so fucking *good*," I manage to somehow moan.

His dark laughter against my pussy raises goosebumps on my overheated skin. "*Yes*. Yes it fucking is." And without another word, he sucks my clit into his mouth, a steady rhythm building in coordination with his fingers that has me coming soon after it begins.

I'm poured honey on my bed as I slide down onto my mattress, exhausted and more than satisfied. Every nerve in my body is a live wire, too sensitive to be touched. But Will doesn't hesitate, flipping me onto my back as if I were nothing more than a plaything of his. And I love it.

He kneels between my legs, pulls my slip off. And when he finally comes over me, Will licks the sweat off my body in one straight line from my bellybutton to my collarbone. He runs his tongue over my erect nipples, stopping to bite and suck and play for a moment.

"...perfect fucking tits, covered in sexy freckles... wanna fuck them so bad and..." he mutters, too low for me to fully understand, utterly lost in my body. He's not talking to me, anyways.

I close my eyes and relish in feeling this wanted, in feeling this need I have for him be matched. His lips keep roaming, tongue keeps flicking, teeth keep biting.

"Are you on birth control?" he asks suddenly. "Because I need to come inside you."

He *needs* it—simple as that. And who am I to deny him his needs?

"Yes," I say with a nod. "Yes, I am. But—"

"I'm clean," Will rushes to clarify. "I haven't had sex since my last physical. You?"

"I got tested after finding out my ex cheated, and even then we always wore protection. And haven't been with anyone since then. Except for you, of course. So... I'm good."

The dark and intense look in his eyes, a clear sign of hunger, is replaced by a soft smile for a moment, only to transition into one of determination. He kisses me and, in its urgency, it's messy and wet and barely even a kiss. But his lips are there just the same as he lines his cock up to my entrance, pushing in just the smallest amount. I hiss, because even just the tip of his cock is wide enough to have me straining—especially after everything he did to me earlier today and just now.

Will catches me wincing, kisses my brow, and whispers that he'll start off slow to help me get used to it. But that once he gets started, he says, "not sure whether I'm gonna be able to stop. To fuck any other way than I want to fuck you, Bridget. And it isn't tender and quiet and soft. Not now. That's not what I want now." He pauses to kiss my temple, inching just half an inch more. "Maybe later, when I've calmed down. When I don't feel as wild as I do now. Okay?"

Eyes squeezed shut, I nod helplessly, my body feeling too empty, needing him more than I've ever needed anything. He kisses me once more, on the lips this time. Will takes a deep breath and tells me he's going to fuck me now right before he pushes in to the hilt, making me cry out in surprise, pain, and of course, pleasure.

It's a tight fit—just like it was the last time. But it feels incredible in an overwhelming, life-altering, joyous way.

Will moves over me, his hips delivering on his promise—a ruthless, steady rhythm that has me pulling my legs up to my sides to give him more room, wrapping around his waist and scratching at his back as my nails seek for purchase. I try to keep my eyes open, to watch him over me, to memorize every detail of this moment, but it's impossible—I'm too overwhelmed by it all. The way he kisses my neck, the words he speaks in my ear, how he fills me inside, our combined scents filling my lungs, the taste of his sweat on my lips, and the knowledge that this is happening with Will—*again*—is almost too much to bear. I fear for one moment that I'm a second away from actual combustion —but the way things are going, it doesn't sound as horrible a death, really.

When one of his hands comes up to rest at the base of my throat, I can't stave it off any longer, losing all sense of control. Will's name bounces off my apartment's walls when it leaves my lips in a loud moan. Once he feels me begin to pulse, I know he's at the end of his line, too. Will's movements grow choppier and faster, he grits his teeth and squeezes his eyes in concentration.

He growls and tells me how many times he's thought about this in the last few weeks: "At least once every half hour, Bridge. At least that." His breathing grows ragged, his words no longer make any sense, and when he finally presses in as hard as he can with his hips, I feel him empty himself inside me, gasping for air as he does.

WILL

It's fucked up, really. Downright diabolical.
Will thought karma had found him by way of this awful job—this
purgatory where he had agreed to suffer until he didn't have to
anymore. He didn't know this purgatory was just setting the scene for
the actual payback the universe had planned for him: meeting her,
falling for her, which would all lead to the inevitability of losing her.
The pain of that was bound to be destructive.
It doesn't matter to him, though. Not really. Not as long as he gets to
experience the good parts first. Surely the memories and experiences
will end up outweighing the costs. Til then, he's in, very much along
for the ride, in any capacity she'll take him for.

23

MY NAME IS BOND. JAMIE BOND

Lena calls me into her office a few weeks later, the urgency in her voice apparent. "Now. I need you in this office now."

I run after her, phone and notebook in hand, my heart racing a little. It's been a while since we've addressed the giant Prada bag in the room—Jenna's betrayal—and I wonder if whatever it is she wants to talk about is related to this. Did she finally find a way to give me the recognition I deserve? Did she find a way to make Jenna pay? Or are we just generally screwed?

"Shut the door and take a seat," she says, motioning for the chair in front of her desks. When we're both seated and calmer, she finally speaks. "I've managed to receive a last minute invite to a work event tonight, and I need you to come with me. I know it's Friday and you probably have plans, but you need to cancel them."

I frown, confused. "Okay?"

"Okay? What do you mean *okay*?"

"I—Well, I thought you were going to tell me there's been some progress with the whole Jenna thing. That you'd figured out a way to..."

"To what, Bridget?" She raises a brow, her eyes shooting icy daggers at me.

"I... don't know, honestly." I sigh, because I *don't* know. What is there to do? I just kind of hoped she would know.

"I told you to leave it to me. And tonight is part of that. I found a way to get invited to Stevenson's anniversary party. It's always this huge gala, and this year it's going to be at the New York Public Library. Dinner, dancing—the works. They're going to be honoring their new CFO. I want to use that opportunity to talk to our clients and yes, maybe undercut Jenna by giving them more attention than she ever could. She doesn't know anything about the account, she doesn't know the ins and outs, and she sure as hell isn't coming up with the golden ideas. But she's recycling everything we say, which means the client thinks she's so devoted to them. I want to go to this party and show up for them, make nice with the buyers and the higher ups, show our faces so they can begin to associate us with this project and not Jenna—or even Sartoria for that matter."

I blink at her, processing her words. "I don't understand."

She sighs and blushes, like she knows her answer will be embarrassing. "I want us to be the girl you can't avoid. I want to make ourselves unavoidable and constantly available. And while that would sound kind of pathetic in the dating world, I don't think standard dating rules apply here. When it comes to sales, I think the opposite is almost always true: playing hard to get becomes a problem, and making yourself constantly available is how you succeed."

I shake my head. "I'm confused. We already signed this deal. We just need to finish it. What are you talking about making ourselves—?" Realization hits me in the chest with the full force of a train. "You mean *us* as in *you and me*?" Did she mean eventually cutting out Sartoria & Co. altogether?

She swallows once. "We just need them to associate this

project with *us*—Lena and Bridget—and no one else. That *we* manage the account. But all while staying hungry; not thirsty." She brings her index finger to her lips in a silent *shh*, looking around in every direction as if there were cameras all around us. "Later."

I nod. "So what's the plan?" I ask in a whisper.

"The plan is we go to this party tonight. We schmooze. And we pull their attention to us. I want to get more info on what Jenna's been feeding them. And I want you to try and find her assistant and bond with her, too. It'll be just you and me—I checked with Jenna's assistant, and she said she was otherwise engaged tonight, so it's a perfect time."

"Okay. Done."

"Do you need a dress for tonight? We might have some black tie dress samples in your size in the closet you could borrow."

My eyes widen, breath catching. "The sample closet?" *Act cool. Act cool. Do not freak out. Do not blow this. You are just a few minutes away from living out your movie montage makeover fantasy.* "I... Yes, I would love to borrow a black tie dress for tonight."

"Okay, then. Tell Marina from product development to give you something—not too boring and not too sexy, please. We don't want them to think you're matronly or a Kardashian."

I snort and nod before leaving her office, walking with purpose to the elevators. While I wait, I text Will:

BRIDGET

Lena's got me on some super secret mission for work, so I'm not gonna be able to hang tonight.

AFTER WHAT HAPPENED BETWEEN US THE NIGHT OF HIS MOM'S birthday party, Will and I had decided that denying the intense chemistry between us was a bit ridiculous. It was obvious there was a spark there, and we both enjoyed more than each other's company.

"We're adults," I'd told him as we'd lain naked in bed, his fingers trailing a path up and down my spine. "We can do this just for fun, right?"

It was a pathetic attempt by me to have whatever part of Will he'd be willing to give me. If I couldn't have his heart, I could at least have his friendship and body, right? The silver-lining of it all?

He didn't look as enthused by the idea as I thought he would —and it stung. "You mean do a friends-with-benefits thing? Are you sure?"

Did he think I couldn't handle myself? That I wouldn't be able to separate sex from romantic feelings for him? I half wanted to tell him that of course I could. After all, I'd fallen in love with him way before I ever laid eyes on him.

"I'm sure." I stretched to kiss Will, to taste him and reassure him that I was in it. "You're kinda my best friend. And also the best sex I've ever had."

This made him laugh, even made his cheeks flush a little. He slinked an arm around my waist and brought me closer to him. "Ditto. And ditto."

"So let's do this."

"Alright," he grinned, though his smile didn't reach his eyes. "What are our rules? We gotta have some rules, right?"

I paused to think, scanning his face for every minute change in his expression, searching for... something. But his face had slipped into a comfortable poker face.

"I don't know," I said finally with a shrug. "I just know I enjoy doing this. Maybe the rule is we keep doing this until we stop enjoying it? Simple as that?"

He bent to place a soft kiss on my shoulder, raising goosebumps on my skin. "I can do that. But what about exclusivity?"

Every muscle in my body tensed, though I tried my best to play it cool. I took a deep breath to regulate my heartbeat before answering to the best of my abilities. "I don't think... I don't think I'd be able to do this if you were still sleeping with other people."

"There are no other people, Bridge." His voice was soft, eyes intense.

"Then why did you ask?"

"Because I wanted to know whether there were other people for *you*. Whether *you're* seeing other people."

"Oh. Well, I'm not seeing anyone."

He smiles. "Well, alright then. The rules are we're exclusive, and we stop doing this once it stops being fun and/or we want to start seeing other people."

"Deal."

And with that, we'd agreed to continue our friendship—and added some serious benefits to it.

Our friendship has remained the same—we still text often, support each other, and hang out all the time. Only now, some of his messages have turned spicy (again) and whenever he comes over, we often end up in bed—or the shower or kitchen counter or the floor or against my damn front door.

Ginger has gotten attached to him, too. Will bribes her with treats and cuddles every time he comes over, and honestly I don't blame her. There's no way anyone could resist a good cuddle from that man. When Will sleeps over, she nudges herself between us if we're spooning, purrs loudly the second he pets her.

We're both head over heels for Will Jacobs and I can feel the danger of it. But I still can't help myself.

Maybe a night away from him will be good after all.

WILL

Oh, yeah, Jamie Bond? You out to kill someone
or something, 007?

I SNORT, GETTING INTO THE ELEVATOR WHEN IT ARRIVES.

BRIDGET

Or something

WILL

It's fine. I was actually going to text you
anyways. I forgot I had plans already

BRIDGET

Awww, Will. You don't have to make something
up just so you don't sound as lame, you know?
That makes it even more pathetic.

WILL

LOL.

Call me when you're done with your mission?
Maybe we can still meet up

BRIDGE

Will do

WILL

K. Talk then

IDIOTICALLY, I BEGIN TO TYPE *LOVE YOU* BUT CATCH MYSELF JUST IN time and delete it in a manic panic. The horror of the moment distracts me from realizing that I've made it to my floor, a virtual shopping center of the most incredible dresses—some samples that never went into production and some that became our clients' bestsellers.

I look around the floor, slack-jawed in disbelief. Like a whole department store floor to myself. I know in a heartbeat this place is going to find something for me.

"COME ON, GINGER. PLEASE EAT. WHAT'S GOING ON WITH YOU?" I groan, pushing my baby's food bowl towards her in an attempt to tempt her. She sniffs at her paté, loaded with beef Churus (essentially just cat GoGurt, if you ask me) to tempt her even more. But she just walks away, jumps on her chair, and curls up with a giant sigh.

Anxiety rips through me as I stand in the middle of my apartment in a huge red floral print taffeta dress with a high slit and black heels. Ginger barely picked at her breakfast this morning, but I thought she was just protesting how I'd given her the same meal three times in a row. So I gave her some treats instead, assuming she'd eat when she was hungry, and went to work. But she won't eat now, either, and it's killing me.

"At least have some water?" I ask, kneeling in front of her chair, placing the water bowl by her, doing my best not to ruin this dress.

She lifts her head and laps at the water a bit, which eases me a little. Maybe it's a virus. Maybe it's nothing. But what if it's something horrible?

My phone vibrates for the eighth time in the last thirty minutes. I would bet my life that it's Lena again asking where I am. I considered telling her the truth, but I'm not sure "my cat is sick" fits the list of acceptable reasons to skip out on work events (or is this a work sabotage? I don't even know anymore).

With a sigh, I place the food and water bowl near Ginger's chair and kiss her on the head, right between her ears. "I'll be home as soon as possible, okay? Like, sooner than as soon as possible."

But she doesn't reply, of course. Doesn't even look me in the eye.

Something about it doesn't feel right, but I ignore my instincts.

With a deep breath, I grab my phone from the bed and stuff it into my clutch before heading out into the chilly spring night.

When I get to the New York Public Library, Lena is out of her mind angry with me. Thankfully, we're in public, so she reels it in, the vein in her forehead close to bursting.

"What the hell took you so long?" she hisses, pulling me by the arm into the hall. "You missed the presentation and the awards. I told you we need to be everywhere."

"I know, I'm sorry. But my cat—"

She heaves a sigh and stops to stare at me. "It's fine. You're here. Go get yourself a drink and scan the party for Iris. If you see her, text me. I'll do the same if I find her first." With that, she turns on her heels and disappears into the crowd.

Checking she's out of sight, I head towards the bar because, if I'm going to endure the rest of this night, I'm going to need a cocktail. And a strong one at that. It's a work event, and of course I need to focus, so I remind myself to keep my drink limit to one. But when I'm hit with a familiar scent at the bar, my whole body tenses in anticipation, head swims with it. Because I would know that orange blossom and vanilla scent anywhere—even surrounded by a crowd.

WILL

Every time he thinks there's no possible way she could be any more beautiful, she ends up outdoing herself.
Her beauty truly is unmatched.
Her heart is one in eight billion.
Bridget Quinn is all he's ever wanted.
And she's here.
Fuck.

24

I LOVE NEW YORK. AND YELLOW CABS. AND YOU.

The image is so impactful, it does something to my soul. Such a welcome surprise. Such horrible timing. Still, how funny is it he's here? Though I shouldn't be surprised—it is the company he works for, after all.

When he sees me standing there, his laugh catches in his throat and he chokes, eyes widened in shock. "What are you doing here?" he sputters.

I take a physical step back, shocked by his reception. "I—I told you. I had a work thing."

He sets his drink down at the bar and mutters some good-byes to his... colleagues? Bosses? I'd say friends, but they all look to be at least twenty years older than he.

"This was your work thing?"

"Obviously."

"But it's a Stevenson thing. You didn't think to tell me? Since I work for the company after all?" His voice is light, but something in his eyes has me unsettled. What the hell is going on?

"I wasn't aware I needed to ask your permission to do my job, Will. Plus, you had originally said you had nothing to do so I didn't think you were going."

He rubs a hand down his face and sighs. "Sorry. I realize how dumb I sound right now. Like I'm questioning you or something. I'm just surprised, is all. I didn't expect to see you here. This isn't something lower-level employees from the company or our vendor's companies usually attend."

"Well, it must be different because you're here tonight, too, right? And I'm just here as Lena's date."

"Oh."

"Yeah."

Something about his less-than-warm reception gnaws at me. Contrary to his reaction, *I* would've been happy to have him here. It would've meant bonding over how much we hate work events. We could've talked endless amounts of shit about our bosses and coworkers together. Without ever spilling too many corporate secrets to each other, that is.

I roll my eyes and wave down the bartender, who looks me over appreciatively before grinning and leaning over to meet my eye.

"What can I get for you, darlin'?" His southern accent is thick, his blue eyes shining bright. If I weren't head over heels for the irritating guy standing next to me, I swear I'd be giggling just from his smile alone.

Will's body tenses at my side, but I ignore him, choosing instead to order a glass of champagne. By the time the bartender brings me a full flute, he still hasn't apologized. I thank the bartender and begin to walk away, only to have Will stop me by gripping the upper part of my arm.

He drags me to the side of the ballroom behind a column, hidden away from the rest of the guests. "I'm sorry. That was rude of me. You caught me off-guard, is all."

I refuse to meet his eye, keeping mine instead on the marble wall across from us. He moves to stand in my eye-line, forcing me to finally look at him.

"Seriously, I'm sorry. I get nervous at these work things because my boss is here, and he's the worst and utterly unpredictable, and you look amazing, and I was blindsided. I'm here solely for work and I swear the first thing I thought of when I saw you was how fucking gorgeous you look and how much I want to take you home. I never would've thought that the worst thing that could happen tonight was to have you here as a distraction, but there it is."

I raise a brow. "Really? The absolute *worst* thing, William?"

The corners of his lips quirk up a bit. "Barring an alien invasion or a humanity-ending meteor? Yeah, kinda."

"You're such a drama queen," I say before taking another sip of champagne.

I roll my eyes, but when he moves to stand closer and his scent envelops me, I find myself losing the little amount of strength I'd built up. I stumble a little in my heels, but he catches me with an arm around my waist, my back to his chest.

"You do, you know," he whispers in my ear, his body pressed up against mine.

"I do what?" I struggle to answer.

"Look incredibly beautiful. You always seem to top yourself, and I have no fucking idea how you're able to do that."

I scoff, but my cheeks blush, and betray my fake nonchalance.

He smiles and glides his nose up and down my neck, inhaling deeply as he does. "You're wearing that perfume of yours," he murmurs. "You almost always wear it, and I miss it so much when you aren't around. When I think about it..." He inhales again against my cheek. "When I think about it and you aren't there, it's like my lungs seize up, paralyzed from missing it."

I squeeze my eyes shut, thankful he can't see me—and no

one else can for that matter. Because it's one thing to have sex with your best friend, but is this part of it, too? The way he speaks to me, the things he says, and the way they make me feel? Is this normal friends-with-benefits behavior?

I have no frame of reference for what we're doing, which sometimes makes this whole thing seem impossible. But then I turn in his arms and stare up into his dark eyes and feel that superhuman tug on my heart. And I know. I know I could never leave him. I know that, no matter how much this hurts me, I would never be able to stop this. It will have to be him. Because with everything happening, Will's my silver lining. And if I don't have him…

My free hand rises to his chest, my eyes following the way my manicured fingers travel over it. "You look good in a tux."

I don't see his wicked smile, but I *feel* it. That's how attuned to each other we are.

"Thanks. You should see me out of it."

This makes me snort. So I surrender and look up, a little thrilled by the way he looks down at me, the way he has me a bit cornered against this column. "Your jokes are unoriginal."

Will laughs softly in my ear. "You love them anyways."

I love you.

I close my eyes and let myself inhale his perfect scent just once. Just enough to hold me until the next time we're together. I let it fill my lungs and heart and brain; let it run through my veins, build beneath my skin like it's the fuel that keeps me going. And in a way, it is.

Finally, I'm able to get myself together. And that's a good thing because I'm at a work event and flirting with the man I've been sleeping with for the past few weeks. I'm supposed to be doing my job, but he's driven me wild to the point of distraction. A clear head is my priority. Or it should be.

"I have to go back to work," I tell him with an involuntary pout.

"Ah. This secret mission of yours. I'm not sure what you think you're going to find here, but if you guys are thinking of stealing some jewels or something, you've got the wrong gala. Maybe try one in a museum?"

I laugh and slap him on the shoulder. "I can't tell you what the mission is."

Will leans against the marble column with one hand and brings the other to push some hair off my face. A chill runs down my spine, and it isn't because the marble is cold. By the smug smirk that flashes across his face, he notices.

"Why's that?"

"We talked about this, remember? We agreed to separate work from this friendship. Besides vague venting about bad days and bosses and asshole coworkers, no details. Neither one of us wants to compromise the deal between our companies. Even though it's not like we have any decision-making level authority."

"You told me about your VP stealing your idea. How is this any different?"

"It just is."

"Are you sure you aren't just making up some excuse because you somehow found out I was going to be here, and you *really* wanted to see me in a tux?"

I press my lips together to keep from smiling. "You don't look *that* good."

It's a lie, of course—the first one I've told in a long time. Because he looks like heaven and hell combined.

"Well, how long do you have to be here for, anyways?" He checks his watch. "Because I've been here long enough that I can Irish exit the shit out of this event, and no one will care. We can go back to your place?"

Spending a Friday night with Will in any capacity is always tempting, but after seeing him in this suit, it's nearly impossible to resist. Still, I'm here for work, and that's important to me.

"I don't think tonight will be possible. I have a really important job to do." I try for my best #Girlboss voice, putting my hands on my hips like Wonder Woman.

He beams at me with the smile he uses when he's being supportive and proud, when I'm pursuing my passion, and he's there for me. "I think that's good, then. We can see each other tomorrow. But I'm going to need you to wear that dress again just so I can see it come off you."

I laugh and shake my head. "You're incorrigible. And you're —" My phone vibrating in my hands cuts me off.

LENA

Iris left and Jenna's here. Abort. You can go home now. DO NOT LET JENNA SEE YOU. I've already left in an Uber.

"Shit."

"What is it?"

"My mission has been aborted."

He raises a brow. "I thought this whole thing was cute at first, but, like, you don't *actually* think it's like a secret mission, right? You're not, like, raiding the New York Public Library, right?"

I roll my eyes and push him out of the way, checking my surroundings for Jenna.

"Wait, where are you going?" he asks, following me closely behind.

"Home."

"Why are you whispering and crouching? Doesn't that make you look more suspicious?"

I stop dead in my tracks and look at him because he's absolutely right.

"Let me take you home the way I usually would if you weren't acting like a total head case right now."

I snort and let him lead me toward the exit with a hand on my lower back, exposed thanks to my backless dress.

When we find a cab, Will gives the driver my address and turns to look at me.

"I'm so happy to see you," he tells me.

And something about the way his eyes shine in the darkness of the car gives me hope that it isn't the possibility of sex that has him excited. That he's actually glad we're spending time together in any way.

"I was genuinely bummed today when I thought we weren't going to get to hang out."

I bite my lip to stifle a grin. "You're just saying that because you wanted to get laid," I whisper, hoping the driver can't hear, but between the partition and his loud music, I'm confident he's in his own world.

Will's smile slips, brows pulled together. "You really think that's the only reason I ever want to see you?"

The city lights zoom past us as we drive down Sixth Avenue, and I stare quietly down at my hands. "I... don't know. Maybe."

"Bridge, hey." Will twists in his seat and reaches over to cup my face. "Look at me." When I do, he shakes his head, eyes soft. "You know that's not the only reason why I want to hang out with you, right? It's not even the main one."

"I—I don't know. Sometimes—"

"No. Never. Don't *ever* think that. You are..." He exhales once, frustrated.

And I get it. I *am* frustrating. He shouldn't have to deal with a needy friend with benefits. FWB are meant to be fun and relaxed. And I feel anything but that right now.

"I *care* about you, Bridget." His eyes lock with mine, causing all the air from inside the cab to disappear. "I care about you and, while I thoroughly enjoy fucking you, I would give it up in a second if it meant not seeing you ever again. We're friends, Bridge."

Friends. Friends friends friends.

"Yeah." I swallow. "That's nice to hear. Sometimes I get a little freaked out, though. That I'm going to lose you."

Will's brows pull together. "Believe me, you're the only one with the power to end things."

I snort, but his face remains serious.

"I mean it. I'm not going anywhere. I'm in this."

"Yeah. BFFs, right?" I shake my friendship bracelet (which I never take off) in front of his face and try for a laugh, but it comes out mangled.

Will makes a sound that's halfway between a groan and a grunt before wrapping a hand around the nape of my neck. One second, we're next to each other in the back of the cab; the next, I'm somehow sitting across his lap, our lips fused together, my fingers deep in his soft hair.

Will holds me steady with one hand, while another travels freely over my body. He starts off at my neck and bare shoulders. Trails a hand lightly over the side of my breast, his thumb reaching out to subtly touch me right over my erect nipple through the luxurious fabric. I suppress a moan when his fingers pinch me right there, because I love the way he turns me into putty in his hands, but I *really* don't want the driver to kick us out.

It's not the driver I should be worried about, though, because it's Will who puts a stop to it all of a sudden.

He pulls away and holds my face in both of his. "Stop. This is

—" He exhales and shakes his head. "This is the complete opposite of what I'm trying to prove. I don't want to be a part of your life because of how amazing our sexual chemistry is or how hot you are," he whispers.

"You think I'm hot?" I can't help the dumb, goofy grin that spreads across my face.

Will rolls his eyes at me. "Bridge, you know I'm a goner for you. I mean, my fucking god, look at this slit." One of his hands comes over my exposed thigh, his rough hands moving dangerously close to where I'm wet and waiting for him. "It's killing me. This dress, the heels. It's all killing me. I barely stand a chance when you're dressed in those cute sweats of yours, and I'm supposed to just act normal when you have the most delicious thigh sticking out like that?" He shakes his head. "No, Bridge. I mean, yes, I'm supposed to act normal, but it's hard. Literally." Will pushes his hips up, and I feel his cock—just like he said, it's *hard*. And waiting for me.

I laugh into his neck before pressing a kiss there. "You're kinda adorable, William."

His arms wrap around me so tight, I whimper a little. He kisses my shoulder and whispers "You're kinda my everything, Bridget."

I pull away to meet his gaze, a stinging building behind my eyes. "Don't say it like that."

"Say it like what?" His voice is soft, but his confusion heavy.

"Like..." I sigh, my eyes studying his face. *Like you have feelings that go way deeper than friendship. Like you're right there with me.*

But I refuse to say it out loud. To bring the subject up. To even mention a hint of the possibility that there might be anything other than friendship blossoming here. Because what if I'm wrong? What if I'm so wrong I go back to being alone?

I can't. I can't lose him.

"Bridge?"

"Nothing. Like nothing, Will." I force a smile, but Will isn't buying it.

"Listen, Bridge. I think we need to have a serious conversation. Things have changed and—"

"We're here. Cash, credit, or tap?" The cab driver interrupts us.

WILL

Tonight.
He'll tell her tonight.
He needs to tell her tonight.
She needs to know he loves her tonight.

25

NO, BECAUSE SHE ACTUALLY ALMOST SCARED ME TO DEATH

"Fair warning, my apartment's a mess," I tell him once we finally make it to my place.

He laughs softly in my ear, his hands on my waist, chest against my back. "It's always a mess, Bridge."

"Why don't we ever go to *your* place?" I ask Will as I struggle to open my front door. I can barely get the words out, much less go through the whole process needed to get inside my apartment, as his lips trail up and down my neck. I can feel his impatience on my lower back, hard and eager, so I push my ass out into him.

He groans and whispers my name, causing a burst of electricity to run through me. When he bites the spot between my neck and shoulder, I shiver and he laughs.

Whatever it was he was going to say before we were interrupted by the cab driver must be far from his mind, because his hands have not stopped touching me since getting out of the car.

"You have Ginger, remember? We can't just abandon her," he reminds me.

I smile at his use of the word *we* until I realize something. *Ginger*.

My heart sinks to my stomach because she's not insistently meowing on the other side of the door when I slide in the keys, scratching and howling for me to come in and feed her. In fact, it is eerily quiet in the apartment.

"Oh my god." I shake Will off and focus on getting the door open, kicking it and jiggling it just like I'm supposed to.

"Wait, what's happening?" he asks, but I'm barely processing his words because once I walk into the apartment, I catch Ginger snoozing on her chair. But she doesn't lift her head to look at me, doesn't open her eyes—doesn't even move.

"Oh my god" I cry again, feeling the start of tears trail down my cheeks. I kneel in front of her and gently pet her head, which earns me a quiet meow—barely even there—and one open eye.

"Is she okay?" Will kneels beside me, petting her back. There's a sense of urgency in his voice I would find adorable if I weren't in a state of panic.

"I need to get her to the emergency room. She's been sick, but I thought it was just a virus or something. But she looks worse. This is bad."

I get up and kick off my heels, pulling on a pair of flats as I frantically search for her carrier in the back of my closet.

"Which animal hospital do you want to take her to?" Will's phone is out, his face pulled into a concentrated frown. He looks so serious right now. So authoritative.

Protector.

Partner.

Safe place.

"I can get us an uber."

"What? No. It's almost midnight, Will. This could take hours."

"I'm not letting you take Ginger to the emergency room this late at night by yourself."

"I can take care of myself." I would sound more convincing if my voice wasn't trembling through tears, my face probably already red and blotchy.

I'm a mess.

He cups my face with one hand, and takes the carrier from me with the other. "I know you can, Bridge. That doesn't mean shit, though. I want to come. For you and for Ginger. I care about her too." Hearing those words is what finally breaks me down—I let myself burst into tears. Will immediately drops the carrier and takes me in his arms.

"I'm scared. I love her so much. Aside from you, she's my best friend in the whole world." I sob once against his tux.

"I know, Bridge. That's why we need to get going so we can help her get better."

"WHAT IS TAKING SO LONG? THEY TOOK HER BACK TO TRIAGE, LIKE, half an hour ago!" I whisper-yell at Will from the waiting room as I pace back and forth. It's past midnight, and I'm feeling more exhausted than I think I ever have in my entire life.

"Calm down, Bridge. They know what they're doing. I googled this place, and they're the highest-rated emergency animal hospital in New York." Will's still wearing his tux, though his bow tie is in his pant pocket and the top two buttons are undone.

I take a deep breath and sit beside him on the uncomfortable waiting room chairs. Closing my eyes, I lean my head on his shoulder, cuddling deeper into his side when he wraps an arm around me.

Just as I begin to settle, as my breathing begins to slow, I hear a man's voice: "Ginger Quinn's parents?"

I rise to my feet so fast, I stumble a little. As usual, Will is there to catch me. He slips his fingers between mine and leads me to the front desk where a James Bailey lookalike in scrubs with a clipboard waits for us.

"Are you Mr and Mrs Quinn?" He asks, a sympathetic smile on his face.

I blush a deep crimson. "N-No."

Will looks mighty uncomfortable as he explains: "We're not together. It's her cat."

Ouch. Just what I needed right now.

"Right." The vet turns to face me and sticks his hand out. "I'm Dr. Sloane. I'm your cat's vet. We've already checked her out in the back, and I know you spoke to our triage nurse already, but would you mind stepping inside this room with me for a chat?"

I swallow and nod, following the doctor into a small room off the side of the front desk with Will in tow. Once inside, I explain how she's been lethargic, how she hasn't wanted to eat or drink much in the past 24 hours.

"Not even those gross cat GoGurts that they make that she's so obsessed with."

Will gasps at my side, because he's gotten to know Ginger well by now and knows just how much she loves them.

"Have you noticed her go into the kitty litter often but not produce any urine or poop?"

"No. I work all day and haven't been home to notice so—" The words get caught in my throat as I realize what a horrible mother I am, leaving my cat behind without supervision. "God, I fucked up." I put my head in my hands and try to calm down. I feel a hand on my shoulder, but I don't need to have my eyes open to realize it isn't Will.

I slowly raise my head to look at the vet, whose eyes have grown soft. "It's going to be okay, I promise."

I turn to look at Will for some reassurance from him as well, but find him a bit too preoccupied. Distracted by the hand currently on my shoulder. It's as if he were doing everything possible to invoke any kind of superpower that could incinerate Dr. Sloane's hand off my body without hurting me.

Honestly, if I weren't so upset, I'd probably find it hot.

"So there's nothing wrong with Ginger? She's going to be okay?" The hope in my voice is dangerous, I realize, when the doctor's smile slips.

"She will be. But she has a urinary blockage. A pretty bad one and quite rare in female cats. But then again, I get the feeling your cat is unique." He tries for a smile, and I want to make a comment about her being part of the small percentage of female cats who are ginger, but can't bring myself to.

"If we don't operate now to drain the bladder and do a urine sample to find out what's going on, something bad could happen."

I gasp, my heart in a sprint. "Okay. Yeah. *Yes*. Whatever you need to do, we'll do it."

"Good. I just need to warn you before we proceed with anything of how much everything will cost. But you have pet insurance, correct?"

For the second time today, my heart sinks with fear.

"I—I only just got health insurance for *myself* a few months ago..." I admit, starting to cry again. "And that was through my job."

His face twists in worry, and he drops his hand from my shoulder, which is fine by me because it frees me to lean into Will's chest. He wraps an arm around my waist, and asks the doctor for an estimate.

"All in all, it could be anywhere between eight- to twelve-thousand dollars."

"*American* dollars? *Human* dollars?" I practically wail.

"This is just an estimate, though. It could be less."

"It could also be more?"

He swallows and nods. I try not to cry even harder. I don't have the money, but Ginger is the most important thing in my life right now, and I'll do anything for her. Even if I have to sell a kidney.

Will tightens his grip on me before he begins rubbing soothing circles on my back. "Do you offer payment plans or...?" he asks. And thank god for him, for his ability to keep a cool head.

"Yes, we absolutely do. You'd have to speak to our finance department once we have a final number and pay a minimum deposit of two-hundred dollars now, but yes. I'll need you to sign this form as an acknowledgment of the possible expenses." He taps on the clipboard before passing it to me.

I exhale, a bit more appeased, and take it from his hands. My credit will make whatever payment plan they offer impossible (thanks again, Roger, you self-serving prick), but there's nothing I wouldn't do for Ginger. She's the only family I have left.

"Done," I say when I wrap up my signature and hand him the clipboard back.

"Great. I'll go back and hand this over to reception and then we'll get to working on Ginger. In the meantime, I'd suggest you go back home and get some rest. We'll call you when we have an update."

"Thank you, doctor."

With a kind smile, he shakes both our hands and walks back through the double doors he came from.

In silence, I tap my debit card to the reader, praying it goes through. Once the two-hundred dollars are paid, we're dismissed. Will calls us a cab and we ride back to my place where I fall asleep in his arms while crying softly into his shirt.

When I wake the next morning, it's because my phone won't

stop ringing. For a split second, I consider throwing it out the window. But when I'm flooded with memories of last night, I fumble around my bedsheets for my cell, noticing that Will is nowhere to be found.

"Hello?" I ask a little breathlessly.

"Is this Bridget Quinn?"

"Hi. Yes, this is she."

"Bridget, hi. This is Dr. Sloane. Declan Sloane."

My heart erupts in a sprint as I clutch the phone to my ear, bracing myself to hear whatever comes next. I'm over pleasantries, but I realize my cat's life rests in this man's hands, so there's nothing I can do but bear it. "Hi, Dr. Sloane. Do you have an update on Ginger?"

"Yes. I'm calling to let you know everything went fine. We emptied her bladder and did a study. Turns out that she had some crystals in her urine, and they were causing the blockage and pain. She had a high fever, but we were able to get it down, and she's stable now. Did you happen to change her diet recently? Because that might be a factor as to why this happened."

I sniff, realizing only now that I'd started crying again. "Not really. I don't know. I mean, I did start giving her these new dry treats, but they're super popular. I didn't find anything on the internet that could lead me to believe they were bad for her. *God,* I'm a terrible mother."

He laughs softly over the other end of the line. "You're not. These things happen. And she's going to be fine, so no worries with that."

I exhale, the weight of the world suddenly off my shoulders. "I'm so relieved to hear that, you have no idea."

"I'm happy I was able to help. Really. Ginger is a beautiful cat. As beautiful as her owner."

Uhhhh... What?

I choose to ignore his comment. After all, my cat is still in his custody. "Now that we've got the good news out of the way, could you tell me the bad news?"

"The bad news?"

"The final number? On the bill?"

"Oh, uh—" He coughs. "I was able to waive most of it, and we were off by a lot from the initial estimate. So you really only have to pay about one-seventy more, I think."

I pause. "What?" Is my luck finally turning? After spending all night crying into Will's chest wondering how I was going to afford it, how much I hated my ex for ruining my credit, and how impossible it was going to get a reasonable interest rate from their finance department, I wake up the next morning and the problem vanishes?

There's a silence over the other end of the line as if he's considering saying something.

"What? What is it? You're making me nervous, doc."

"Please. Call me Declan."

"Uh. Declan."

"I just... am going to be extremely unprofessional here, but... Are you seeing someone, Miss Quinn? Bridget?"

I nearly drop my phone. Did he seriously just—?

"Um."

"Because if you aren't..." Is this really happening? "I would love to take you to coffee." His voice is tentative; cautious. Like he knows this is as insane as I think it is. We've only spoken about my sick cat, and based off of *that* he wants to go out on a date?

"I... would need to think about it." But it's a no.

WILL

He would've paid ten times the price. More. He would've emptied his bank account for her. Because what good is it to have all this money if you can't use it to at least help the people you love? Or their cats?

THE DOCTOR WILL SEE YOU NOW

The receptionist at the animal hospital shoots me a look when I pay the remaining balance—such a small fee in comparison to what I was initially quoted.

When I ask how they were able to manage to lower the price of the final bill considering how much imaging was done and the kind of procedure they had to do on Ginger, she winks and whispers, "Well, I'm not supposed to say, but just know you have a secret admirer." She smiles and hands me my receipt as I frown.

Dr. Sloane did this? He covered the cost? Did the work pro bono?

Shit, should I have said yes to the date?

"Is... Is the doctor still here? I'd like to talk to him, if possible." At least to thank him.

I place Ginger's carrier on the counter. While my legs and ass are toned from living in a walk-up, I don't have the upper body strength to lug a twenty-six pound cat everywhere without a break.

"Did the vet tech not give you clear enough instructions for your cat's post-visit, dear?" she asks, her voice soft. "Because, if so, I can ask her to come back and—"

"No, no," I quickly stop her. "She was fantastic. I was just wondering whether the vet was still here, so... so I can thank him?" This is so awkward, but I should at least say thanks. If the initial estimate was a minimum of eight grand, and I only had to pay for less than four-hundred...

She smiles and gives me an *I get it now* look. "Oh, I see. He should be. He was pulling a double tonight. Covering for a friend. He's such a *nice* man." She gets up from her seat, the fondness in her voice genuine. "Let me get him for you."

I thank the woman and wait, but set Ginger down on a chair.

After just a few minutes, Dr. Sloane comes out with the receptionist in tow.

"Bridget." His grin is wide and genuine. His five o'clock shadow is very much present and the bags under his eyes make it obvious he's been here far longer than he should be. Even so, his eyes seem to light up when he sees me, his whole demeanor perking up.

"Hi, Dr. Sloane. I just wanted to thank you for everything you did for Ginger. For going the extra mile, too."

I look to the side, checking the other patients in the waiting room or the receptionist aren't listening in on our conversation. I don't think cutting every patient a discount is something he can do all the time, so I don't say it outright. No need to start a riot.

"Honestly, it was no problem. It's clear you really love Ginger, so I was happy to help." He looks at her carrier, a fond smile on his face. "And even though she may have given us a little attitude for a moment there, she's super charming."

I laugh softly. "Yeah, *charming*. I don't know about that, but she's sure got some personality."

He smiles and sighs. "So... Have you—" He swallows and

clears his throat. "Have you given my proposal any consideration?"

"Your proposal?"

Shit.

His tired smile is hopeful, enthusiastic. Almost as handsome and perfect as Will's. "The coffee date? I'd love to take you out. It could honestly be a five-minute water one, even. I think I can prove to you I'm not a creep in four, and then we can enjoy the remaining minute planning our next date." His grin is sexy, his confidence unshakable, and maybe I'd find it all charming if I weren't so down bad for my best friend, a man who appears to be very okay with our friends-with-benefits situation. With it never evolving into anything more.

And maybe I've reached my limit. Maybe I need to follow Will's advice and stop settling for the silver lining. Because here's this perfect man—attractive, smart, funny, likes animals—and I'm turning him down because I have feelings for a guy who didn't care enough to stay the morning after this whole thing happened? Who just disappeared and hasn't called since, despite knowing how traumatic this whole experience was? Sure, it's only six am, and he's probably sleeping or something. But waking up without him after everything that happened, given how close we are, was unacceptable.

It's clear he's never going to care for me in the same way I care for him. And it's also clear I need to start moving on. So why not start with this vet?

And it's for that reason, and for that reason alone, that I say "How about dinner?"

GINGER AND I SPEND THE WHOLE WEEKEND VEGGING OUT, cuddling in bed, watching reruns of our favorite dumpster fire reality TV shows. We indulge in snacks—chocolate for me, cat GoGurts for her—and nap often. We also spend the entire weekend ignoring Will Jacobs's texts and calls—which proves to be much simpler than I expected. Turns out, outrage is a great motivator.

After scheduling my date with the vet for next weekend, I decide the best way for me to help myself get over Will is to completely cut him out of my life. And while it's a horrible thing to do, especially without having a conversation about it first, it was even worse of him to disappear for almost twenty-four hours. Which is exactly what happened.

I don't get a single text or missed call from him until early Sunday morning. *Sunday.*

By then, I'm still unsure of my decision to go on a date with Dr. Sloane—*Declan*—the following Friday. But Will's almost relaxed text message asking me how Ginger was enraged me. So I cut him off.

All week, I've been ignoring his texts, sending his emails into my trash bins, and rejecting his calls. I don't read the messages, and I don't listen to the voicemails. I know it would be easier to block him, but I still can't make myself do it. You don't fall out of love with someone just because you're angry at them, and while I'm making progress, I'm not able to carve him out of my heart just yet.

It's difficult and takes nearly every ounce of energy that I have, but I manage to get away with it. I manage to listen to what my heart is telling me: it's time to move on and let go.

It's what I keep reminding myself of as I put the finishing touches on my makeup for my date with Dr. Sloane. We're not going anywhere fancy—just his favorite Mexican place on the

Lower East Side—but it's the first date I've been on in almost a year, if not more, and I want to put some effort into it.

When my apartment intercom buzzer goes off, I freak, though. The doctor is ten minutes early, and I am far from done. My hair is still a mess, and I have my left cat eye to complete, which isn't something you can do in a few seconds. It takes time. Dedication. Complete silence and concentration. Maybe even a prayer here and there. One does not simply slap on a cat eye. Not if we want it sharp enough to kill a man.

With a sigh, I press the buzzer and tell him, "I'm not ready yet, so can I buzz you up? I'm sorry, but I think you're like ten minutes early!"

He doesn't reply, but I hear the gate open through the inter-com. I unlock my front door and leave it cracked—a risk in this building, but whatever—and run back into the bathroom to finish getting ready.

When I hear the front door open and close, as well as the sound of male footsteps walking into my apartment, I call out, "I'll be ready in a sec and then we can go!"

"Who are you talking to?"

My hand freezes mid-*swish* of my liner at the sound of Will Jacobs's voice. This, of course, results in a cat eye that rivals the mask of any member of The Incredibles team.

I gasp quietly, my whole body tensing.

"What the fuck is he doing here?" I whisper to myself.

"Uh, you know, your bathroom door is open. And this apart-ment is kinda small—*really* small, actually. So even your whis-pers are pretty audible. And I think you fucking know why I'm here or you wouldn't be frozen like that, unable to even face me." It's clear by his voice that he's angry with me. And honestly? Who can blame him? I did something really horrible. I ghosted him. That's not something nice people do.

I haven't been nice.

I drop the eyeliner on my small counter, completely forgetting about my horrible makeup, and exit the bathroom to find him standing by the door, looking absolutely delicious. He's in a suit and tie, which makes me believe he came here straight from work.

He's working late again? On a Friday?

I grimace, wanting to chastise him for the hundredth time for not putting his mental health before work but then realize: Jeez, I've got some balls when I'm probably contributing to some of that stress.

"I—I'm sorry. But I can't talk about this now."

His lips press together, his hands fisting at his sides. "You can't talk about this now? Seriously?"

I clear my throat and check the time on the oven, silently begging to universe to somehow keep Dr. Sloane occupied until I can get rid of Will.

"I... I have to finish getting ready."

Will looks me over slowly, as if drinking me in, wanting to absorb the way I look. Something about the desperation in his eyes makes me want to burn his expression into the side of my brain.

"You look so fucking beautiful," he says in a gust of a breath, like he tried his best to keep it in and failed.

"Thanks. But you need to go." I clear my throat once. Swallow twice. "I... I have a date."

He sucks in a breath. The look in his eyes is almost... devastated. But it makes no sense. None of this makes any sense.

"A date? What do you mean you have a *date*? With who?"

"With... Dr. Sloane."

"Who the fuck is—" His eyes widen in realization, the anger and horror clear on his face. "*The fucking vet?* The fucking vet who hit on you while I was right fucking there and *touched* you? *He* asked you out? And you said yes? To *him*?"

Now *I'm* upset. I put my hands on my hips and take a step toward him, fire running through my veins. "I know it's hard to believe anyone would want to date me, William. But yes, he did ask me out. And yes, I did say yes."

He squeezes his eyes shut and pinches the bridge of his nose between his fingers. "Why did you say yes? I thought we agreed to do this friends-with-benefits thing exclusively."

"Well, you disappeared Friday night, and he asked and he was really nice and stuff with everything he did for Ginger, so I said yes. You were gone the next morning without a single word, so I just figured you wouldn't care."

"You figured I wouldn't—? I— I was *so* exhausted. I had been working like an insane person that entire week—you *knew* that. Then I had that event—which you also knew about since you were there. And I stayed up all night while you cried yourself to sleep, trying to make sure I heard your phone in case they called. I only got about an hour's worth of sleep before I had to wake up to run an emergency errand. So I went and did what I had to do, then decided to go home to shower and change—I was still wearing that tux, if you remember—fully intending to check up on you after. I was desperate to know how Ginger was doing and how I could help, but I fell asleep immediately after my shower, as soon as I sat down on my bed for a second. I've been working myself down to the bone lately. For Christ's sake, I was so tired I slept for almost fourteen hours straight and—" He stops mid sentence to take a breath, almost angry. "I didn't mean to disappear. That was a mistake, which I tried to correct. Yours was intentional. And it's the *second* time you pull something like this. The first sign of trouble and you cut and run."

I press my lips together, unsure whether I believe him. "Fine. I'll agree that what I did wasn't nice. But we agreed this would stop once we decided we wanted to see other people or this stopped being fun. This is me wanting to see other people," I lie.

I don't know how I get the words out without them shaking even a single time, but they do. They sound like those of a determined, strong woman—the complete opposite of how I feel. Deep down, I know that I'm weak and fragile, because if he pushes just a bit, just the smallest amount, he might be able to convince me to go back to our original arrangement. It would rip me to shreds, but I'd do it. Just to be near him. Just to have any piece of him.

God, I'm pathetic.

He looks at me and narrows his eyes. "Is this you thanking him for taking care of Ginger or you wanting to see other people?"

"I-I—Both? But why does it matter? You and I aren't—You— And *he*—Plus, he didn't just *take care* of Ginger. He also managed to get them to lower the cost of my bill. Remember that estimate? Well, it went from eight-thousand to almost a total of four-hundred dollars. He was kind enough to do that."

Will's nostrils flare, his pupils black. "He fucking told you *he* was the one who got you a discounted price on her treatment? And *that's* why you're going? Did he make you feel obligated to go on this date to pay him back for his alleged help?" he practically roars, his face redder than I've ever seen. "Because you don't owe that guy a fucking thing, Bridge. You don't owe anyone anything. Not even if they somehow cover your vet bill." He wipes a hand over his mouth, eyes a little manic.

I shake my head. "It's fine. He's a cool guy and—"

"You like him?" he cuts me off. "Can you stand there right now and tell me you like him?"

I shrug once. "He's nice."

"High praise," Will deadpans.

I roll my eyes and cross my arms in front of my chest. "He also happens to be successful and handsome and charming and smart and into animals. So."

"Okay, well, I'm all those things, too. So why not me? Why not me, Bridget?"

I stop breathing and drop my arms. And jaw.

My heart races in my chest, trying to catch up to his words.

"W-What did you just say?"

Will swallows once, eyes wide, the whole world on his shoulders. So beautifully devastated, my love.

He steps toward me and takes my hands in his, kissing each one before speaking. "Why. Not. Me? I'm here. And I have been *aching* to be yours for fucking *months*, Bridget Quinn. And five seconds after meeting this guy, you decide *he's* the one who gets to break through to your heart? I've been trying to chip away at this shield around it, trying to find my way in since the beginning of time, it feels like. And I was fine just being your friend, I think. Friends who fuck was even better. But I can't be your friend if you're with someone else. I can't see you with him or hear about you together and be okay with it. To play second fiddle to some guy who will never get close to deserving you. Because you are just that amazing, Bridget. I can't see anyone deserving you. Not even me.

"But is that why you ghosted me? Because you decided you liked this guy?" Will's grip tightens around my hands, desperate, like he's afraid if he lets go I might float away. For good. "Am I so easy to dismiss?"

"Will," I whisper, "what are you talking about? Of course you're not. You're the most important person in my life," I confess.

"Then why the ghosting?"

"I... don't know." It's all I can manage to say, the storm of emotions moving too quick and wild for me to pin down a single thought.

He stares at me quietly for a moment, his eyes bloodshot as he rolls his lips before nodding once. "Okay," he says, dropping my hands. "Okay. If that's what you want, I'll let you go. I just want you to be happy."

"Wait, what is even happening? Can we go back to what you said before? What do you mean you've been trying to chip away at my... what was it? The shield around my heart? What do you mean?" I realize my voice has reached a tone of desperation that is almost comedic, but his words don't make sense because... "Wait, wait, wait. Are you saying... Do you have feelings for me?"

Will rolls his eyes at me. Classic. "I just told you I did. And I've *been* telling you for months. In actions *and* in words. *Yes*, I fucking have feelings for you. Of course I fucking do. I am *desperate* for you, Bridget Quinn." His hands come to my waist, fingers digging into me in that way they always do when he holds me there.

Desperation is such an accurate choice of words to describe the pain and yearning of being with Will but not *being* with Will.

"I... but I do, too. Have feelings for you. And I'm desperate for you, too." The stinging in my eyes becomes nearly unbearable before I feel the first tear on my cheek.

"Then what the fuck are we doing, Bridget?" he asks, slinking his arms around my waist, pulling me in so tightly I can barely even breathe. Though maybe it isn't the way he's holding me that's keeping oxygen from flowing into my lungs. Maybe it's the fact that my heart is so full there's simply no room for it in my chest cavity. Maybe this love has grown so large there's no room for anything else.

"I don't know what we're doing. But I know what I don't want to do." I sniff, my hands traveling up his shoulders to link my fingers behind his neck.

"And what's that?" He kisses away a tear, and then another.

"I don't want to be friends-with-benefits anymore. Or friends. I mean, we can be friends—I think it would be nice to be friends with your partner. But I don't want us to be together as anything other than being a couple. I want to be your girl-friend and I want you to be my boyfriend."

It's a risk to use the proper terminology before we've even been on a single official date, but in the spirit of not settling and being overtaken by the joy of this moment, I decide going for broke is the only way to play this. If there ever were a time to put it all out on the table, it's now.

For a split second, my stomach tightens in knots, and the fear of rejection begins to wash over me. But then, Will's smile turns into something truly blinding, filling every corner of my being with light.

"I wholeheartedly agree with everything you just said." He leans down to press his lips to mine, holding me tighter than he ever has before.

When I sink into the best kiss of my life, I realize he doesn't know I'm not going anywhere. The way he grips me to him is almost like he's scared someone will snatch me away from him any second now—or that I'll run away. But Will doesn't realize that this is it for me—I'm already his. And I can't let him go a second longer without him knowing. So I tell him with the way I press myself into him. I tell him by reaching up higher on my tiptoes to get to his lips better. I tell him by moaning when I feel his tongue swipe against mine and his dick harden against my stomach.

He moves down to kiss my jaw, trailing kisses down my neck, pushing my top's strap off my shoulder, exposing it so he can nibble and kiss there.

"You're so beautiful," he groans into my skin, his voice gravelly as he speaks. "You're always so fucking beautiful, but tonight is one of those nights where it hurts to even look at you."

Suddenly, I realize something in horror. Will moves back up to kiss me again, but I stop him with a hand against his lips. "I have a date tonight."

He pulls back, expression fierce. "What? No, you fucking don't. Unless it's with William Jacobs and it involves a bed and lots of sex and great takeout, no you fucking don't. You need to cancel."

I sigh. "*Obviously* I don't want to go on this date with Declan—"

"Dr. Sloane." he interrupts, clearly not enjoying the familiarity.

"—and I'm obviously going to cancel when he gets here but he's due any minute and—"

The buzzer on my intercom goes off, and we freeze. I look up into Will's eyes, into the pool of melted dark chocolate I could throw myself into, and he stares back down at me.

"You need to go, Will. You can't be here."

"If you think for one fucking second I'm going to be okay with this, then—"

I sigh. "Of course you won't. Because I wouldn't either. I just need to..." I begin to pull away, and for a moment, his grip tightens, unwilling to let go. But after half a second, he reconsiders. "I need you to leave, take a couple of walks around the block. When you come back, he'll be gone, and we'll be ready to start something new. The *right* way."

"I don't want to leave you alone here with some other guy and—"

"Will." I peck him once in an effort to silence him, and it works. "You were right. I don't owe him this date, but I do owe him some respect. As a human and as the man who saved Ginger's life." We both turn to look at my cat, who watches our interaction from her seat. "I am not going to do this in front of you. It wouldn't be fair to him."

Will exhales deeply once and nods. "It gets harder to leave you the more I know you, is all."

I smile and kiss him on the cheek. "Ditto."

WILL

It's been three blissful weeks of Bridget and Will. Sure, Bridget and Will have existed before. Independently. Then as friends. Then as friends-with-benefits. But never as a unit. As Bridget-and-Will. As something said almost in the same breath, one word, one meaning. Three weeks of the same things they had before, without hiding the way they feel about each other.

Everything is ten times better. Everything is ten times more visceral. Everything is her.

Will hasn't been this happy in... He can't remember how long. Certainly not since his mother's accident and maybe even long before then.

And while he's aware it could all come crumbling down any second now, he knows he only needs to last a few more weeks. Then, it will all be over. All the stress, all the hiding, will be done. He won't have to watch what he says, and will be able to just... be.

He knows he's an awful man for not telling her yet, but he's just protecting her. And protecting them.

Shit, who the hell is he kidding? He knows he's mostly protecting himself.

27

TWENTY-FIRST CENTURY LUXURIES

"Such a good girl... you're *such* a good girl." Will's whispered voice breaks through my sleepy stupor, a slow, lazy smile spreading across my face. I snuggle deep into my covers and continue to pretend to sleep while my boyfriend (yes, you heard that right—we started calling it what it is) praises my cat and gives her treats.

Three weeks ago, Will and I decided to finally come clean about how we feel about each other. Since then, we've been together nearly every free moment we've had. Sure, I had to break up with Dr. Sloane first—or whatever the hell it's called when the guy actually shows up for the date but you reject him before you even go out on it—and it was awkward AF. Though I have to admit, he was a super great sport about it.

"I should've known," he said after I informed him I couldn't go out with him.

I told him Will and I had *just* had a talk about how we felt about each other, and it turned out we wanted to explore that. I wanted to be as honest as possible. In a city full of grifters and fuck-boys, Declan Sloane was an outlier—a good guy. He deserved the truth.

"The way he looked at you... the way you looked at him for support. I should've known. Especially after the whole—" He waved his hand vaguely in the air and shook his head. "Never mind."

I grimaced, feeling the bile rise in my throat because I am an *awful* person. I mean, who agrees to go out on a date with someone when they have feelings for someone else? Horrible people, that's who.

But once he assured me he understood the situation, and I apologized for the third time, I told him he seemed like an extraordinary man who any person would be lucky to have. Dr. Sloane smiled and hugged me, wishing us both the best of luck.

It was all very civilized.

I don't really know Dr. Sloane, but it was nice to get *someone's* blessing for our relationship. After our argument, Molly and I hadn't exactly been on speaking terms. Besides team meetings we were forced to attend together, we hadn't shared the same space in a while or said more than a passing "Hello." She was avoiding me, and I refused to allow a "friend" to treat me like a joke. And since I was no longer the going out type, my other friends from before Roger were nowhere to be found.

Besides Will, lately, I've been feeling like my close friend circle has dwindled down to... Well, no one, actually. Once I began to ghost Will, Loneliness became my constant companion.

I'm glad he's back in my life. But more than that, I'm glad that he's back in my life the way that I want him in my life. *Not* as my pen pal. *Not* as my best friend. Not even as my friend with amazing benefits.

He's in my life as my partner, and I've never been happier.

Ginger purrs loudly from the foot of the bed where I watch through one eye as a shirtless Will smiles down at her. They look completely enamored with each other, which makes me fall deeper for him still.

Ginger hated Roger. Ginger hated all of my exes, actually. But I have a feeling she'd go to the ends of the earth for Will. I have a feeling she'd give up her favorite banana catnip toy for him.

"Your mommy and I love you *soooo* much," he tells her, his voice slipping accidentally into baby talk. I melt into the mattress—I'm sure of it. "We love you *soooo* much."

I can't help it any longer. I sit up and crawl toward him, wrapping my arms around his waist from behind.

"Good morning," I whisper in his ear before pressing a kiss to his neck.

I sense his smile when his hands come over mine, holding me to him. "Good morning."

"Are you trying to buy my cat's love?"

He scoffs. "No need to. I already have it."

Ginger jumps off the bed and retreats to her chair, giving us space.

I snort and kiss him a second time. A third. Suck into the place between his shoulder and neck. When he moans my name, a shot of heat courses through my entire body.

My hands begin to travel over his abs down to where I can tell he's already hard and waiting. But he catches them before I meet the waistband of his pajama bottoms with a groan.

"Baby," he begs, his breathing growing ragged. "I can't. I have to go in early today. Remember? I told you."

I sigh and let go of him, throwing myself with a frustrated huff back onto the mattress.

With a laugh, he crawls up my body, raising his undershirt that I wore to bed as he goes. With every inch of skin he exposes, he places at least one kiss. When our bodies line up perfectly, Will places a soft peck on my nose, drops his forehead to mine.

"I'm putting in my notice today," he whispers, his eyes tight, brows pulled together.

I gasp, pushing us both up to sitting positions, my shirt riding back down. "Are you serious?"

He nods and runs his fingers through his hair, looking out the window briefly as he settles onto his heels.

"But... I mean, how long have you been thinking about this? It can't be that long, since I'm just finding out. Maybe you should take some time to think it through. I know you're tired and have been working some crazy long hours, but you should probably find another job before and then—"

He takes my hands in his and places a soft kiss on my lips to cut me off. "Bridge," he starts again. "I've been thinking of doing this for a while—just been waiting for the right time to leave. I'm sorry I haven't told you. But we've been trying to separate work from our personal life, remember? We agreed not to go into too much detail."

I nod once before he continues.

"Honestly, it's overdue. Things are crazy, my boss is insane and borderline abusive, and I don't like the practices they set forward in their everyday business operations."

I raise a brow, intrigued. "What do you mean? If they're doing something sketchy, you need to tell me because Sartoria & Co. shouldn't—"

He laughs once, rueful. "See? I couldn't go into much detail because it would've caused potential conflicts."

"Will, if Stevenson is doing anything illegal—"

"It's nothing like that. They're fine, and your company isn't at risk working with them, other than that they're extremely diffi-cult—but I'm sure by the number of orders you'll receive it's bound to pay off. Somehow." He sighs before continuing. "Hon-estly, it's more so that they're greedy. And the new corporate structure values margin and profit over reputation and morals—

I'm sure you've seen it in the email exchanges and the one meeting you were at. And I mean, I get it. It's a business. The entire point is for them to make money. But I feel as though there should be *some* shred of integrity in what we do, right? Like, there should be a point where you stop trying to stretch the margin."

I understand his frustration—but only to a point. I've only seen the cost-cutting, profit-hungry side of Stevenson from our side, as vendors. I haven't experienced the day-to-day demoralization of employees through new company policies that sully their brand name. But I believe it because the attitude is there. The frustration is evident in every single email response from the client, in everything their Chief Merchandising Officer and her team says and does. Iris insists it's the higher-ups putting pressure on them, which tracks with everything Will tells me.

He lets out a groan and throws himself on his back, staring up at the ceiling.

Sensing he has more to say, I remain quiet and let him take a moment before he continues.

"I hate the constant battle of putting out shitty products and doing layoffs, making people work three different jobs because we want to cut corners when we don't need to. Management thinks they're doing all this to set the company up for success but, in my opinion, all it's doing is setting it up for failure.

"Employees are unhappy, which means they care less, so their work is subpar. Turnover is increasing rapidly. The quality of our products is going down—be it because we ask our vendors, like Sartoria & Co., to lower their own standards or because we don't have as many people doing QA tests so many issues slip through the cracks. I mean, we first went to you guys to revamp our private label brand because you have an outstanding reputation for quality and sustainability. And suddenly they want to cut corners left and right, completely defeating the purpose of why we did it. Make it make sense, you know?

"And honestly? I fucking hate the job in general. I hate being the bad guy. I hate it when my boss makes me do things I don't want to do and then tells me to claim the ideas as my own. I hate what it entails. Yes, the money has been fantastic, but I'm good now and none of it is worth any of this anymore. And while, if I'm being honest, I don't have a single fucking idea what I want to do with my life, I know for damn sure it isn't this."

His eyes are wild, his breathing a little shaky. I've known he's been frustrated with work for a long time, but never to this degree. Because of our agreement, Will has kept a lot under wraps, it seems.

"How long have you been feeling this way?" I ask. "I mean, you had mentioned it before—to an extent. But how long have you felt so unhappy?"

"Pretty much since the day before I even started working there," he admits in a whisper.

I gasp. "Will. You mean to tell me that for *five* years you've hated every second of your job?"

"Yeah."

"Why didn't you leave sooner?"

Something flashes in his eyes. Uncertainty. Hesitation. "I— I made a commitment, remember. And I simply wasn't in a position to leave."

And that's Will, always loyal, no matter what. Even if it hurts him, he stays true to a fault.

But loyalty aside, five years is *a lot*. I find it difficult to believe Will wasn't in a position to leave. Did he mean he couldn't find a job? I already told him once before his intelligence and charm would make him a shoe-in anywhere. But maybe that's just my love for him talking. Though I find that very difficult to believe. Besides the occasional cover hogging,

Will has proven to be nothing short of perfect every day that I've met him.

"You could've left sooner. No one would've faulted you for it if you were unhappy."

He stares up at the ceiling, pensive for a moment. "Maybe not. But I wasn't in a position to."

"And you are now? Financially, I mean? Since I suppose that's what you're talking about."

He nods. "That's also part of why I've waited so long. I had some... stocks that officially vested this morning. Now I can sell them and put the money somewhere safe. That, combined with everything I've saved over the years should be enough to hold me for some time. More than enough. I had an unexpected big expense recently but..." He looks at me. "It was worth every penny. And I can manage for a bit."

"Huh? What unexpected expense?"

He sighs, eyes glazed over. "I just... need to figure out what's next."

I nod and lean down to give him another kiss. Softer, this time. Gentle. "It'll be okay," I whisper against his lips.

He shrugs. "I'm sure this all sounds super attractive, right? A man in his thirties who has no idea what he wants to do when he grows up?"

I snort. "Who the hell *does*? That's such a luxury, Will. Don't you think? Most of us..." I take a deep breath. "Most of us are just *surviving* ninety nine percent of the time, Will. That's why I try my hardest to focus on the good. The silver lining." I bend down and kiss him on the cheek this time.

He rolls his eyes, but there's a small smile on his face. "You and your silver lining."

His frustration makes me laugh. "Seriously. Like, doesn't it feel like an enormous privilege? Being in the exact industry you want to be—*knowing* what you want. I find it hard to believe that can exist for the majority of people nowadays."

"You seem to be in the right industry. In the right job."

I purse my lips for a moment as I think through his words. "Yes. I think I am—at least for now. I think it's the first time I feel *passionate* about something, and I'd love for it to turn into something bigger. But who knows where I'll be in a year? Or five. Or ten, for that matter. And that's a horrible thing to say, but sometimes it feels like the truest thing. We're all here, doing the best that we can. All we can do is live life the best way we know how, surrounded by the people who make us happy."

He smiles and pulls me down to his chest, wrapping me in his arms so that I can fit snuggly into that perfect nook that I've claimed as my own. "Like you?" He kisses the top of my head. Inhales deeply, filling his lungs so much my head rises with the movement.

My smile is goofy and embarrassing. "I make you happy?"

"You make me the happiest, Bridge. Always. Forever."

I press my lips together to physically keep myself from revealing how I *really* feel. How much I care about him.

LATER, AT WORK, WILL'S WORDS FROM THIS MORNING HAVE ME living in a love-filled haze. If I were a cartoon, I'd bet everything I own, every last dime in my bank account, I'd be surrounded by a cloud of pink fog with hearts in my eyes and a goofy grin slapped on my face. I'm sure I'd almost be running into anything I walk by, not paying attention to a single thing around me while a chorus sings nothing but love songs in my head.

Yeah, I've got it bad.

So bad, in fact, I don't hear Lena the first three times she calls my name from her office. It's not until she walks over and shakes my shoulder that I realize anyone is even talking to me.

"What the hell is wrong with you?" she hisses.

"Sorry, I— I spaced out."

With a roll of her eyes, she scoffs. "Come on. We need to go."

"Need to go... Where exactly?" I ask, a bit terrified by the manic look in her eyes.

"Let's take a coffee break. Outside. Coffee shop a couple of blocks away."

"Lena, what's happening?" I let her drag me to the elevators, coats left behind.

"I can't talk about this on company property. So let's go."

WILL

Few things can match the feeling of freedom. Though is what Will has truly freedom? Sure, after the agreed upon six week transition period, he'll officially be unemployed and can cut ties with the people who fill him with so much toxic energy. But the fact remains that he lied—a lie of omission, but a lie nonetheless. And while the lie isn't an issue now, it's something he will have to carry on his shoulders for the rest of this relationship—which, by the way things are going, could mean the rest of his life.

At least he hopes so.

28

IT'S LIKE GUERRILLA WARFARE—JUST REPLACE THE COMBAT BOOTS WITH STILETTOS, AND THE CAMO WITH A FLORAL PRINT (IT IS SPRING, AFTER ALL)

"You're freaking me out," I tell Lena while we wait for our orders at a coffee shop nearby.

She looks around nervously, checking our surroundings as if we're five seconds away from being invaded by aliens. Or the FBI. Or something.

"I have a plan," she whispers, despite the fact that no one from the office is around. "A plan to take down Jenna. To have her get her just desserts."

I've never really understood that expression before. I mean, dessert always sounds amazing. How is it used synonymously with justice being served?

Regardless, I sit up straight in my seat, interest peaked.

"You're finally going to tell HR? Or you're going to let me go to HR? Did you find all the evidence we would need to get her in trouble?" The need to be vindicated is clear in the speed and enthusiasm with which my words pour out of me.

Lena smiles—but something about it is unsettling. It's the smile of someone in the know, yes. But in the know of something almost... nefarious? It can't be, though.

Just a couple of months ago she agreed she had been way too

hard on people. She agreed she would be making an effort to be less harsh on her coworkers and subordinates. And she *has* been—for the most part. It's been a minute since I've seen anyone leave her office in tears. She's also kept the passive-aggressive comments to a minimum in meetings. And I know this all sounds awful, but it *is* an improvement.

I narrow my eyes at her. "What are you talking about? A plan to take her down?" I don't like this. I don't like lying or manipulating people, and something about the look on her face tells me it will somehow involve this and more.

Lena's smile falls. "It's not bad, I promise. I just mean that I've come up with a way to vindicate ourselves after what happened. Jenna made us look like we screwed the pooch in front of Stevenson's Chief Merchandising Officer and our CEO so... I came up with something. To show that she took your idea. Our ideas. And claimed them as her own. I have a plan."

I don't like where this is going. Jenna may be a shitty person, but I'm not one to fight fire with fire or to play dirty.

"What sort of plan?"

"Well, after everything went down I realized she must still be pulling the same shit she used to back in the day—especially with all the rumors flying around that corporate hadn't been happy with her in a while. Meaning, she's probably been making a lot of waves in the office with everyone, taking credit for other people's work, kissing the CEO's ass, making everyone think she's hot shit off of the work from other people's backs. And the other day she asked for me to follow through on your idea and manage the implementation process. Which, like, whatever. She's a VP so I get that she's not gonna get into the details of a project whether it was her idea or not, but you can understand my frustration. So I—"

A waiter comes by with our coffees and sets them down in front of us, cutting her off. Lena thanks him with a smile so bright, he flushes. She checks him out as he walks away with a small smile on her lips.

How diabolical can you be to be talking about revenge and get sidetracked by a waiter at a coffee shop mid-conversation?

She flicks a Splenda packet a couple of times before pouring it into her coffee and continues once the waiter is out of sight. "As I was saying, I decided to speak to people around the office, to see whether she had ruffled any feathers recently. And it turns out she has. And the people I spoke to were more than willing to work with me on this. They were more than willing to fib on a few things about the so-called implementation process to create chaos. They are much more than willing to help bring her down."

I suck in a breath, my stomach dropping. "I don't like this at all."

Lena sighs. "Bridget, it's fine. It's just a little revenge."

"You don't think that's a bit—"

"It's not a big deal, alright?" Lena snaps, her eyes blazing.

"But what's going to happen to Jenna? I don't like her, but I don't want to ruin her life. And what about Stevenson? You seem awfully sure whatever it is you planned is not going to make them angry enough to fully cancel our contract. I mean, this has all been super hard work. We're close to meeting our first delivery of items for the pre-season. And you want to risk it all at the one yard line?"

Lena rolls her eyes at me with a sigh. "Jenna will get fired and she'll find another job, but she'll be fine. We'll come out looking like heroes to the client after the clusterfuck that's currently going down now—don't check your email just yet, by the way; not unless you want to read some seriously messed up threats as a response to what's going down—"

"Wait, you haven't even told me what's—"

"—and we're not going to lose the account. I already have the fix and a plan. So many others are already on board with this. Just stick with me today and all will be right in the world."

"I... don't know what to say." I gnaw on my lip because this is insanity. What the hell? A revenge plan? And *several* people are involved? What the hell is this? This can't be normal. I know that Will often tells me I settle for less than I deserve when I focus too much on the silver lining of things and don't fight for what's mine. But this isn't right, and I'm sure he'd agree. Revenge does not seem like an acceptable response to something as mild as stealing credit for an idea. We're not saving lives here, people; we're just making clothes.

"Can I at least get some more details?" I ask. The Oscars should contact me for how cool I'm acting right now, when in reality there's a storm brewing beneath my skin.

"Of course," Lena tells me with a smile. "So, as you know, we had that plan to cut costs for the client by working with the factories and reselling materials leftover, correct?"

"Among other things," I mumble, annoyed.

"Well, obviously we had to go through the whole ordeal of adjusting our die cutting processes for our factories in Asia and creating a new strategy to resell the materials—which, *god*, is so fucking genius because it gives us even more clout around being sustainable *and* makes them even more money. Seriously, Bridget, what an amazing job."

Glad you're now going to sully it by enacting revenge.

I had chosen to let this go, to move on, and now we're back to this?

"So anyway, that's done. And we did get the pricing down quite a bit from it. But when we passed on the new HTS codes to get the correct duty on the first cost, our pricing team might've... fibbed a little." Her smile is more mischievous than any kind the Cheshire Cat could come up with. "We gave them the wrong codes, which had a *much* lower tariff attached to each material.

And to be fair, it's not an unlikely mistake. They change the damn duties and codes every couple of years—it's really annoying—and you now know that the *slightest* change in composition for an article of clothing can completely change the duty import rate." She rolls her eyes and takes a sip of her coffee as if she thinks messing with our customer's orders' Harmonized Tariff Schedule codes isn't a big deal. But of course she knows it's bad. If she didn't, she wouldn't have enacted a whole revenge plan around it.

"Anyway, so we input the orders, bought everything, started production, and now we just got notice that the duty is much higher despite our promise to Stevenson to deliver on a lower price. And we—*Stevenson*, actually—might be getting fined by the government if we don't fix it soon. And since all roads lead to Jenna not being on top of things, it will make Stevenson hate her and want nothing to do with her. Then, we'll get them to want to work with us because of all the time and effort they know we've put into their account. Jenna's time at Sartoria will be over. And our time has finally come."

I inhale a low gasp, because trying to pull a fast one on customs is incredibly bad. And finding out they have to pay more after everything we've gone through is going to be the last straw for Stevenson. I doubt they'd be down to stay with us after all of this. To be honest, Lena's "solution" sounds more like a delusion than anything else.

"But we negotiated based off of that new duty number. And this entire deal has been like pulling teeth because the finance department at Stevenson have been unreasonable dicks who wouldn't approve our prices, and when they finally do, it's because we lied? This is fucked. You're going to blow up this deal. To throw all the progress we've made out the window, Lena."

I want to cry. I want to cry because I loved this job in practice, but oh my god, what the hell? What is *wrong* with people? Betrayal and revenge plots? This isn't medieval times! It's *just* clothes.

She rolls her eyes once more. "You're exaggerating, Bridget. And you need to relax. Today is going to be perfection, you'll see. Now finish your coffee, girl. You're going to need the caffeine for what I've got planned. We've got someone's job to destroy."

IT DOESN'T TAKE LONGER THAN A FEW MINUTES FOR ALL HELL TO break loose once we get to the office. Stevenson has been emailing and calling for the past half hour, freaking out—as they should.

Lena walks away, cool as a cucumber, into her office, and I take a seat at my desk in a numbed-out state while I wait for the inevitable moment in which Jenna's wrath will rain upon us.

I don't work. I don't talk to anyone. All I do is hold my phone in my hands, wondering whether I can even text Will. This is… a serious problem between both of our companies. And while it's not my fault, I don't want to put him in a position where he would need to lie to his bosses about what went down and why. Not just because I feel the need to call him to vent and freak out. Even if he *is* putting in his notice today. It would be extremely selfish of me, wouldn't it?

And while I fight the superhuman urge to text him, I come to the realization that *he* hasn't texted me in a few hours either. Which… makes sense, actually. Maybe he's doing the same thing I am. Maybe he's trying to avoid putting *me* in an uncomfortable situation. I'm still hoping to keep my job here, after all.

I jump with a start when the two front doors of our floor

burst open, a seething Jenna walking through them, calling out for Lena at the top of her lungs. She can't see her yet, so our lovely VP misses the smirk on my boss's face as she hears her approach. My blood runs cold because I know shit's about to go down.

I watch Jenna stalk toward Lena's office, a murderous look in her eyes, right as my phone rings.

"Can you come in, please?" she asks, without so much as a greeting. "Pretty sure we're about to get bombarded by a few questions. Need you here to field them, to be a witness in case HR is involved, and to hold a united front."

"I..." How exactly did I get *so* involved in this revenge plot? Why does Lena need *me* for this? I mean, aren't I a junior employee? Why am I being used as a scapegoat? "Sure. Be right there."

Jenna and I reach Lena's office at the same time. When she looks at me, I truly wonder how it's possible I'm still alive—surely one glance from her should've been enough to kill me.

Once all three of us are inside, door closed behind us, Jenna doesn't spare another second to make herself heard.

"What the hell was that? I thought I told you to handle this whole operation. This is a massive fuck up and now Sascha is losing her mind because *she's* getting calls from Stevenson's CEO. Over a tariff problem. How the hell am I supposed to tell our CEO that we gave our client—our biggest fish that we managed to reel in but have been struggling to keep before even delivering our first season—a wildly different price for every single SKU they ordered of every single style? Do you have any idea what that means? I think you do, given how many years you've been with this company."

Lena smiles innocently. "I'm so sorry, Jenna. I thought we gave them the correct duty codes and based them off of the weight of the new, more efficient die cutting process. I guess there was some mistake there."

"I had a meeting last week with Sascha, and she asked about this account. I told her everything was handled and that I made sure our client was happy and now *this* happens? I have Stevenson threatening to not just cancel our orders, Lena, but to sue us. Unless we pay for the difference, they're going to send their lawyers after us for ruining their collection. Not to mention what this will do to Sartoria's reputation. To *my* reputation. This is a small industry. Word will get around."

Jenna's phone vibrates in her hand and all three of us look down to see it's our CEO calling. I'm speechless as all three of us watch Jenna, wide-eyed, ignore her boss's call.

"I... Are you going to get that? Because I think it'll be worse if you don't," I ask.

I. Am. An. Idiot. Why did I think it would be okay to say anything at this point? Both Lena and Jenna's heads whip in my direction to shoot me equally terrifying glares.

"You." Jenna points a very sharp fingernail in my direction. "Why are *you* here? You have nothing to do with any of this."

"I—I—" But my mind has gone blank, the only thing that penetrates my brain is the awareness that Jenna's phone has finally stopped vibrating.

"She was the one who came up with the idea *you* stole as your own. I thought she should see you finally getting what you deserve."

Jenna gasps. "So you *did* plan this."

"Of course I did." A disturbing smile spreads across my boss's face. "And it was about time, too."

Lena's phone vibrates on her desk, our CEO's name flashing on its screen. With the same smile, gaze locked on Jenna's bloodshot eyes, she answers it.

Sascha is so upset, every single word out of her mouth comes out clear as day, even though the call isn't on speakerphone.

"*—have the entire management team of Stevenson calling me about tariff penalties and fines and—*"

"*—want to know where the hell Jenna is and what you guys are going to do to make this all right. I swear to god, Lena, if we lose this client, all of you are losing your jobs. I'm giving you until end of day to get it together before we meet with HR and your time at Sartoria & Co. is over.*"

And even though Sascha never backs down, never once retreats, Lena remains constant, her expression stony and calm. And I know right then and there that she is truly, deep down, a hundred times more terrifying than Jenna could ever be.

Cold. Hard. Ruthless. That's the type of person who wouldn't hesitate to ruin someone's career. It's the type of person who would relish in it.

I was so wrong about her. She wasn't trying to be better— this is just who she is—and I'm disappointed in myself for believing in another person who ended up letting me down.

Suddenly, it's not just Jenna who's tearing up at the situation. At this nightmare.

I just want today to be over. I just want this whole ordeal to be done. I just want to be lying in bed with my cat and Will and cuddle into that space on his chest and shoulder that's mine alone and just *be*.

Jenna leaves with a huff, without saying another word, and Lena looks at me with the triumph of a ten-time Olympic gold medalist in her eyes. "We have something to finish. Let's go."

"Go where?"

"Stevenson HQ."

WILL

Will's had some bad days at work—terrible ones, actually. Truly soul-sucking ones. But they've been fewer and farther in between since he and Bridget officially got together. He's been too busy being happy to let his miserable job get to him.

But today. Today has been a royal nightmare that has rivaled every single bad day he's ever worked at Stevenson. Today, right after handing in his resignation and having to face two hours of his dictator "boss" yelling at him about shirking responsibilities and questioning his character—"Where's your loyalty, William? What kind of man are you? After everything I've done for you?"—the whole deal with Sartoriu blew up. Today is bound to rank in the top five worst work days of his life. At least his professional life, for sure.

All he wants right now is to hear Bridget's voice. To talk to her and hear her say everything's going to be alright.

It's a strange realization, but he's come to accept that she's become this core part of who he is. That by falling in love with her, she has made a permanent spot for herself in his heart that will never belong to anyone else. The simple idea of Will belonging to another person is, quite frankly, ridiculous. He will forever be Bridget's.

And he needs her now. Desperately. But there are fires to put out—for

her sake and his—and damage control to tend to. After that—after this whole fucking mess is over and after the transition period is finalized—he'll tell her everything.
He knows it's a risk, but in order to give himself fully to this, he knows it's necessary.

29

SO, THAT HAPPENED

This is a bad idea. A bad, nonsensical idea.

"I don't see how just showing up is a good thing, Lena. I mean, what if they're busy? What if they can't see us?" I ask.

Though, really, I'm just terrified of facing another person's wrath for the third time today. The more I look at people's behavior around me, the more horrified I am. I mean, is this specific to Jenna and Lena? Or is this an industry thing? If I stay in this long enough, is this who I'll turn into? And where is the silver lining in all of this? My handy little survival tool is failing me now because I can't see the good at all.

Lena scoffs as we exit the Uber, pushing a pair of oversized sunglasses over her head in the way that makes some women's hair look straight out of a shampoo commercial. Her tailored red floral dress hugs every single one of her curves as she walks in the sharpest heels I've ever seen—and they have to be sharp, since she's dressed to kill. Lena is channeling Head Bitch In Charge energy, which I'd normally respect. But not now. Not when her intention is to hurt someone and relish in their pain.

"Follow me."

I'm so caught up in the turmoil of this whole situation that I don't *really* realize I'm walking into *Will's* office until our elevator ride all the way up to the thirtieth floor—the top of the building.

"Shit," I mutter, pulling out my phone to text him as fast as I can while Lena is distracted by the receptionist at the front desk. I hear her demand to see the merchandise team, claiming "They'll know what it's about." Which, duh, of course they will.

BRIDGET

I'm sure you've become aware there's some sort of shitstorm going on between our two companies (not sure how much your boss chose to share with you), but it's so bad my boss just dragged me to your HQs.

Anyway, if you see me around, remember no one is supposed to know we're together. HUGE conflict of interest. Especially now.

Just want this day to be over so we can be together. It's been a total mess.

Also, Lena is fucking insane. Just wanted to clarify that for the record.

Also, also, I really miss you

Also, also, also, I would very much like a repeat of this morning for when you come home tonight, but maybe after a hot shower and a cuddle sesh because today has been a nightmare

WE'RE ASKED TO TAKE A SEAT IN THE OFFICE RECEPTION AREA while we wait for the team. In the meantime, I zone out, searching through my socials for my favorite cookie content creators (yes, it's definitely a thing, no matter what Will says).

Watching the way the artists flood their designs with more icing, the way their crisp lines delineate whatever image they're trying to recreate, usually soothes me. But I'm worn down and wound tight and no amount of decorated sugar cookies is going to change that. All I keep telling myself is that, no matter what, at the end of the day, I'll have Ginger, Will, and a comfortable bed —and that's all I need.

And snacks. I'll definitely need snacks after this.

"IRIS WILL SEE YOU NOW," THE WOMAN AT THE FRONT DESK SAYS before leading us to an empty conference room. "Wait here."

Once she's left us alone in the room, Lena hisses at me to hand her the folders we prepared for this impromptu meeting. Plain cream folders filled with delivery schedules, product line sheets, cost breakdowns, and some additional info Lena slipped into each one before we left. Info she's counting on to help us keep Stevenson on as a client while completely avoiding a lawsuit, she said. Lena hasn't let me in on her plan, but she seems to be channeling all the confidence of a mediocre white man, and we all know how things end up working out for them most of the time.

(They turn out well, in case you weren't clued in.)

When the Stevenson team finally arrives, I stand there, back ramrod straight, as we watch person after person take a seat with stern expressions on their faces. The last one in, of course, is Iris, Stevenson's Chief Merchandising Officer.

The room goes quiet, an eerie blanket of tension falling over us. Suddenly, I begin to wonder what kind of dark magic Lena has up her sleeve that she thinks we can get by unscathed.

Iris introduces everyone on the team to us. At first, I find the move quite polite and almost welcoming, despite her cold glare. But when I realize she's brought on one person from each department—*three* from Stevenson's in-house legal council—I realize this is far from civil. She pulled in all her best generals, ready to tell us how we messed everything up. Ready to tell us how they're going to mess *us* up.

Will isn't here to represent the finance department, but it makes sense—this is an upper management only meeting, and he was supposed to put in his notice today. There's no reason why they would call him in, is there?

Part of me is relieved—I won't have to pretend I'm not in love with the man across the table while my guard is down. It's already so hard when we're alone together. Another part of me is extremely disappointed, wanting instead to have had him here in the same room as me. I know his presence alone would've helped in this stressful moment.

"Lena, is it?" Iris asks.

Lena flinches as she realizes that her plan to make herself ubiquitous in all Sartoria-Stevenson interactions did not work. It's clear Iris barely knows her name. But still, Lena carries on with the same confidence she had when she first walked into this room, snub forgotten.

"Yes, Iris," she continues with a tone of familiarity, an air of confidence I've never seen on anyone before—definitely not in someone on the precipice of losing their job. "I know there's been a slight misunderstanding between Sartoria & Co. and Stevenson due to a minor miscommunication, but I believe we can solve this issue."

Iris scoffs and shakes her head. "A minor miscommunication? Is that what you call it?"

Lena shrugs, unbothered. "No reason to give it more importance than it deserves. Not when the solution is clear."

"And what solution is that, exactly?" she asks with a raised, perfectly filled in brow.

Lena smiles broadly. "Simple. You pay the fine. You pay the difference in pricing. And Sartoria keeps your contract as is for this season."

The Stevenson team bursts into laughter while my jaw drops.

"Is she for real? Who is this woman?" one of the lawyers asks.

"You must be out of your goddamn mind if you think we're going to do that. And who even are you again? Why isn't Jenna here? More importantly, why isn't Sascha here? She's your CEO, and she should be solving this for us."

"I wasn't done just yet." Lena gets to her feet and puts her hands on the conference room table, leaning over it, staring right at Iris as she does. "See, the thing is, Iris, Sascha isn't my CEO. I don't work for Sartoria anymore."

I gasp, my hand flying to my mouth. "What?" I whisper, but Lena ignores me.

"I've started my own environmentally conscious private label—The Green Tailor. And I'm here to show you that you need to dump Sartoria and come with me."

I blink up at her from my seat, awestruck. *What is happening today?* "This is coconuts!" I whisper-yell.

She shushes me before taking the stack of folders and passing them around the room. "I know you're wondering why you would work with me after all of this happened, but I think it's important to remember that Jenna was the one who took special interest in your account, despite my opposition to her involvement. Therefore, any mishandling of it is purely her responsibility. Anything that fell under my jurisdiction for this project has gone off without a hitch, as you can see. With the exception of pricing and duties, which she took over supervision of, all manufacturing has been perfect, all orders are scheduled to be delivered on time, and the quality of production is unmatched. All abilities I will be taking with me to my next endeavor—including connections with the best factories around. I also have a team of former Sartoria & Co. employees—all rockstars—currently submitting their immediate notices to the company, ready to take you on. We'll have other clients, of course, but we would love to be able to make you our main stars. The only catch is that yes, you would have to pay the fine that Sartoria's mistake caused and the balance between the original price quoted and the actual one. But I am ready to offer you a contract right here, right now, saying that we will pay you that amount in full in exchange for your commitment."

Speechless.

I am absolutely, positively speechless.

Is this real life? Is this seriously happening?

Talk about cutthroat.

Of course Iris is going to say no, right? She and Sascha have been friends for a long time—it was so evident in the meeting when they came over to look at the samples in our office. She would never double-cross her friend so suddenly like this. And certainly not with said friend's former employee. No person in their—

"I see." A slow smile spreads across Iris's face. "I gotta say, you've got moxie, Lena. I like that."

Is she for real?

Lena smiles triumphantly. "We're ready to take you on. And we understand that you might need time to think about it, but the offer to pay the fine and the balance is only valid until I walk out your front door. Those were my investors' terms. Other than that, there's a proposal tucked in that folder there for you to review."

Iris thumbs through the proposal with pursed lips,

surprising me by giving it what appears to be serious consideration. Lena takes her seat beside me again, a smug smirk on her face.

"What the hell is going on?" I ask her in a whisper.

"Don't worry about it," she whispers back. "All will be well. And I know I haven't looped you in yet, but I just couldn't risk things being blown. But of course I want you to come on to my company and work with me. Once we're out, I can finally tell you everything."

I look down at my hands in my lap, not knowing what to say or do. I'm flattered she'd want to take me with her, but this? This method of operation is definitely not my style. Especially not after it's been done to me too many times over. No matter how shitty Jenna acted, I would never want to turn into the type of person who schemes and sabotages and doesn't do the right thing.

After a few minutes of studying, Iris sets the proposal down on the table and squints at Lena, whose energy has not faded.

"Okay," Iris says. "Okay. But this is a conversation we need to have with a completely different team." She looks around at the people in the room and dismisses most, with the exception of two of the lawyers, someone from finance, and another from merchandising.

She then proceeds to address someone I assume is her assistant. "Please get the Liams in here. We have much to discuss."

While we wait for "The Liams"—whoever the hell they are —Lena and I sidebar quietly. Fiercely.

"This isn't right," I tell her, my voice full of conviction.

"I thought you wanted to get justice for Jenna stealing your idea." She rolls her eyes like she still believes I'm that "green" new girl who knows nothing about the industry. And while of course there's so much more I need to learn, no one needs to tell me that what just happened was wrong.

"Justice, yes. But this isn't justice. This is revenge. Justice is reporting her and getting her on probation or suspended or fired. It's not destroying her. It's not sinking to her level. Or lower. It's following the right course of action. Due process. Let the system do its job."

Lena shoots me a half murderous, half shocked look. Clearly, she never expected me to go against her.

"The system?" She scoffs. "In what world do you think you live in, Bridget? Reporting her would've gotten you fired."

"Maybe," I say with a nod. "But you don't know that for sure. And even if it had, at least I'd still be able to look at myself in the mirror tomorrow morning. How are you going to manage that?"

"Oh, I'll manage just fine," she bites back.

"You're making a mistake, Lena." I shake my head in disbelief. I can't believe I looked up to her. I should've known there was nothing beneath her hard exterior but an even harder, colder interior.

"I don't think so." She laughs once, tossing her hair behind her shoulder. "So I gather you're not joining my ranks then?"

"Thank you for the opportunity, but I have to get back to the office. Pretty sure I've just been fired, thanks to you. So I need to go gather my things."

"Don't bother," she sneers. "I got a text from Jenna before we went into the conference room that our things had been boxed up and will be shipped to us."

I scoff and get to my feet, throw my bag over my shoulder as I ready to head out. But just as I do, two men in suits walk into the conference room.

"Ah, here they are," Iris says with a smirk. The energy shifts in the room, though. The air seems to grow colder, and the tension seems to have increased on the Stevenson side, as if the rest of their team is *not* as happy to see the two men as Iris is.

Even the lawyers look terrified.

I'm so taken aback by the change, it takes a moment for me to process the two men. One of them is in his early seventies. I've never met him before, but I know exactly who he is after having done some minor research on the company when I first started: Liam Stevenson, the CEO and third-generation owner of the family-run department store. The second man is in his mid-thirties—heartbreakingly handsome, a smile that can bring me to my knees, so gorgeous and charming he can get me to do nearly whatever he wants with it. I know this because the second man is none other than Will.

My boyfriend.

Soon-to-be ex, actually.

WILL

Oh, shit.

30

THE ACTUAL BIG REVEAL

Will sucks in a sharp breath when he sees me standing in the corner of the room. I, on the other hand, have stopped breathing altogether. Every single inch of my body is paralyzed in shock. As for the rest of the people in the conference room, no one's said a word, choosing instead to wait on one of "The Liams" to speak first.

From the corner of my eye, I watch the older man squint at Will with a questioning look in his eyes. Not surprising, since the man I woke up next to this morning has gone as white as a sheet, his unblinking eyes never leaving mine. "Liam? What's wrong?"

Will blinks once before swallowing, rolling his lips before turning back to... his father? No, he mentioned his father was dead. His grandfather, then? Is that who he is?

Yes. Yes, he's Liam Stevenson's grandson. Liam Stevenson has a grandson and I know this because—

I gasp. The gala. The stupid event at the New York Public Library was for *him*. No wonder he was freaking out when he saw me. He was afraid I'd find out he's been lying to me.

He's been lying to me.

But why? What was the reason behind keeping me in the dark about who he really is? And changing his name? Why would he tell me his name was Will if he goes by Liam?

But, wait… His mother calls him Will, too, so…

Oh, god. Oh god oh god oh god.

My brain spirals as it attempts to catch up with everything. With the lies. With the misinformation. With my own damn stupidity. As soon as I begin to have one realization about what this could mean, as soon as I begin a single thought, another comes crashing over me. The shock rocks me so deep in my core, I wobble on my feet.

Will takes a step toward me, reaches out a hand to catch me even though we're on different sides of the room. His concern should be heartwarming, but it turns my confusion into anger because—

The fucking audacity.

He wants to act like he still cares about me? After clearly having lied to me since late January? You don't treat someone you care about like that.

Oh my god, it's been months, and I've believed every single thing out of this man's mouth without hesitation or question. And how dumb was that, trusting a stranger off the internet? With my luck, I should've known better. I should've known the universe was bound to send me yet another person who would ruin my life.

I feel the stinging in my eyes grow stronger, the tightness in my throat so intense I can barely swallow. Because betrayal has never hurt this much. Not when Roger stole all my money and ruined my credit, leaving me out on the street. Not when it was Molly letting me down as a friend, never believing I could achieve anything big in life unless it had to do with failure. Not Lena, for breaking my heart and turning out to be a nightmare instead of the mentor I needed. Not even when it was my own mother who used to leave me to fend for myself on her bad days, or make me have to take care of us both on her worst ones.

No. Will's betrayal hurts so much more than all of those combined. And maybe it's because of how deeply I trust him. *Trusted* him. Until this very moment, the idea of Will pulling this level of deceit was unimaginable. Unthinkable.

Honestly, if future me had traveled back in the past to warn me about this moment in time, I would've thought the craziest part about our interaction would not be proof of the existence of time travel, but that she was making these claims.

Will? Lie and deceive in such a gigantic manner?

No.

Except that he did. Except that I am about five seconds away from bursting into tears because I trusted this man with every fiber of my being. With every single one of my thoughts. I let him into every nook and cranny of my heart only for me to realize I have no idea who he is.

I need to leave. I need to leave, to get out of here and find some sort of foothold on reality because—Jesus Christ, what the hell is going on?

Will stands by the conference room door, blocking my only exit out. There's no question that, in order to get away from him, I'm going to have to go through him, and it will take every ounce of strength in my body to fight him if he asks me not to go. But it's a necessary evil, since I don't think I could stand to be here a minute longer.

"I—" I begin to address the room. "Excuse me, I have to..." But I never finish my sentence as I power-walk toward the conference room door and walk out, pushing myself in between Will and his grandfather—the Liams.

Once I clear the door, I start running and don't stop.

I don't stop when I hear him call my name.

I don't stop when I reach the front doors of their offices.

I run like a madwoman to the elevators and wait impatiently, praying that for once in my life—once in my entire fucking life—luck will be on *my* side.

I hold my breath and only release when the elevator dings and the doors begin to open. I practically jump into the elevator and frantically punch the lobby button. But despite my best efforts, Will still manages to jump in right before the doors close.

"Bridge," he says, devastation clear on his face. "Bridge, I'm so fucking sor—"

"*Do not*," I cut him off, my voice breaking as tears begin to stream down my face. "Do not even *try* to apologize," I hiss. "You've been lying to me for *months*. And for what? Some sort of fucked up corporate espionage thing? Just so you could get information and have the upper hand in negotiations? I mean, Jesus, all that talk about corporate greed this morning was just talk, then. I guess I never expected it from the guy I fell in love with." I shock myself—and Will—for revealing that last piece of information in such a careless manner. But his betrayal has finally cracked me open and there was no way to keep it in anymore. "Guess that guy doesn't exist, though."

Will rears back, eyes widening. "What? No! No way, that's not what happened. Not at all. We were—we fucking *are*—real. Realer than anything I've ever had in my life. I was not using you."

"Really? Because it kind of looks like you were. On *several* occasions we went into detail on pricing, did we not? Even though we agreed to try to keep work talk to a minimum. Yet you still used me to get whatever scraps of information you could."

"That's ridiculous! I absolutely did not."

"Throughout the entire development of this season's collection, we've been getting pushback from *your* company's finance team. They've been making my team's life impossible. And guess what? You are the literal head of that department. *You* were making my work harder than it had to be."

"It was my job, Bridge. It was my job to make sure we got the highest margins, and it's not like I *wanted* to make your work life miserable. These weren't my decisions. They were—" He groans. "None of that matters. None of the work shit matters. What matters to me is that you know that this is real. That my feelings are real. And I'm still me. It's still *us*. Give me time to explain. I was—"

But just as he begins to spew whatever excuse he could muster up at the drop of a hat, the elevator dings and the doors open. Immediately, I sprint out, my heels clicking and clacking on the marble floors. Will is on my tail, calling out my name, begging me to stop. But I'm so close. I'm so, so close to the revolving doors, to the streets of New York, to catching the first subway outta here. Except my shoes weren't made for running and I'm an absolute klutz, so I wipe out in front of everyone, falling face and wrist first on the ground.

Of course, because why would the universe let me get away with at least a single shred of dignity? Why wouldn't it give me the chance to leave with my head held high after the chaos I just witnessed happen before my eyes?

For what feels like the hundredth time in an hour, I ask myself, "Where is the silver lining in all of this?"

The tears are hot as they stream down my face, no end in sight. I've finally hit my limit, I think. So I surrender and sit on the floor, cradling my left wrist to my chest with my right hand. I never lie, it's true, but I tell myself that most of these tears stem from the pain shooting up and down my wrist and hand, and not because my heart feels like it's been torn to shreds and my mind has been put through a blender.

My eyes are closed as I softly sob in the middle of this cold lobby, but I sense Will's warmth and scent—so familiar to me now—as he sits beside me on the marble floor.

"Does it hurt?" His voice is honey and sweetness, and I want to seek comfort in it.

But I don't trust it or him—or even myself, for that matter. After all, I'm the one who keeps getting myself into these situations with the wrong people.

It's clear that I'm the problem, here.

"Yes," I whisper back. "Yes, you hurt me."

His breath hitches. "I—I meant the wrist. But... Yeah. I know." I can hear the pain in his voice, and I resent it. He doesn't get to feel pained over hurting me.

Finally, I gather enough strength to open my eyes and look up at him. Through my tears, his face is blurry, but I can still see how deep his regret goes as he looks back at me.

"You lied to me," I whisper.

"I didn't. I just didn't clarify a few things."

I scoff at the audacity, but he at least has the decency to look miserable as he says it.

"Lie of omission, then."

Gently, he takes my injured wrist in his hands and examines it. "It's swelling up, Bridge. We need to go to a doctor. Or at the very least we need to ice this immediately."

I pull it back, wincing in pain. "*I* need to ice it immediately. Back home. In my apartment. Alone."

"Bridget, please. Just let me take care of you. We can go to my place—it's just around the corner—and we can talk. Baby, we can talk and I can explain everything and you can yell at me and call me an ass—because I am. I know I am. But please, come home with me and let me explain everything while I take care of you and—"

"Stop. Just... Stop. Will—or is it Liam?—I really don't want to hear it right now. Just let me go home. Let me have this." The exhaustion and heartbreak must be clear on my face because Will's eyes grow glassy, his brows pinching as if in pain.

After a moment, he nods. "Okay. Okay, Bridge."

"Okay."

Will presses his lips together, as if searching for the perfect words to make this better, but we both know there aren't any. At least not now. Maybe not even ever.

"Can I at least take you? Make sure you get home okay?"

"It's fine," I tell him when he tries to help me to my feet. "I'll take the train, and it will all be fine."

"What? No. You can't take the subway like this."

I snort. "Well, I'm certainly not going to take a cab. It's almost four o'clock—the start of rush hour—so there's no way I'm going to be able to find one now. And if you're worried about the fact that I look like a tear-streaked lunatic, no one on the subway is going to be shocked by a woman crying in their car. This is New York. It'll be like any other Tuesday afternoon on the F train."

"I—" He hesitates, struggling to speak. "I actually have a car service. Which we could take. To your apartment, if you'd like."

I gawk at him. "*Car service*? Just how rich are you?"

"I'm not rich." He groans, looking away in embarrassment. "The car service comes with the role of CFO. Which is new. Or *was* new, since I put in my notice today. My grandfather wanted me to use it during business hours so people think I'm hot shit or something. But I only use it for trips to and from work."

"Nepobaby." I scoff again and he flinches. "Is it a limo?"

"It isn't a limo," he says with a frustrated sigh. "But it does come with certain... amenities. One of which is a fully stocked minibar and ice for drinks. Which means if we take my car, we'll be able to ice your wrist on our way to your place so we can talk."

"*I'll* be able to. *I'll* be able to ice my wrist. Without you."

"Bridge—"

"You can't seriously believe that things are going to go back to normal after what just happened, can you?"

"Obviously not. But I would love to have the chance to explain myself. I was going to tell you after it was all over."

"I still don't know what *it* is!" My voice echoes in the lobby. Suddenly, I realize there are one too many people staring at us and I *really* don't feel like being someone's slow motion car crash they can't look away from. "I'm not even sure I understand what's going on. All I know is that you aren't you, and you've been lying to me about pieces of who you are for some reason."

"So let me explain. You don't want me in your apartment? I totally get it. But let me take you home, ice your wrist while we talk on the way back to your place. Give me the car ride home to tell you everything."

It's his use of the word *home* that gets me. I hate myself a little for folding so quickly, but it's true. Since having him in my life, since our relationship took that next step, my apartment— my shitty, six floor walk-up, bug infested, miniature apartment, where nothing ever works—has quickly turned into a *home*.

I swallow once and squeeze my eyes shut, trying to process the different layers of pain my body is made up of. My wrist is definitely sprained at the very least. But my heart? That's for sure broken.

In all honesty, I don't want to spend a second more with Will than I have to. The embarrassment cuts too deep. But I know I'll drive myself crazy with questions that will be left unanswered if I don't give him a chance to explain himself. Sure, there's a chance they'll all be lies, but I'll at least have something to go off of. And right now, I need that.

I take a deep breath to steel myself because I know that this car ride will be agonizing in more ways than one. Still, it needs to happen.

"Get the car. I'm only giving you the ride back to my place to tell me everything."

WILL

Over the past five years, Will's grandfather, Liam Stevenson III, has taught him how to command the room in front of the industry's biggest titans. He's taught him how to speak clearly and concisely—get to the point in an assertive and confident manner. To do it in a way that could terrify both the smallest employee at the company to the chairman of any board. The elder Stevenson has taught him to be the perfect orator, to be utterly persuasive.

But even so, Will already knows from the look in Bridget's eyes that not even the best speech, not even the most perfectly strung set of words, will get her to forgive him.

And honestly, especially given the way she found out, he wouldn't blame her.

It's not like he doesn't hate himself, too.

31

IT'S REALLY NOT THE END OF THE WORLD, JUST THE END OF AN ERA

The car ride to my apartment starts off eerily quiet. After I scoot into the spacious back seat of Will's—the *company's* —tricked out, gas-guzzling, black monster of an SUV, he wordlessly helps me click my seatbelt into place. Being so close, a wave of his scent falls over me. And it takes a godlike effort to ignore the way it brings back every single incredible feeling to the front of my mind, every unbelievable memory that we shared, but I need to right now. Because I can't let my feelings for Will—or at least the Will I thought I knew—get in the way of whatever is going on here.

When he pulls away to secure his own seatbelt, it's a massive relief.

Just like he said, the car—or tank, more like it—has a fully stocked minibar, tucked somehow between our seats. It's clear from the set-up that this was a very, very special custom model. Will takes enough ice into a cloth napkin he finds on top of the bar and knots it into a makeshift ice pack. With extreme care, he takes my injured wrist from me and gently presses it to my skin. I jump from the contact, but I lie to myself by thinking it's because of the coldness and *not* because the touch belongs to the man I gave my whole heart to only to have him rip it to shreds.

Which reminds me...

"I think it's time for you to explain what the hell is going on."

"I don't even know where to begin."

"How about the obvious part? Your name. What's your real name?"

He laughs once, humorlessly. "You *know* what my name is. Will Jacobs."

"If that really is your name, then why did they call you *Liam Stevenson* up there?"

He takes a deep breath, seems to ready himself. "It's... complicated. Kinda."

"Try me."

"Right. Well. It's a bit of a cliché and a really long story, but I'll start from the beginning."

"That's usually the best place to start."

His mouth barely twitches into a smile, but disappears when I remain cold, brows permanently pulled together.

"So, when Mom married my dad, my grandfather Liam wasn't super happy about it. Dad was the son of a factory worker and homemaker, had no college education, and had been working as an hourly employee in Stevenson's HQ's mailroom. Which, to add insult to injury to my grandfather, is where my parents first met.

"Mom was visiting my grandfather at his office when she ran into my dad in an elevator. She says it was love at first sight." He shrugs and shoots me a look. "I don't know about that, but I know my grandparents were far from happy with the situation. Pretty sure my grandfather fired my dad and everything when he found out about them. Mom was used to being surrounded by wealthy men with Ivy League graduate degrees—not ones who came from blue collar families. And my grandfather was pretty clear that if she wanted to continue a relationship with my grandparents, she'd have to fall in line. She was their only daughter, so they had their society's expectations of her marrying some dude from American royalty, basically."

I scoff and shake my head. "Classic."

"Yeah, I know. But that's how it is with these families. It's like happiness comes second to what other people in their society think. But who cares about that?" He huffs, frustrated. Either at himself, his family, or this entire situation in general, I don't know. "In the end, Mom decided to run off with my dad, obviously. They got married and didn't speak to my grandparents until she found out she was pregnant. Mom had been trying to make things right between them for a while and finally managed to when they realized they would be missing out on having grandkids. So, in honor of their rekindled relationship, she named me after my grandfather."

I wonder how it made Will's dad feel to have his child named after a man who had so strongly rejected him. Immediately, the thought makes me sad for Sandra, because it couldn't have been easy to balance conflict between the people she loved.

"He was elated I was born a boy and named after him because he thought he was going to pass on the family company to me. But I never showed any interest in business."

"Didn't you major in Econ?"

"Yeah, but... I did it because my grandfather offered to pay for college, and that was a condition. He said I had to study something 'realistic,' something I could apply to business. And I was good at it—you saw all those Mathlete trophies in my mom's house—which is why I didn't mind so long as I would be able to double-major in art.

"I never expected him to hold it over my head, though. Paying for school, I mean. But the second I graduated college, he kind of... called on me? To start working with the family company. Started calling me Liam instead of Will. It was like he had this whole life planned out for me. And I hated it. I felt like I owed him so much and almost wished he had never offered to pay for school."

Money can turn the kindest of people into the worst. While I'm seething in anger and betrayal from what he hid from me, I love the Will that I got to know enough to feel deep sadness for him.

"I didn't grow up with the best example of what a family's supposed to look like—you know that—but that doesn't exactly sound like the kind of love you'd want to receive," I tell him. "And while there was obvious financial support, there didn't seem to be much emotional support. I didn't grow up with much of anyone, but the one grandparent I did have gave me every-thing. I'm sorry you didn't have that."

He nods, eyes sad. "I still have my mom, though. Don't forget."

That makes me smile a little, because it's true. Sandra Jacobs is one of the most amazing people I've ever met, and I loved her the second I met her. Since her birthday party, I've been to her house two more times (as Will's official girlfriend) and every time she makes me feel more and more loved, more welcome.

"Your mom *is* amazing."

His grin is wide. Proud. "The best." But the happiness that was so clear on his face disappears in a heartbeat when a dark cloud seems to fall over his face. "So when I didn't answer his '*call*,' he took it personally. Mom got upset because he was back to his conditional love ways and my grandmother had passed already, so she wasn't there to soften him up this time around. So we fought. We stopped talking. And I was kind of adrift already—you already know that—not really knowing what I wanted to do in life. So I took up a teaching job in my hometown and just... did that for a while."

"What does this have to do with anything? With you lying to me and—"

"*Omitting.*" He takes a deep breath. "It has to do with it because after several years of not talking to my grandfather, I had to go back to him, tail between my legs, and ask for help. After I crashed my car and paralyzed my mother, leaving her with hundreds of thousands of dollars worth of medical debt and a lifetime of additional health problems, I went to him for money.

"Mom was too angry to do it herself, so I did it. I went to him for money for *his daughter* and he flat out refused to give it to me. Told me it was my responsibility to figure it out. And you know what? I don't blame him. It's my fault she's in the wheelchair. It's my fault I'm in this situation. And if you tell me to fuck off, I'll hate it, and I'll hate myself even more than I already do for the rest of my life, but I'll understand because I know it was all my doing."

"Are you trying to make me feel sorry for you? Because, yes, it makes me sad for your mother, but what you did to me and us—"

"*No.* No, I'm being serious. I'm owning up to my mistakes. I've known for a long time that this day could come. That it *would* come. I just... My grandfather promised he'd give me the money for my mother under the condition that I work for him for five years minimum. It was a starting bonus, the already high salary, and at the end of the five years, another massive bonus. He also specified that because Stevenson was a public company, but family-run, it might be best for people to start referring to me professionally as Liam Stevenson, as well. 'To keep the tradition alive,' he'd say. 'For the shareholders.'" Will has the decency to roll his eyes in disgust. "Obviously, it was all about appearances for him. Always has been. And I guess he was hoping I'd fall for the high salary, perks, and promotions he kept giving me.

Not that I wasn't good at my job, but it was very evident that it was all a way to train me to take over. To entice me. To save face after 'losing' his daughter to a 'commoner.'

"But I never wanted to stay in the job. I saved every penny I could after helping pay off some of my mom's bills just in case she ever needs more. With the exception of Ginger's medical bill, I have not spent a single dime of that money on anything for myself because I feel like it isn't mine. So no, Bridget. This wasn't about corporate espionage. This wasn't about gaining secrets in order to make your job more difficult by having the upper hand in negotiations. This wasn't about tricking you to get laid. But I did keep things from you because you just assumed that I was a middle manager, and it didn't seem relevant to clarify at the time—we were just strangers on the internet. And once things started changing for us, we had already talked about how much you hated upper management, specifically my finance team—run by *me*—for making your job impossible. So what was I to do? I had only a few months left of obligation to my grandfather and didn't want to mess that up and lose out on the bonus he promised—I had to stay for my mom. I also didn't want to mess things up with you. And yes, I was a coward. But I was always going to tell you. After all this was over, after I had quit and finished up this role, I was going to tell you."

"You... *You* paid Ginger's vet bill?" I ask in a whisper. My brain is overloaded with information, but this is what stands out from everything he just told me.

He sighs, exhausted. "Yeah. Yes. I had to. It was over nine grand and just..."

Nine grand??

"It wasn't Declan?"

His eyes tighten. "*Dr. Sloane.* And no. It wasn't him. It was me. That errand I had to run that morning... It was to go back down to the animal hospital and pay off the bill. I only paid off part of the bill to make it believable. Left those couple hundred for you to pay. Then I spoke to the office and begged them not to say anything and—"

I scoff, cold and furious. It completely throws Will off, has him physically recoiling as much as he can in his seat.

"Do you see how incredibly manipulative you've been? All the lies and just... the controlling ways in which you've behaved over the last few months?"

"Bridget, no. I wasn't trying to manipulate you by—"

"Lying to me about who you are. Lying to me about the vet bill. Which, yes, is *incredibly* generous of you, and I'll find a way to pay you back eventually, but you should've told me and—"

"I never lied! And you would've never let me pay if I'd offered and—"

"Because it would've revealed who you were, right? That's mostly why you didn't want to tell me. Because by picking up a nine-thousand dollar bill you'd have to reveal that you were working at the executive level, making a shit ton of money."

"Bridget, I didn't do it to manipulate you. I did it because I lo—."

I suck in a breath. There's no way I can keep the tears at bay any longer. They streak freely down my cheek, warm and wet.

"Don't. Don't you even dare say it." It's like lightning striking a tree right down the middle—my heart has been stricken and split in two—raging, burning. "Maybe your intentions were good, but your actions..." I shake my head. "I get why it didn't matter as much when we first met virtually, but things changed quickly. You should've come clean then. And in not doing so, you managed to blow up our entire relationship. I feel like I've been tricked into falling for you when I have never been more open and honest with anyone in my entire life."

"I never lied about who I was—not to my core. I omitted *details*—"

I scoff. "Details!"

"Yes, details! Because what I do for a living is just a fucking detail. It's not who I fucking am. A job isn't an identity. I took you to my mother's house. I showed you my childhood. I've shown you my heart, Bridget. You fucking know who I *am*." He takes my good hand and presses it to his chest. Beneath my palm, I can feel his rapid heartbeat, racing to catch up with the madness. "We talked endlessly about everything from goat videos to our biggest traumas. You know everything there is to know about me. And I love you and everything that you are. This isn't some silly fling for me. This is it. You are *it*. It can't end because of something so dumb."

It's the wrong thing to say, and based on the way he winces, Will realizes it, too.

"You think this is dumb? After all the times I've been lied to and used by the people I've loved? You think it's irrational of me to be angry at this?"

He exhales, dropping his face in his hands. "I didn't mean that. Your feelings are valid, and I'm definitely a dick, but I did it out of love. Because I was scared. Can't you just see that I did this because I'm in love with you—so fucking in love, Bridge— and I would've done anything to not lose you?"

I take a deep breath and squeeze my eyes shut, pressing myself against the back of the seat. This is so hard. And it hurts. It hurts more than any other betrayal. Because I am so goddamn in love with him. With the Will I thought I knew.

I feel Will's large, warm hand come over my thigh. "Baby, please. Tell me you're willing to work this out. Tell me this isn't it." His voice breaks. "You see the silver lining—the positive—in everything. In the worst situations, you keep your head held high. You're able to keep moving. Is there any way you can do the same here, so we can move past this? I'm not saying it won't take work and time and—"

"You're the one who taught me to stop settling for the silver lining, Will. To demand more from life than just accepting the bad and focusing on the good. So why would I stay with someone who has hidden part of who they are *for months*? If you and I were still just friends and I were dating a man who did the same thing, would you be telling me to stay with him?"

Will's eyes are bloodshot and wide when he swallows once. His voice breaks again when he answers, "No, I wouldn't. I'd tell you you deserve better."

I nod between tears. "Exactly."

When I wipe my nose with the back of my hand, I realize we're just a block away from my place, and what perfect timing. I take a deep breath and really look at Will. Get my last fill of the only man I've ever truly loved before I walk away from him and what I thought was the best relationship I ever had.

WILL

He always knew getting his heart broken by his own stupidity would be a risk. But seeing her face, tear-streaked and pained, cut through him sharper than any knife ever could. He hadn't prepared for that kind of pain.
His blood runs cold, his own tears run hot as he watches her exit the car, and all he wants is to throw himself at her feet and beg for forgiveness. But he knows it won't do any good. Nothing will, now. He's lost her forever.

32

HOW TO HEAL A BROKEN HEART: ONE TUB OF NUTELLA + ONE TUB OF PEANUT BUTTER + AN OLD FRIEND

Being fired and breaking up with the man of your dreams on the same day is really not recommended for your mental health. In fact, if there's a way to avoid it, I would do so altogether. Space it out, if possible. Because normally, if you lose one, you'd at least have the other to throw yourself into. Distract you from the loss. Otherwise, you'd find yourself in my situation: wrapped in a blanket in your bed, can't remember when you last washed your hair, on your computer looking for jobs, licking a mixture of Nutella and peanut butter off a spoon (like a melted Reeses's cup). You'd be stuck thinking nonstop about how much of a loser you are, all while your cat judges you from afar. And while, a week later, I don't regret standing up to Lena for what I believe in or ending things with Will, it still sucks.

I sigh and look over at the kitchen counter, where a heap of Will's apology gifts have started piling up. A whole collection of items filled with reminders of how well he knows me or things tied to inside jokes. Friendship bracelets, sketches, a gorgeous vintage Oscar de la Renta dress in my size, a book on tambour embroidery (a new technique I've been experimenting with on used clothing I've purchased recently), and flowers. So many flowers—all cat friendly, of course.

While they're all beautiful and fill my depressing apartment with an amazing scent, all they serve as is a reminder that he hurt me. Betrayed me. That the man I fell in love with and gave myself to completely was a liar. Just like the ones before.

"I'm going to have to throw it all out, aren't I, Ginger?"

My cat lifts her head to glare at me from the chair. She doesn't understand why Will hasn't come by in days, and I think she hates me for it. We both grew too attached when we should've known better.

With a sigh, I use my non-sprained hand to dip my spoon into the peanut butter again, followed by the jar of Nutella, and then shove the whole concoction in my mouth.

"I need a job. STAT."

AFTER A LOT OF INTROSPECTION AND WEEKS OF RATIONING THAT bring back nightmares of times when I experienced food insecurity as a child, I finally find a job. And while it isn't working at the corporate level, it's still somewhat in the fashion realm. Somewhere I quickly excel at and am passionate about.

Necessity is the mother of invention—that was my childhood's motto. With my mother being so unreliable, I had to learn early how to work with what I had, which is what gave me such great instincts and a knack for creative problem-solving while working at Sartoria. It's also why I decide on a job working in retail again—this time at a second hand shop.

The salary as a sales associate isn't enough to cover all my expenses, but I use my discount to buy the pieces that aren't moving on the floor that I know I can do something with. After that, I work my magic on them and resell the pieces either in the same store or online for a pretty reasonable profit.

It's fun, a fantastic creative outlet, and it almost distracts me from the fact that I am absolutely miserable.

Because I am. Miserable, that is.

Three weeks after our blow-up, Will stopped trying to contact me. No more flowers, no more gifts, no more calls. And while I never once wanted to call him back or reach out, it killed me. His gifts were the only remaining connections I had to him, the only way of knowing that he was even still alive. I mean, what if something had happened to him? What then? We had no friends in common who would've been able to communicate it to me.

I struggle to not let myself go down that rabbit hole, but some days are harder than others. As the early days of summer are fast approaching, I'm saddened to think that all the fantasies I dreamt up of the things we'd do once the warmer weather hit won't be happening. No outings to the beach. No picnics outdoors. No weekend trips up to Connecticut to visit his mom.

Despite still being mad at him, more than anything, I'm devastated to think that after just a few weeks of trying to apologize, he's given up on us when I haven't stopped loving him for a single second.

Not one.

The first week of May, I come home from a shopping spree to my favorite vintage shops and craft stores to find a visitor waiting for me on my building's stoop. I stop dead in my tracks just a few feet away, because the last time we spoke feels like so long ago, I have no idea what to say.

Molly sees me approach, and her eyes widen as she gets to her feet.

We're both quiet for a moment, unmoving. But when the bags of clothes and materials start to tire my arms, I break the silence.

"What are you doing here?" I ask.

Molly winces, but I feel like it's a fair question to ask. It's been well over a month since we last spoke, and I haven't received so much as a single text. Not even after I was fired for my association to that psycho, Lena.

"I—I just want to talk. To apologize. To figure out what went wrong and how we can fix it."

My breath hitches, my eyes suddenly stinging with the possibility of more tears—they already ache from this morning's cry fest in the shower.

Molly sounds sincere, but I've been burned before.

"I mean, *I* know what went wrong. You weren't a good friend."

It's a low blow, but not untrue.

"That's fair. I deserved that." She nods solemnly. "Can we go up to your place? To talk?"

I look down at my feet, processing. Because a break-up with a significant other always hurts, it's true. But you never expect a friend break-up to cut just as deep. Sometimes it makes you question things about yourself maybe even losing a significant other would never make you question about yourself. The grief of it all can be just as bad or worse.

Maybe that's why losing Will has been especially difficult. Because he wasn't just some guy I'd been dating. He'd become my best friend. The person I'd grown closest to.

"Please, Bridge." Molly takes a deep breath and pulls out a bottle of champagne, a small bottle of orange juice, and a paper bag from my favorite deli from her enormous purse. "Brunch?"

That finally breaks me, a dam of tears immediately spilling. It might seem like such a silly thing, but it speaks mountains to me. Because what's better on a weekend than bottomless mimosas and brunch with your friend for a full life catch-up? And I haven't had that in forever.

I drop my bags on the sidewalk and my face in my hands, breaking out into sobs. Not more than a second later, Molly's arms are around me, holding me to her.

"Bridge, I'm so sorry."

I nod against her neck because I know. I know Molly isn't a bad person deep down. If she were a bad person, we never would've become friends in the first place. And I need this. Need her. Need a friend.

It's been weeks of loneliness and heartache and a solitude so sharp and deep I feel like it's hard to breathe sometimes. Like my lungs have frozen and refuse to stretch to make room for air. Like every single person who's ever left me or betrayed me is pressing down on my chest and windpipe.

Between sobs, Molly leads me to the building, carrying my stuff for me all the way to my apartment. Once we're inside, Ginger shoots her an ugly look as if to say "I know how you treated my mother" and steers clear of her.

I take a seat on my bed, a blubbery mess, and tell her, "She's here to apologize. Chill."

Molly smiles fondly at me as she puts my bags and our coats away. "Ginger mad at me, too?"

I nod and wipe my nose with the back of my hand. "I don't think *I'm* mad anymore, though." *At you or Will*, I think. "Just sad. Sad at how things turned out."

Molly frowns and takes my hand. "I want to talk. But I think we should do it over some glasses of mimosas and some food. Let me make the drinks and I'll get us some plates."

"We can eat in bed. Maybe turn on a TV show in the background?"

"Deal."

We don't really talk about anything until after our bellies are full, and we're both a little buzzed. Instead, we watch episodes of The Bachelor and discuss how this season has been quite possibly the most boring and why. It isn't until Molly mentions one of the girls at work is considering applying, that our conversation stalls.

"How is work, by the way?" My voice is small, cautious.

She throws back the rest of her drink, and sets the glass on my nightstand. "They asked me to come here, you know."

I blanche. It takes a few moments to process this information. "What? I thought you... Oh. So you're not here to apologize." Another painful slash across the heart.

"No, I am," she says quickly. "I definitely am. I've been wanting to forever. I just... haven't had the courage to yet. Until today. I've been a coward."

She pauses for a moment before continuing. "I don't know what happened with the whole Lena drama—I mean, there are rumors, but no one really knows, and you don't have to tell me—but the whole company was a mess for a while. I heard talk about a lawsuit and layoffs. Legal was interviewing every single person who had touched the Stevenson account.

"Then, last week, things changed. They settled down. I got pulled into HR, and I swear to god I thought I was going to get fired. But it turned out it wasn't anything like that. The meeting was about you."

"About me? What?" I sit up, intrigued.

"HR knew you had been hired based off of my referral and they wanted me to go and convince you to say yes when they asked you to come back. They asked me whether I had stayed in touch with you. Whether we were still friends. Whether I knew if you had already found a job or not." She shakes her head in disapproval, the whole thing sounding a bit too... sketchy. "I told them we were on the outs. Also, I may have pointed out how manipulative that was. There was no way I was going to show up to your place and beg you to come back to work when we hadn't spoken in weeks. When I had acted like a total bitch to you."

"They were going to beg me to come back to work?" Why would they *beg* me to come back to work? Yes, I was good at my job, contrary to what Molly initially thought I would be. But it's not like I wasn't replaceable. Especially now, with Lena gone. I'm smart and capable, but I was only just learning and Sartoria wouldn't have had a hard time finding my replacement.

She exhales heavily and refills her glass. Polishes off the last of the champagne. "I'll tell you everything, but I want you to know that I've been wanting to apologize to you since the second you walked out of that bathroom door. I've felt so ashamed for how I behaved. Not just in that moment, but in general. You are one of the most resilient people I know, Bridget Quinn. And to suggest that *you're* the reason why shit falls apart around you was fucked up and horrible of me not just to say, but to think, too."

"It's not a crazy assumption to make," I say with a self-deprecating shrug. "I *am* the common denominator in every single one of the crazy things that has happened in my life. The less-than-stable parent. The laundry list of odd jobs here and there and how I lost them. The list of men I thought would change but never did." *And the one I thought was perfect but broke my heart.*

"Stop. While that may be true that you're the common denominator, it's purely coincidental. You are... an exceptional woman. A great friend. And a fantastic employee. I don't know what came over me that day—that place is toxic and warps my thinking sometimes—but I do know that you didn't deserve it. And you deserve much better from a friend."

"Thank you." I sniff.

"Everything I said was all about me and my insecurities. Not about you."

I nod and wrap my arms around her, pulling her close into a hug I think we've both been needing for a while. "Thank you for being honest."

When our long hug is over, she breaks the silence first. "I saw on socials you have a new job. At Houston's Closet, right?" I nod and Molly smiles. "I feel like that's perfect for you."

"It really is. I need to tell you all about it." And for the first time in a while, I feel a genuine smile spread across my face. "The pay is nowhere near as much as what I was making at Sartoria, but I love it."

"That's amazing, Bridge." She smiles, but it's quickly followed by a sigh. "I'm jealous you found something you love. Because that meeting I had with HR was actually the straw that broke the camel's back for me. It made me realize what a manipulative place we worked in and how it had turned me into someone I didn't like. I just..." She shakes her head. "I don't know what got into me. The competitiveness. The betrayal. Like, it's not a soap opera or a high stakes industry. We're not—"

"Saving lives," I finish the sentence for her.

This makes her laugh and bump her shoulder against mine. "Exactly. So I quit. Immediately, I wanted to call you, but I felt I needed time. To work on myself. To work out what I wanted to say, exactly. And I knew that whatever had happened at work must've been serious enough that you probably wanted your space, too."

"Yeah. It was... a lot."

"But I'm here now for myself and for you and for our friendship. I want it back. I want you back. I want to be friends again. Do you think you can forgive me?"

I reach out and wrap my arms around her. Hold her once more, eyes squeezed shut. "Yes, Molls. Of course. We're human. We all make mistakes. And I've seen firsthand what that place can do to people. Let's give this a second chance."

"Thank you, Bridge." She pulls away and smiles, eyes red.

"Now that we can put this all behind us..." I get to my feet with more excitement than I probably should. "Can I show you something amazing for dessert?"

She laughs and sniffles, wipes her nose with the back of her hand. "Sure. You have frozen thin mint cookies or something?"

"Even better." I run to my kitchen cupboard and pull out the jar of peanut butter and Nutella.

"I appreciate you coming here to see me. To apologize after everything," I tell her between spoonfuls of peanut butter and chocolatey goodness. "I... I've been going through a rough time lately—I don't just mean the craziness that happened at Sartoria, which I promise to tell you all about one day—but just... I'd been seeing this guy..."

A slow smile spreads across Molly's face. "I thought so. All the giggling while texting. How busy you were on the weekends. The goofy smiles at your desk when you spaced out."

I sigh wistfully, a flood of memories with Will—good ones— filling my brain. "Yeah. He was... He was amazing."

Molly frowns. "If he was so amazing then what happened? And why didn't you tell me?"

I feel my face twist in pain. "I don't even know where to

begin," I confess. "I guess I didn't tell you at first because he worked for Stevenson."

Molly gasps. "What?"

I laugh once. "Yeah. We kind of met through work. Which is why we agreed that it would be a conflict of interest given everything that was going on between the two companies. Neither one would approve. And I didn't tell you because I didn't want to put you in the uncomfortable position of knowing I was doing something wrong. But also... it was all so amazing, part of me just wanted to keep it to myself. I know that doesn't make sense, but I wanted to hoard my relationship. Protect it, you know?"

"No, I totally get what you mean. You wanted to keep it safe in a bubble. Not let the outside world interfere." She nods pensively, dipping her own spoon into the tubs of chocolate and peanut butter before licking it clean.

This is certainly not the most... shareable dessert, but fuck it. If you can't share germs with your friends, are you really friends?

"Exactly. Which is ironic, since telling someone might've helped avoid things exploding the way they did. Because, maybe if I had told you about him—if I'd told anyone—I'd have found out sooner who he really was. Since my clueless butt wasn't able to put two and two together."

"Oh my god, Bridge." Molly gasps; she brings her hands to her mouth in shock. "Please tell me he wasn't another grifter trying to steal your money."

I snort. "No, he wasn't. He turned out to be Stevenson's CFO."

Molly blinks at me a few times, too stunned to speak for a moment. "What?"

With a sigh, I walk over to the fridge and pull out two beers. "We're gonna need another drink for this story."

MOLLY SIGHS ONCE. "LISTEN, I'M NOT EXCUSING HIS BEHAVIOR, but—"

"Nope."

"I get what you're saying, Bridge, but—"

"Molly."

"The man loves you. He loves you and you love him and—"

"*No.*"

Molly huffs in frustration. "Why are you so willing to forgive me but not him? You just told me you fell in love with him. You just said you thought he was the love of your life. That's not something to take lightly or let slip through your fingers."

"*Was.* Past tense." I get up to grab another beer, wobble to the fridge. It's seven P.M. now, which means we've been drinking for eight hours. I don't even know how we're alive at this point. I guess thanks to the DoorDash gods and Chinese food for providing sustenance to absorb all the cheap champagne and beer we've consumed today.

"Okay," she says, getting up to her feet on the bed, holding out her hands for me to toss her a can. I do and miss, but it falls at her feet. She doesn't seem to mind though. "Okay, but, like. Remember what you said when I thanked you for forgiving me? You said 'Molly, goddess divine—"

"I did not use the words 'goddess divine'"

"Shh! This is my story. You said 'Molly, you goddess divine, everyone deserves a second chance.'"

"I did not say *everyone.* I said *let's give this a second chance,* but—"

"Did you or did you not say that?"

"I *just* told you what I actually said. Dude, I think you're drunk."

"Your face is drunk."

We burst out into peals of laughter on the bed, struggling for breath. "God, I needed this kind of silliness. I missed you a ton," I tell her.

Molly smiles. "Me too." But then she sighs and all humor leaves her face. In its stead is only concern for a friend who's hurting. "I'm serious, Bridge. You love him, don't you?"

I swallow and throw myself onto my back on the bed, looking up at the ceiling as the tears start to stream down my face. They come so easily these days.

"More than I've ever loved anyone before in my life. It's like..." I try for a deep breath and fail again. There's just no room. "It's like nothing I've ever known, Molls. Like... I feel like half of me is gone. That it's with him. And I'm scared I'll never get it back. Worse still, I'm scared I won't ever want it back."

"Forgive him, Bridge. You're so good at seeing the good in everything—in people and in every horrible situation you've been in. Why can't you do that here?"

"Honestly, I think it's because of that very reason that I don't want to. He once told me looking too often at the bright side of things can result in settling. That I'd settled too much in life, accepted too many bad things. That I should fight for what I deserve. And wouldn't me just accepting that he kept who he was from me—even if it was with good intentions—be settling?"

"Yeah, but wouldn't you be doing the same if you don't? He doesn't want you to settle because he wants happiness for you. He wants you to fight for what you deserve. So wouldn't you *not* forgiving him leave you settling for an incomplete life without him?"

In a twisted way, I can see Molly's point.

"But what does it say about me if I forgive him? If I take him back after all of it? Doesn't it say I'm a pushover?"

"I think it says that you love him enough to try and make things work. Like a real couple would. I think it says that a life without his love would be unacceptable." She takes my hand in hers and squeezes it. "Bridge, if you're able to forgive him and move on, I think it says that your relationship can withstand anything life throws at you."

WILL

He's tried everything he could think of to get her to talk to him, but nothing's worked. Will hasn't been able to get Bridget to answer the phone, call him back, or reply to his messages. After a few weeks, he's realized she would never get back to him. And why would she? She deserves better.

Which is why he picked today to be the day he says goodbye. Goodbye to her and to the life they maybe could've had together if he'd been honest from the beginning.

He doesn't deserve happiness—that's for sure—but Bridget deserves the world. She deserves peace.

Will won't move on from this—he can't. You don't get two loves of your life. Bridget was it for him and he's just going to have to live with the fact that he's lost her forever.

And though just the thought of that makes his knees weak from the emotional toll it's taken on him, he's decided to take a page out of Bridget's handbook and look at the bright side for once. The silver linings:

First, even though he lost it, Will found his love—something many people spend a lifetime searching for. He will always treasure every moment he and Bridget spent together even if she will forever be the one who got away.

Second, despite accepting he's destined to live a life of solitude, he can now focus on what's next for him. Relationships will no longer be a distraction for him because there's no way he could ever love anyone the way he loved Bridget. And if that kind of love isn't possible, he doesn't want it, anyway. Not when he's known what it's really like to love someone.

Third, Will is definitely never working for his grandfather again. He's spent the last few weeks trying to figure out what he wants to do now that he's freed of the shackles that bound him so tightly and is still coming up short, but he at least knows that he'll never go back to the family business. And he's ecstatic about it.

Yes, these are the good things he can focus on now to get him out of bed in the morning. Still, he'd give it up in a second if it meant being with her.

33

MY DELIVERY GUY HATES ME

My conversation with Molly about Will has been playing in my head on a loop for days. I was able to forgive her, but not Will? A man who's loved me more than anyone ever has. The only man *I've* ever truly loved.

And maybe that was the reason I wasn't ready to forgive him yet. Because it hurt so much. But was I really willing to let a potential life partner go because of a mistake? A big one, no doubt, but one where the intent wasn't a malicious one?

He'd proven several times over in the past that he was dependable and kind. Even with the whole vet bill thing—though misguided—he did it so I wouldn't have to keep struggling. Because he sees me and could tell just how tired I am of things falling apart all around me—even if I've been in denial about it myself.

Sigh.

I don't know much of anything anymore. All I know is my head is a mess, and my heart is confused and bruised, and I miss him like crazy.

Though talking to Molly was incredibly helpful, ironically

enough, he's the only one I want to hear from right now. And I guess that just goes to show how supportive Will has always been with me that I still ache to talk to him.

I contemplate all this as I serve myself a Diet Coke while I wait for my Chinese food. It was a long day at work, but it's finally the weekend, and I'm mildly excited for it. I don't have big plans other than completing a few projects I started last weekend—a threadbare Missoni knit dress that can use a revival, a Halston wide-leg white silk pant that's unfortunately yellowed with age and needs to be lightened, and a pair of vintage Doc's from the eighties that need a good buffing and maybe a cool paint job—but I'm looking forward to it.

When my intercom's buzzer goes off, I very nicely ask the delivery man to bring it up.

"No, ma'am," he says. *Ouch. Ma'am? Really?* "Six floors is too much. You come down and get it."

"No, I totally understand. And normally I would. But, see, I would really appreciate it if you could bring it up because I'm exhausted—I've been on my feet all day—and was wondering whether just this once you'd be able to make an exception and—"

"*Ma'am.*" Oh my god with the ma'am. "What do you think I do for a living? Sit in a comfy chair all day?"

"I—I guess not. I'm sure you've probably been all around the city delivering food, huh?"

"Exactly. So why don't you come and get your food? If not, I'll leave it here on the stoop but I am not coming up."

"Please. I know it's—"

"I got it," a familiar voice cuts through our discussion. "I mean. If that's okay with you, Bridge. For me to come up."

I'm silent for a moment, shell-shocked. "Will?" He's here?

"Yeah, I..." He clears his throat. "Listen, you don't even have to talk to me if you don't want to, but I can bring your food up to you if you'd like. I can leave it just outside your door. I also have something I wanted to give you, if that's okay."

"I—"

"Fantastic! Here you go my friend. I'm off."

Silence. I still haven't buzzed him up. "Did the delivery guy just...?"

"Leave? Yeah." He sighs. "Listen, if seeing me is too much, just buzz me in so I can at least leave your food in the lobby. I don't want to leave it on the stoop and have some random stranger take it while you're on your way downstairs. At least if it's inside you have a better chance of it surviving theft."

"In this building? Not a chance," I say with a laugh. And it feels so good to laugh, even if it's not a full-bellied one.

Will also laughs on the other end of the intercom, and it sounds like heaven.

"So, what do you want to do then?" he asks. "I promise you I won't pressure you into anything."

I press my forehead against the door frame by the intercom, thinking. I could just do what he says. Buzz him in, ask him to just leave the food inside the building for me to pick up once he's gone. Avoid seeing him altogether. Or I could embrace the fact that he's here so we can... I don't know. Talk? I'm not sure what the right move is here.

All I know is that I miss him, and if he's here to say something, I want to hear what it is, regardless of whether or not I'm *supposed* to want to hear it or not. At the end of the day, my love for him didn't just disappear into thin air. It's still here, every day, in everything that reminds me of him and us. In every small moment we spent together I treasure, and every big gesture he ever made. From late nights spent talking well into the next morning, to teasing him about the way he ate his cereal—something I still don't get to this day. From the way he loved my cat to the way he stood up for me every time he felt I was wronged.

I take a steeling breath and make my decision. "Come on up."

WILL

In all honesty, he never expected her to agree to see him. He's only here to drop off the present he had commissioned months ago with a final note where he apologizes once again and tells her goodbye.
But now that she's willing to talk? There's no way Will's going to let that opportunity slip away. He has a second chance to make things right, and he's going to try his best to do so.
If, after everything, she still asks him to leave, he'll go without further argument.
After, he'll go on as planned, loving her until the day he dies.

34

———

I DESERVE LOVE

For what seems like hours, I wait for Will to come up the stairs, back pressed against my front door. When I hear footsteps approaching from the hallway, I squeeze my eyes shut and press the palms of my hands to the frame. On the other side, I hear Will take a steadying, deep breath before knocking gently.

I take one as well.

My hand trembles as it wraps around the doorknob, heart racing and twisting as I pull the door open.

And there he is.

Will Jacobs in all his glory.

Handsome. So handsome.

Dark curls damp from the late spring showers. Chocolate brown eyes cautious, staring up at me through thick lashes. Kind and full of... *something*—something I don't know whether I want to name, since I'm not quite sure whether I want it or not. Whether I'm ready to receive it.

Will puffs my name from his lungs, like he's been trying to keep it in for the longest time. "*Bridget.* You look..."

I look down at myself, try to see what he's seeing. But it's just me. In my sweats.

"Like a slob?" I blush.

"Perfect. You look perfect. I love you in those sweats. It's you." There's a slight ache in his voice that seems to match the one in my heart. A longing that drains every last bit of my energy at the end of the day.

My face twists in half pleasure, half embarrassment. "You caught me off guard." *In more ways than one.*

"I—Yes. I'm sorry I didn't call. I figured you wouldn't want to talk to me, and I brought something for you and—" He sighs and shakes his head. "How's your wrist, by the way?"

This is awkward.

I look down at my left hand and twist it in the air. "Good. It was just a sprain, so I had it wrapped up for just a couple of weeks. All back to normal." I give him some spirit fingers, which makes him smile tightly.

So awkward.

He makes a little frustrated groan noise. "We don't have to talk, if you don't want to. I can leave now. Leave you alone to your dinner. And to this." He laughs once, sheepish, nervous, as he hands me my takeout and a blue bakery box with the words *Annie Rose Cookie Designs* on top.

I gasp.

"You got me Annie Rose cookies?" I ask, practically tossing my dinner onto the kitchen counter, hunger completely forgotten, so I can properly hold the luxurious box with two hands. I don't want to risk dropping it and breaking what's bound to be a set of the most gorgeous cookies inside. I stare at it in awe, admiring the shimmering box and silver foil logo.

"I did, yes." He scratches the back of his neck, avoiding eye contact. "I, uh, actually reached out to her a few months ago, but was only able to get her to make these last week. She has a massive waitlist. Turns out you were right: there is such a thing as a cookie influencer."

"I told you," I say with a small smile.

He smiles back. "You did. And it was a little crazy to me to see how in-demand she is for commissions." He laughs once.

My eyes snap up to him. "Commissions? You had these commissioned? You didn't buy her regular designs?"

Will looks down at the box, rolling his lips with his brows pulled together. "No, I didn't buy her regular designs," he says quietly. "I asked her to do something special. For you. For *us*, actually. They were meant to be a gift for when I—" But he cuts himself off. "But it doesn't matter now."

"For when you what?"

Will clears his throat once and meets my gaze, eyes red-rimmed and glassy. "I signed up months ago before I blew things up between us. I was going to give them to you when... When I said I love you for the first time. It was something I had planned out, but then... Well, you know what happened."

I look down at the box again, my throat constricting. God, what is it about *him* and *us* and *this* that makes it impossible for me to breathe?

"Either way, they wouldn't have been ready on time. I was practically bursting at the seams before our fight, trying not to say it before I could get off the waitlist. There was no way I was going to last another week before I blurted it out, let alone a couple of months." He huffs. "I'm not ecstatic about *how* it came out—I would've rather accidentally told you in the middle of making love to you or a romantic moment instead of while I was begging for forgiveness." He sighs and shakes his head while I remember how awful hearing him say he loved me back felt. It wasn't supposed to be that way. It wasn't supposed to be in a situation where he was trying to apologize for hiding part of who he was.

"Oh." It's all I can say.

I want to ask more questions—the kinds that have been

burning inside me after weeks of mutual radio silence. Mostly, I want to ask whether he still feels the same way. But what does it mean that I want him to still feel the same way? What does it mean that of everything I need clarification on, this is the one thing that screams above all others?

"These must've cost you a fortune," I say.

"They were more than worth it."

Right. I forgot he's probably loaded—CFO and all that.

"I guess you can afford it." Immediately I grimace because I didn't mean to bring it up—I really didn't. But the ease with which he was able to drop what is likely to be a couple thousand dollars on just *cookies* (because no matter what Will thinks, Annie Rose is a big deal) just serves as a reminder of his lies. Or omissions.

He huffs once, frustrated. "You know I'm not that guy, right? I may have... *misled* you about my job, but I'm not the type of guy to give a shit about money. The car and driver, the fancy apartment—yes, there was a fancy apartment, and yes, that's why we always stayed at yours—those were paid for by the company. And any money I made all went into paying off my mother's medical debt and growing a savings account in case of emergencies. I'm not—" He stops to run his hands through his hair. "I'm not like that. I'm not that guy. I don't care about fancy shit. *Yes*, I spent a lot of money on these cookies. But I'm crazy about you—fucking gone in love with you—and this qualified as an emergency to me."

I can't help the small, cautious smile that spreads across my face. "I know you're not that guy, Will. I know who you are."

He inhales sharply, because he knows what I said carries more weight than it would've just a few months ago.

"You do?"

I sigh, defeated. "Yeah, I think I do."

"I never used my powers for evil, Bridge. Except— Except maybe once."

I raise a brow, surprised. "Once?"

"I— I may have told Sartoria that the only way Stevenson would drop the lawsuit after that whole tariffs fuck up is if they hired you back."

I gasp. "Are you serious?"

He nods. "I know it was super bad and manipulative, but I felt awful, and I couldn't believe that something that had nothing to do with you ended up costing you your job. You didn't deserve that. I knew you loved working there and were probably devastated about losing your job. I wanted it to be the last thing I got done before leaving my official post as CFO. It was manipulative and gross, but I figured you weren't speaking to me anymore, so..." He shrugged. "I wanted to use my evil powers to make you happy, Bridge."

For some reason, this makes me laugh. The thought of Sartoria's corporate offices freaking out over having to find and rehire a fired assistant in order to avoid a lawsuit gives me more satisfaction than it should.

"My friend Molly mentioned being pulled into a meeting with HR to get me to come back. But they never called."

He grins. "I know. When I saw you posted a photo on Instagram with the caption 'First Day at new job!' or something like that, I called it off. You looked really happy— happier than I ever saw you at Sartoria when things were still good."

"Did you guys sue them?"

"Nah. We paid the fines and they covered the loss. Everything ended up okay. In that regard, I mean."

I ignore that last comment when I suddenly realize something. "Wait, hold on. So you have an Instagram, now? I thought you were fully off socials."

He looks like he extremely regrets telling me this. "It's new. I don't really post anything."

"I haven't seen any follow notifications in a while…"

"I don't. Follow you, that is. If I did, I'd be stuck to my phone all day. But I do check up on you," he explains. "I wasn't trying to go all creepy stalker. But I just wanted to see how you were doing." He pauses while I gawk at him. "And now that I hear myself say it out loud, I realize how creepy I sound."

Surprising myself, I laugh once more. "A little bit. But kind of cute."

Now *that* surprises him.

"Do you like your new job?" he asks.

My smile is big and genuine. "Love it."

"Good," he says, smiling back.

"What about you? What are you going to do now that your time at Stevenson is done?"

"I'm not sure yet. But I look forward to finding out."

I nod, loving this journey of self-exploration he's embarked on. He deserves it, no matter what anyone says. Including himself.

Will looks at me with a wistful smile before speaking again. "Anyway, I guess I'll leave these cookies here with you and— Wait, what are you doing?" he asks in a panic when he sees me carrying the box over to the kitchen counter.

"Opening the box, obviously."

"Can you wait 'til I'm gone, please? It's— They're a little embarrassing. I don't want you to think I'm crazy and—"

"Not a chance."

"Bridget, *please*. I don't want—"

But it's too late. I pull the lid off and—

I gasp, bringing my hands to my mouth.

Speechless. Utterly speechless.

Because the second I pop the lid open, I see the most

gorgeous collection of iced cookies. I don't know if I'm biased because of its designs, but I'm pretty sure this is the best Annie Rose has ever produced.

"Will, I..." I shake my head, in shock. "Are these...?"

He takes a deep breath before answering. "They're all special moments to us. Or things from our relationship that made me fall in love with you. Inside jokes, too," he whispers.

"They're... *beautiful,*" I breathe. Beautiful is an under-statement.

I can't bring myself to look at Will, but I feel him shrug beside me, his breathing faster than it should be. "Yeah." His voice comes out a little mangled—unnatural.

My hands hover over the icing paintings of different things we've shared together, too scared to pick one of the cookies up and accidentally drop them. Like I'd destroy the memories I've treasured so much in my heart if I did.

An extremely detailed cookie of Ginger in her green tufted chair—my heart grows two sizes, leaving me wondering how that's even possible when I haven't been able to get a full breath in weeks.

A Star Trek logo painted in edible gold that has my cheeks blazing red at the memory of what we did on his bed.

Two friendship bracelets, one on top of the other, with BFF beads on them that remind me of the best friend I ever had.

A bowl of chocolatey cereal makes me snort, the way he serves himself one of my favorite Will quirks.

Cartoon figures of a man and a woman—Will and me— cuddling in bed with an orange cat on the edge—perfect morn- ings together that had me wishing for more days like that.

The same couple standing with their faces close together, a floral dress similar to the one I wore that first night we met in real life—the night we first made love.

And a pop-up window with a sentence from one of the first

emails he sent me where he called me a breath of fresh air, taking me back to all those months ago. When I was lonely, when I still had Molly but didn't feel understood. When I was finally getting my life together but hadn't yet met the stranger who would change it for the better. Who would make me feel seen. Who would steal my heart and soul, when I would've given it to him willingly, anyway.

Will.

"I—I know they're a little corny," he says in a low voice. "In retrospect, maybe I should've cancelled the commission because of everything. But I just couldn't. I couldn't bring myself to."

"I'm glad you didn't," I manage to say in a whisper. "They're incredible."

I pick up the cookie with the email reverently, my eyes tearing up.

He sighs beside me, both of us carefully inspecting the fine details in the lettering, the perfect blend of colors. "Even then," his whisper is deep, with an ache to it. "Even then I knew, Bridge. I knew you were special. I knew you were going to save me."

I don't dare breathe, because I'm scared of what I might say if I have enough oxygen in my lungs.

"I understand why you dumped me. Believe me, I do. If some other guy would've done this to you, I would've—" He tenses, and I look over to find his eyes squeezed shut as if he were in pain. "You deserve better."

When he finally looks at me, we stare quietly at each other for a moment. As his eyes travels all over my face, I wonder whether he's getting his last fill before I ask him to leave my apartment—and my life—forever.

Except that I don't think that's what I want anymore. I don't think that's what I've wanted for a long time.

"You're right," I say, my voice breaking, Molly's words

suddenly making more sense than anything ever has. "I do deserve better. You taught me that. To stop settling."

Will swallows, his eyes full of hurt. "Yes, I did. And I still believe that, Bridge. I'm not gonna—" He sighs, frustrated. "I'm not here to try to convince you to come back to me. To forgive me and let me love you for the rest of our lives, no matter how badly I want to. I know what I did. And what I didn't do, for that matter. I know I hurt you and fucked everything up, and I love you enough to know you deserve better." He pauses. "I will always love you. And I will always pick you over my own happiness."

"So you agree? That I deserve not to settle? That I deserve to be happy, no matter what?"

"*Yes*. Always. Of course, Bridge."

"Then why are you pushing me away?" The first tear of what I suspect will be many streams down my cheeks. "If you want me to be happy—if you want me not to settle—then why are you pushing me to lead a life without you in it?"

Will's eyes widen, slack-jawed. "What?"

"I—I was angry, Will. Am still angry, a little, I think. But... I love you."

"You... love me?" He takes a careful step forward.

"Yes," I say between soft sobs. "Yes, very much. And I'm pretty sure it isn't going to go away anytime soon. Maybe ever. I tried for a while and..." I shake my head. "It didn't work. I didn't like it."

"Bridge."

"And while you were... a total *dick*. I get that intent matters. I can understand where you were coming from. It was stupid and moronic, but I can see why you were scared. And maybe because of it, you don't deserve me. Maybe because of it someone on the outside looking in might say that you don't get to have the woman you love. But see, I think it's about time the universe be kind to *me*. And I think it's high time I get what *I* deserve. And I deserve love, for once. I choose love. And I'm pretty damn sure that you will make me happy, if I give you the chance. Because I know that after this whole thing, you'll never lie to me again, will you, Will?"

"Never, Bridge. I will never fucking lie to you or keep something from you ever again, Bridget Quinn." He tentatively reaches out, his hands hovering over my waist, trembling from holding back.

Will looks like he's seen a ghost. It's clear from the expression on his face he cannot compute this is happening, and honestly, part of me can't either. But at the end of the day, the person who needs to decide whether she can live with it, whether she can forgive, is me. No one else. And just like I told Molly, some people deserve second chances. And he definitely does. Just because he made one mistake doesn't negate all the other times he came through for me. All the other times he was a wonderful friend and partner and lover. And I'm not about to throw that all away over a fight.

With a wet laugh, I take his hands in mine and wrap them around my waist, behind my back, pulling him to me.

"So what do you say? Do you think we can finally turn my luck around?" I press my lips to his chin, smile against his skin as I inhale his scent.

"Baby, I *swear* to you I will spend the rest of my goddamn life doing everything possible to give you the world."

"I don't want the world, Will. I just want us."

"And Ginger."

"Duh."

WILL

When people ask Will and Bridget how they met, they often look at each other with a mischievous grin and answer "online dating." Other times, they tell the story of two friends who ultimately fell in love and got together.

Bridget prefers the former, whereas Will loves to talk about the latter. How he knew from her first email that she was special, how madly and quickly he fell for Bridget, his friend. He loves showing off by telling everyone that, while he did suffer in the friend zone for some time, it was worth every second because it set the foundation for the best relationship he's ever had. He likes to show off how they're able to solve conflict because their relationship wasn't born out of passion at first (though he can guarantee they have passion in spades now). It was built upon solid ground. Only two people who really care enough to forgive could've gotten over the worst mistake he's ever made in his life. Only a true friend and partner could've loved him through that. Will and Bridget are both going through a huge transition period right now. Bridget calls it their "search for purpose era" where they attempt to turn their passions into their livelihoods —everyone's dream. He loves that Bridget's on this quest to find exactly what she's meant to do. And personally, Will thinks she's found it. Her creativity and resourcefulness knows no bounds, which is why her idea of opening a store with reclaimed and repurposed clothing sounds perfect for her. There's not a doubt in his mind she won't be able to make it an instant success.

Meanwhile, Will has been looking into pursuing grad school opportunities—but not an MBA, as his grandfather had hoped. After talking more with Bridget about what he enjoyed specifically about art and school, he realized he wants to explore different classes at the Continuing Education level. Maybe from there, he'd be able to determine more where he'd like his professional future to look like. Go to proper grad school. Find the right job for him.

"And it's totally okay that you're still not sure, babe," Bridget tells him one night over his favorite pasta dish. "I told you, you deserve to give yourself time to figure things out."

He smiles and reaches over to wipe some tomato sauce from the corner of her mouth before licking it off his thumb. It gives him ideas for other plans later tonight—he's sure there must be a can of whipped cream in the fridge somewhere.

"I know, Bridge. But I think I've already found my life's purpose."

"Really? What is it?" she asks around a mouthful of penne alla vodka, eyes bright and excited.

"Loving you."

Bridget rolls her eyes, but Will grins when she can't help that goofy, lovestruck smile of hers.

EPILOGUE: GINGER

Ginger wakes just as a ray of sunlight hits her eye, alerting her to the start of the day. She drowsily lifts her head and looks over her shoulder at her humans in bed. Human #2 lies with his arms wrapped around Human #1 from behind, a small, satisfied smile on his face. Like she's his whole world.

Ginger finds it cute, she guesses. The way Human #2 loves Human #1 makes her happy. For several reasons, which include *her* not having to have the sole responsibility of taking care of the redhead anymore.

Ginger ponders this as she begins her morning bath. When she's done, she sees that the humans remain in bed, unmoving.

Something inside her makes her stomach drop, the sudden fear that they're dead causing her to jump with the spryness of a wild jungle cat from her chair and onto the bed. Her mission is clear: revive these two humans. After all, who's going to feed her if they're dead?

She begins her attempts at revival by calmly rubbing her face against Human #1, pressing her cold, wet nose against her freckled cheek.

But nothing. No movement except for a little frown. Good. Good. At least there's movement, though not much of it.

Ginger decides to take it even further and jumps over to Human #2's side of the bed, pawing at him, gently scratching at his bare back—just enough to wake him up and not break skin. Ginger has to be extra careful with these fragile humans. After all, they have zero protection against the world—weak patches of hair in odd places all over their body covered by strange pieces of fabric. Nothing like Ginger's *glorious*, thick orange mane.

Human #2 groans, eyes still closed.

Meoooooowww.

"Ginger, Mommy and Daddy are trying to sleep. It's still early. I'll feed you in a bit."

If Ginger could snort, she would. She doesn't understand many of the sounds the humans make, but she *does* know "Mommy" and "Daddy." These two humans call themselves her *pawrents*, but it's clear over the years that she's been the one taking care of them. First, Human #1—or Bridget, as Human #2 calls her. Then, about a year ago, she started taking care of Human #2, too. Will, she thinks his name is.

Ginger sits patiently for about forty-five seconds by Will before head butting him, nipping softly at his ear with her sharp teeth.

Meeeeooooowww.

With another groan, he presses a kiss to Bridget's bare shoulder before sitting up. He glares at Ginger, but scratches the back of her ears in the way that makes her lean into his hand and her entire body purr.

"Okay," he whispers. "I'll feed you now even though breakfast time isn't for..." He checks the odd contraption connected to a cable on the nightstand her humans seem to be glued to several times a day. "Your breakfast isn't even due for another hour!" he whisper-yells.

Ginger watches the way he begins to reconsider feeding her early, and doesn't like it one bit. She doesn't like it at all. In fact, she can't believe she ever considered promoting him to Human #1 at one point.

Ridiculous.

Ginger has one more tool in her tool box to convince him, though, so she goes for it: she widens her eyes and looks up at Will with a soft *meow* before rubbing her entire body, tail in the air, against him. Now all she has to do is throw herself in his lap and—

His goofy smile is immediate. "Alright, you little dictator. Breakfast it is."

Will scoops her up in his arms and carries her to the kitchen counter, even if she doesn't need the help—she's not complaining, though.

Based on the way the tone of his voice and demeanor change —higher pitched than normal, more cuddles and ear rubs, something she's heard Bridget call "baby talk"—Ginger knows that she hasn't just succeeded in getting her breakfast delivered to her an hour early or in hitching a ride to the kitchen counter. Nope, she knows she's gotten Will to give her a couple of treats after she finishes her wet food, too.

Bridget wakes and sits up in bed, rubbing her eyes. "Will? Are you feeding the cat? Do you need my help?"

"Go back to bed, baby," Will whispers before going over to place a peck on her lips. "You need to rest before the movers get here. Big changes are ahead."

GINGER ROLLS COMFORTABLY ONTO HER BACK, PAWS IN THE AIR. She lets the warmth of the sun that comes in from the window sink deep through her layers of fur.

It's her special time. Part of her new daily routine. Right after breakfast, she goes into the living room to sleep on that one strong ray of sunshine that makes its way onto the one specific spot every day.

Ginger was definitely not a fan of this new place when they first moved in—it was so big, it terrified her sometimes (though she'd never admit it out loud even if she could speak).

She's often heard Will say things she didn't understand about her, like that maybe Ginger had agoraphobia after living in such a small space for so long, and "it's good we moved out of New York. More space for all of us."—but now she's a fan. She no longer needs to constantly see how disgustingly in love the humans are with each other.

The way Will struggles to not have at least one inch of his skin touching Bridget at all times. The way she constantly turns red and grins wildly whenever he looks at her a certain way or says the right thing. Things that Ginger has heard them use with her sometimes—*love*—but she doesn't go crazy over it like they do over each other. Mostly, she's glad she can walk away from their mating rituals when they happen. Before, she could only turn away and go back to sleep. Now, she can go downstairs and stare at the family of squirrels in the backyard. Plot their demise. The squirrels' demise, that is.

"Will? Do you have everything?" Ginger hears Bridget ask.

Her voice is an octave higher than it usually is, anxiety dripping from every word.

Curious, Ginger turns onto her side to watch their interaction through the doorway.

Will slings a backpack over his shoulders before taking her by the hips, pulling her tight against him. He presses his lips against Bridget and she moans, arms looping behind his neck as she inhales deeply. As if trying to memorize his scent.

Ginger almost wishes she had a hairball she could throw up right now.

She likes that her *paw*rents care about each other, but *jeez.*

"Yes, Bridge." He smiles against her mouth while they both attempt to regulate their breathing.

"Lunch? Books? Notebooks and pens?"

"Check. Check. Check and check."

Bridget blushes and tries to look away, but he won't let her. Instead, he grabs her by the chin and kisses her long and hard once more.

"I just want to make sure your first day back to school goes well," she murmurs against his lips.

He pulls back a bit to grin down at her. "I know. And it will. I promise."

"I forgot who I was talking to, sorry. Mr. Charisma can get anyone to love him."

Whatever she said makes him laugh. "I don't know about that, but the only person I care to have love me is you."

There's that word again. They use it so often around the house, it's become kind of the theme. Though Ginger's still not sure what it means. "I don't care about anyone else. What I do care about is making you proud. I care about your happiness in general, but especially about you liking it here in Rhode Island." He pauses for a moment. "But I also care about getting through the next two years of grad school before AI takes any future jobs."

Bridget laughs at his last comment. "I can't speak for the future of AI and architecture, but I can speak for myself. I'm happy we left New York. I'm happy living a small life here on campus, opening my own thrift store. I liked the thrill of New York's fashion world once, yes, but it's been three years and a lot of perspective. Plus, my love for it all changed when I saw what it does to good people—even Molly quit. She went to a smaller company with a better culture. So I'm more than happy revamping vintage clothes and reselling them. And I love being here for you while you pursue something you really like. I love you."

"I love you, too."

With a final kiss and a wistful look in his eyes, Will steps out of the house and into the crisp fall air.

FROM THE KITCHEN COUNTER, GINGER ENJOYS HER DINNER. SHE remembers with horror how Will started putting her food on the floor when they first moved here. Did he expect her to eat her meals like some common street animal or something? Sometimes she wondered whether he truly understood the family hierarchy. But then she reminds herself that he's still relatively new here.

Both humans sit at the table enjoying their dinner—something called Taco Tuesday that Bridget has not stopped talking about all day. Ginger chomps down as she watches them interact, each one customizing this "taco" according to their preferences. She notices that Will prefers more meat, which Ginger can't blame him for. But Bridget goes crazy for what looks like a thick cream.

"We need to talk to the landlord about the shower," Bridget says.

Will seems mildly alarmed, but is too busy building his taco to pay full attention to Bridget. "The water pressure not working again?"

She sighs. "Not really. It's like... trickling. A drizzle, really. Really messing up my hair math days."

He snorts, but is otherwise focused on drizzling the perfect amount of a red sauce over his food. "After we get married, I'll make sure that we buy a house with the perfect water pressure so your hair math days go off without a hitch."

Bridget's eyes widen, her whole body freezes—taco mid-air, mouth open. After a beat Will is clueless of, she blinks a couple of times. "We're getting married?"

Will sits up straight and drops his carefully crafted taco on the plate in front of him. It takes him a second to answer before looking straight at her. He wipes his hands on a napkin. Takes her hands in his. Looks her in the eyes and smiles sheepishly. "Aren't we?"

"You... haven't asked," she whispers.

He nods with a slight frown. "I am very much aware of this." He raises her hands to his lips before placing them softly on the table. He goes back to eating his taco, leaving Bridget stunned.

"Are you planning on asking sometime soon?" Her voice is high. It trembles.

Why?

Will takes a bite of his food and takes a considerable amount of time chewing. Is he doing it on purpose or is human food really that bad that it requires ages to chew?

Once he swallows, he wipes his mouth to reveal a smug smile. "Very soon."

Bridget exhales, eyes on her lap. Her skin changes color that way it always does—Ginger has never seen another human do it quite like her—though she must admit her exposure to other humans has been limited (thank god).

"Okay. Sounds good."

With a soft laugh, Will leans over and kisses Bridget, digging a hand into her red hair. "I love you, Bridget Quinn. I'm going to love you forever. Thank you for being the best friend, partner, and lover a guy could ever hope to have."

She sniffles once. Swallows twice. "Ditto."

THE END

ACKNOWLEDGMENTS

My, what a fun book this was to write! Besides the fact that I got to revisit my past life when I worked in fashion, I feel like Will and Bridget's loving, solid friendship-to-partners relationship progression lit something up in me. It brought me a lot of joy!

Reply All wasn't even supposed to be a novel! It was written as a five-chapter short story for an anthology I wanted to write. I fell in love with Will and Bridget so quickly, that it turned into a novella. Then I wanted more and promised myself to keep it at 75k words. What you just read was 93.5k. Ha!

And while this story came from some need to bring about more light and swoon, it wouldn't have ever happened without the love and support from this community. Because yes, authors write the books, but friends are the ones who keep the authors sane. So, I think it takes a village, sometimes.

Which is why I need to address the group chat, The Hottest, my lovely friends, coworkers, and crazy ladies: Maria Rigou and Hailey Dickert (if you're reading this, you should check out their books, too). It's been an awesome ride, and I am so thankful to have had each other through every high and low. Let's do that Florida signing soon!

To Tracey: You are a goddess! Thank you so much for working through plot points with me, your attention to detail, and your ability to listen to me rant for hours until we come up with a solution. You are the only person I trust with an alpha version of my book, because I know you'll always see beyond the shitty first draft but will also give me your honest opinion. That is invaluable.

To Cassie, thank you thank you thank you for everything that you do. You have helped more than you know, relieving me of a huge chunk of my mental load. There are no words for how thankful I am for you keeping me in check. Seriously. I love to tell everyone I work for you, because Cassie tells me what to do and when. If she didn't, things just wouldn't get done. You're a queen.

As always, a huge thank you to my husband for enduring several months of me going into what I call "Gremlin mode"—locked in my writing cave, have not seen daylight in years, have not spoken to anyone in decades, and life is a mess. Also, for being the most supportive husband ever. You're what keeps me going through the toughest times and no thank you will ever cover how much I appreciate it.

A big thank you to all the people I worked with in my past career. Thankfully, they were nothing like Lena and Jenna. I was lucky enough to be surrounded by incredible women and men who worked hard, were incredibly intelligent, and made me feel proud to work alongside them every day.

Thank you to Rosie Danan for helping me fix my blurb and teach me a solid lesson on what makes a good one!

Quick shoutout to my two cats, Señor Kitty and Salem, and the new addition to our family, our dog Tilly. You're a little demon child, but I love you so much already.

And lastly, thanks to you, dear Reader!!!! I hope you enjoyed this story.

All the best,

C

ABOUT THE AUTHOR

Caroline Frank is a Venezuelan indie author and self-proclaimed shoe addict. She currently resides in Philadelphia with her husband, two crazy cats, Señor Kitty and Salem, and her German Shepherd, Tilly.

She spends her days reading, crocheting, crafting, writing, and biking. Her favorite things include the first sip of an iced-cold Coke and using self-deprecating humor to get through the day.

Though she always planned to eventually take over the world, she thinks writing fun stories every day is pretty freaking awesome and plans to continue to do so for the foreseeable future.

Happily Ever Disaster (Novella - Book 2.5)

Second Chance Snowmance (Book 3)

<u>Standalone Contemporary Romance:</u>

Reply All

CAROLINE FRANK
Reply All